"Kelric's difficulties . . . exploring the reaches of the interstellar Skolian Empire, are a whole lot of fun to read about. . . . Well-written, entertaining, classic science fiction fun."
—*Cleveland Plain Dealer*

"A smoothly absorbing space opera that mixes high-tech gimmickry with galactic politics and plenty of romance. . . . This one packs in lots of action along with its many romantic interludes and diversions into speculative genetics."
—*Publishers Weekly*

"This intriguing novel combines hard speculative science with romantic adventure."
—*Library Journal*

"Ms. Asaro reveals fascinating new aspects of her talent with each new book, and readers can always expect something fresh, different, and absolutely wonderful."
—*Romantic Times*

Tor Books by Catherine Asaro

THE SAGA OF THE SKOLIAN EMPIRE

The
Last
Hawk

Catherine Asaro

TOR®

A TOM DOHERTY ASSOCIATES BOOK
NEW YORK

This is a work of fiction. All the characters and events portrayed in this book are either fictitious or are used fictitiously.

THE LAST HAWK

Copyright © 1997 by Catherine Asaro

Edited by David G. Hartwell
Map by Ellisa Mitchell

A Tor Book
Published by Tom Doherty Associates, Inc.
175 Fifth Avenue
New York, NY 10010

Tor Books on the World Wide Web:
http://www.tor.com

Tor® is a registered trademark of Tom Doherty Associates, Inc.

ISBN: 0-812-55110-9
Library of Congress Card Catalog Number: 97-15568

First edition: November 1997
First mass market edition: December 1998

Printed in the United States of America

0 9 8 7 6 5 4 3 2 1

To my daughter, Cathy,
with love

Acknowledgments

I would like to acknowledge the readers who gave me input on this book: Dr. Lynne Deutsch, Dr. Steve Goldhaber, Dr. Margaret Graffe, Dr. Kate Kirby, Dr. Malcolm LeCompte, and Mr. Tim Oey. I give special thanks to the above because they were the first ever to see my fiction and their insights helped me learn to write. My thanks also to Dr. Joan Slonczewski, to Eleanor Wood of Spectrum Literary Agency, to Scovil, Chichak, and Galen, and to the staff at Tor, in particular Tad Dembinski and David G. Hartwell. A loving thanks to my husband, John Kendall Cannizzo, for his care and support.

Contents

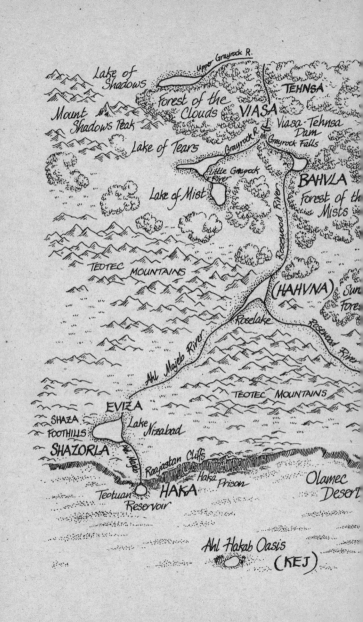

Prologue

The ship's controls wobbled in and out of focus. Kelric tried to rub his eyes, but his arm refused to respond. The exoskeleton on his pilot's seat had jammed around his body. When he fumbled for the catches, his fingers just scraped over the mesh.

On his fourth attempt, the exoskeleton opened and he fell forward, sprawling across the weapons grid in the cockpit. The only illumination came from the red warning lights that glowed all over the control panels, bathing the cockpit in a dim crimson radiance that didn't reach its shadowed recesses.

One green light shone among the red. An engine. One of his inversion engines. It was the only fully functional system on his ship.

It was also why he still lived.

"I'm inverted," Kelric mumbled. The same hit that had crippled his Jag fighter had kicked it from the sublight universe into inversion, hurling him away from his attackers before they could blast him into slag.

The medkit above him hadn't released. He reached for it, but his arm faltered in midair and dropped back onto the grid. Not that it mattered. He needed far more help than a kit could give, more help even than provided by his nanomeds, the tiny cell-repair machines in his body.

Pain throbbed in his arm, from a bone-deep gash. In the exoskeleton he had been numb, probably because it injected him with an anesthetic. Or perhaps the biomech web in his body had released a drug that blocked pain receptors in his brain. It would give him only so much of the drug, though, before its safety routines cut it off, to prevent an overdose or brain damage.

Now his arm hurt too much to move. Even if it intended to stay put, though, his ship was going somewhere. At least it had taken him away from the Traders. He had been out alone, on reconnaissance, when the Trader squad caught him. He hoped they all inverted into the gravity well of a star and finished their careers as kindling for the local furnace.

An alarm sputtered. Lifting his head, he saw that the green light had turned yellow. The last inversion engine was failing.

Kelric swallowed. He had to find a place to land. Closing his eyes, he tried to clear his mind.

Bolt, respond, he thought.

The computer node in his spine answered. Attending. Its messages traveled along bio-optic threads to his brain, where tiny bio-electrodes in his brain cells converted the signals into neural firing patterns. It worked in reverse as well, letting him "talk" to the node.

Status of nanomeds, he thought.

Nanomed series G and H functional but depleted, the node answered. Series O nonfunctional. All other series exhibit decreased function.

Kelric grimaced. His nanomeds repaired his body. Each med consisted of two parts, a molecule designed for a particular task and a picochip, an atomic computer that operated on quantum transitions. Altogether, the picochips formed a picoweb that told the meds what to do and how to replicate themselves. But it was Bolt, his spinal node, that ran the show. Like the conductor of a symphony, it directed his entire bio-mech web, which consisted of the picoweb, the bio-optics threading his body, and the bio-electrodes in his brain. The system had been integrated into his body fourteen years ago, when he was twenty, the year he received his officer's commission.

Bolt, he thought. *What happened to my biomech web?*

You were linked into the ship's Evolving Intelligence brain when we were hit, so your web took a lot of damage. I am making repairs, but the malfunctions are too extensive for me to fully correct. Proceed immediately to an ISC medical facility.

If he hadn't hurt so much, Kelric would have laughed. *Wish I could do that.* He swallowed. *Can you give me a status report?*

Accessing optical nerve, Bolt answered.

A display formed in Kelric's mind, with different views of his interior systems. Then the display "jumped" out in front of him so it looked like a ghostly image hanging in the cockpit.

Posterior tibial artery damaged. Bolt highlighted a diagram of his circulatory system, showing a torn artery leaking blood.

Kelric exhaled. His best hope to repair himself came from the final component of his internal systems: his Kyle centers. Unlike the biomech web, which had been created for him, he had been born with Kyle mutations, courtesy of his unusual genetics. Microscopic organs in his brain made it possible for his brain waves to interact with those of people nearby, letting him pick up their moods and on rare occasions their thoughts. He could also enhance the output of his own brain and so exert increased biofeedback control over his body.

Kelric concentrated, trying to augment his biofeedback training. He helped speed structural components to the damaged artery, control his blood flow, and bring in nutrients. When he finally surfaced from his trance, he felt steadier, enough so he could sit up, holding his arm against his chest.

An alarm warned again of the dying engine.

"Navak," he said. "Take us out of inversion, into sublight space."

No response came from the navigation-attack node in the ship's Evolving Intelligence brain.

"Navak," he repeated. "Initiate navigation mode."

Silence.

Bolt, give me the ship's emergency menu, he thought.

Bolt produced a display of emergency psicons, like computer icons but in his mind instead of on a screen. He concentrated on the emergency-shutoff psicon for the inversion engines, the symbol of a running cheetah turning into a crawling snail. Only one of each animal appeared in the display, a reminder that he had only one functional engine. The cheetah was blinking off and on, warning it would soon disappear as well.

Toggle emergency shutdown, he thought.

Nothing happened.

Bolt, toggle it!

A twisting sensation hit Kelric, as if he were being pulled

through a Klein bottle, the three-dimensional equivalent of a Möbius strip. The effect intensified with a nauseating mental wrench and then stopped.

Bolt? he thought.

We have dropped into normal space, Bolt answered.

Kelric sagged in his seat, hit with an urge to laugh. Sublight. Safe. He was safe.

He was also lost. None of his holomaps worked and too many files in the ship's EI were degraded. He couldn't get accurate data. He knew only that he was light-years away from his previous position, drifting in space like interstellar flotsam. What he needed was a beach to wash up on.

"Navak," he said. "Respond."

Nothing.

Kelric slid his hand around his waist, searching his lower back. Sockets in his spine, wrists, and ankles let him connect his biomech web to exterior systems, such as the EI brain of his ship. When a connector prong clicked into a socket, it linked his bio-optics to the ship's fiberoptics. The sockets could also act as infrared receivers and transmitters, a less reliable form of communication than a physical link, but better than nothing.

When he had fallen out of the exoskeleton, its prongs had pulled out of his body. He tried to push one back into his lower spine, but the prong wouldn't stay put.

Activate infrared receptors, he thought.

IR nonfunctional, Bolt thought.

Kelric swore. He was running out of options. Taking a breath, he marshaled his thoughts. With his Kyle enhancements, maybe he could couple the fields of his brain directly to those of the ship's EI brain. It helped that he was inside the ship, essentially on top of the EI; the electrical forces that dominated his brain activity fell off rapidly with distance.

Concentrating, he tried to kick the EI awake with his mind.

A ghostly green marble appeared in the air in front of him, casting eerie light over the cockpit. It took him a moment to recognize it as a holomap's crudest default display.

Kelric exhaled. "Planet," he rasped.

Navak's audio made a scraping noise.

He tried again. "Planet."

Nothing.

Navak, he thought. *You have to respond.*

A sentence formed in the air, green words in Navak's default font. HAV#"%SPOND IS AN UNIDENTIFIABLE COMMAND.

Relief washed over Kelric. PLANET, he thought, with more intensity. The word appeared under Navak's response.

PLANET WHAT? Navak printed.

FIND ME ONE. OR A BASE. SOMEPLACE HABITABLE WE CAN REACH BEFORE ENGINE FOUR DIES.

SEARCHING, Navak printed.

Kelric waited.

And waited.

Maybe no place was near enough. Or Navak was too damaged to answer. Or the engine couldn't—

OBJECT 85B5D-E6-JHEO SATISFIES YOUR REQUIREMENTS, Navak printed.

WHAT IS IT?

DOES 'IT' REFER TO OBJECT 85B5D-E6-JHEO?

For pugging sake, Kelric thought. *What else would I mean?*

NO DATA EXISTS ON 'PUGGING S %' AS AN OBJECT, Navak printed. HOWEVER, 'PUGGING' APPEARS IN LANGUAGE FILE 4 UNDER PROFANITY. DO YOU WANT TO KNOW MORE?

WHAT I WANT, Kelric thought, IS EVERYTHING YOU'VE GOT ON OBJECT 85B5D—he squinted at the screen—E6-JHEO.

IT IS A PLANET. NAME: COBA. INHABITANTS: HUMAN. STATUS: RESTRICTED.

Kelric swallowed. Inhabitants. Help. He just might survive this mess after all.

TAKE SHIP TO COBA, he thought.

BOOK ONE

Years 960–966
of the Modern Age

I

Dahl

1

First Move: The Golden Ball

Deha Dahl, the Manager of Dahl Estate, was playing dice. She placed a cube in the structure of balls, pyramids, and polyhedrons on the table. Her opponent, one of her more intrepid Estate aides, wiped sweat from her forehead as she studied the dice.

While Deha waited for her aide to make her move, she glanced around. They were in the Coral Room, a round chamber twenty paces in diameter. Painted a deep rose near the floor, the walls shaded into lighter coral hues and then into white at the top. Mosaics were inlaid in the domed ceiling high above them. The room's three doorways each arched to a point and then curved out in a circle graced with a stained-glass window. The doors were solid amberwood. Deha insisted on only the best for these chambers where she played the dice game of Quis with her aides, her peers—and her adversaries.

Their audience of Estate aides sat in carved chairs around the table. They watched the game in silence, some no doubt wishing they could take the perspiring aide's place and others grateful it wasn't them in this duel of minds. All knew she had called this session to see how her opponent, an aide due a promotion, handled the pressure of playing against a Dice Queen.

A hand touched Deha's shoulder. She looked around, surprised to see an aide who wasn't among the group she had selected to view the session.

The aide bowed. "I'm sorry to disturb you, ma'am. But Captain Hacha thought you would want to know immediately. A craft crashed up in the mountains near Dahl Pass." She paused. "It doesn't appear to be from Coba."

There was a time when Deha would have shipped the bearer of such news off to the setting-sun-asylum for the mentally diminished. No longer. She stood up. "Have Hacha meet me in my office." She glanced at her dice opponent. "We will continue later."

The aide nodded and started to speak. Then she stopped, her gaze shifting to a point beyond Deha. She stood up and bowed, not to Deha but to someone else. Following her gaze, the rest of Deha's aides stood up, in a flurry of moving chairs, and bowed.

Deha turned to see who evoked such a reaction from her staff. A retinue had appeared in one of the doorways, soldiers in the uniform of her CityGuard. A girl stood in the center of the group, a gray-eyed child on the verge of womanhood, with fiery hair curling around her face and falling in a thick braid down her back. Tall for her age, she looked like the reincarnation of an incipient warrior queen who had transcended the millennia and stepped from the Old Age into the modern world.

Deha crossed to the girl and bowed. "Ixpar. What brings you here?"

Ixpar's face was lit with contained excitement. "I heard about the craft that crashed near Dahl Pass. I came to help the rescue party."

Deha silently cursed. It would be foolishness to let Ixpar join them. This was no normal child. Ixpar Karn: it meant Ixpar from the Estate of Karn. Of the Twelve Estates, Karn was largest, bigger even than Dahl. It was also the oldest. Its Manager not only ruled Karn; as Minister she stood highest in the hierarchy of the Estates. And she had chosen this girl to be her successor. Someday Ixpar would rule Coba.

But if she didn't let Ixpar come with them, she risked alienating Karn. The girl was already a force in the flow of power among the Estates. Rumor claimed the Minister had been known to place her young successor's opinions above those of her senior advisers.

Political prudence won out. "Very well," Deha said. She raised her hand as Ixpar's face lit up. "But I want you stay with my personal escort at all times." She glanced toward the mountains. "We have no idea what crashed up there."

* * *

In her guest suite, Ixpar changèd into hiking clothes: a sweater, leather pants, and a leather jacket. When she left the suite, she found her escort in the entrance foyer, four tall guards armed with stunners. They accompanied her as she walked through Dahl. Always guards. At times she was tempted to hide or slip away. But she resisted the urge, knowing she was the only one who would find it entertaining.

Guards or no guards, though, she enjoyed the walk. It was hard to believe the Estate had once been an armed fortress. Its harsh interior had long ago given way to its present beauty, its stone floors softened with carpets and its formerly barred windows replaced by faceted yellow glass. Some corridors formed the perimeter of large halls, set off from them only by widely spaced columns. Just as the ancient warrior queens of Dahl had ruled from the Estate, so Deha and her staff now used it as their residence.

They left the Estate and walked through the city. Blue cobblestones paved the streets, which wound among buildings made from pale blue or lavender stone, with turreted roofs. Spires topped the turrets and chains hung from their tips, strung with metal Quis dice. When the wind blew, which was almost always, the chains swung and clinked, sparkling in the sun.

They passed bright temples dedicated to the sungoddess Savina or the dawn god Sevtar, and saw ball courts filled with exuberant players, men and women laughing in the wind. The day was bright, gusty, and fresh. She wanted to jump. Shout. Get into trouble. Of course she couldn't. But it was still a glorious day.

Ixpar knew the route to the airfield well; the Minister often brought her to visit Dahl, which had long been an ally of Karn Estate. This time Minister Karn had sent her alone. It was about time. Ixpar felt as if she were straining in a harness, struggling to fly in the currents of power among the Estates.

Other feelings also stirred within her, less comprehensible than politics. She felt painfully awkward, tall and gangly, with big feet. She grew so fast lately, like a spindlestalk plant. She thought of the youth Tev, with his lean muscles and curly hair. At night she tossed in bed, reminding herself that a woman's intentions toward men should always be honorable. It didn't help. She couldn't stop herself from thinking up ways to convince him that he should let her compromise his honor.

The growl of an engine interrupted her thoughts. Beyond the end of the street, the airfield waited. With her retinue, Ixpar crossed the last stretch of pavement and walked onto the tarmac. Crews were wheeling out two windriders, aircraft painted like giant althawks, with wings of red plumage edged in black, gleaming gold heads, and landing gear as black as talons. They looked ready to leap into the sky.

The rescue party was assembling near a hangar. In addition to Deha, the group included Rohka, who was the Estate Senior Physician, and the young doctor Dabbiv, his gaze intense as he spoke with a pilot. Deha's personal escort stood by the hangar door: Hacha, captain of the escort; Rev, a broad-shouldered man who towered over most everyone else; slender Llaach with her night-black hair; and Balv, youngest of the four.

Ixpar soon found herself in the same craft as the escort, with Balv as pilot. He went about his preflight checks as if what he were doing was perfectly normal. Well, this was Dahl. Things were different here. Modern.

Hacha sat next to Ixpar. As tall as Rev, but leaner, the captain looked like her name: tough and craggy. Following Ixpar's gaze to Balv, she chuckled. "He's a pleasant one to look at, heh?"

Ixpar reddened. "I was just watching his flight preparations."

Deha settled into the copilot's seat and leaned back to talk to Hacha, saving Ixpar from more embarrassment. Discreetly, so as not to be caught staring again, she watched the Manager. A braid of black hair hung to Deha's waist and tendrils curled about her classic face. A dusting of silver showed in the hair at her temples. Her most compelling feature was her eyes; huge and black, they drew attention.

The rider soon lifted off, its wing slats spreading like giant feathers to catch the wind. The dome of the Observatory passed below them, glistening in the sunlight. As the ground dropped away other towers became visible, spires reaching into the sky. Seen from above, the Estate looked like a sculpture: bridges arched in frozen lace over courtyards, battlements glowed an antique gold in the sunlight, and curving walls added scalloped edges to the design.

Then the parks set aside for the Dahl Calanya came into view.

Ixpar pressed her nose against the window, straining to see the forbidden Calanya. Surrounded by a massive windbreak, the parks made a tapestry of lawns and lakes dotted by a myriad of colorful flowers. She could just make out a fountain, a hazelle stag rearing on his hind legs. Arches of water curved up from his horns and fell sparkling into a basin.

The view widened to include the city of Dahl nestled in its mountain valley, its streets accented by the specks of pedestrians. The rider soared higher and Dahl receded until it was no more than a pattern of colors in the panorama of the Teotec Mountains. Ahead, peaks climbed so far into the sky that she grew dizzy trying to sight their tips; behind, forested slopes plunged down until, out of sight beyond the horizon, they became cliffs that met a desert whipped by the wind.

It was out there, a day's ride into the desert, that the strangers had built their starport.

Starport. It had an eerie sound. People from above the sky. Ixpar had seen them years ago when their military commanders came to Karn, imposing warrior queens with hard edges to their personalities. *Skolians* they called themselves, even though they looked like Cobans. Their talk of building a port in the desert had troubled Minister Karn. Now Ixpar sensed unease in Deha as well, an apprehension that whatever had crashed in the mountains was not born of Coba.

"There!" Deha had to shout to be heard over the engines. "I saw something below that crag. A glint, like metal." She glanced at Balv. "Can you take us down?"

He squinted into the glare from the snow. "There's room behind those rocks."

The rider descended, its wing slats drawing together like huge feathers. The snowskis unfolded with a grind, sailing over the snow, jolting the cabin when they skimmed over patches of rock. As they shot past a huge drift, Balv snapped the wings in flush to the hull. After they were clear again he opened the metal pinions and braked against the wind until the rider skidded to a stop.

Captain Hacha disembarked first, followed by Balv, then Deha and Ixpar. Llaach and Rev came last. Not only had the guards hung stunners from their belts, Rev carried a honed discus in a sling over his shoulder and Llaach had a dagger on her boot.

The second rider landed, bringing more guards and the doctors. With Hacha in the lead, they hiked to a hill of boulders that hid the downed craft. Ixpar clambered up the mound, dislodging rocks in her hurry. She reached the top—and looked out at the wreckage of a starship steaming in the melted snow.

Incredibly, it was hardly bigger than a windrider. Even as a wreck, hints of its former grace showed, making it look like an alabaster sculpture broken against the mountain.

Hacha reached it first. She vanished through a hole in the hull, but reappeared almost instantly. "There's a pilot in here," she called. "I think he's alive."

They sped in a sliding run down the hill, their boots kicking up flurries from patches of snow. At the ship, Rev grabbed a twist of metal and shoved it upward, widening the rent in the hull so the others could enter. The interior was chaos: crumpled bulkheads, sparks jumping from panels, broken shards everywhere. The pilot lay collapsed across his forward controls.

Rohka, the Estate Senior Physician, knelt by the man. "He's still breathing."

"We better get him out of here," Llaach said. "If this craft is like a windrider, these sparks could start a fire. The whole ship could blow."

"I doubt starships run on petrol," the doctor Dabbiv said.

Rohka glanced at Rev and Hacha, the two tallest people in the group. "Can you carry him?"

Working together, Hacha and Rev eased the man out of his seat. They took him out of the ship and carried him to a wall of rock Ixpar thought surely must be thick enough to protect against even the explosion of a starship. After they set him gently down on the ground, the doctors went to work on his wounds.

Ixpar knelt to look at the pilot. He was metal. His skin and hair shimmered like gold. His face could have been a mask of the wind god Khozaar; it had that same flawless beauty. But where myth claimed Khozaar was as supple as the wind, this man was huge, bigger than Rev even, with a massive physique to match.

She laid her palm on the pilot's cheek, checking for fever. Despite its metallic cast, his skin felt warm. Human. She wanted to touch him more, to stroke his hair and face, but she held back. Instead she helped the doctors untangle him from his torn jacket. She uncovered his arms—and dropped his sleeve, gaping at him.

Llaach made an incredulous noise. "That's impossible."

"I don't believe it," Balv said. "He's a *Calani*."

Ixpar didn't believe it either. But the evidence was inescapable. The man wore three gold armbands on each of his upper arms.

"Three bands." Rev's voice rumbled. "He's a Third Level Calani."

"For wind's sake," Dabbiv said. "He can't be a Calani. He's not even from this planet." The doctor pulled scraps of cloth away from the man's waist. "They don't have—hey!" He dropped the scraps. "Look at that."

A weapon, huge and black, glittered on the pilot's hip.

"That's some stunner," Llaach said. "What is a Calani doing with a gun?"

Captain Hacha frowned. Then she headed back to where Deha and the other guards were examining the ship. Apparently the Manager didn't believe it might explode; they were all walking in and out of the wreckage.

Ixpar turned back to the pilot. She wasn't sure which she found more unsettling: an offworld Calani or a Calani with a gun. She ran her fingers over the engravings on his armbands. "These hieroglyphics are Skolian."

Dabbiv glanced up from the splint he was setting on the man's leg. "You can read Skolian?"

"Minister Karn had me learn it."

"Can you make out the name of his Estate?" Balv asked.

"Something about an office," Ixpar said. "It's a title—Third

Office, I think. It must mean his Calanya Level." She pieced out the inscription. "Jagged Imperial Third Office. No, it's *Officer*, not *Office*. Tertiary Officer?" She studied the glyphs. "Jagernaut. That's what it says. Jagernaut Tertiary, Kelricson Garlin Valdoria. Imperial Space Command."

"What does it mean?" Llaach asked.

"If we don't get him to a Med House," Dabbiv said, "that won't matter. He'll be too dead for it to make a difference."

Manager Dahl's voice came from behind them. "This man is an Imperial citizen. You all know their Restriction laws. We are forbidden interaction with him. We must take him directly to their starport."

Ixpar stood up. "He's hurt. He needs our help."

"The starport has medical facilities," Deha said.

Senior Physician Rohka looked up from the leg she was splinting. Ixpar could guess the doctor's thought; it would take nearly a day to reach the port.

"He will die before we get there," Rohka said.

Deha considered the doctor. Then she turned to Ixpar. "Would you come with me?"

The Manager led her to an area behind another outcropping. Hacha and Rev were both there, studying a panel from the wreckage. A symbol glowed on it, a black triangle inscribed by an amber circle. Etched within the circle was the gold silhouette of an exploding sun.

"Do you recognize this symbol?" Deha asked her.

"It's called the Ruby insignia," Ixpar said.

"What does it mean?"

Ixpar thought back to what the Public Affairs Officer from the Imperial delegation had told Minister Karn. "*Ruby* refers to the rulers of an ancient empire that predates the Imperialate. The Ruby Dynasty."

"I thought a council ruled the Skolian Imperialate," Deha said.

"Now, yes. The Assembly." Ixpar brushed her fingers across the insignia. "The Ruby Empire collapsed five thousand years ago. Apparently only ruins remain."

"This insignia is part of the pilot's identification."

"When the Imperialate was forming, about four centuries

ago, they decided to use the Ruby symbol for their insignia."
Ixpar shrugged. "They put it on everything."

Deha regarded her uneasily. "But this comes from his personal ID."

Personal ID? That intrigued Ixpar. "Maybe he descends from the Ruby Dynasty."

"Does that have any significance?"

"I'm not sure." She considered the thought. "We had better get him to Dahl."

"If he recovers, it won't be long before he realizes no reason exists for the Restricted status we convinced his military to give us." Deha grimaced. "What if he decides to notify Imperial Space Command? Right now they think something is wrong with us. It's the only reason they leave us alone. Do you really want ISC to institute formal assimilation procedures for Coba? You've met their warrior queens, Ixpar. They conquer. Period. The Restriction is our only protection."

"They aren't all warrior queens. Half their military are men." Ixpar glanced at the pilot. "An army like that can't be harsh."

"That assumption is based on our culture. Not theirs."

Ixpar turned back to her. "If we take him to the starport, we'll be returning a dead man. These Imperial warrior queens you so fear aren't just going to show up, take his body, and forget we let one of their sons die." She thought of how his cheek had felt under her hand, how it made her want to touch him more. "And just look at him. He's so beautiful."

"Just because he's a handsome young man instead of a craggy old Manager doesn't make the danger less." Deha considered her. "Does anyone at the port monitor these mountains?"

"I don't think so. The port is automated. No people. Every now and then we hear that a ship came in to refuel, but the crews never leave the port."

"According to his ship's log, he was lost when he crashed."

Ixpar understood what Deha left unsaid; if they buried the pilot and destroyed his ship, their anonymity was safe. But when she looked at him, he brought images of desire and fatherhood to her mind. Her instinct was to protect him.

"Deha, no. What if we take him to Dahl and never let him go? His people sent him out without any protector. It's their own fault he ended up like this. He's ours now."

"He might escape. We can't risk that."

The doctor Dabbiv came over to Deha. "If we're going to save his life, we have to leave for Dahl as soon as possible."

Deha looked at the Skolian. In the sunlight, his skin, hair, and armbands gleamed like gold. Softly she said, "He truly is a beauty."

Her voice returned to its matter-of-fact tone. "Very well. Put him in my rider. We will take him to Dahl."

2

First Structure: Orb's Circle

It was an ice forest of blue, its branches a lacework of filaments.

Gradually Kelric realized the forest was a blanket lying across his eyes. He considered pulling it down. As he drifted in and out of sleep the idea lodged in his mind, until finally it translated into action. His head moved, just barely, but enough to make the blanket slip so he could look beyond the blue.

He saw more blue; a wall, painted sapphire near the floor, shading up through lighter blues until it blended into ivory at the top. Sunlight streamed through a window patterned from diamond-shaped panes of frosted and faceted glass. Breezes rippled its curtains, revealing glimpses of sky and mountains. A table stood near the window, surrounded by four chairs carved with leaf designs.

A girl moved into his line of sight. All he registered at first was the glorious mane of red hair that cascaded to her hips.

"Who . . . ?" he asked.

Coming closer, she spoke in accented Skolian. "You are awake?"

"Not sure . . . Are you real?"

"Very real, Kelricson." She laid her hand across his forehead. "I am Ixpar."

"How know my name?"

"From your armbands. They are part of your uniform, yes?"

"Yes . . ."

Her fingers trailed to his cheek and lingered. Then she withdrew her hand. "We found you when you crashed above Dahl."

He wanted to ask what was a Dahl, but it was too much exertion. So he soaked in the warmth of the covers. Ixpar blotted the sweat on his forehead with a cloth.

After a while he said, "Not Kelricson."

"Kelricson is not your name?" she asked.

A fragment of memory drifted in his mind: he was being announced at a session of the Assembly. His heritage gave him an honorary seat and a sense of duty prodded him to attend, but he felt painfully awkward, an oversized soldier out of place among the councilors. Neither politics nor public speaking had ever come naturally to him. So he sat silent through the entire session.

"Not-Kelricson?" Ixpar asked. "You are still here?"

He looked up at her. "What?"

"You were telling me your name."

The man in his memory continued to announce his title, so he repeated it. "Kelricson Garlin Valdoria kya Skolia, Im'Rhon to the . . . to the Rhon of the Skolias."

"So many names. Do you wish I use them all?"

"Just Kelric." His eyelids felt heavy. "In dreams . . . don't need baggage."

The girl smiled. "I will tell Deha you think her Estate is a dream."

"Deha?"

"She is Manager of Dahl. She led the rescue party that rescued you."

"Will you tell her something else?"

"Anything you like."

Softly Kelric said, "Tell her I am forever in her debt." Then he passed out.

Darkness alternated with light. Kelric was only vaguely aware of his surroundings; whatever medication the doctors were giving him blurred his mind and melted the days into a haze. His nanomeds weren't trying to deactivate the drugs, though whether that was because Bolt had decided the medicine helped him or because the system wasn't functioning, he wasn't sure. Bolt made no response to his queries.

On a night when warm breezes sifted through the curtains, he drifted out of sleep to see a tall figure standing by his bed.

"Ixpar . . . ?" he asked.

"She sleeps," the woman said. She spoke Skolian with such a thick accent he barely understood it, but her resonant voice pleased the ear and her aura of power penetrated even his drugged haze. Starlight sifted through the window and silvered her slender form. She wore a simple robe that covered her body without hiding its natural grace. Her features were regular: high cheekbones, straight nose, sculpted planes. Her eyes riveted his attention; huge and dark, with faint lines around them, they looked like black pools, drawing him into their depths.

Kelric concentrated on the stranger, but his Kyle receptors caught nothing more than a name. Day? Deha? Then pain sparked in his temples, forcing him to relax his attention.

Deha sat on the bed and laid her palm on his forehead.

"It's hot," he mumbled.

"Much so," she agreed. "Your fever refuses to leave."

"How long been here?"

"One tenday and a bit more."

"Ten days?" He tried to sit up. "Need contact my squad."

Deha nudged him back down. "What you need do is rest." She brushed a curl out of his eyes, then stroked her hand over his hair. "Golden Calani," she murmured.

"Calani?" he asked. But he fell asleep before she answered.

Straining against the body cast that covered him from chest to toe, Kelric vomited into the basin that his nurse was holding.

After the spasms eased, he sank down onto the bed again. People crammed the room: his nurse cleaned his face, another nurse took the basin, guards hulked by the door, doctors conferred in whispers. He wished they would all go away and let him be sick in private.

A man said his name. Looking up, he saw the doctor Dabbiv and the guard Llaach watching him. The doctor spoke again. Although Kelric had learned a few words of their language, he had a long way to go before he could understand even simple sentences. When he shook his head, the doctor slowly repeated the phrase.

Translate, Kelric thought, hoping Bolt's recovery had continued along with his own.

I can't, Bolt answered. My transl^%´´ó@—+

What?

My library hasn't built up enough Coban words or grammar.

Kelric shook his head at Dabbiv again, hoping his meaning was clear. The doctor considered him, then turned to Llaach. After conferring with the guard, Dabbiv nodded to Kelric and took his leave of the room.

Llaach lifted a glass of water off the nightstand and offered it to Kelric. He shook his head, but she persisted in trying to make him drink. They went back and forth that way for a while, until Dabbiv reappeared with Ixpar at his side.

The girl smiled. "My greetings, Kelric."

He exhaled with relief. "Can you tell me what they want?"

"Dabbiv says you are deehi—what is the word? Dehydrait?" She took the glass from Llaach and tilted it to his lips. "Dried up."

Kelric pushed it aside. "No."

"You should do what Dabbiv says. He is a good doctor."

"Does he put anything in my food? Drugs?"

"Of course not. He brings your medicines for you to drink."

"Are you certain?"

"Yes. Why do you ask?"

"I think the food and water are what make me sick."

She frowned. "You would not say this if you knew how much care the cooks use with your meals."

"I appreciate their efforts. But I'm not Coban. What's

harmless to you could be poison to me." Particularly now, when his nanomeds were deactivated or dormant.

Ixpar talked with the doctor, then turned back to Kelric. "Dabbiv says he will try to find you a better diet. And we can boil your water. Do you think this would help?"

He smiled. "Yes. Thank you."

"We will right away talk to the cooks. But now you should rest. I will tell all these worried-looking people to leave."

Good luck, Kelric thought. He had been trying all morning to make them go.

Ixpar spoke a few words to the others—and they left. Then she bowed and took her leave as well, without another word.

Kelric blinked. Just like that, his room was empty. What about his young nurse commanded such a response? It wasn't Ixpar's appearance, exactly; she was awkward with adolescence, all arms and legs. But she had a quality about her, something indefinable that made her seem larger than everyone else.

In any case, the privacy was a relief. He lay back, gazing at the ceiling, which was painted blue, with clouds and a flock of birds. Skyroom. This was far better than a grave, which was where he would be if these people hadn't helped him. That Deha and Ixpar both spoke Skolian suggested an Imperial presence on planet. He had to report back to headquarters. By now Imperial Space Command must have listed him as lost and presumed dead.

A dim image formed in his mind: a floating green sphere. When he concentrated, it faded away.

Retrieve image, Kelric thought.

The memory has suffered degradation, Bolt thought. I will try to improve resolution.

As the sphere reappeared, a blur under it resolved into a line of hieroglyphics. It was a message his ship had printed before the crash. Something about Coba. Restriction. Yes. That was it. Coba was under Imperialate Restriction.

It made no sense. The planet was obviously habitable and Kelric recalled no military briefing about a world called Coba. From what he had seen so far, it was a pleasant place, certainly no candidate for quarantine.

Then again, he had only seen one room and a few people. Coba definitely bore investigation. It had gone unnoticed too long.

With the help of the boy who had brought him lunch, Kelric managed to sit up, wincing as the edge of his bodycast jabbed his chest. Pugged primitive, wrapping his body in plaster. Normally his nanomeds would speed the healing of his broken bones, but he wasn't sure how active they were after the damage he had taken during the attack and then the crash on Coba.

As his nurse adjusted the pillows behind his back, Kelric shifted the tray on his lap and waved at the door, continuing his "conversation" with the boy. "You must know what I mean. The guards outside my room, the ones who always sit at that table, gambling or something. I see them every time someone opens the door. What are they doing?" He knew the boy didn't understand Skolian, but he talked to him anyway. He had little else to do. Although he still slept most of the time, he felt well enough now to stay awake a few hours each day.

The youth regarded him curiously. Dressed in blue trousers and a white shirt, he looked more like a schoolboy than a nurse. Only the medic's patch and Dahl suntree emblem on the shoulder of his shirt said otherwise. He poured Kelric another glass of tawmilk and offered it to him, but Kelric shook his head.

As the boy persisted, a laugh came from the other side of the room. "Maybe milk is not so good, heh?"

Kelric looked to see Deha Dahl standing in the door arch. She spoke to the nurse in their language and he bowed. Then he withdrew, leaving Kelric alone with the Manager.

"My greetings, Prince Kelricson." She came over to the bed. "Or perhaps you prefer a military title? Tertiary Valdoria?"

"Actually, I prefer Kelric."

"Kelric." She smiled. "Dabbiv says you seem better since we worked out this special menu for you."

"Much better." He hesitated, grappling with the awkwardness that always plagued him when he wanted to express something important—like gratitude to the person who had saved his life. "Manager Dahl, what you've done for me—I won't forget."

She watched him with an inscrutable expression. "Do not be so quick to thank me. Almost we didn't bring you here."

"Because of the Restriction?"

"Yes." She sat next to him on the bed. "When we ask for the Restriction, never did we imagine you would happen."

"You *asked* to be Restricted? Why?"

"We don't want your ISC occupying our world."

He stared at her. "As part of the Imperialate, you would have access to our technology, sciences, arts, nearly a thousand worlds—all of it. You gave that up because you didn't want ISC here?"

"You use loaded words." She spoke carefully. "Others use words such as *military dictatorship* for your Imperialate."

He tensed. "The Imperator is not a dictator."

She considered him. "Tell me something. What are you prince of? An ancient dynasty, yes?"

"The Ruby Dynasty. But the Rhon has no power anymore."

"The Rhon?"

"My family. That's what the Skolian people call us."

"And what do the Skolian people call the Imperator?"

He regarded her warily. "The Imperator."

"You play games with me. He is your brother, yes?"

Kelric inwardly swore. It would have been better for him had these people been less adept at digging information out of his ship's wreckage. "Half brother. Kurj and I have the same mother. But he came to his position through work. Not heredity."

"Kurj?"

"The Imperator."

"So," she said. "You call the Imperialate's dictator by his personal name."

"He's not a dictator, damn it."

"No?"

"No." The nature of his brother's violent rise to power was territory he had no wish to trod with this stranger. She was already too unsettling.

Heart rate and blood pressure anomaly, Bolt thought. It accessed his optical nerve and a translucent display appeared, superimposed on Deha, with diagrams of Kelric's vital signs.

Terminate display, Kelric thought. *You can give a synopsis.* Had Bolt been working right, he wouldn't have needed to ask for brief mode; he had long ago set that as the node's default.

The display vanished. Your hypothalamus is producing certain hormones, which in conjunction—

Skip the tech-talk, Kelric thought. *Just tell me what's wrong.* Nothing is "wrong." Unless you consider sexual arousal a problem.

He flushed. Just what he needed, a voyeuristic computer in his spine.

"Kelric?" Deha asked. "Are you all right?"

He scowled. "I'm fine."

"You look tired." She reached out to brush a curl out of his eyes.

In pure reflex, Kelric grabbed her wrist. As she froze, his mind caught up with his reflexes and he stopped. Bolt's combat libraries could direct reflexes far more complex than grabbing a wrist and the hydraulics that controlled his skeleton could as much as triple his response time. Any more would have required greater than the few kilowatts of power produced by his internal microfusion reactor, generating too much heat for his body to dump even with the reflective adaptations of his skin.

Deha sat utterly still, watching him. Disconcerted, he loosened his grip.

"I didn't mean to startle you," she said.

He rubbed his thumb over her palm. "My reflexes overdo it sometimes."

Her face gentled. Then she withdrew her hand and cleared his lunch tray, setting the remains of his meal on the nightstand. She took a pouch out of her robe and set it on the tray. "I bring you gift."

A gift? He picked up the pouch, making its contents rattle and click.

Deha had the same type of pouch hanging from her belt. She took it off and emptied a profusion of small shapes onto the tray: balls, cubes, polyhedrons, pyramids, disks, squares, rods, and more, in every color of the rainbow.

Intrigued, he poured a similar set out of his pouch. "What are they?"

"Dice."

"What do we do with them?"

"Play Quis."

"Is that a gambling game?"

"Sometimes." She pushed the pieces to the edges of the tray, then set a blue cube in the center the tray. "Your move."

"If they're dice, don't we have to roll them?"

Deha shook her head. "We say 'dice' because many centuries ago the pieces, they have numbers on them, and these numbers, they tell you what moves you can make. You pick a piece, roll it out, and the number that comes up tells you—" She paused. "What is this word I want? Elections? No . . . Options! Yes. This is the word."

"The number gives you options for doing something?"

"This is right. Options for placing your piece in a Quis structure." Deha lowered her voice, as if revealing a confidence. "Back then, Quis takes less skill. Now we build structures using strategies based *only* on rules. It takes much more work by the brain." She grinned. "But still we gamble on who wins. So. Make your move."

He laughed. "I've no idea how to play."

"Try anything. We see what happens."

Enjoying himself now, he set a bar on her cube. She pushed a purple cube up against her blue one. He placed a purple bar and she responded with a magenta cube.

"You know," he said, setting a square in the structure. "I have no idea what we're doing."

"I explain when we finish." Deha snapped her fingers. "But I forget. We must make a wager." She considered. "Two tekals. Is reasonable for beginner."

"What's a tekal?"

"A coin. One tekal buys you a sausage at market."

"I don't have any tekals."

Deha smiled. "You owe me then."

"I might win, you know."

She placed a red cube against her magenta cube. "We see."

He put a disk on top of her cube. "Your move."

"Not my move." She set an orange cube by her red cube. "My game."

"It is?"

"Very definitely."

He counted the dice. "You made more moves than I did. Don't I get to finish the round?"

She regarded him with approval. "Is true, you can finish. But is no way for you to beat me now."

"How did you win?"

"I made a small spectrum." She tapped her cubes. "Blue, purple, magenta, red, orange."

This was certainly a better diversion than arguing with her about his infamous brother. "What does it mean?"

"A spectrum is like a rainbow: red, orange, yellow, green, blue, purple. Then starts over with red again. Also you can put—what is the word? Interm?" She paused. "Intermediate. You can use intermediate colors if you want, like magenta between purple and red. For small spectrum, the line of dice must be more than four pieces. A grand spectrum is ten or more dice."

"Suppose I had blocked your line of cubes?"

"Ah." She nodded. "You learn fast. A block would stop me. Then I must go in another direction."

"Can you use different shapes?"

"Not in a spectrum. You can in a builder. Color stays the same in a builder and shape changes." She tapped a cube. "The number of sides is the order. Cube has six sides, so it is sixth order." She made a line of dice on the tray: pyramid, pentahedron, cube, heptahedron, octahedron. "This run follows order so it is a builder. If it follows both color and order, it is a queen's spectrum."

He grinned. "If I make a queen's spectrum, will I win back my tekals?"

Deha chuckled. "Maybe." She made a sweeping motion of her hand. "Many more structures and patterns exist. Spectrums and builders are only a start."

"I'd like to learn." He picked up a handful of dice. "If you have time to teach me."

"We all teach you. Everyone's Quis has a different personality." She lowered her voice again. "Really, it is more than gambling. The better one plays Quis, the greater her influence.

We . . . I keep losing the words. Talk? We talk with Quis. It is like a net that spreads to everyone. The better a person plays the net, the better her position in life."

"Is that why you manage Dahl? Because you play Quis well?"

Deha shrugged. "I have some ability. It is one reason the previous Manager chose me as her successor. But it works both ways. Managing Dahl gives me knowledge that aids my dice."

He regarded her, fascinated. "It sounds like more than a game."

"This is true. If you play Quis well enough, it can tell you stories." Deha considered. "I give an example with Varz Estate." She set a black dodecahedron on the tray. "Varz is a too-powerful Estate, second only to Karn. Varz has always challenged Karn for the Ministry. So we must help Karn gain advantage against Varz."

"Why not help Varz?"

She snorted. "I would help a scumrat before Varz."

"Ah." He smiled. "I see."

"So. I build structures that tell about, say, inequities in Varz import practices. I sit at Quis with my aides, they sit with their aides, their aides sit with others. Soon my input into the Quis spreads like ripples in pond. It reaches a logger in Viasa and she says to merchant, 'You know, I read much in the Quis lately. Much about Varz and all of it bad. It is a good thing Karn has the Ministry.' "

"Which doesn't sit well with Varz, I take it."

"Ah, but Manager Varz makes her own ripples." Deha lifted a handful of dice. "So the merchant tells the logger, 'You play Quis with dull-wits. If Karn keeps running things, soon we will all pay so much for goods we have no money left for Quis. Then, my friend, you never get paid what I owe you.' "

"Who wins?"

"This is the crucial point, yes? Everyone is in the Quis net. With so many people, ripples bounce back and forth, reinforce, cancel, make new ripples." She paused. "Perhaps that is our ultimate wager. Power. Control the Quis and you control the Twelve Estates."

Kelric wanted to ask more, but he was tiring. He leaned back in the pillows to gather his strength for new questions.

"Ai," Deha murmured. "I should let you rest."

"It's all right." He regarded her. "I meant to ask you—what news is there about the starport?"

Her inscrutable look came back. "I wrote the Ministry, as you ask. They verify what I tell you. After your people made the Restriction, they took away their ships. I am sorry. We have no port here."

"There must be some outpost."

"None."

"They would have left a base," he said. "I can find it with equipment on my ship."

"The crash destroyed your ship."

That wasn't what he wanted to hear. ISC had started to experiment with combining the EI brain of a Jag starfighter and the biomech web of its Jagernaut pilot. So the Jag's routines could run on Bolt and Bolt's could run on the Jag. When he disconnected from the ship, it usually felt like the mental equivalent of logging off a computer. What he felt now was different, a void, as if part of him had vanished.

Bolt, he thought. *Have you had any luck reaching the Jag?*

No. However, at this distance from the crash site, it is unlikely I will pick up any significant signal.

Surely you can get at least a residual interaction.

This is a logical assumption. However, I detect nothing.

Kelric considered Deha. "If the crash destroyed my ship that thoroughly, how am I still alive?"

"You don't remember? You ejected."

Bolt, did the Jag eject me?

It considered that option. My records of the crash are too garbled to determine what actually happened.

Kelric felt an unexpected grief at the Jag's destruction. It was an effect he ought to report. The ship's designers needed to know their latest modifications were creating a complex mental symbiosis between the ship's brain and its pilot. But Deha claimed no ISC personnel were on planet for him to contact. No starport, no base, no outpost, no nothing.

He didn't believe it.

Prepare Kyle probe, he thought.

Your Kyle centers are injured, Bolt thought.

Kelric tensed. *Why didn't you say anything before?*

I was too damaged. As I effect repairs to myself, I can better monitor you.

If his Kyle centers were injured it meant he had suffered brain damage. Kelric had always known that linking a bio-mech web to his brain had its risks, but realizing that in theory and facing the reality were two different things.

His Kyle centers were microscopic organs, the Kyle Afferent Body and Kyle Efferent Body. KAB and KEB. The KAB acted as a receiver, its molecular sites activated by fields produced in other people's brains. The KEB acted as a "transmitter," strengthening and modulating the fields his own brain produced. Everyone had a KAB and KEB, but in most people the organs were atrophied. In rare cases like his, the genes that controlled KAB and KEB growth were mutated, unable to carry out their duties. So the Kyle organs continued to grow.

Having an enhanced KAB and KEB, however, wasn't enough to make a Kyle. The brain also had to interpret the signals those organs received and sent. That function was carried out by specialized neural structures called *paras,* aided by the neurotransmitter psiamine. Most Kyle operators could only decode the moods of other people, but a strong operator could pick up intense thoughts if they came from nearby, particularly if the sender was also a Kyle operator.

Focusing inward, Kelric sensitized his KAB to Deha. It was like brushing the outer seawall of a hidden grotto. Bubbles surfaced in her thoughts: sexual arousal, thoughts of her Estate—

Pain seared his head, vaporizing the link. Blotches danced in his vision.

"So quiet," Deha said. "Is something wrong?"

"I'm just tired." Given his uncertain situation here, he had no intention of revealing his diminished capabilities.

She set aside his tray and helped him ease under the quilt. Sliding in to him, she tucked the covers about his body. Having her so close unsettled him. His last tour of duty had been a nightmare of skirmishes separated by extended periods of isolation while he ran reconnaissance. He hadn't touched a woman in a long time and Deha was no ordinary woman.

When Deha leaned over him, Kelric laid his hand on the small of her back. She stiffened as if a pulse of electricity shot up her spine. She didn't pull away, though. Instead she looked down at his face, her expression gentling.

Then she kissed him.

At first he was too startled to respond. When he recovered, he slid his arms around her waist and returned the kiss.

Warning, Bolt thought. *Amorous interaction with a potential enemy is unwise.*

Bolt, go away.

I am inside your body. I cannot leave.

Busy with the kiss, Kelric didn't respond.

After a while Deha raised her head, holding herself up with her hands. She reminded him of someone, but he couldn't place who. He caught a wisp of her mood, a sense of affection. Something else was there too. Regret? When he tried to concentrate, a headache lanced his temples. He dropped his arms, his forehead knotting with pain.

"Ai," Deha murmured. "I am sorry. I must let you rest." She stood up by the bed, watching him with her gentle expression, one he had never seen her use with her staff. She touched his hair, her hand brushing his curls. Then she withdrew. As he closed his eyes, he heard the door whisper closed.

Bolt, he thought. *I need an analysis of this situation.*

The analysis is simple. You shouldn't be kissing someone you don't trust.

Ah, but, what a kiss. Kelric smiled. *I still need an analysis of what she told me about there being no ISC base.*

You need to sleep. I will run calculations while you are down.

He had given up telling Bolt that humans didn't "go down" like computers when they slept. Bolt had decided its coinage was appropriate and resisted changing it. So Kelric simply closed his eyes and let sleep settle over him.

This ought to be interesting, Captain Hacha thought. They couldn't move Kelric to the dice table, so they moved the table to him, a blue lacquered stand with legs a handspan in length. It was easier for Kelric now that the doctors had removed his bodycast and put him in lighter casts that only went to midthigh. He sat up in bed and they set the table over his lap.

They were six players: Hacha and Rev pulled up chairs near the bed, Balv and Llaach sat on the bed, and Ixpar sat cross-legged between Balv and Llaach. Kelric blinked at them, seeming unsure what to do with so many people.

At least he had shown some modesty and put on a shirt. During the heat wave that descended on Dahl, he had been sleeping bare-chested, wearing only pajama trousers split up the sides to accommodate his casts. Although watching him that way had its pleasures, Hacha otherwise failed to see why Deha found him so attractive. He was too big, for one thing. Men shouldn't be taller than women. The idea of a male warrior repelled her.

Llaach adjusted the pillow behind his back and spoke slowly, so he could understand their language. "Are you comfortable?"

He answered in his heavy accent. "Yes. My thanks."

They each picked a die from Hacha's pouch, and Rev ended up with the highest-ranking piece, an orange heptagon. He opened the session and the game took off.

Hacha built her defense from polyhedrons, a wall blocking the other players. Her offense thrust forward in a phalanx of wedges. Rev attacked with bar-builders, battling her back and forth across the board. Balv tried to make a spectrum, but it kept running afoul of Ixpar's defensive walls. Llaach floundered after only a few moves and Kelric placed his dice randomly.

Then Hacha saw it; Ixpar was taking advantage of her battle with Rev to sneak in an attack. Hacha diverted her phalanx toward a weak spot in the girl's defense. Ixpar deflected the attack, but Hacha had slowed her down. Turning her attention back to Rev, she finally trapped him with one of her favorite moves: hawk's claw—a ring of dice closing like a claw around his highest-ranking structure.

"Heh." Rev exhaled. "The win goes to you, Hacha."

Balv smiled. "For a while there I thought Ixpar would get you both."

Hacha nodded to Ixpar. "You played well." It felt strange to omit the title *Successor Karn* when she spoke to the girl. But she agreed with Deha's decision; it was best not to reveal Ixpar's position to Kelric. The less he knew, the better.

Balv studied the board. "It looks like Rev is second and Ixpar third." He grinned. "But I beat you, Llaach."

Llaach peered at the pieces. "Pah," she grumbled. "You did."

Kelric was obviously trying to follow the conversation. He spoke with halting words. "I am last?"

"Yhee," Balv said. "I'm afraid so."

"I understand not *yhee*," Kelric said. When Ixpar started to answer him in Skolian, he shook his head. "Coban. So I learn."

Hacha frowned. "Coba is the name of the world. We don't speak 'cabon.' We call our language Teotecan. *Yhee* is a formal form of the word *yes*."

"The informal form is *yip*," Balv added. "But you only hear it in slang."

Kelric tried the word. "Yhees."

"Yhee," Rev said.

"Yheez," Kelric said.

Llaach laughed. "It's all right. Say it however you like. Your accent is beautiful."

"And don't be discouraged about losing the game." Balv motioned toward Hacha and Rev. "You're playing with Dahl's best."

"Kelric didn't lose," Ixpar said. "He made a flat-stack. That ranks over Llaach's toppled builder."

What was this? Hacha looked where Ixpar pointed and saw a neat stack of blue disks nestled behind one of Rev's towers. A perfect flat-stack and she had missed it. That irked her. She hadn't expected Kelric even to start a structure.

"I can't believe I never saw that," Balv said.

Kelric tapped the table. "Is—" He hesitated, then asked Ixpar something in Skolian.

"Blue," Ixpar said.

"Table is blue." Kelric tapped his stack. "Also blue. So it hides."

Rev's laugh rumbled. "A camouflage. You'll do well, Kelric."

"I don't believe it," Llaach said. "I got caught by a camouflage."

Ixpar smiled. "Maybe you had other thoughts distracting you."

As the others laughed, Llaach reddened. "Blow off, you oafs."

When Kelric gave Ixpar a questioning look, she said, "Llaach recently took a kasi."

"Kasi?" he asked.

"Husband," Hacha said. "Llaach wed the youth Jevi." It didn't surprise her that Llaach was distracted, married to a man as handsome and charming as Jevi. He reminded Hacha of her own husband. The similarities between the two men ran deeper than appearance; both were dice players in the Dahl Calanya. She and Llaach had served on the Calanya honor guard for a time, giving them the rare opportunity to court a Calani. It was true that in letting her wed a Calani, Deha had bestowed her with great honor. But what good was honor when Hacha could only visit her husband instead of living with him? It made her crazy. On top of that, she was stuck with this disagreeable assignment, guarding Kelric.

"Ask Balv or Rev," Ixpar was telling Kelric. "They can show you."

Balv pushed up his sleeve, revealing a gold band around his wrist. "It symbolizes the vow that joins the woman and the man. A man who wears the bands is called a kasi."

Kelric glanced at the bands on Rev's wrists. "All of you have someone?"

Llaach laughed. "We've all been caught." She winked at Ixpar. "Most of us, anyway."

The girl smiled. "I'm keeping my options open."

"You sound like Deha," Balv said.

Kelric's reaction was so subtle that Hacha suspected only she caught it. But she had no doubt; the moment he heard the Manager's name he stiffened.

"Manager Dahl is alone?" he asked.

Hacha spoke brusquely. "By her choice. Deha has loved only Jaym."

"What happen to him?" Kelric asked.

"He died of a fever several years ago," Balv said. "Since then Deha has been—well, different. More distant."

"She doesn't want another Akasi," Hacha said.

"Akasi?" Kelric asked.

"It's the title of a Manager's husband," Ixpar said.

Glancing at Ixpar, Hacha saw the flicker of jealousy on the girl's face. She had been around long enough to recognize that look. It seemed the Ministry Successor was as taken by this offworlder as Deha.

As far as Hacha could see, that meant nothing but trouble.

3

Double Circle

Deha stared out the window of her office into the Estate gardens. Maybe she had a fever. Or it was the weather. Or else she was just crazy. Kelric was too different. Too young. And too forward. Several times since she had first kissed him, he had initiated a return of affections. In her day, the rules were clear: women made the advances. Everything was different now. Young people had their own rules, few of which made sense to her. Besides, Kelric was an offworlder, half brother to the Imperator, for wind's sake. Who knew what rules he lived by? She might as well heave the old ways out the window for all the help they gave her now.

"Manager Dahl?"

Deha turned to see Hacha in the door arch. "Captain. My greetings."

Hacha bowed. "Do you have a moment?"

"I was going to see Kelric. Walk with me."

They walked along open halls with high ceilings. Made from stone and lit only by high windows, this wing of the Estate remained cool despite the heat.

"I'm concerned about Successor Karn," Hacha said. "I don't think it's wise she spend so much time with Kelric."

"I didn't realize she was there that often," Deha said.

"She translates for him. But he knows enough now to manage on his own."

"Has he done anything to threaten her?"

"No. Nothing. But we should take no chances where her safety is concerned."

Deha thought for a moment. "Tell Kelric she's been neglecting her schoolwork and won't be able to see him as much."

"As much?"

Although Deha knew she could stop Ixpar from seeing Kelric, she had no desire to antagonize the girl. "Brief visits are all right, if guards accompany her into the room."

"I'll take care of it."

They walked in silence for a while. Eventually Hacha said, "How are you feeling?"

Deha glanced at her. "Fine. Why?"

"Senior Physician Rohka asked me to talk to you."

Deha scowled. Not this again. Ever since that minor heart attack of hers last year, her staff had been acting as if she were a blown-glass Quis die. Don't work so hard, don't stay up so late, don't push yourself. To listen to them talk, a person would think she was a doddering old woman instead of a vigorous Manager in her prime.

"I'm fine," Deha said.

"Just don't go playing Quis with ghosts."

Deha smiled. "I won't." She considered the captain. "How are your Quis sessions with Kelric?"

Hacha spoke grudgingly. "He does have talent."

"That was my impression also." It wasn't only his obvious knack for the game. Deha had never met anyone who learned rules and strategies so fast. At times she had an odd sense, as if he kept a record in his mind of what he learned and paged through it when he had a question.

At the skyroom, she left Hacha outside with the other guards. Inside, she found Kelric asleep, lying on his back in the sweltering heat with the covers thrown off his upper body, leaving his chest bare. She quickly closed the door, giving him privacy.

For a while she just sat on the bed, watching him sleep.

Eventually the temptation became too great and she slid her hand across his chest. His gold nipples glittered and felt more metallic than normal skin. The hair curling on his chest wasn't as stiff as true metal, but it had a smooth, cool texture to it.

Kelric opened his eyes. With a drowsy smile, he slid his arms around her waist and spoke in Teotecan. "My greetings, Manager Dahl."

Deha leaned over and kissed him. When he pulled her down next to him on the bed, she stiffened, knowing it was wrong to take advantage of his being laid up this way. But he was so *willing*. As they kissed, she slid her hand along his side, down to his leg. He was wearing sleep trousers, well-washed linen that felt downy under her palm. She stroked his muscles through the thin material. Such a pleasure, touching him this way.

As his kiss grew more passionate, Kelric rolled her onto her back and stretched out on top of her. Put off by his aggressive response, Deha pulled away her head. She eased out from under him and sat up.

Kelric blinked. Then he drew himself into a sitting position, his plaster-sheathed legs sliding under the quilt. He spoke in halting Teotecan. "Something is wrong?"

She paused. "No, it's nothing."

He looked puzzled, but his face gentled as she closed her hand around his. He said, "Jag, news you?"

"I don't understand."

He tried again. "My Jag. My ship. News have you?"

So. He ventured into even more difficult territory now. "We went through every bit of debris we found," she said. "I'm sorry, Kelric. But it's all slag. Any communications equipment was destroyed."

"I need look myself."

Not a chance, she thought. Although they had blown up his ship, she had no intention of letting him near the remains. Who knew what he might salvage?

He watched her with an odd look, as if he were concentrating on a monologue he could barely hear. Then he gasped and doubled over, his palms pressed against his temples.

"Kelric!" Deha leaned over him. "What's wrong?"

His face knotted. "Head . . . hurts."

"I'll get the doctor."

"No." He lowered his arms. "Nothing she can do."

The door swung open and Captain Hacha strode into the room. As soon as she saw them on the bed, she stopped. "My apologies." She left quickly, closing the door behind her.

"Kelric, I'm sorry." Deha slid off the bed. "I shouldn't have put you in such a compromising position." She touched his shoulder. "I'll have Senior Physician Rohka bring you a potion for your headache."

"What about ship?"

"There's nothing we can do."

He watched her closely. "Your words, they make tricks of light."

"What do you mean?"

"Are they part lies? I don't know."

You know more than you realize, she thought. "You should get some rest." She kissed him again and took her leave before he could ask more questions.

Deha found Hacha waiting outside the skyroom. She motioned for the captain to walk with her. When they reached the privacy of the vaulted corridors, Deha said, "You wanted to see me?"

"Kelric's guards gave me a strange report about Ixpar Karn," Hacha said. "This morning they saw her come out of his room. But they never saw her go in."

"Probably she was in there before they came on duty."

"They looked at the start of their shift. He was alone. They closed the door and a while later Ixpar walked out."

"Check into it." Deha thought of Ixpar's political clout. "But be discreet."

They continued walking through the halls. Finally Deha said, "What is it?"

Hacha glanced at her. "Ma'am?"

"I know you. You're worried about something."

"As captain of your escort, I have no business concerning myself with your private life."

"Then tell me as my friend."

Hacha exhaled. "To use a man for your pleasure, especially a man in so vulnerable a position as Kelric—it is unlike you."

"What makes you think my intentions toward him are dishonorable?"

"You certainly can't make him your Akasi."

"Why not?"

Hacha laid her hand on Deha's arm, drawing the Manager to a stop. "He isn't worthy of you."

Dryly, Deha said, "I suspect the Rhon would disagree with you as to who isn't worthy of whom."

"I'm sorry to be blunt. But how many other women's beds do you think he's been in?"

Deha shrugged. "I will learn to deal with his past."

"What about the rest of it? He's a Jagernaut. Up until now, he's been in no condition to do much more than sleep. But he's getting stronger. When he realizes we never intend to let him go, his reaction won't be mild."

"Everything you say is true." Deha paused. "But he will be my Akasi, Hacha. Whether he consents to it or not."

Scroll in hand, Ixpar knelt in front of the stone wall. The Estate dungeons were a few paces to her right, damp and unused for centuries. She unrolled the scroll, a copy of the ancient Estate plans she had filched from the Dahl museum. Yes, there it was; the distance between this wall and the nearest cell as shown on the diagram was less than the actual distance she had just measured on the wall.

Ixpar grinned. She had begun this game years ago when she discovered the museum at Karn housed copies of the plans used to build the Estate. Comparing them with the real Karn, she found hundreds of inconsistencies. Most were changes made over the centuries, but a few were inexplicable. She finally uncovered their secret: hidden passages honeycombed the Estate.

Now the Dahl plans were giving up their secrets. Running her hands over the stone, she found a crumbling niche where the wall met the ground. She dug her finger into it and jarred loose the cracked remains of a switch, clicking it to one side.

Holding her breath, she waited. Sometimes the ancient mechanisms were broken or jammed—

The clink of stone hitting stone sounded inside the wall. Bracing her feet against the ground, she leaned her weight into the wall. With a grating protest, as if wakened from a long sleep, a massive block slid inward and ponderously swung to one side. Beyond it, a passage stretched into darkness. She gathered up the scroll and squeezed into the tunnel, then pushed the door back into place. Lifting her oil lamp, she surveyed the latest addition to her collection of hidden passages.

An unassuming tunnel made of rough stone extended in front of her for a few paces and then turned to the left. She followed it around several turns, until the passage terminated in a dead end. An examination of the wall uncovered three niches near the ceiling. It took her a while to figure out the sequence for flipping the switches, but her efforts were finally rewarded with the clink of releasing pins. She pushed in the wall, leaving a circular hole big enough for her to crawl through.

Ixpar recognized the passage beyond. She had explored it a few days ago. The light from her lamp made huge Ixpar shadows on the walls, giving the tunnel a barbaric aspect, as if an ancient warrior queen might step out of the shadows any moment and challenge the intruder in her domain. Ixpar imagined the queen; fierce and vital, gleaming in her bronze and leather armor. With a flourish, she whipped out an imaginary sword and dueled her opponent up and down the passage, thrusting at the air until she vanquished her invisible foe. Then she dropped to the ground, laughing and gasping for breath.

I should bring a real sword, she thought. It would make the game even better. Then again, how would she explain why she was walking around Dahl with a sword? Better to bring something she could hide under her shirt, perhaps a blunt-edged discus in a sling. You couldn't fight a duel with it, but discuses were always good for knocking down enemies while you were skulking around in the shadows.

She wondered why the ancient queens made these passages. Secret escape routes, in case an enemy took the Estate? Maybe warriors prowled around down here engaging in Estate intrigues. Or perhaps a queen made this passage so she could sneak into the bedroom of her concubine. Ixpar smiled. No wonder her imaginary opponent had fought so hard. She was protecting her lover.

But I won, Ixpar thought. I get to claim the prize.

The tunnel took her to a dead end that she already knew was a secret door. Easing it open, she peered into the room beyond. Her prize lay fast asleep, unsuspecting of the warrior queen sneaking into his boudoir, his gold chest rising and falling in deep breaths.

Ixpar smirked, remembering how Kelric's guards had gaped when she walked out of his room yesterday. She had enjoyed it immensely. Still, it was best not to do it again. Hacha was probably trying to figure out how she managed it. She doubted the captain would solve the puzzle, but she intended to take no chances.

Leaving the door ajar, Ixpar slipped into the skyroom. She went over and sat on the edge of the bed, contemplating Kelric's sleeping form. Faced with the reality of him, she had no idea how to proceed with her courtship. In fact, she was so discreet about courting him, she suspected only she knew she was doing it. But how could she make her intentions known with guards hulking around her all the time? She couldn't pay suit to him with an audience.

Voices outside the door brought her jumping to her feet. She ran into the tunnel, barely managing to close it up before the skyroom door scraped open. With her ear pressed against the wall, she could just hear Deha's voice as she talked to Kelric's guards.

Pah, Ixpar thought. If she didn't make her intentions known to Kelric soon, it would be too late. Deha was also courting him—and doing a much better job of it.

4

Orb Starburst

Morning sun filled the skyroom as Kelric's nurse pushed aside the curtains. An autumn breeze fluttered the boy's shirt and rippled through the pants he wore tucked into his sky-blue boots. The gentle picture he made only added more jolt to his words.

"Exploded?" Kelric pushed up on his elbow. "What do you mean, exploded?"

"The fires after the crash," the boy said. "Like when fuel tanks on a windrider catch fire."

"Starships don't run on petrol. And if the antimatter on my ship hadn't properly deactivated, it would have taken half the mountain range when it blew."

"The mountain is still there," the boy said. "But your ship did blow up. Captain Hacha said so herself."

The hell it did. What his nurse described was impossible, unless someone set the blast *after* the crash. What was Deha up to? He pulled away the quilt and swung his cast-covered legs off the bed.

His nurse tensed. "What are you doing?"

"Getting up."

"You can't get up."

Kelric leaned on a chair and stood up on his plaster-encased feet. Then he grinned. "Care to bet on that?"

"You have to stay in bed."

"Why? Every time I get up you people tell me to lie down. Every time I talk about my ship the subject gets changed. No one will tell me a thing. So I'm going to find out for myself."

"You can't," the boy said. "Not with plaster on your legs."

"Good point." Kelric sat down and banged his legs against

the metal rim that bordered the bottom of the bed. Plaster sprayed out over the floor.

"Stop it!" The nurse grabbed his leg in midswing. "You'll break the bones again."

"Not bones." He tugged away his leg and unpeeled strips of plaster in powdery chunks. "Just casts."

A grating noise came from the wall.

Kelric stopped. "What was that?"

His nurse turned to the wall. "I don't know."

The noise came again. Then a panel in the wall opened and Ixpar stepped into the room.

"Hey," the boy said.

Ixpar pushed the panel closed, leaving a smooth blank wall. She spoke to the nurse. "Get the guards. *Now.*"

As the youth strode to the door, Kelric went back to work, peeling the last chunk of plaster off his legs.

"Kelric, stop," Ixpar said.

"Not a chance." He stood up and tried an exploratory step. His legs held up, so he limped across the room to a long mirror with Quis designs etched around its edges. A man in blue sleep clothes looked back at him, a thinner man than he remembered.

When the increased flow of blood tingled in his legs, at first it puzzled him. Then he almost laughed in relief. His nanomeds weren't dead; they were responding to his weakened condition, trying to help him.

"What are you doing?" a voice said.

Kelric turned to see Captain Hacha in the door arch. "Standing," he said.

She used what was apparently meant as a placating voice. "We don't want you to hurt yourself. Why don't you get back into bed? I'll send for the doctor."

Kelric limped toward the door. "I don't need a doctor."

"I'm sorry." She blocked his way. "You can't leave."

"Why not?" He looked around as Rev, Llaach, and Balv stepped into the room. "Why are you keeping me locked up?"

"You need to recuperate," Hacha said.

"No I don't."

The last semblance of placation disappeared from her voice. "Get back into bed."

Combat mode toggled, Bolt thought.

Kelric caught sight of Ixpar inching toward the door. Moving with enhanced speed, he grabbed her arm. When all four guards whipped out their guns, he didn't have time to wonder at the vehemence of their response. Bolt's reflex libraries took over and bypassed his brain, sending commands straight to the hydraulics that controlled his body.

As the guards fired, he dove to one side, swinging Ixpar into the nurse so both she and the boy stumbled back into the room. Although he avoided most of the shots, one caught him in the shoulder. When the tiny needles punctured his skin, Bolt thought: Alert: injection of chemicals into bloodstream. Synthesizing possible antidotes.

As Kelric staggered, Rev wrenched his arms behind his back while Llaach leveled a stunner at his chest. The armlock was one Kelric had learned to break in basic training. He twisted free, went for Llaach—

—and his legs collapsed.

Kelric fell, taking Llaach with him. She shoved her gun right up against his chest and fired. Then she went limp in his arms, passing out as he choked her. Numbness spread through Kelric's torso.

Switching to full hydraulics, Bolt thought.

Kelric's legs jerked as the hydraulics took control of his body. They kept him moving, like a machine, despite the drugs coursing through his veins. Even as he jumped to his feet, Balv was lunging at him. He grappled with the younger man, rolling him over his shoulder and slamming him to the ground. At full strength, the throw would have killed Balv. As it was, Bolt calculated only the force necessary for a knockout and sent that data to Kelric's hydraulics, all within a fraction of a second.

Then he was wrestling with Rev and Hacha, crashing back and forth across the doorway. He twisted the stunner away from Rev and emptied the last of its charge into the gigantic guard. As Hacha knocked the gun out of his hand, he kicked up his leg and caught her in the stomach, hurling her into the wall. Again Bolt calculated for a knockout rather than kill.

Gasping as his hydraulics faltered, Kelric sank to his knees among the unconscious guards. The nurse also lay in a heap, caught in the cross fire of a stunner.

Motion flickered in his side vision. He jumped to his feet and grabbed Ixpar just before she darted out of the room. Shoving her back inside, he closed the door.

"You'll never make it out of Dahl," she said. "There are guards all over the Estate."

"They won't shoot." Kelric sagged against the door, taking a labored breath. "Not if it means hitting you." Keeping his attention on Ixpar, he picked up Balv's stunner and took Llaach's knife out of her boot. "The charge needed to knock out someone my size could do you a lot of damage. And I have a hunch." He straightened up. "I think your safety is a lot more important around here than anyone lets on."

"That's ridiculous."

"I've spent my entire life among people with power, Ixpar. I know it when I see it." He tilted his head toward the wall. "Where does your secret door lead to?"

"I don't know how to open it from this side."

Kelric pulled her over to the panel. "Open it."

"No."

He didn't bother to argue, he just heaved his bulk into the wall. After being rammed a few times, it buckled in to reveal a stone passage. He pulled Ixpar inside and limped down the tunnel, bringing her with him.

As they walked, he brooded. He had finally figured out who Deha reminded him of. His first wife. An Imperialate admiral over twenty years his senior, Corey had died ten years ago, assassinated by Trader terrorists. One day she was a passionate, powerful woman; the next she was gone. Now he had the damn-fool idiocy to see her in Deha.

The tunnel exited into a tower. A staircase spiraled up on the right and a door stood on the left. He motioned at the stairs. "What's up there?"

"One of the storage wings," Ixpar said.

With his gun poised, he stood to one side and opened the door, revealing an empty garden. Leaving the door open, as if they had gone out of it, he pushed Ixpar toward the stairs. "Up. You first."

Doors appeared at each landing. The first three were locked, but the fourth opened into a room filled with graceful urns as tall as his waist. Dusty light filtered in a window midway up the opposite wall.

"This is crazy," Ixpar said as he pushed her inside. "It's like backing yourself into a box. Why didn't you go through the garden?"

"It's the first place they'll look." He shut the door. "I want some answers. You can start by telling me why Coba is Restricted. What is it you're all trying to hide?"

"Nothing. What Manager Dahl told you is true."

"That you don't like ISC? You'll have to do better than that."

She clenched her fists. "Did it ever occur to you that our freedom means more to us than your Imperialate? Or maybe conquerors prefer to forget that about the conquered."

"You people never intended to let me go, did you?"

"You were dying. We had to make a decision. We gave you your life." She met his gaze. "But we won't trade our freedom for yours."

Kelric knew ISC wouldn't Restrict Coba and then leave it untended. That his Jag's EI brain directed his ship to this region of the planet suggested ISC had made contact with the Twelve Estates. That meant the base or port would be somewhere nearby. Given the local mountainous terrain, it was probably in the desert. What he needed was transportation.

"Where is the airfield?" he asked.

"Across Dahl. On the other side of the Calanya."

"What's a Calanya?"

"Some parks and buildings. Dice players live there."

Dice again. He shook his head, then stiffened as pain shot through his muscles. The stun shots were wearing off.

She watched him. "You ought to be out as flat as a Quis disk right now. Four hits you took and that one time Llaach had her gun shoved right into your chest."

Kelric made no response. Instead he pulled her to a bench under the window and made her step up onto it. Looking out, he saw mountains towering over the city. He moved to one side, out of view, and motioned at the latch on the pane. "Open it."

When she pushed the latch, the window banged open and wind rushed into the room. As Kelric slid off his shirt, she flushed. "What are you doing, taking off your clothes?"

"Making a holster." He fastened the stunner and Llaach's knife into the shirt, then tied it around his waist. "We're going to climb down the tower."

She stared at him. "Those little cracks in its wall won't support me, let alone you."

"I've climbed down worse in training drills." He grasped her around the waist and lifted her onto the sill. "Turn around so you're sitting with your legs hanging outside."

Sweat beaded on her forehead. But she did as he said, with more composure than many adults he had seen in similar situations. Leaning out, he saw a courtyard four stories below them. Beyond it, the city spread out on all sides.

"Where is this Calanya?" he asked.

Ixpar indicated a distant wall across the city. "On the other side of that windbreak."

Kelric climbed over the sill and lowered himself into the wind, facing the tower. He probed the wall with his toes until he found a foothold. Then he tugged Ixpar off the sill, holding her as she maneuvered around to face the wall. They descended slowly, Ixpar about half a meter above him.

Suddenly an avalanche of pebbles cascaded over him, accompanied by a frantic scraping. Looking up, he saw a toe-hold under Ixpar's foot disintegrate. He worked his toes deeper into a crack and clenched the wall with a vise grip that, courtesy of his biomech, would take a powered wrench to release. Even so, when Ixpar slid into him, he had to strain to keep from being knocked off the wall.

She eased her weight away from him. "I'm all right."

Releasing his breath, Kelric resumed the climb. When he felt packed dirt under his feet, he let go of the wall, then swayed, spots dancing in his vision. As Ixpar slid down next to him, he sagged against the tower. She tried to bolt, but he caught her around the waist.

"Kelric, listen to me," she said. "You'll never make it to the airfield. Give it up before you rebreak your legs." More gently she said, "We won't hurt you."

You have no idea, he thought. His fight with the guards had unmasked a portion of his hidden enhancements, but Deha and her people didn't know the extent of his abilities. It left him room to bluff. But he had to get help. The longer he went without repair, the more it aggravated the damage to his internal systems.

Holding Ixpar's arm, he drew her to the gate. A plaza lay outside the courtyard, bordered by pale blue houses. In the center of the plaza, opening to the sky like a flower, a white fountain glazed with accents of color brought to mind lakes, forests, and sun. Water arched up from it, whipped by the wind into a mist of rainbows.

He set off in a limping jog across the plaza, pulling Ixpar with him. On the other side they entered a maze of narrow cobbled lanes that wound among stone houses three and four stories high, with windows full of plants. As they ran, the crisp mountain air cleared his head. Once the sound of laughter reached their ears, and an instant later a flock of children dashed into the lane, too intent on their game of chase to notice two people hiding in the shadows of a recessed doorway.

A lawn separated the city outskirts from the wall Ixpar called the Calanya windbreak. The barrier stood as high as three adults and was thick enough for two people to walk abreast on its top edge. It curved off in both directions for kilometers. Holes sculpted in the stone provided glimpses of landscaped parks beyond.

"It should be easy to climb this," Kelric said. "We can cut through the parks."

"No!" Ixpar said.

He blinked. That was the strongest emotion he had ever seen her show. "Why not?"

"It is a violation of the Calanya," she said. "You will contaminate the Quis."

Contaminate a dice game? He drew her over to the windbreak. "Climb."

Ixpar scowled. "May a giant hawk pluck you off the mountain and feed you to her babies."

He couldn't help but smile. "I hope not."

The wind grew stronger as they scaled the wall, tearing at their clothes and hair when they reached the top. It died away as they descended the inner side. At the bottom, a lush carpet of grass sloped down from the windbreak. Groves of trees heavy with gold fruit were scattered at the foot of the hill and far across the parks the windows in a cluster of buildings sparkled like liquid diamonds.

They set off across the lawn. He was limping more now, his still healing legs growing more fatigued. He glanced at Ixpar. "You said dice players live here?"

"The men in a Calanya are all expert Quis players," she said. "You could call them advisers. To Deha. Quis advisers."

"And Quis is power." When Ixpar nodded, Kelric smiled. "This park isn't a bad setup just for being good at dice."

They were crossing a carved wooden bridge that arched over a stream when they saw the man. He was sitting on a stone bench on the other side of the stream, relaxing in the sun.

Kelric halted with Ixpar on the bridge and drew his gun. "Who is that?"

"A Calani," she said. "A dice player who lives in a Calanya."

The man stood up, watching them. He was slender, having gray hair and the look of a scholar. His clothes were simple, with an appearance of wealth about them: suede trousers and knee boots, a darker suede belt tooled with Quis designs, and a white shirt with embroidered cuffs. Guards made from what looked like solid gold circled his wrists and two gold armbands showed on each of his upper arms.

"Those bands make him look like a Jagernaut," Kelric said.

"You insult him," Ixpar said.

"Since when is that an insult?" With Ixpar at his side, Kelric walked down to the Calani and spoke in Teotecan. "You are the only one out here?"

The Calani watched him in silence.

Kelric glanced at Ixpar. "Why won't he talk?"

"Calani never speak to Outsiders." She crossed her arms. "In the Old Age, the penalty for breaking into a Calanya was death."

Kelric frowned. He neither needed nor wanted another hostage, but he couldn't leave the man free to sound an alarm. So he fired the stunner. Surprise flashed across the Calani's face as he collapsed.

"No!" Ixpar dropped on her knees and felt for the man's pulse.

"I'm sorry." Kelric rubbed his temples. "But I can't take chances."

The look she gave him could have chilled ice. "We can't leave him like this."

"He'll be all right." Kelric drew her to her feet. "He'll just sleep for a few hours." He headed for a single-story building made from amberwood and blue stone. Potted plants hung from its eaves and the shutters were open, revealing windows of gold glass bordered by copper.

Inside, they walked down a hall painted in green and shadow-gray, dappled like a forest glade with sun filtering through the foliage. It ended at a sunroom; the walls shaded from amber at the floor into white-gold at the top. The ceiling was blue, with clouds half covering a sun. In one corner, a youth sat at a table playing Quis solitaire.

"Get up," Kelric said.

The youth looked up as if surfacing from a dive. When he saw Kelric, he blinked and stood up.

Kelric glanced at the meter on the stunner. He couldn't keep knocking out people; the gun's charge was almost exhausted. So he motioned at a papery screen painted with trees and birds that blocked a doorway across the room. "Open it."

With Kelric and Ixpar following, the youth backed toward the screen. He pushed it aside to reveal a larger sunroom with two huge doors in the opposite wall. In one corner of the room a boy sat listening to the talk of a man with a halo of white hair. In the center, seven men sat at a table playing Quis.

Kelric silently swore. The odds were now eleven to one and some of the dice players looked formidable. When they saw him, they rose to their feet. None spoke—except Ixpar, who let out a shout loud enough to wake the next planet.

The doors across the room slammed open and four guards strode into the room. As Kelric fired, the stunner sputtered. He managed to knock out the guards, but as soon as the dice players realized his gun was empty they started toward him.

Kelric grabbed the youth from the sunroom and jerked back his head. "If anybody twitches, I'll snap his neck."

The Quis players froze. Still holding the boy, Kelric took Ixpar's arm and pulled his hostages across the room to the double doors. As soon as they were outside, he shoved the youth back into the Calanya and closed the doors, then locked everyone inside.

Ixpar twisted in his grip. "You can't do this."

"Watch me." He headed down the hall, drawing her with him. He opened the door at its end onto gardens and lawns. Several hundred meters away he saw a line of trees, and beyond them an airfield tower rose into the sky.

They were halfway to the trees when shouts broke out behind them. Spinning around, Kelric saw guards pouring out of the Calanya. He broke into a run, pulling Ixpar, and she huffed for breath as she struggled to keep up. His hunch about her proved correct; no one fired at them.

They ran through the line of trees and onto the airfield. Sprinting across the tarmac, he headed for the first hangar. When he saw it was empty, he ran toward the next.

An octet of guards burst out of the control tower ahead of them. Kelric stopped so fast it would have jolted Ixpar off her feet if he hadn't caught her. A glance back showed the guards from the Calanya closing in on them from behind. So he backed up toward the hangar they had just passed, coming to a stop against its rough wall. The guards surrounded them, forming a semicircle three rows thick, with the closest guards about ten meters away.

Holding Ixpar with her back against his front, Kelric laid his knife across her neck. "Come any closer," he said, "and I'll open her throat."

Ixpar went rigid, her dismay reaching even his injured Kyle

centers. He had no intention of carrying out his threat; he would go into combat mode if he had to fight, relying on his enhancements to avoid capture. But he had a hunch the bluff was his strongest weapon right now.

The guards parted and Deha appeared, coming forward. "Let her go. An Estate Manager will make a better hostage."

"No," he said. "Call off your guards."

"I don't believe you would hurt her."

"Are you willing to bet her life on that?"

Deha turned to a guard captain. "Clear the field."

"You stay," Kelric said.

The area cleared with remarkable speed. When he and Ixpar were alone with Deha, Kelric tilted his head toward the next hangar. "Over there."

They walked to the structure, he and Deha watching each other, his knife against Ixpar's neck.

When they reached the hangar, he saw a windrider inside. He pulled Ixpar over to the aircraft and pushed her at the hatch. "Get inside."

"Kelric, no." Deha swallowed. "She's just a child. Leave her here and take me."

Not a chance, he thought. He had no doubt that Deha unarmed was as dangerous as her guards were armed; her intellect was more potent than a stunner. Ixpar made a safer hostage.

He waited while Ixpar scrambled into the rider. Then he stepped up into the hatchway, keeping close watch on Deha.

Strain showed in the Manager's face. "Kelric, don't do this."

Warning: Bolt thought. Posture and voice inflections of agent below suggest a threat behind you.

Kelric spun around—in time to see Ixpar hurl a blunt-edged discus at him. He dodged, but at such close quarters he couldn't evade it even with enhanced speed. The discus hit his temple and he plunged into blackness.

5

Queen's Spectral Tower

Jahlt Karn stood before the wall of one-way glass. To avoid a glare, lights on both sides of it had been lowered. In the dimness, her gray eyes darkened to jet. Gray streaked the braid of ebony hair that hung down her back. Dressed in black trousers, black tunic, and gray boots, she blended with the shadows. She stood tall and gaunt, spoke in a quiet voice, and as Minister she ruled the Twelve Estates.

Deha stood next to her. Below them, in the room beyond the glass, Kelric lay unconscious on a bed.

"Imperialate law is clear." Jahlt turned to Deha. "The Restriction forbids us contact with Skolians. You should have taken him to the port."

"He would have died before we reached it," Deha said.

"All Coba will suffer the consequences of your decision." Jahlt shook her head. "As long as he lives, the chance exists he might escape. Then what? Neither he nor his notorious family will appreciate our attempts to hold him prisoner." She regarded Deha. "We have no choice. He must not live."

Deha tensed. "We've had no executions in decades."

"Nevertheless. It is either execution or life in prison, and I see no reason to take chances."

Deha spoke carefully. "There are many forms of prison."

"Meaning?"

"Consider the one institution our ancestors guarded more closely than any prison."

"Put him in a Calanya?" Jahlt snorted. "You might as well roll a firebomb with your Quis dice."

Deha had her rebuttal ready. "He would be kept separate from the others. Until he adapts."

Jahlt studied her. "I begin to wonder if other factors affect your decisions about this offworlder."

"Such as?"

"He is a remarkably striking young man."

"I don't appreciate your implication."

"Then tell me something," Jahlt said. "If you swear this man to your Calanya, will he be Calani? Or Akasi Calani?"

Deha crossed her arms. "Whether or not I make him my Akasi is my business."

"It becomes my business when I think your hormones are impairing your judgment."

"My judgment is fine."

"Yet you want to swear a man into your Calanya who can't play Quis."

"He can play Quis. He had nothing else to do while he was recovering."

Jahlt shrugged. "To know the rudiments of dice and have the talent for Calanya Quis are two different things."

"True," Deha said. "But consider this: he had no money to bet when he was learning, so he wagered planets instead." She smiled. "After a few days my escort owned half the Imperialate."

Dryly Jahlt said, "I'm sure ISC will gladly pay the debt when Captain Hacha shows up to collect."

"There is no debt. Kelric won back his planets."

Jahlt moved her hand in dismissal. "It wouldn't be the first time a handsome face swayed Hacha into letting a lesser player win."

"Hacha doesn't like him. Besides, he's never won a game against her. But he's beaten both Llaach and Balv and they're no beginners. He even beat Rev once." Deha paused. "I've played him myself, Jahlt. He has a true gift."

The Minister put her hands behind her back and paced across the room. "Have you considered the effect he will have on the Quis?"

"What effect do you mean?"

Jahlt turned. "I don't know. That's the problem." She came back to Deha. "And if he escapes? No talent is worth that risk."

"He won't escape."

"The last time you told me that, he kidnapped my successor."

"It won't happen again."

Jahlt's voice hardened. "It certainly won't."

"If we send Kelric to prison," Deha said, "it will be an abominable waste of his life and his genius. Resurrect the death penalty and we put Coba back centuries."

The Minister considered her. Then she went to the window and looked down at Kelric. After a moment she said, "I will trust your judgment, Deha. But think well before you make your final decision." Jahlt turned back to her. "If you swear him to the Calanya, he will be there for life, with all that will mean for you, for Dahl, and for Coba."

Chankah Dahl, Successor to the Dahl Manager, was a young woman, though not so young that the years hadn't honed her skills in Estate politics. With a position at Dahl second only to Deha, a kasi and two young daughters to her name, and the respect of her peers, Chankah was well satisfied with her life.

Today she walked along the Ivory Hall with the doctor Dabbiv. "You should tell all of this to Deha," Chankah said.

"I have told her," he said. "She says that under no condition am I to stop sedating Kelric. She's afraid if he wakes up he'll try to escape again."

"Are you sure the drugs are poisoning him? Maybe the dosage is just too high."

"That's what Deha said. But the dosage is only half that needed for a man his size." Dabbiv came to a halt. "It's all wrong. I have trouble bringing him out of sedation so he can eat. When I do get food into him he can't keep it down, not even what he could eat before. And his blood has a violet tinge to it. Maybe that's normal. Maybe it means he's dying. I just don't *know*."

Chankah laid a calming hand on his arm. "Did you ask him why his blood is purple?"

"He said something about a chemical reaction of 'nanomeds' with nitrogen in the air. It makes no sense."

"Perhaps you should talk to Deha again about your concerns."

"It won't do any good. She doesn't take anything I say seriously."

"Of course she does. Why else would she appoint you to the Estate staff?"

He snorted. "I have no idea. If she had her way, we'd be back in the Old Age and I'd be locked up in a Calanya."

Chankah raised her eyebrows. "That's absurd. She practically dotes on you."

"I don't want to be *doted* on. I'm not a pet."

"It can't be that bad."

He scowled. "How would you know? You've never experienced it. If I said 'Deha, the wind is blowing,' she'd say 'That's nice, Dabbiv.' If you said 'Deha, the wind is blowing,' she'd say 'A profound observation, Chankah. One worthy of my successor.' "

"Dabbiv."

"It's true." He took a breath. "That's why I need your support. She listens to you."

Despite Dabbiv's reputation for being excitable, Chankah considered him one of the most promising physicians in Dahl. It had been her own recommendation that Deha appoint him to her staff. If he was this worried, she ought to speak to Deha. "All right. I'll need to see his medical records first, though."

"You'll have them. And Chankah—there's something else."

"Yes?"

"Are you familiar with the work being done at Varz Estate?"

"Some experiments with blood composition, isn't it?"

Dabbiv started to walk again. "They've isolated several blood types. At least three."

She walked with him. "I wouldn't take this claim too seriously. Not when it originates from Varz."

"Just because there's hostility between Varz and Karn, it doesn't make the Varz biochemists incompetent."

"It's the uses Manager Varz intends for the research that I question."

Dabbiv cleared his throat. It sounded like preparation for battle. "I want to send a sample of Kelric's blood to their labs for analysis."

"Impossible."

"Why?"

She frowned. "Which reason do you want first? That Minister Karn forbids us to let it be known we have a Skolian here? That Deha would object to correspondence with Varz? Or simply that it would be a waste of time?"

"If Kelric dies," he said, "none of those reasons will stand up against the wind."

"Heh." She felt like an airsack going empty. "You think it's that important?"

"Yes."

"I'll see what I can do. But I make no promises."

"There's one more thing."

"Any more and Deha will send me to dig rock on a quarry crew."

Dabbiv made a frustrated noise. "It's her health. She won't listen to anyone. If she has another heart attack like the one last year, it could kill her."

"She's sensitive about it. She will think I imply she's too weak to manage Dahl."

"If she doesn't slow down," Dabbiv said, "she won't be too weak. She'll be too dead."

Chankah exhaled. "All right. I'll talk to her."

Usually the Quis patterns engraved on the walls of an Estate hall fascinated Ixpar. Not today. The carvings sped past in a blur as she strode through the Lower Halls of Dahl. Nothing could erase the memory of Kelric's words: *Come any closer and I'll open her throat.* How did she reconcile the Jagernaut who had dragged her across Dahl with the man she had watched learning Quis? It seemed ludicrous now, the way she had courted him.

Tomorrow Jahlt was taking her back to Karn, and in a few more days Kelric would be sworn to the Dahl Calanya, forever forbidden to her. So for the first time, she was going to disobey a direct order from the Minister.

Ixpar walked to the AmberTower and climbed its spiral stairs, around and around the cramped turns. At the top she followed the curve of the wall until she came to a window of one-way glass. On its other side, the AmberRoom glowed, with gold walls and a goldstone floor. Plants in baskets hung about the windows and sunlight sifted through the foliage, making patterns on the walls. Kelric was sleeping in a bed with yellow sheets and a green velvet cover.

Ixpar went on, walking around the tower until she found the door with its octet of guards. Captain Hacha bowed to her. "My greetings, Successor Karn."

Ixpar nodded. "I've come to visit Kelric."

"He's asleep."

Ixpar knew he wasn't asleep. He was drugged senseless. "I still wish to see him."

Hacha shifted her weight. Ixpar had given her a no-win choice; antagonize the Ministry Successor or disobey the Dahl Manager. After considering for a moment, Hacha pressed panels on the door handle in a complicated combination. A bolt thumped and she swung the door open. But as Ixpar walked forward, Hacha motioned at the guards and they fell into formation around her.

"You may all wait Outside," Ixpar said.

Hacha shook her head. "I'm sorry, Successor Karn. We can't leave you alone with him."

Ixpar knew Hacha well enough to realize she had pushed the captain as far as she would go. "Very well. Wait by the door."

Hacha nodded, satisfied with the compromise.

Ixpar sat in a chair next to Kelric's bed and spoke in a voice too soft for the guards to overhear. "I came to tell you goodbye, Kelric. I'm sorry about what we've done to you. But we had to. I wish I could make it better for you." She swallowed. "I wish I knew how to stop caring about you."

"Ixpar?" His lashes lifted and he looked at her with eyes like liquid gold.

She leaned closer. "How are you awake? The doctors gave you a sleep potion."

"Sleep?" His eyes closed. "I thought . . . poison."

"Poison? Kelric, no. It must be a mistake."

"Ixpar . . ."

"Yes?"

"Was bluff." The drugs slurred his speech, heightening his accent. "I wouldn't have killed you."

She wondered if he had any idea how much that meant to her. As he sank back into sleep, she touched his cheek. "Good-bye, Kelric."

Senior Physician Rohka paced in front of Deha's desk. "I wish you would put him somewhere with fewer stairs."

"The exercise is good for you." With Kelric asleep in the tower and guards posted on every landing, Deha's mind was more at ease. They had come too close to disaster. Who would have guessed Ixpar could search out secret tunnels unknown even to the Estate archivists? Had the girl not been carrying the discus as part of her "quest" game, Kelric might now be on his way back to ISC headquarters.

She regarded the doctor. "Why does he have that limp?"

"One leg healed with a slight twist," Rohka said. "His bones had so many breaks, it's a miracle they set properly at all."

A buzz came from the desk's audiocom. Deha switched it on. "Manager Dahl."

Chankah's voice floated into the air. "Can you come up here?"

"Is there a problem?"

"He woke up," Chankah said.

Deha glanced at Rohka. "I thought you gave him a seda-tive."

"I did. He should have been out until tonight."

They found Chankah outside the one-way glass in the tower. Inside the AmberRoom, Kelric was sitting up in bed rubbing his eyes.

Deha activated the audiocom by the window. "Kelric?"

He looked around. "Where are you?"

"Outside. How are you feeling?"

He scowled. "Like I've been poisoned."

She glanced at Rohka. "Can there be something in what Dabbiv says?"

"Dabbiv overreacts. Kelric obviously isn't being poisoned to death."

"But?"

Grudgingly, Rohka said, "The medicine does seem to bother him." She thought for a moment. "There is another sleep potion. It doesn't usually work as well, but I can try it."

"All right." Thinking of how Kelric would react to yet another potion, Deha added, "But put it in his tea."

After the doctor left, Chankah spoke to Deha. "I wish you would reconsider swearing him to the Calanya. Send him to prison."

"For what? He hasn't done anything wrong."

"For Coba's safety. For your safety. Winds, Deha, he could snap you in two as easily as if you were a stalk of grain."

"He won't."

"You don't know that. At least take precautions."

"Such as?"

"I'll show you."

Chankah took her down to the Old Library. As always, the room soothed, with its shelves crammed full of books, old and new, gilt edged, bound in leather. A display case by the wall held a set of exquisitely tooled Calanya guards as ancient as the Estate.

Chankah opened the case and lifted out the guards. "Give these to him."

Deha blinked at her. "First you want me to send him to prison. Then you say I should honor him above all other Calani."

"I don't suggest this for his honor. These are the only guards we have that are made in the old way."

"Meaning they can be locked together?" Deha scowled. "That's barbaric."

"We're talking about your *life*." Chankah clenched the guards. "What if he turns violent again?"

For a long moment Deha considered her successor. Then she exhaled. "Let me think on it."

The room was a smear of gold dotted by bits of emerald. Kelric tried to focus, but blurred vision apparently came as a side effect of the battle going on inside his body. One species of his nanomeds eliminated chemicals—like unwanted drugs—that his biomech web hadn't authorized. The biochemistry sounded simple: a med locked onto an invading molecule, deactivated it if possible, usually by changing its molecular structure or taking it apart, and flushed the debris out of his body.

It rarely worked that smoothly. The meds first had to find the invaders, then get rid of them without producing hazardous byproducts. It also took energy, and fighting an invasion this severe drained him. Nor could the meds immediately capture every drug invader. According to Bolt, the sedative molecules that had so far escaped were destroying enzymes he needed to metabolize certain foods. The Coban diet made it worse; the unboiled water contained bacteria that attacked his digestive system, and some of the spices and sauces would have required intervention by his meds even if he had been in perfect condition.

His condition was far from perfect. Bolt's memory was corrupted, some bio-optic threads in his body were experiencing attenuated transmission, his hydraulics had sustained structural damage, and his meds were replicating too slowly. Worse, some meds were replicating improperly, forcing others to treat them like invaders.

The sound of an opening door broke Kelric's concentration. Two blurs were approaching him. "Hacha?" he asked. "Rev?"

"We brought you lunch," Rev said. As he came nearer, a blur in his hands resolved into a tray. He set it on the nightstand.

Kelric regarded the food without interest. At least the Tanghi tea was made with boiled water. After the guards left, he drank the Tanghi and then lay down again, exhausted from his battle with the drugs.

It wasn't until he opened his eyes that he realized he had fallen asleep. Morning sunshine was pouring through the window when a moment ago the shadows of late afternoon had filled the room.

"How do you feel?" Deha asked.

Disoriented, he rolled over and saw her standing by the bed. As he sat up, his wrist caught on a blanket. When he pushed away the cloth, his hand slid over metal. Puzzled, he looked down at his wrists.

Guards. Calanya guards. The gold was welded together so cleanly around each of his wrists that its joining blended into the engraved designs on the metal. Yanking away the covers, he saw his ankles similarly guarded by gold. He swore, swung around to Deha—and hands shoved him down on his back. He looked up into the bores of Rev and Llaach's guns.

"Try anything," Llaach said, "and we'll put you out like an avalanche on an airbug."

"Let him go," Deha said.

Rev released him, but Llaach looked as if she wanted to dump him out the window. When she finally let go, Kelric sat up and regarded them implacably, then gave Deha the same look.

The Manager sat on the bed. "I know you don't want to be a Calani, Kelric. But winds, it's better than the alternatives. Most of my advisers think you should be sent to prison. Jahlt Karn almost ordered your execution."

He stared at her. "The Minister wants me killed?"

"Yes."

"For *what*?" He felt as if a cage were closing around him. "Don't you realize what will happen if the Imperial Assembly learns what you people are doing?"

"That," Llaach said, "is why the Minister wants you dead." She touched her gun to his temple. "Dead like that Calani whose neck you threatened to break."

Deha glanced at her. "Perhaps you and Rev should wait Outside." When they started to protest, Deha shook her head. With obvious reluctance, the guards withdrew. Llaach paused at the door, looking back at Deha, but when the Manager frowned, Llaach went out and closed the door.

Deha turned back to him. "I'm sorry. They don't trust you."

"And you do?" he asked.

"It would do you no good to take me hostage. My guards have orders to stop any escape you attempt even if they have to shoot me."

"This is crazy. You can't lock me up."

"Your Oath ceremony is tonight."

"I'm not taking any damn oath."

"Another man will speak for you." Deha paused. "In the Old Age the Oath was always given through a surrogate, supposedly because Calani were too exalted to speak in public." Dryly she added, "I suspect the real reason was to avoid questions about whether or not the Calani was there of his own free will."

He snorted. "That figures."

"Kelric, I truly am sorry." She stood up. "I wish it was your choice to stay."

He couldn't give the answer she wanted, so he said nothing.

After she left, Kelric lay back, trying to subdue his vertigo. He wished they would stop with their potions. His head felt strange, like an earthquake fault under pressure. He needed to think, but he was too tired to sit up and every time he lay down he drifted into a fitful sleep.

That evening, while he lay in a drugged daze, the door opened. Rev and Balv came in, followed by a boy carrying a pile of clothes. The boy approached shyly and showed him the garments. "For the ceremony, sir."

Rubbing his eyes, Kelric made himself sit up. Both Rev and Balv had their guns out, but they needn't have bothered. His battle with the drugs left him too drained to fight anyone.

With the boy helping like a valet, he dressed. The shirt was made from burgundy velvet. Its sleeves fit tight around his Calanya guards, then widened out from wrist to shoulder. The collar opened halfway down his chest, but crisscrossing laces held it closed. Almost closed. A gray suede vest went over the shirt, its snug fit accenting his physique. The trousers, made from a rich gray suede, were odd. The outer seam of each leg was unsewn but kept closed by small flaps that buttoned across it. Suede knee boots finished off the picture. Kelric was no expert on the messages given by clothes, but even he recognized the ones in these: sexually provocative, in a subtle manner designed to suggest high social class.

He almost refused to wear them. But he already had a pounding headache, and he didn't want to make it worse by getting into a contest of wills.

When Kelric finished dressing, Balv ushered the valet out of the room. But Rev remained.

"I wanted to tell you," the guard said.

"Yes?" Kelric asked.

"About tonight," Rev said. "For a normal ceremony you would have chosen an Oath Brother."

"Oath Brother?"

"Your closest friend." Rev hesitated. "I know you have no reason to call me a friend. But you shouldn't have to stand alone."

"You would stand as my brother?"

"Yes."

The offer caught Kelric by surprise. It was true he felt a kinship with Rev; not only were they alike physically, they also shared a similar awkwardness with words. But he had thought his escape attempt blotted out any friendships he had with his guards. He felt it most with Llaach, whose hostility was so intense he could almost touch it.

He spoke quietly. "I would be honored to have you stand as my brother."

Rev bowed to him. "The honor is mine."

After Rev left, Kelric fell into a half sleep. At Night's Midhour the escort and four more guards came for him. Not only did they carry stunners now, they also wore ceremonial curved swords with glistening nacre inlaid in the hilts.

No one spoke as he stood up. Captain Hacha stepped behind him, drawing his arms behind his back. Metal pins clinked— and his wrist guards locked together, binding his arms behind him.

"What the—?" He tried to pull apart his wrists. "What are you doing?"

No one answered. Instead they escorted him from the room. They descended the stairs that spiraled around the tower, a guard on each side keeping a steadying hand on his arm. At the bottom they walked through halls lit only by torches that sent shadows flickering on the walls. When they reached a recessed archway, Rev pulled back the bolt in an ancient door there and leaned his weight into the heavy portal until it creaked open.

A great hall stretched out before them, lit by no more than the starlight pouring through its crystal walls. Radiance shimmered in the air, reflected off the marble floor, glimmered in the shadows of a ceiling so high above their heads Kelric could barely make out its vaulted spaces.

A retinue of robed figures drifted toward them from the far

end of the hall. Deha walked at its front with a younger woman at her side.

"Chankah," Rev said, following Kelric's gaze to the unfamiliar woman. "The Dahl Successor."

The shimmering air, the starlight, and the shadowy retinue all combined with his drugged haze to make him feel as if he were floating in a surreal netherworld. When Balv prodded him with his gun, Kelric walked forward. The retinue parted so he was passing down an aisle of people.

Deha led them back the way they had come, to a large dais at the far end of the hall. Made from black marble and veined with crystal, the disk scintillated in the starlight. The rows of finely carved chairs that circled it held an aura of age, as if they had guarded the dais for centuries.

The retinue withdrew to the chairs, and Deha climbed the dais with Chankah. When Balv prodded him up the steps, Kelric stumbled and with his wrists bound behind his back he couldn't catch his balance. As he fell to one knee, his guards drew their swords. He froze, acutely aware of the honed steel only fingerspans away from his body.

Deha spoke. "Help him up."

Hacha slid her hand under his arm, supporting him as he rose to his feet. With their swords still drawn, the guards escorted him up the stairs. They followed Deha and Chankah to a depression in the center of the dais, a circular area about a meter in diameter and a handspan deep. A rail at waist height circled it, with an opening just wide enough to let a person step through. In the shadows on the far edge of the dais, the vague outline of a table curved in a semicircle. Glitters came from the blades of the guards' drawn swords.

Deha spoke to the retinue. "Ekaf Dahl, approach the Circle."

A man came forward and climbed the dais. When he reached Deha, she indicated a place to the right of the circle. "You will Speak from here." Then she and Chankah walked toward the table, becoming blurs as they receded into the dark.

A moment later, her voice floated through the air. "Sevtar Dahl, you may enter the Circle."

As far as Kelric knew, no one named Sevtar stood on the dais. But Rev nudged him forward. With the guard at his side, and the drawn swords all around him, Kelric stepped through the gap in the rail, down into the sunken area.

A pipe began playing, caressing the night with notes as delicate as a lover's touch. Its melody flowed through the hall, sweet and haunting. Then it receded, growing fainter, until it vanished.

Deha spoke out of the shadows. "Does one here stand as Oath Brother to Sevtar?"

"I stand for him," Rev said.

"What are your words?"

Kelric realized then just how much Rev's offer meant. The taciturn giant made no secret of his discomfort with public speaking.

Rev's voice rumbled. "I speak thus: Sevtar may differ from us, but the quality of his character transcends differences. His inner strength is as great as his outer. He will honor your Calanya."

Chankah spoke softly. "Your words are heard and recorded, Rev of Dahl."

The guard bowed. Then he stepped out of the Circle and vanished into the darkness.

A bell chimed, two notes, high and clear, vibrating in the silvery air. Chankah began speaking, what sounded like a chant in a language other than Teotecan, verses with an ancient sound, a hypnotic rhythm. When she finished, the bell chimed again, a musical echo of the radiance filling the hall.

Deha spoke. "Hear my words, Sevtar, but before you give them back to me as Oath know that your life is bound by them."

Even if Kelric had intended to answer, he was too dazed to think of a response. It didn't matter. Ekaf spoke. "I hear and understand."

A glow appeared on the table, a flame in a bowl of oil. Ruddy light flickered across Deha's face. "For Dahl and for Coba, do you, Sevtar, enter the Circle to give your Oath?"

"I do," Ekaf said.

"Do you swear that you will hold my Estate above all else, as you hold the future of Dahl in your hands and your mind?"

"I swear."

"Do you swear to keep forever the discipline of the Calanya? To never read or write? To never speak in the presence of those who are not of the Calanya?"

Saints almighty, Kelric thought. What is this?

"I swear," Ekaf said.

"Do you swear, on penalty of your life, that your loyalty is to Dahl, only to Dahl, and completely to Dahl?"

"I swear," Ekaf said. "With my life."

A chime rippled like a waterfall. Deha passed her hand over the oil, and the flame flickered and vanished.

Kelric felt as if he were floating in the shimmering air. Deha and her successor seemed to materialize out of nowhere, walking toward the Circle. Chankah carried a box of carved wood. When they reached the rail, she opened it to reveal two armbands lying on velvet. They looked like solid gold.

Deha regarded him. "In return for your Oath, I vow that for the rest of your life you will be provided for as befits a Calani." Then she nodded to Hacha. When the captain moved behind him and lifted his manacled wrists, Kelric stiffened. But all she did was release him. Bringing his arms in front of his body, he rubbed his sore muscles.

"Kelric." Deha spoke softly. "You need to put your hands on the rail."

He set his palms on the wood. It felt cool and smooth under his palms.

"The bands I give you are those of an Akasi Calani." Her face gentled. "May you someday wear them of your own free will." She took an armband from the box. Picking up his hand, she slid on the band and pushed it up his arm until it stopped on his biceps. She slid the second band onto his other arm.

"Sevtar Dahl," Deha said. "You are now a First Level Calani of Dahl."

6

Night's Move

The escort returned Kelric to the AmberRoom the same way they had taken him from it; in complete silence, his wrists locked behind his back, without Deha or her retinue. The journey up the tower seemed endless. He couldn't even use his hands to lean on the rail as he climbed.

Inside the AmberRoom, Hacha freed his wrists. Brusquely she said, "Don't try to leave. An armed octet will be posted Outside at all times." She turned and walked toward the door, motioning for the others to follow.

Rev spoke. "I'll stay a while."

Hacha glanced back and shrugged. "Suit yourself." Then she left with the others, closing the door behind her.

Kelric sat on the edge of the bed. "Is she always that abrupt? Or is it just me?"

Rev said nothing.

"Ekaf took the vow of silence," Kelric said. "Not me."

"I have no right to speak with you."

"Hacha just did."

"Only because she is now captain of your Calanya escort and Deha has allowed it. But she can't talk with you. Only to you."

Kelric exhaled. "I don't understand any of this."

"You can speak with other Dahl Calani," Rev said. "And with Deha. But not to anyone Outside."

"You do it too."

"It?"

"Say *Outside* as if it were a title."

"It is," Rev said. "Those within the Calanya are Inside. The rest of the universe is Outside."

Dryly, Kelric said, "That leaves a lot of people Outside."

"Yes. You are one of a very few."

"Great," Kelric muttered.

Rev sat in a chair. "Kelric, it is considered a great honor among our people." He stopped. "I should call you Sevtar now."

"Why Sevtar?"

"He is the dawn god, a giant with skin made from sunlight. He strides across the sky, pushing back the night so the sun-goddess Savina can sail out from behind the mountains on her giant hawk." Rev smiled. "Deha thought it appropriate."

"What's wrong with the name Kelric?"

"Kelric isn't Coban."

"You're right, he isn't. But my name is Kelric."

"You have a new name now."

Kelric shook his head. This was getting him nowhere. He ran his fingers over his right armband. Akasi? Deha reminded him too much of Corey, his first wife, stirring ghosts better left buried. Corey had been a well-known figure, a hero of the people. During the long days after her death, at the ceremonies and state funeral, all broadcast to a grieving public, he had stood silent in his black dress uniform, a widower when he was barely twenty-four. On display before everyone, he had kept it all inside, how it tore him apart to lose her. In the ten years since, he had gradually regained his equilibrium. Now Deha came along, throwing everything off balance.

It was safer to think of other things. He regarded Rev. "I thank you for your speech."

"It was my honor."

"I'm glad someone feels that way. I think Llaach wants to heave me off a cliff."

"There is the matter of Jevi," Rev said.

"Jevi? He's her husband, isn't he?"

"Yes." Rev paused. "He is also the youth whose neck you threatened to break in the Calanya."

Kelric winced. No wonder Llaach was angry.

Across the room the door swung open, leaving Balv framed in its arch, with torchlight flickering behind him. He stepped aside and Deha walked in, her silken robe from the Oath Ceremony rippling in the dusky light.

Surprise flashed across Rev's face. "Well. Ah." He stood up. "I will go now."

As Rev crossed the room, Hacha and Llaach joined Balv in the archway. When Rev reached them, the four guards stood looking at Deha, who had stopped halfway between Kelric and the door.

The Manager smiled. "Do you four plan to stay there all night?"

Hacha regarded her. "Ma'am—"

"Yes?"

Hacha started to speak, stopped, then said, "If you need us, we're right outside."

"Thank you, Captain," Deha said. "Good night."

The guards shifted their feet, glancing at Kelric. Finally they closed the door.

Deha turned to him. "It seems they still don't trust you."

"Maybe you shouldn't either," he said, though in truth he wanted her to stay.

She walked over to the bed. "I don't."

"Then why are you here?"

She dimmed the lamp on the nightstand until only stars lit the room. Then she knelt next to him on the bed. "I don't trust that you would do what is best for Coba if you left here. I do trust the quality of your judgment. You won't hurt me."

"How do you know that?"

She brushed the back of her hand over his cheek in a gesture of intimacy he had come to know well. "I've played Quis with you."

Kelric took hold of her wrist. He had started with a half-formed thought of pushing her away, but instead he drew her into his arms, as he had done so many other times recently. In the starlight her eyes made large pools of black.

Deha eased off his vest, then undid the laces on his shirt and let it fall open. Laying her hand against his chest, she murmured, "Your skin is so much like metal. How can that be?"

He brushed his hand over her hair. "My grandfather's ancestors fiddled with their genes to make themselves reflective. To help dump heat. They lived on a hot, bright planet."

"I don't know what genes are." Smiling, she nudged him down on the bed. "But the fiddling sounds good." When Kelric gave a soft laugh, she stretched out against his side and kissed him, her tongue tickling his mouth until he let her come inside.

Eventually, when they paused, Deha spoke near his ear. "You truly are a beautiful man. Your eyes are like liquid sunshine. They grace a face that would shame Khozaar, most handsome of all gods."

Kelric blinked. He wished he were more adept at the sort of words lovers spoke to each other. She didn't seem to expect a response, though. She tugged down his shirt until it tangled around his elbows and then she traced her finger through the hair on his chest. "So beautiful. But so tall. Are all Skolian men as large as you?"

"Not most." At six feet seven, he was large anywhere, even on Coba where most everyone was tall. He extricated himself from his shirt, pulling out his arms, but when she started to stroke him again, he caught her hand. "Deha."

"Hmmm?" She slid down his body until her head was level with his chest. Then she took his nipple into her mouth.

"Ah . . ." He stared at the shadowed ceiling while she played with his nipple, kissing and gently biting it. After a moment he remembered what he was going to say. "We can't keep pretending this is a normal wedding night." Closing his eyes, he added, "Do the other one too."

She moved across his chest. Eventually he said, "You can't force me to stay on Coba. ISC will look for me."

Deha stopped kissing him. "Not if they think you're dead." She slid back up to look at his face. "You are a prince among your people, yes? I have made you one among mine. Is that really so terrible?"

"I have my own life." He undid her braid, letting her glossy hair pour over their bodies. "I want it back."

"I can offer you a better one. No more being alone."

Kelric brushed her cheek with his thumb. Although he had no intention of staying on Coba, at this moment "no more being alone" felt just fine. He opened her robe, revealing a satin shift underneath. Her breasts were firm, the nipples erect under the satin. As he rubbed them, her eyes closed. Pulling her forward, he took her breast into his mouth and suckled it through the satin. She made a satisfied noise deep in her throat, somewhere between a sigh and a moan.

When he paused for a breath, Deha started to play with the flaps on the seams of his trousers. "You are discreet in how you wear these," she said. "Old-fashioned. I like that."

He could guess how those less "old-fashioned" wore the style: fasten the flaps looser and the pants revealed a strip of skin from the man's waist to foot. He wondered if she saw the contradiction in giving him clothes that were deliberately provocative and then expecting him to wear them in a way that hid what they were designed to show. He suspected not; all he picked up from her was desire, mixed with relief that perhaps he wasn't as "modern" as she had believed.

It was soon obvious, however, that his clothes were also designed so that a woman who knew what she was doing could make removing them as erotic as she wanted. Deha took her time unfastening the flaps, her hands caressing his thighs and legs until he was so aroused that Bolt started up with warnings about elevated physiological responses. Kelric told the node to shut up.

When he tugged at her clothes, Deha sat up on her heels and slid off the robe, then pulled the satin shift over her head. She had well-toned curves, slender and lean, with long, muscular legs. Kelric trailed his fingertips across her flat stomach. The hint of stretch marks showed at her hips, indicating she had given birth.

"Your body is lovely," he said. "How do you stay so fit?"

"Morning walk. Evening walk." Wryly she added, "Arguing with my doctors."

"Your doctors?"

"They worry too much." She smiled. "It gives them something to do."

Deha finished taking off his clothes, then lay next to him and slid her hand up his inner thigh. While she caressed him, he rubbed his hands over her backside and his cheek against the top of her head. Then she slid on top of his body, straddling his hips, and eased onto him.

They made love slowly, building together. Her touch was

skilled, first gentle, then urgent. When he used his Kyle senses to match his response to her emotions, she murmured in Teotecan, her words too blurred to distinguish, simply noises of affection.

One time he caught a memory that came into her mind, the image of himself laughing, with sunlight in his hair. At that moment she paused, pensive as she raised her head to look at him. Then she lay down again and kissed him. Kelric hugged her, stroking her hair.

As they built to their crest, Kelric tried to open his mind to her, to share his pleasure. Then the orgasm broke over him and he lost his senses in her embrace and the silver night.

Later when they were drowsing in each other's arms, he tried again to reach her mind, with no more success than before. Deha simply wasn't a Kyle. It didn't mean he couldn't feel affection for her, but it did leave him with a sense of incompletion.

Still, he almost felt content. Only a dull throb in his temples kept him awake. It intensified every time he used his Kyle senses on it. Whatever brain damage he had taken was growing worse.

Kelric watched Deha sleep, wondering how much he should tell her. He had no illusions about why these people feared him. They kept their autonomy because Coba was inconsequential enough that some overworked ISC bureaucrat had let the Restriction through. But the Twelve Estates didn't merit a status meant for places so uninhabitable or hostile they required quarantine. As soon as ISC took closer notice, Coba's evanescent independence would evaporate. Absorption by the Imperialate would bring the Cobans advanced technology, but it would also mean military occupation and obedience to Imperial law, as well as opening their world to Imperial use.

He wasn't sure why the guards had hesitated to shoot Ixpar. But he felt Deha's resolve; if he took her hostage and forced his guards to choose between letting him go or risking their Manager's life, they would follow her orders to stop him— even if it meant killing her.

"No," he said.

Deha opened her eyes. "You are still awake?" She stretched against his side. "You seemed so tired at the ceremony."

He smiled, savoring the feel of her skin sliding against his. "I guess you revived me."

Her face gentled, that expression she showed only him. "You look pensive."

He chose his words carefully. "I have a system inside my body. It's called biomech."

Deha pushed up on her elbow. "We wondered, after your fight with the guards. You seemed beyond a normal human." She watched his face. "But why does that make you pensive?"

"The system needs maintenance." That wasn't really the problem, but it came close enough without revealing his weakened condition.

"What will happen if it doesn't get it?" she asked.

"It could injure me."

She tensed. "Kelric, anything I can do to help, I will."

He wondered if she realized she was calling him Kelric rather than the Teotecan name they had given him. "You can't provide what it needs. I have to leave Coba."

Softly she said, "We can't let you go. You know that."

"Even if refusing causes me harm?"

Her voice caught. "I'm sorry."

Looking at her, he almost wished he hadn't said anything. He felt her anguish. Again he caught one of her memories, a glimpse of her former Akasi, this time lying still and lifeless on a funeral bower.

"Ai, Deha." He touched her cheek. "I'm not going to die."

"Anything I can do here on Coba, I will. I mean that."

He pulled her into his arms. "Just lie with me. Like this."

Eventually they slept. Sometime later he was awakened by her moving about. Opening his eyes, he saw her sit up and reach for her shift.

"Are you cold?" he asked.

"No." She drew the shift over her head. "I have to finish some paperwork in my office."

"On your wedding night?"

Deha gave him a rueful smile. "Dahl won't stop even for

that." She pulled on her robe, then leaned over and kissed him. "Sleep well, my Akasi."

After she left, Kelric lay staring at the ceiling. The throb in his head kept shifting and resettling, as if adjusting to an inner pressure. Finally he got up and paced around the suite. In an adjoining chamber he found a bathtub the size of a swimming pool, tiled in green and gold, with statues of three-legged animals at its corners. He started toward it—

—and pain rocked through his head like an earthquake.

Kelric gasped and fell to his knees by the pool. In the water he saw the reflection of his face contort in agony. Shocks hit him again and again, built and subsided, like blows from a hammer. It went on and on until he wanted to cry out. But he made no sound, no motion, barely even breathed.

Gradually the tremors came farther apart. Their force eased, lessened, died away. For a long time afterward he remained still, afraid to move lest it start again.

A ray of light touched his face. Looking up, he saw the dawn through a window across the room.

Kelric closed his eyes. *Bolt.*

No answer.

Bolt, what just happened?

I'm not sure. I am d%#&—

What?

I am damaged. The bio-electrodes in your brain are also malfunctioning. The seizure you just experienced was due to their making your neurons misfire. I can't ^^^&

You can't what?

I can't fix it. You must go to a biomech repair facility. If you don't, you may lose all function.

Kelric knew that without his biomech, he had even less chance of escaping. He had to make his move now, despite his unhealed injuries, before it was too late.

He returned to the bedroom and dressed, not in the sexually suggestive outfit from his Oath ceremony, but in some old clothes he found in the bureau. He braced himself against the door and sensitized his Kyle organs to the guards outside, using his biomech to amplify the signals from his KEB. When his link with the guards faltered, he clenched his teeth against the pain, overrode the safety toggles in his web, and let a burst of power surge out of his brain.

A cry came through the door; Bolt had miscalculated and applied too much force. With his injuries Kelric couldn't barrier himself against the shock of the attack as it reflected back to him. It hammered at his mind until he groaned and spots clouded his vision. Half blinded by pain, he threw his bulk into the door again and again, until it flew open with a bang.

Outside, his guards lay unconscious on the floor. He limped around their bodies and headed for the stairs.

7

Hawk's Flight

Deha sat behind her desk, bathed in the morning sunshine slanting through the window at her back. Piles of folders waited and a full day faced her: city meetings, Estate conferences, Quis sessions. She reached for the audiocom—

Another hand came from behind her and bent back the com switch until the wood snapped off with a crack.

Deha spun her chair around—to see Kelric a few paces away, aiming a stunner at her head. Behind him, curtains billowed out from an open window that should have been closed. She stared at him, remembering how he had felt in her arms. He looked far different now, his expression closed to her.

"I came for my Jumbler," he said.

"Jumbler?" It sounded like a description of himself, or at least what he did to her emotional state. How had he escaped the tower?

"My gun," he said. "I must have been wearing it when you found me."

She thought of the monster weapon they had found on him. "We left it on your ship. The explosion destroyed it." In truth, she had stowed the gun in her safe. Her experts said it didn't work. But then, they were only experts when it came to stunners.

Kelric looked as if he were straining to hear a muttered conversation. Softly he said, "That's what I needed," followed by, "Forgive me, Deha."

Then he fired.

The guards who had formerly watched the AmberRoom now stood clumped before Deha's desk. Dabbiv stood with them, his hands in the pockets of his white sweater where Deha knew he always put them when he was tense.

"Escaped." Deha was standing behind her desk, her head pounding in the aftermath of the stun shots. Kelric had pumped her with enough charge to put her out for the entire morning. "Where were all of you while he was escaping?"

"Kelric knocked them out," Hacha said.

Deha scowled. "How could he knock out every guard in the tower, sneak into my office, knock me out, rob my safe, and disappear? My entire CityGuard can't find one man?"

"We have every available unit out searching," Hacha said. "I also doubled the detail at the airfield. We'll catch him."

"You'd better." Deha turned to Dabbiv. "And you. Insisting we stop his medication. No wonder he escaped."

"The drugs were poisoning him," Dabbiv said.

"If he was in such terrible shape, how did he manage this phenomenal escape? I want him back on sedation the instant he's found."

"Deha, no." Dabbiv pulled his hands out of his pockets. "There's no telling what cumulative effect the drugs will have on him."

She forced out the words. "That may be. But we have no choice."

"My calling is to heal. Not harm." He took a breath. "I'd rather you put me on a city crew than ask me to go against that."

Deha pushed her hand through the tendrils that had escaped her braid. "Fine. You're no longer on his case. You're reassigned to the city." She glanced at Hacha. "I want reports from the search teams every hour."

"You'll have them," Hacha said.

"Very well. You may all go."

As they left, Deha took a breath, trying to calm the pound of her heart and ease the pain behind her breastbone that radiated into her neck, jaw, and arms. She watched the departing guards bow to a woman who stood just inside the arched doorway.

"Chankah," Deha said.

Her successor closed the door. "Dabbiv told me you sent him to the city." She came over to the desk. "Deha, why? He does a good job here."

"We—disagreed."

"Do you really intend to dismiss him from the Estate?"

"No. No, I don't." She exhaled. "Everything is a mess. If Kelric makes it to the port we're finished."

"There's no way out of Dahl except by air. We'll catch him when he goes for a rider." Chankah paused. "When we do, we must put an end to all this."

"Lady Death already stole Jaym from me. I won't give her Kelric too."

"Whether Kelric dies or goes to prison, he will be gone." More gently Chankah said, "From what I've seen, he's a good man. But that doesn't change the danger he poses us."

"So." Deha crossed her arms. "You would lock him up in the Haka prison."

"That's right."

"And which Estates are strongest, Chankah?"

"I don't see how that—"

"Answer the question."

"Karn and Varz are strongest."

"Karn and Varz. The two Estates whose relations define the word *antagonism*. And after them?"

"Haka and Dahl."

"Haka. *Haka*." Deha scowled. "You want me to hand a Quis genius to the most powerful ally of Varz? What other presents would you give Manager Haka?"

"He'll be in her prison," Chankah said. "Not her Calanya."

Deha lowered her arms. "A dice player as gifted as Kelric belongs in a Calanya."

"I hope you're right," Chankah said.

So do I, Deha thought.

Hidden by a moonless night, Kelric leaned against a clump of boulders. Rocks littered a trail that wound down the mountain until it leveled out into cultivated fields far below. Beyond the fields, Dahl gleamed like a sculpture of spires. Lights on the aircontrol tower blinked in the night, beckoning—and unattainable. Too many guards were out searching: in the city, on the Estate, everywhere.

Hunger gnawed at him. Although crops flourished below, eating them made him sick, as did drinking water from fountains in Dahl. His resources were almost gone. He still had the Jumbler that hung heavy at his hip, but to activate it required that he key his brain to a neural chip in the gun. Designed with his own DNA, the chip picked up waves sent by his KEB and filtered by his biomech web, making them more distinctive than fingerprints. It ensured that only he could fire the gun. But that vaunted safety feature had put him in a no-win situation; using his Kyle senses and biomech would further aggravate his injuries, but if he didn't do it now he might never have another chance.

He sent a probe to the gun.

Contact—no, he lost it.

On the second try, his probe clicked into synch with the weapon. A menu flashed in his mind:

Fuel: abiton
rest energy: 1.9 eV
charge: 5.95×10^{-25} C
magnet: 0.0001 T
max radius: 0.05 M

The menu wavered, came into focus—and melted. Gritting his teeth against what felt like a mental version of ripping his tendons, he yanked his link to the gun back in place.

Then he set out for Dahl.

Deha leaned against a rail on the airfield, brooding in the morning sunlight. Hacha stood at her side, watching her guards patrol the hangars. Then she looked up into the mountains. "He can't stay out there forever," the captain said. "He has to come back in sometime."

And then? Deha wondered. Kelric was a windstorm they had trapped in a bottle. Cracks kept fracturing the glass, and every time she tried to repair one, two more appeared.

Balv came out of the tower and walked over to them. "Llaach just reported in. She and Rev are still at the Calanya. Everything is quiet."

Deha nodded, struck by the irony of having Rev guard her Calanya. In past ages, a dice player with his brilliance would have been *in* it. His Quis expertise was why she had chosen him for her escort. A Manager could learn much from what her bodyguards picked up in the Quis.

Shouts came from across the field, as guards converged on a hangar, forming a semicircle. "That's it," Deha said. She took off, flanked by Hacha and Balv.

At the semicircle, they made their way to the front. Ten paces away, Kelric stood backed up against the hangar with his weapon drawn.

Hacha stepped forward. "Be reasonable, Kelric. We know your gun doesn't work."

"It works," he said. "It shoots abitons. Antimatter particle of the biton. And guess what, Captain. Every electron in your body contains hundreds of thousands of bitons. I shoot, you get annihilated."

Deha glanced at Balv. "Do you know what he's talking about?"

"I've no idea," Balv said.

Hacha took another step—and Kelric raised his gun.

The Dahl guards fired in unison, and though Kelric lunged to the side, many of the shots hit him. Yet it had no discernible effect. Holding his gun in both hands, with his feet planted wide, he fired across the ground separating him from the octets. Orange sparkles lit the air in a narrow beam—and where the beam hit tarmac, the ground exploded in a flash of orange light. Rocks and dust flew into the air. In a second, a chasm stretched the length of the field, with debris crumbling from its edges in miniature avalanches.

"Winds above," Balv muttered.

Deha swallowed. Apparently his gun worked much better than they had thought.

Kelric looked at her. "Order the guards inside the hangar to come out."

"There aren't any," Deha said.

He aimed into the building. "You have two seconds. Then I shoot."

"Wait." Deha raised her voice. "Unit three, come out of the hangar."

Three guards walked out.

"All of them," Kelric said.

"That is all of them."

"There are five more."

"No one else is in there," Deha said.

Kelric brought his thumb down on the firing stud.

"No!" Deha raised her voice again. "Unit five out."

Five more guards appeared. After the octet backed away from the hangar, Kelric motioned at Balv. "Send him over here."

"There's no way you can leave Dahl," Deha said.

"Send him here," Kelric said.

"No."

Kelric didn't argue, he just fired at a nearby hangar. His target exploded in a blast of orange light.

Deha swore under her breath. Watching her, Balv said, "I better do what he wants, before he starts shooting at people."

"We have to stop him, Balv. No matter what it takes. If you're in the rider when we catch it—" Deha left the rest unsaid.

"I understand."

"All right. Go." Softly she added, "Wind's luck to you."

He touched her arm. Then he headed for the edge of the field, where the chasm narrowed enough for him to cross.

Deha turned to Hacha. "Have the guards block their takeoff. And get the other riders ready to go."

"I have crews standing by."

"And Captain. If you can't recapture him—" Deha forced out the words, hearing them as if another person spoke. "Force his rider into a crash."

Kelric loomed above Balv in the hatch. "Put your stunner on the tarmac."

Balv set down the weapon.

"Now climb in here," Kelric said.

Balv climbed, acutely aware of the gun Kelric kept trained on him. Inside, the cabin seemed cramped, dwarfed by Kelric's size.

Kelric motioned him toward the pilot and copilot's seats in the front. "You fly."

As Balv sat in the pilot's chair, he looked through the windshield and saw guards running along the fissure. By the time he finished his preflight checks, several octets were massed outside the hangar. When he started the engines a line of people solidified in front of the rider.

Kelric was standing by the seat, his gun poised near Balv's head. "Go."

"I can't. I'll run over the guards."

In response, Kelric yanked on the throttle. The rider jumped into motion.

"No!" As Balv grabbed the wheel, people scattered in all directions. Mercifully, he regained control of the craft before it hit anyone. As the area cleared, he taxied out of the hangar and accelerated alongside the chasm. Kelric sat down in the copilot's chair, still with his gun trained on Balv. Within moments, they had lifted off the tarmac and were sailing into the gales of the Teotec Mountains.

Static burst from the radio. "This is the Dahl Sunrider. Come in, Skytreader."

"Don't answer," Kelric said.

Below them, the mountains unrolled in a jagged panorama. In his side mirror, Balv saw a flock of craft rising from the airfield. They looked like specks against the cliffs towering over Dahl.

"Skytreader." Hacha's voice crackled on the com. "Land now or we'll force you out of the air."

"Outrun them," Kelric said.

"I can't," Balv said. A fist of wind grabbed Skytreader and tossed it upward like a child playing with a dice cube. "This is crazy. We have to land."

Kelric touched his gun to Balv's temple. "We're going to the starport you all claim doesn't exist."

"You can't shoot that thing in here. You'll destroy the rider."

"No. Just you."

"I won't fly." Balv swallowed, wondering if he were about to die.

For a moment there was silence. Then Kelric said, "Get up."

Balv stared at him. "What?"

Kelric flipped over his gun and held it like a club. "Get up."

"You'll kill us both."

"You have five seconds. Then you go to sleep."

It only took Balv an instant to imagine lying unconscious in a craft flown by someone who had never handled a rider, let alone battled the winds of the Teotecs. Then he slid out of the pilot's seat. As Kelric took his place, the rider lurched like a drunk gambler.

"Let me take us down." Balv motioned to a cluster of cloud-wreathed crags below. "I know places we can land."

"The only place I'm going is home."

"We can't make it." As Balv slid into the copilot's seat, he looked back through a window. Painted eyes and wings showed on the pursuing riders. "You know they'll catch us."

Kelric made a fast scan of the controls. Then, with no warning, he pulled Skytreader into a nearly vertical climb. Pressure built in Balv's ears and he had to yell to be heard over the straining engines. "You're going too high!"

Kelric ignored him, taking the rider up in a dizzying half loop, the horizon careening past the windshield as the craft turned upside down. Just when Balv began to fear altitude would finish them as surely as a crash in the Teotecs, Kelric rolled the rider right side up and angled into a descent, headed the opposite way from their previous direction. Skytreader streaked into the upper ranges of the Teotecs, leaving their pursuers far behind.

They landed high in the mountains, in a pocket of rock fenced by crags and icy patches of snow. Balv stared through the windshield at a finger of basalt thrusting into a cobalt sky. "I thought we were going to the port."

Kelric cut the engines. "So did Hacha. Once she gets turned around, she won't have any idea where to find us."

It almost made sense; locating a craft up here was virtually impossible unless the pilot wanted to be found. But Kelric had missed one "minor" fact—the starport was in the desert.

"You're going to fly me there," Kelric said. "When it gets dark."

"Fly you where?"

"To the starport."

A chill ran down Balv's back. How did Kelric always know what he was thinking? "And if I refuse?"

"You won't."

"Why not?"

"Because you want to live."

Balv had no answer for that.

Kelric loosened the collar of his shirt. "Does this craft carry oxygen?"

"Oxygen?"

"Air."

Balv knew a weapon might be stored in the cabin locker. He stood up. "I'll check in back."

Kelric raised his gun. "Sit down."

Balv sat.

"No pilot stores emergency air out of reach." Kelric's voice rasped. "The air. *Now.*"

Balv heard the edge of desperation in his voice, recognized the danger in it. "The panel is above your head."

Kelric ran his fingers along the hull until he found the catch. When he clicked the panel open, a mask dropped out, hanging by a hose. He clamped it over his face and drew in huge lung-fuls of air.

When Kelric finally lowered the mask, his tension had visibly eased. He spoke in a calmer voice. "The air is so thin up here."

"Thin?" Balv had never heard of thin or fat air.

"The concentration of oxygen is low for me."

"Air is an element. Its composition can't vary."

"It's a mixture of elements, Balv. Oxygen and nitrogen, with traces of other gases."

Balv had no intention of arguing. "All right."

"I don't get it." Kelric's voice was growing hoarser. "Your science is only in the rudimentary stages, yet you people can build machines as sophisticated as these riders."

"You sound terrible. You need a doctor."

"What I need is the starport."

Balv had no response to that. So they sat silent, Kelric periodically breathing from the mask.

After a while Balv said, "Can I ask you something?"

"What?"

"You are a soldier, yes?"

"That's right."

"Who do you fight?"

"Eubian Traders."

"Why?"

"We have something they want."

"Why not trade?" Balv wondered what ISC considered worth more than the lives lost to keep it. Wealth? Power? What pushed them, that they ruled so much and still wanted more?

"You think it's greed?" Kelric said. "If the Traders had found Coba before we did, your life would be a lot different now. I'll tell you what we have that they want. People."

"People?"

"They sell them. You want to be a slave? I'd rather die."

That made Balv pause. It had never occurred to him that the Imperialate lived with its own nightmares. He chose his words carefully. "During our Old Age, the Estates were always at war. Managers made their captives into slaves. Calani were bought and sold like prized goods." He grimaced. "I am glad I live now and not then."

"I had the impression there wasn't much warfare here."

"Now, yes. But in the Old Age, Managers were warriors. They nearly fought one another into extinction. Now we fight with Quis."

Unexpectedly, Kelric smiled. "Political hostilities submerged into a dice game. That's quite an accomplishment." He glanced at Balv's wrist. "Is that your kasi band?"

Balv looked down. He had pulled the gold out from under

his cuff and was twisting it around his wrist. "Yes." He wondered if he would ever see his wife again.

Kelric touched his own shirt where the outline of an armband showed under the cloth. "Why are yours on your wrists?"

"It's not the same thing. The armbands mean you are a Calani." Balv stopped twisting his band. "Of course, nowadays some kasi refuse to wear these."

"Why?"

"In the Old Age a kasi was his wife's property. He wore wrist guards with her name engraved on them. Some men feel the bands are a remnant of those days."

Kelric pushed back his cuff, uncovering his wrist guard with its engraving of the Dahl suntree hieroglyph. "Like this?"

Balv shifted in his seat. "Well—yes."

"I take it that means I'm Deha's property."

"Yes." Balv felt the need to add more. "Many of us consider the Akasi Laws barbaric."

"I won't argue with that," Kelric muttered. Sweat trickled down his neck.

Balv wondered why Kelric was so hot. The cabin was cold and all Kelric wore were flimsy old clothes. He ought to be freezing. Balv peered at the skin above Kelric's wrist guard. "Can you roll up your sleeves?"

"Why?"

"I want to check something."

Watching him warily, Kelric pushed up his sleeve—and revealed an inflamed rash of red dots all over his arm. "What the hell?" He looked at Balv. "What is that?"

"Kevtar's disease, I think. Most of us get it as children."

"I'm sick?"

"It's not serious. You'll be fine by tonight." Balv winced. "I should apologize. You must have caught it from me."

"You don't look sick."

"I'm not. But Rev and I were at the Med House this morning visiting his children. All three of them have Kevtar's."

Kelric grimaced. "Thirty-four is a little old for me to catch a child's illness."

"Thirty-four?" Balv stared at him. "You can't be that old."

"Why not?"

"The way you look—we all assumed you were younger."

Kelric shrugged. "It's just biotech. And good genes."

"Oh. Of course." That made no sense to Balv.

"Little Kelric," he muttered. His voice sounded like sand scraping glass. "Baby of the Rhon. Youngest and biggest." He wiped sweat off his forehead. "Gods, I'm burning up."

By evening Kelric's rash had spread until it covered his chest and neck. He paced across the cabin, shivering now, his voice even hoarser than before. "I thought you said I would feel fine by now."

"You should," Balv said. "I've never seen Kevtar's affect anyone this way. We have to get you to a Med House."

"Not a chance." Kelric shifted his Jumbler from hand to hand. "We're leaving for the port."

"We don't have enough fuel to reach it from here."

"Maybe not. But we have enough to get damn close." He motioned with the gun. "Get in the pilot's seat."

Balv knew this might be his last chance to make a move. He stood up, stepped away from the copilot's seat—and lunged for the Jumbler.

Kelric jerked away the gun, his movements mechanical, as if he were a puppet acting on reflex. It happened so fast that despite the accuracy and speed of Balv's lunge, his hand closed on air.

Kelric leveled the Jumbler at Balv. "Sit."

Balv froze. "You don't want to shoot me."

"That doesn't mean I won't."

Balv sat in the pilot's seat, his mind racing to find a solution. What if Kelric reached the port? Were the tales true, that entire worlds had been punished for an offense against the Rhon? If Kelric was their youngest, the one they felt most protective toward, their wrath would be even greater.

He looked up at his abductor. "I won't fly you to the port."

"Fly or I shoot."

Balv took a deep breath. "Then you'll have to shoot."

"You're willing to die to keep me here?"

"Yes."

Kelric stared at him as if he were trying to extract the truth of Balv's words from his brain. Then he jerked his gun toward the hatch. "Take what you need to survive and get out."

Balv jumped out of his seat and strode toward the back of the cabin, moving fast, before Kelric changed his mind. Kelric had already taken the stunner from the locker, so Balv grabbed a jacket and a box of flares to signal the search parties.

When Balv heaved open the hatch, chill wind blasted through the cabin, throwing back his hair. He jumped out onto the ice-encrusted rocks around the rider, where the snow that melted during their landing had refrozen.

Within seconds the rider was airborne, leaving Balv alone in the freezing wind.

A burst of static from the com jolted Kelric awake. One glance at the controls told him the craft was losing altitude. As he brought up the nose, the radio crackled again, with a voice buried in the static.

A Skolian voice.

". . . identify yourself. You are approach . . . Restricted zone off limits . . . identify . . ."

"I'm a Skolian citizen," Kelric rasped. His fever was worse now and his voice had grown so hoarse he could barely talk. "Do you read? I'm an Imperialate citizen."

". . . off limits to all Coban . . . identify yourself."

"Is anyone there?" he asked. "Anyone?"

The message continued to repeat.

The rider faltered, coughing and spluttering. A fast check showed what he had feared would result from his erratic flying: the fuel tanks were empty. As he opened the wings and rode the wind like a hawk, the desert sped upward in a blur of red.

Kelric did his best to control the dive, trying to glide on the wind. At the last moment, he hunched over and covered his head with his arms. With a shriek of splintering metal, the rider hit ground and plowed through the sand. The impact nearly tore him out of his seat despite the harness. The craft rolled over, wrenching him from side to side, and the crack of breaking glass added its cry to the chaos.

With a final shudder, the rider rocked to a stop. Slow and cautious, Kelric raised his head. The windshield was broken and the cabin looked like a storm had hit it. Equipment lay thrown all over the deck. Two passenger seats had ripped loose and his Jumbler lay smashed under a crumpled section of the hull. His Quis dice were scattered everywhere, most of them crushed.

Kelric untangled himself from his seat, moving stiffly, both from the damage he had sustained during the crash and from the fever raging in his body. He limped across the cabin, picking his way over the debris. The rider rocked, then listed to one side, leaving the deck at a slant that sent him sliding into the hatch.

The buckled door came loose under his shove and fell out onto the desert. Scorching wind poured into the cabin, accompanied by a rain of sand that insinuated itself everywhere. Raising his arm to protect his eyes, he climbed out into the heat.

Red desert stretched everywhere. Nothing but sand, sand, sand, and the towers that reached into a pale blue sky like fingers from a giant buried hand—

Towers?

Kelric squinted in the heat shimmer of the air. Then he grinned.

It was the starport.

Lift one foot. Put it down. Again and again and again . . .

The impact of his body against sand jarred Kelric out of his daze. He rolled onto his back and stared at the twilit sky. The stars dazzled. It didn't matter that Coba had no moon. She had enough stars to light a hundred nights.

"Port," he mumbled. He climbed back to his feet and resumed his trudge.

Deceptive sands. He had forgotten how a desert could lie. The towers had taunted him all day with their distance, coming closer with maddening slowness. But he was almost there now. He could make out the ISC insignia on the tallest structure. Even in a fully automated port, regulations required at least one shuttle be available for transport.

Fevered thoughts darted through his mind. When he reached HQ, he had to report on Coba. ISC would take a long look at the Twelve Estates. It was obvious Coba claimed rich resources, both in material terms and the harder-to-quantify value of human mind and culture. Had the Cobans been more accommodating in their first contacts with ISC, Coba might have earned Imperial citizenship, but now he had no idea what would happen. ISC would see their unpredictable behavior as a potential threat.

And Deha? Imperial law recognized marriages on any planet under ISC jurisdiction, including Restricted worlds. Dissolving his union with Deha would require legal action, and if he revealed the circumstances of its formation she would come up on criminal charges. Given his titled position within the Imperialate, she was in serious trouble. He didn't want her destroyed that way. Hell, he wasn't even sure he wanted the marriage dissolved.

He would have to make his report with caution, when his mind was clear. Stress how these people saved his life. If he wasn't careful, he could destroy the Cobans because he was too clumsy with words to choose ones that would ward off the wrath of ISC and his family. When this fever cooled he could think better.

What would happen if he got into space and the fever grew worse? Any shuttle in an automated backwaters port like this would be bottom-of-the-line, with minimal medical facilities. The fever was devastating his system, raging faster than his crippled nanomeds could fight it. If he didn't cool it off, the shuttle would deliver a corpse to ISC. Then what would happen to Coba?

The growl of an automated crane lifting freight interrupted his thoughts. He was close enough now to see it moving within the port.

But there was still another rumble.

An engine?

Kelric spun around and stared at the sky. Stark against a crimson sunset, the black silhouette of a rider was growing in size.

"No!" he shouted. "Not *now*."

Combat mode toggled, Bolt thought. Whirling around, Kelric ran for the starport, using enhanced speed.

Warning. Bolt created a display of statistics. Femur, tibia, and fibula hydraulics malfunctioning. Sciatic fiberoptic thread: 48 percent loss of efficiency. Auriculotemporal thread misfiring. Estimat&*−3##

The growl behind him swelled into a roar. Then a shadow passed over his head. He shouted a protest, his voice lost in a thunder of engines as the rider skimmed along the ground in front of him. Even before it rolled to a full stop, its hatch burst open and his escort was jumping out, Balv included.

Kelric tried to veer away. Bolt should have analyzed the terrain, his reflex libraries should have guided his feet, and his hydraulics should have supported the abrupt direction change. Somewhere the system failed. He tripped and fell forward, slamming into the sand.

As he struggled to his knees in the evening's fading light, he saw the guards running toward him.

Kyle magnification activated, Bolt thought.

Deactivate! Kelric thought.

Preparing attack.

No! He shouted the thought. *You can't use my brain for that! STOP!*

But he had pushed his injured systems too far one too many times. The safety protocols failed and an attack exploded out from his Kyle centers, amplified so far beyond what his brain could tolerate that Bolt quit trying to calculate the resulting damage and just flashed red warnings all over the disintegrating display of stats. Uncontrolled, the attack slammed into the escort with a force only a member of the Rhon could summon.

Kelric tried to stop the onslaught, cut it off, swamp it out, anything to end the nightmare. But his damaged systems refused to respond. The signal held true, unrelenting, dragging him further and further into his link with the escort, until their identities merged.

He was Hacha, level after level of personality, each peeling back like a skin: strength, traditionalism, pride in her work, love for her husband and child. Rev's mind was a complex of dice patterns, shifting, unceasing. He lived Quis, thought Quis, dreamt Quis . . . Balv thought of flying, of his family, of his job. Impressions of Llaach lanced though the barrage; newest member of the escort, least confident. Deeper down he found her love of her husband: Jevi, Calani.

Like a runaway web virus, Kelric's amplified signals ate away at their minds. Llaach buckled first, her neurotransmitters going wild, attacking her own brain cells. As she died, Kelric screamed, dying with her, experiencing every instant of it, unable to break the link that bound the five of them together.

And when the other three guards began to die, Kelric finally, in desperation, broke the link by breaking his own mind.

8

The Square

"The Tribunal of Dahl," Chankah said, "is now convened."

She stood in the Hall of Voices, a large room paneled in wood, filled with a sense of antiquity. The table in front of her reflected light from amber-glass lamps overhead. At her back, a rail set off a gallery filled with benches. An empty gallery. This Tribunal was closed to the public.

The Estate aide Corb stood at her side, adjusting his spectacles. About five paces in front of them, the judges sat at their high bench, looking down from its gleaming expanse of darkwood. Their robes rustled as they moved. For this case there were six judges instead of the usual three: two on defense, two on prosecution, and two neutral, including the Elder Judge.

The Elder regarded Chankah. "Successor Dahl, do you agree to act as Estate Manager until Deha Dahl can once more assume her duties?"

"Yes," Chankah said. No, she thought. Not this way. But no choice existed. Deha—her lifelong mentor—lay near death in the aftermath of a massive heart attack brought on by whatever had happened three days ago, out in the desert.

One fact remained clear: Llaach was dead. Although the Tribunal would focus primarily on her death, the ramifications of any decisions made here would go much further than Llaach. The future of the Twelve Estates was at stake.

"We shall begin," the Elder said. She waited until Chankah and Corb sat down, then said, "Bring in the Tribunal party."

An Estate aide pulled back the bolts in a door to the left of the bench and leaned her weight into it. With the creak of old wood, the portal slowly swung open.

The Voice entered first, a tall man in a violet robe, his silvered hair swept back from his face. The witnesses came next: guards from the city, airfield personnel, doctors Rohka and Dabbiv, and captain Hacha. The captain looked pale, but her walk was steady.

They brought Kelric in last.

Dressed in a black prison uniform, he walked surrounded by an octet of guards. A chain four handspans long joined the iron manacles fastened around his wrists above the gold gleam of his Calanya guards. Watching him, Chankah felt a sense of grief. So much was lost, both for Dahl and for Kelric, all because he had the misfortune to crash on a world where he was both coveted and feared.

The Voice crossed to a table on Chankah's right and the aide directed the witnesses to the gallery. The Square of Decision stood to the left, a chair surrounded by a wooden rail. The guards seated Kelric in the chair and took up posts around the rail.

The Elder spoke. "Before we begin, do any here have petitions that concern this Tribunal?"

The large number of people who approached the gallery rail worried Chankah. How could there be so many petitioners when so few citizens knew what had happened? She had kept the incident quiet, backed in her decision by the Ministry. If knowledge spread about Kelric's identity, it could start a panic. News of Llaach's death had leaked into the Quis, but most people believed she died apprehending a Dahl citizen who had stolen a windrider. Chankah had revealed the full story only to a select few: city elders, top officials, and Deha's kin.

Four people stood in the first group: two women and two men. "Please identify yourselves," the Elder said.

"I am Yeva," the first woman answered. "Two decades ago, before Deha Dahl became Manager, she worked in the Children's Cooperative. During that time she was my primary guardian."

"I am Tabbol," the first man said. "Manager Dahl was my guardian in the Cooperative."

"I am Sabhia," the second woman said. "Manager Dahl was also my guardian."

The younger man spoke last. He watched the judges with familiar eyes, huge and black, like dark pools. "I am Jaymson. Deha Dahl is my mother."

Chankah stared at him. It had been longer than she realized since she had seen Jaymi. He wasn't "Jaymi" anymore. Deha's son, her only biological child, had grown into a man.

"What is your petition?" the Elder asked.

Yeva read from a document in her hand. "If Manager Dahl dies as a result of her heart seizure, Sevtar Dahl should be tried for her murder as well as that of Llaach Dahl."

Chankah almost swore. Did they realize what they were asking? Whether they acknowledged it or not, Kelric was their stepfather. All they saw in him was the conqueror incarnate, a nightmare come to life. Watching Jaymson, she felt a deep loss. She suspected he would have liked Kelric once he had the chance to know him, but that would never happen now.

"Your charge is severe," the Elder said. "On what grounds do you bring it?"

"On the grounds," Yeva said, "that Manager Dahl's condition is a direct result of the accused's actions."

The Elder considered her. "This is not a murder trial. We are met to determine what transpired in the desert, why Llaach Dahl died, and what our response should be." She paused. "Given the far-reaching ramifications of any decisions we make here, your petition will require a private conference by the Bench."

"I understand," Yeva said. "We await your decision." She gave her document to the Tribunal aide and withdrew with her group.

Chankah recognized the second petitioner: Avahna Dahl, Speaker for the Calanya. The painful duty of telling Llaach's husband that his wife had died had fallen to Chankah. When he requested to see the Speaker, she thought he wanted to send a message to Llaach's kin. Avahna's presence here was an unwelcome surprise.

The aide Corb spoke to her in a low voice. "Are you going to allow this? What if Jevi demands Sevtar's life for Llaach's?"

Chankah pushed her hand through her hair. "It's Jevi's right to petition. Just pray we don't have to intervene."

Avahna said, "I speak for the Calani Jevi."

"What is his request?" the Elder asked.

"He asks," Avahna said, "that if the Bench acquits the accused, then Sevtar never be allowed to live in the Dahl Calanya. Should this be unacceptable, Jevi asks to leave Dahl for the Calanya of another Estate."

Sympathy gentled the Elder's face. When she glanced toward the table, Chankah nodded, relieved.

The Elder turned to Avahna. "You may tell Jevi his petition is granted."

Avahna bowed. "Thank you, your Honor."

The final petitioner was a woman with coppery curls spilling down her back. She wore the blue jumpsuit of a guardian from the Children's Cooperative and looked ill at ease in the severity of the court.

The woman took a breath. "I am Chala Dahl. I represent the Elders of the Dahl residences: the Women's House, Men's House, Couples' House, Parents' House, and Children's Cooperative." She shuffled her papers self-consciously, then read from one. "Although we abhor the nature of the events that led to this Tribunal, we feel compelled to make this statement: there have been no executions for centuries. If Sevtar Dahl is given such a sentence, it will set us back to an age when violence was our way of life. For this reason we exhort you to refrain from any such ruling."

Yeva jumped to her feet. "I object to this girl's claim—"

"You are out of order," the Elder judge said.

"Your Honor, I apologize," Yeva said. "But this girl claims to represent all Houses of the city when in fact she speaks only the naïve opinions of a few people."

Chankah stood and the petitioners fell silent. She considered Yeva. "Do you claim to represent the Houses of Dahl?"

"Successor Dahl." Yeva bowed. "All I state is this: the severity of the crimes brought before this Bench require measures of equal severity when dealing with the perpetrator."

Perpetrator. Chankah frowned. Yeva spoke as if Kelric's guilt were already decided. The hearing hadn't even begun and already they had convicted him. It undermined the very foundation of a Tribunal, which was that the person who sat in the Square of Decision should receive a fair hearing. They needed to cool off the courtroom, give the tension time to ease. Chankah turned to the Elder and the judge nodded, understanding her unspoken message.

The Elder regarded Yeva. "If you wish to present a statement, you may do so prior to the morning session tomorrow." She turned to Chala. "We will take your petition into consideration."

Chala and Yeva nodded. After everyone had taken their seats, the Elder picked up a mallet and knocked it against a small gong on the bench. "This Tribunal is now in session." She turned to the Voice. "Evid Dahl, step forward."

The Voice went to stand before the Bench.

"Do you swear to remain impartial when you question the witnesses?" the Elder asked.

"I swear," Evid said.

"Please call your first witness."

Testimony of officers from the CityGuard filled the morning, and after Midday recess the airfield personnel were questioned. The witnesses laid out a list of Kelric's actions; fights, threats, assaults, abductions—it all formed a violent picture incongruous with the quiet man who sat in the Square of Decision.

"And so the matter before this Tribunal," Yeva finished, "is one with no precedent in modern history. As such, it requires unprecedented justice. Yesterday it was claimed we regress to barbarism if we deal with the accused as he has dealt with us. I answer with this: if his crimes go unpunished what message will that send out? *That a person may murder without censure?*"

Mutters rumbled among the witnesses. The Elder waited

until the noise died down and then spoke. "No one would deny we must avoid such a message. However, we remind you that Sevtar Dahl has been convicted of nothing."

"I understand, your Honor," Yeva said. But as she returned to her seat, others nodded their support to her.

The Elder turned to Evid. "Summon your next witness."

"I call Dabbiv Dahl," Evid said.

Dabbiv went to stand before the Bench. The Elder said, "The Tribunal oath requires you tell the facts with truth. Do you swear to do so?"

"Yes," Dabbiv said.

"Be seated then."

The Square of Witness, to the left of the Bench, looked much like the chair where Kelric sat. However, no guards stood around its rail. After Dabbiv was seated, Evid said, "Doctor, in what capacity do you know Sevtar Dahl?"

"I was his physician," Dabbiv said.

"Was? You no longer are?"

"Manager Dahl took me off his case."

"Why?"

Dabbiv hesitated. "We disagreed about his treatment."

"Disagreed how?"

"She wanted me to give him drugs that made him sick."

Evid raised his eyebrows. "Manager Dahl wished to poison her Akasi?"

Dabbiv flushed. "Of course not. The drug was a sedative, a powerful one, but safe under proper supervision. Safe for a Coban, that is. Kelric, I mean Sevtar, isn't a Coban."

A prosecution judge beckoned to Evid. He talked with her, then turned back to Dabbiv. "When was the last time you gave Sevtar the drug in question?"

"The day of his Oath ceremony," Dabbiv said.

"After which he escaped from a locked room at the top of a tower, knocked out all of his guards, shot Manager Dahl, wrecked the airfield, kidnapped a pilot, and flew to the starport?"

Dabbiv reddened. "Yes."

"Since these events, do you believe the drug had any effect on him at all?"

"I don't know how he managed to nullify it, but it *was* poisoning him."

A neutral judge bent to Evid. He listened, then spoke to Dabbiv. "Could a side effect of this drug be to induce psychosis?"

"It made him physically ill," Dabbiv said. "Not mentally."

"But is it possible?"

"I don't know."

"Could his adverse reactions, both to food and medicine, be psychological in origin?"

"I doubt it."

Evid leaned forward. "Then tell me this. Can a change in eye or skin pigmentation dramatically alter the way a person reacts to sedation?"

"I don't know. It doesn't seem likely."

"Yet," Evid pounced, "the only difference between Sevtar and you or me is coloring. Why then should a substance that is harmless to us poison him?"

"He only *looks* like us." Dabbiv thumped his fist on the chair. "What do I have to do to make you people see? This man isn't from another Estate. He's from another *world.*"

"Young man," the Elder said. "Please control yourself."

Dabbiv scowled at her.

A prosecution judge beckoned Evid. He listened, then turned to Dabbiv. "Are you still a member of the Estate staff?"

The doctor stiffened. "No."

"What is your position?"

"Medic for the city maintenance crew."

"Manager Dahl dismissed you from the Estate?"

Tightly, Dabbiv said, "Yes."

"I see." Evid glanced at the judges for confirmation, then said, "We have no further questions, Doctor."

Chankah frowned. The more she heard, the less impartial Evid sounded. She rose to her feet. When the Elder nodded, Chankah said, "It should be made clear in transcript that Manager Dahl fully intends to recall Dabbiv in his position as one of her physicians."

"Very well." The Elder glanced at the Scribe. He sat to the right of the Bench at a Quis table recognizable by its distinctive structure, a round top on a fluted pedestal. The Scribe dipped his quill in ink and turned Chankah's words into hieroglyphs on his parchment.

The next witness was Senior Physician Rohka.

"His reaction was severe," Rohka said when questioned about Kelric's bout of Kevtar's disease. "The night they brought him back here his fever was so high we had to pack him in ice. Without treatment, he would have died."

"Do you know what caused it?" Evid asked.

"He probably lacks immunities we're born with."

"Can't emotional stress make some people sick?"

Rohka considered the thought. "It's possible."

"Could that have led him to attack the escort?"

"It would take more than stress to explain how he killed Llaach Dahl." The doctor blanched. "Every blood vessel in her brain was ruptured."

A murmur rumbled through the petitioners and witnesses. Evid waited until it quieted, then said, "We have no more questions, Doctor."

After Rohka left the chair, Evid bowed to Chankah. "I now call the acting Estate Manager of Dahl."

So, Chankah thought. It was a rare occurrence for a Manager or her successor to be called in a Tribunal. But then, this was no normal Tribunal.

When Chankah was seated, Evid said, "Successor Dahl, please describe the events that led to your discovery of the escort."

"I was with the two riders that found Balv," Chankah said. "After he took over as pilot for the other craft, it outdistanced the one in which Manager Dahl and I rode. We found it that night near the starport."

"And the escort?" Evid asked.

"Their bodies were on the ground nearby."

"What was Sevtar doing?"

"Kneeling in the sand."

"That's all?"

"There wasn't much else he could do. He was catatonic."

Evid frowned. "Then what caused Manager Dahl's heart seizure?"

"It happened when she realized Llaach was dead. She knelt next to the body." Chankah steadied herself against the memory. "Then she said, 'No, I'm not ready,' and collapsed."

"Ready? For what?"

"I think she realized she was having a heart attack." Quietly Chankah said, "She meant she wasn't ready to die."

"How did Sevtar react?" Evid asked.

"Her voice roused him. He tried to go to her. But he could hardly move."

Evid considered her. "Successor Dahl, your statement indicates that besides Manager Dahl and the escort, only Ixpar Karn knew Sevtar well. Since Minister Karn refuses to let her successor testi—"

"Her *what*?" Kelric's interruption vibrated in the air.

Silence followed the words. The Elder looked down at Chankah, her face flushed. "Perhaps you should . . . ?"

The request startled Chankah as much as Kelric's outburst. By law, no witness could intervene with any person in the Square of Decision. Then she understood; as acting Estate Manager only she could speak to a Calani.

Chankah hurried over to Kelric. "Please. You mustn't disrupt the testimony."

He clenched the rail in front of him. "Ixpar is the Minister's *heir*?"

"Not heir. Her successor to the Ministry."

"Why isn't she here to testify? Her word could make a lot of difference."

"Sevtar, please. Now isn't—"

"My name is Kelric."

"Outbursts like this only hurt your case."

He regarded her with the look of a man who expected to die. "What case? They've already convicted me."

Chankah regarded him. Then she returned to the Bench and spoke to the Elder. "We need a recess."

The aide Corb sat on the bench that circled the alcove, watching Chankah pace across the small room. Sunlight slanted through the arched window and reflected off his spectacles.

"Kelric is right," Chankah said. "They've already decided his guilt. Evid is hardly any more objective than the petitioners who want an execution."

"They're afraid," Corb said.

"That doesn't excuse the charade going on in there." Chankah stopped. "Ixpar Karn should be here. Her testimony is important."

"I don't see how the Minister can refuse our summons."

Chankah grimaced. "She's the Minister, that's how."

"You should talk with Elder Dahl."

"Good idea. Check with her aides. See if we can meet before the Tribunal reconvenes." She went to the window, watching the hawks drift in lazy circles above the city. "Tell me, have you ever seen an althawk?"

He adjusted his spectacles. "Well, yes. Of course. A lot of them nest in the peaks above Dahl Pass."

"Not the common hawks. I mean the giants. The beasts our ancestors rode through the skies."

"How could I? They're extinct."

She turned to him. "Legends say a hawk chose one warrior and one warrior only whose touch he would tolerate. He killed anyone else who tried to catch him."

Corb studied her face. "Why do you bring this up now?"

"Because the giant hawks aren't extinct, my friend. One came down from the stars." She rubbed her hands along her arms. "We caged him with an oath and pinioned him in gold. Now we're so terrified of what we've done, we're afraid to let him live."

The Elder lifted her robe off the chair in her chambers where she had draped it during the recess. "To say your suggestion is unusual, Chankah, is an understatement."

"Who else is there to speak in Sevtar's defense?" Chankah asked. "Only Successor Karn, and the Minister forbids it."

"Dabbiv spoke for him."

"And Evid did his best to make Dabbiv look like a fool. We have only prosecutors in this hearing. No defense."

The Elder settled the robe on her shoulders. "Perhaps because there is no defense."

Chankah wondered what had happened to the Elder's vaunted neutrality. "Or because we wish to see none."

"To let Sevtar take the Witness Chair would violate his Oath."

"As acting Estate Manager I can allow it."

A tap sounded on the chamber door. "Elder Dahl?" a girl called. "The other judges are ready to enter court."

"All right." The Elder regarded Chankah. "I must think more on your suggestion."

When the Tribunal reconvened, Evid summoned Hacha. Watching the captain take her seat, Chankah felt as if a weight descended on her. Hacha's word carried authority in Dahl. And from the beginning she had despised Kelric. Her testimony would destroy him.

Evid spoke. "Captain, you were the only witness to Llaach Dahl's death. Can you describe what happened?"

"Sevtar affected our minds," Hacha said.

"He had a weapon that worked on your brain?"

"No. He did it himself."

"He attacked you physically?"

"No. He didn't move."

"Then how did he kill Officer Dahl?"

"I'm not sure," Hacha said. "It was an accident."

Evid frowned. "You mean the deceased 'accidentally' burst every blood vessel in her brain?"

"No," Hacha said. "I mean Sevtar never intended for it to happen."

"Then why is Officer Llaach dead?" Evid demanded.

"He only meant to knock us out," Hacha said. "But he couldn't break his link with our minds. So he broke what created it. He burnt out his brain."

"Ah." Evid relaxed. "I see." He almost smiled. "You believe he used—what is the word? Telepathy?"

"I don't know what it was."

"Llaach Dahl suffered massive brain hemorrhages," Evid said. "Isn't it possible the accused's weapon affected your brain as well, making you think this mental force existed?"

"He wasn't carrying any weapons."

"Wouldn't it be more accurate to say he had no weapons you recognized?"

Hacha snorted. "Is that any less absurd? An invisible gun that explodes blood vessels in the brain?"

Evid leaned forward. "No more absurd than a gun that does nothing until fired by the accused, at which time it tears holes in airfields and disintegrates hangars."

"He didn't shoot us."

Evid studied her. "The fact that he let you live must make you grateful."

"I defend him," Hacha said, "because he didn't commit murder."

"No?" Evid demanded. "A member of our CityGuard—an officer in *your* command—is dead."

Hacha leaned forward. "All four of us would be dead if he hadn't sacrificed himself to save our lives."

Evid's voice grew louder. "Murder is no sacrifice."

"Llaach's death was an *accident*."

"How can you defend a murderer?" someone yelled.

Looking out at the gallery, Hacha raised her voice. "I'll mourn Llaach for the rest of my life. But killing Sevtar won't make her live again." She turned to the Bench. "If you execute him, it's you who are the murderers."

One of the judges flushed. "You dare make such an accusation?"

"Winds above," Chankah muttered. The rumbles in the gallery were growing loud and harsh. Several of the witnesses stood up, staring at Kelric with hostility bred by fear. Watching him pull at his manacles, Chankah's mind formed the ugly image of a mob attacking a man trapped in chains.

She strode to the Bench. "Stop the Tribunal. *Now.*"

Rising to her full height, the Elder banged her mallet on the gong. A sonorous note pealed out above the din.

"This is Tribunal," the Elder boomed. "Not a contest of lung power." When the room quieted, she said, "We are in recess until tomorrow morning. If an outbreak like this occurs again we will close these proceedings completely."

"And so it is our decision," the Elder finished, "that Sevtar be allowed to make any statement he wishes. Anyone who interrupts him will be expelled from this courtroom."

Chankah looked out over the gallery. The watchers sat in silence, as if subdued by the capacity for violence they had discovered in themselves the previous day.

As Kelric sat in the Witness Chair, he pushed a curl of his hair away from his eyes. His sleeve slipped, revealing both his Calanya guards and manacles, cold iron paired with gold. Murmurs of dismay came from the witnesses.

Is this how Dahl will become known? Chankah brooded. As the Estate that put a Calani in chains?

Kelric took a breath. "I come before you with—with great regret."

His voice was deep and husky, with a lilting accent. From a normal man such a voice would have captivated. From a Calani, it devastated. Hearing him, Chankah could believe the legend of the warrior who, after coaxing only one word from her queen's Akasi, became so enamored of him that she committed suicide because he was unattainable.

But after his first words, Kelric froze. The Elder waited, then motioned for Dahl's acting Estate Manager.

Chankah went to the Chair. "Kelric? What's wrong?"

He swallowed. "I'm not sure I can do this."

"But why?"

"Speaking in public—I could never do it well. I'm a soldier, not an orator. And now I'm—I've a neurological problem. The electrodes in my brain. They're damaged. They're making my neurons misfire."

"I know what an electrode is," she said. "But how could you fit something so big in your brain?"

"They're small. You can't even see them with the unaided eye."

Chankah wondered at the marvels his people had achieved. But at what price? "You're talking to me."

He twisted the chain that joined his manacles. "Public speaking—it makes my tension jump. I can't—it's triggering something in my brain that affects the electrodes. They make my neurons misfire. Then I stutter. Or lose my thoughts."

Although Chankah knew his reaction had no connection to his oath of silence, the instincts it evoked in her went deeper than logic. Every time he stumbled with his speech, it was as if he struggled against breaking his Calanya Oath. It made her want to protect him, care for him, assure him everything would be all right.

It was, in fact, an effective defense on his part.

"Going ahead with this could help you," she said.

He rubbed his palms on his knees. "I'll try."

After she returned to her table, Kelric said, "Manager Dahl and her guards—they saved my life. I have the greatest of gratitude for that. I never wanted—I never meant for Llaach's death to happen. If I could change it—undo it—if only . . ."

If only, Chankah thought. So many *if onlys*.

Kelric glanced at the petitioners who wanted his death. "Deha is my wife. I would never—how could you believe I would try to kill her?"

Spots of red touched Jaymson's cheeks and even Yeva looked subdued.

Kelric took a breath, then continued. "My mind has injuries. I've described it—to your doctors. It is real. I needed—need even more now—I have to get treatment. And I—the food. The water. I can barely even *eat* here."

He pushed back his curls, looking like a Calani out of an Old Age legend. "In the desert—the link Captain Hacha described—it was real. I—I malfunctioned. I became the escort." He swallowed, his face pale. "When Llaach died—I died with her. I couldn't make it *stop*." His voice cracked. "For the rest of my life I'll live with the memory of her dying."

Then the only sound was the scratch of the Scribe's quill.

Chankah wondered if the others realized the full impact of his words. His own mind had imposed a sentence on him worse than any a court could issue. He would live with Llaach's memories until the day he died.

When it was clear Kelric had no more to say, the Elder spoke in a subdued voice. "This Tribunal is now in recess until the Bench reaches its decision."

The clang of metal woke Kelric. He lifted his head from the cot and peered into the darkness. A glow lit the end of the hall outside his cell. It came closer, resolving into a guard who carried a lamp. Captain Hacha walked with her.

When they reached the cell, the guard peered through the bars. "I think he's asleep, Capt'n."

Kelric sat up, swinging his legs over the edge of the cot. The guard blinked at him, then turned to Hacha. "If anyone finds out I let you in here I'll be in more trouble than a fly in a vat of hot wax."

"I won't stay long," Hacha said.

The guard muttered under her breath. But she opened the door and withdrew down the hall, leaving Hacha alone with Kelric.

The captain came into the cell. "Rev and Balv ask that I give you a message."

"Yes?" Kelric asked.

"They thank you for their lives." Quietly she added, "As I do for mine."

He wasn't sure what he had expected from the captain, but this wasn't it. "Are they all right?"

"Yes. They're both out of the Med House now." She sat on the other end of the cot. "Kelric, I don't understand you. I doubt I ever will. But I know what happened out there. The only thing preventing you from reaching the starport was the four of us. To escape Coba, all you had to do was let us die."

He spoke quietly. "In the past, I've wondered what I would do if I ever faced such a choice. I always assumed I would save myself." With an edge of bitterness, he added, "I was wrong. Now I'm going to die for it."

She regarded him. "There is a phrase. *Chabiat k'in.* It comes from an ancient language, older even than Old Script. The literal translation is 'the day is guarded, watched over.' But it is more than that. It is a spiritual thing, a guarding of life. My ancestors used it to mean the life a warrior gives by offering her own to save others." Lamplight flickered on her face. "There is that between us now."

The guard appeared in the doorway. "We've done with changing shifts, Capt'n. You got to leave or I'm in trouble."

Hacha stood and spoke in a low voice. "I won't forget, Kelric."

Then she was gone and the door clanged shut.

* * *

Fatigue creased the Elder's face as she stood, looking out at the courtroom. "We are met today to issue a decision in the case of Sevtar Dahl."

Chankah sat with Corb, her hands clenched in her lap. A tense silence filled the hall.

The Elder continued. "It is true that Sevtar's actions led to Manager Dahl's injuries. However, he is responsible for neither her heart condition nor her decisions. We thus bring no charges against him for any calamity that results from that illness."

"No!" Yeva Dahl stood up. Two guards moved away from the wall and started toward her. She looked from one to the other, her face flushed. Then she sat down.

The Elder waited until the murmurs among the witnesses quieted. Then she said, "We may never fully understand Sevtar's abilities. We lack the background to determine whether or not he misused them. For our decision in the matter of Llaach's death, we must rely on the testimony we have heard about Sevtar's character and our judgment of the statement he made to this Bench."

When the Elder paused, Chankah could almost feel every person in the room leaning forward to hear her words.

"It is our conclusion," the Elder said, "that the accused did not intend to kill Llaach Dahl. We therefore rule her death as accidental manslaughter."

So, Chankah thought. The penalty for manslaughter varied, but the maximum sentence was a lengthy prison term. She was surprised how much it relieved her to know that Kelric would live.

"In deciding sentence for this case," the Elder continued, "we are faced with an unprecedented situation. If Sevtar ever escapes—no, if Kelricson Garlin Valdoria, third heir to the military rule of Imperial Skolia ever escapes, all Coba will suffer the consequences." She spoke in a strained voice. "We have no wish to pass sentence on a Calani. Nor do we desire to revive punitive measures unused for centuries. And it is clear the accused is a man of good character." She sounded as if she were struggling under a weight. "But against our desire for leniency we must weigh the safety of our world."

Her final words fell into the air. "The Dahl Bench therefore sentences Sevtar Dahl to execution by honed discus, to be carried out on Halften, at Night's First Hour."

9

Queen's Arch

Ixpar walked along the sunhall, soaking in the sunlight that poured through its many windows. An arched door swung open farther down the hall, making a pleasing shape. Then it closed, leaving Jahlt Karn behind in the hall.

"Ixpar." The Minister waited for her. "I was looking for you."

She came alongside Jahlt. "I just finished my physics tutorial."

The Minister walked with her. "Avtac Varz is coming to visit."

Ixpar thought of the Varz Manager; a steel-gray woman who knew her power well and pitted it against Karn often. "Why?"

"A good question. If you ask Avtac, she will say she comes to discuss mining rights on the Miesa Plateau." Jahlt snorted. "The real reason she comes is to make trouble. As usual."

Ixpar almost smiled, wondering if the Varz Manager said the same thing to her staff when Jahlt visited Varz. "Is she bringing her successor?"

"Yes, Stahna comes. Manager Varz has suggested you and Stahna exchange Quis."

"They know I've never played Council Quis before."

"They also know Stahna has twice your age and experience." Jahlt paused. "There will be no loss of honor if you decline."

And back down to Varz? "I'll play."

Jahlt gave her a look of approval. "Avtac has no idea of your gift with the Quis. You will dice spirals around Stahna."

Ixpar didn't know about that, but she intended to spend all her free time in preparation. "Tev will be impressed."

"Tev?"

"He's in my mathematics tutorial."

"Ah. He." Jahlt smiled. "Tell me about him."

Ixpar warmed to the subject of Tev. "He's beautiful. His eyes are brown. Like hazelle eyes. They almost look gold when the light hits them right."

Jahlt's smile vanished. "I thought you left that behind."

"Left what behind?"

"The Skolian."

Ixpar stiffened, and silence accompanied them for the rest of their walk.

An Estate aide was waiting in the antechamber at the end of the sunhall. She bowed to the Minister. "A construction forewoman is here to see you, ma'am. Something about a contract for her crew."

"All right." Jahlt turned to Ixpar. "The file on the Miesa mining treaties is in my desk. You should read it before Avtac arrives."

Ixpar went on alone to Jahlt's office, a corner room filled with sunshine. Armchairs upholstered in fine old leather stood on the rugs and bookshelves lined the walls. The top drawer of the desk contained a clutter of quills, two ink bottles, and a pendulum watch. The Miesa file lay tucked into a corner.

As Ixpar took the file, the door opened. She turned to see an aide enter the room.

The woman bowed. "Successor Karn." She gave Ixpar a letter. "A rider delivered this at dawn. The pilot said it was urgent, to be opened by you only."

Curious, Ixpar turned the envelope over. The gilt stamp of the Dahl suntree emblem gleamed in one corner. Who in Dahl would send her a secret communication? Kelric? The instant the aide left, Ixpar tore open the letter.

The message was from Captain Hacha.

Jahlt opened the door of her office and found Ixpar staring at her from the center of the room. The girl held a crumpled paper clenched in her fist.

"It's a lie," Ixpar said.

Jahlt frowned. "What?"

"A lie." Ixpar's usually vibrant voice was flat with fury.

"What are you talking about?"

"Have they killed him yet? *Murdered* him for the good of Coba?"

So. Ixpar knew. Whoever caused this trouble would soon regret it. "Who were you talking to?"

"No one. The Miesa file wasn't in your desk so I looked for it. I found this." Ixpar raised her fist with the paper. "Why didn't you tell me about the Tribunal? I should have testified."

Jahlt closed the door. "You must accept that Kelric is gone."

"No! You can't let them execute him tonight. It's *wrong*."

Jahlt went over and pried the paper out of her fist. It was the letter Chankah had sent after the Tribunal. "Let those with the necessary experience decide his guilt or innocence."

"I know him. Better than any of you."

Jahlt laid a hand on her shoulder. "You see only what you want to see. The handsome prince in need of a protector. It isn't reality. It doesn't even come close."

Ixpar shrugged off her hand. "What happened to your words about justice? How can I believe you when you don't follow them yourself?"

Jahlt motioned to a dice table by the window. "Sit down." She would engage Ixpar in a Quis session. The evolving structures would tell the story of the Imperialate, revealing far better than words what it would mean for Coba to become an occupied world.

After they were seated, they rolled out their dice. Jahlt set an orb in the center of the table. A gold orb, for Kelric. She watched Ixpar, waiting to see how the girl responded.

Jahlt knew Ixpar would try to convince her, through the dice, that they should let Kelric live. But Ixpar had never faced the full power of her mentor's Quis. It was no coincidence Jahlt ruled Karn: none could hold their own against the unmitigated force of her dice, especially not a child. She had hoped to spare the girl the blistering pressure of such a session. But Ixpar was coming of age and it was time she learned the ways of power. She had lived her entire life in freedom and was too young to comprehend from her history lessons what it meant to be subjugated by conquerors. Caught in her infatuation, she refused to see the danger Kelric posed.

It was time the girl faced reality. Then she would understand why Kelric had to die.

Still breathless from running, the aide leaned on the table in Chankah's suite. "The message came over the air tower com. The rider must have broken every known speed record."

Chankah forgot the dinner she hadn't been able to eat anyway and left with the aide. They strode through the city, tall figures passing through the falling dusk, and reached the airfield in time to see a windrider descending in a glare of lights, buffeted by angry winds. The craft bore the Karn symbol: a giant althawk with its wings spread in soaring flight.

As soon as the rider landed, the hatch swung open—and the Minister of Coba stepped out into the night.

Leaning against the wind, Chankah crossed the tarmac. She bowed to Jahlt. "You honor my Estate."

Shadows hooded Jahlt's face. "The execution. Is it done?"

"No. In an hour."

The Minister said, "I want to see him first."

Kelric heard the prison door clang open. Boots sounded on stone in the hall outside his cell. He stood up and gazed out the high window of his cell, at the stars that gleamed between the bars. Good-bye, he thought. Then he turned to face his executioners.

Chankah was coming down the hall with an octet of guards. An unfamiliar woman accompanied them, a tall and gaunt figure in black trousers and jacket.

After a guard unlocked the cell door, the gaunt woman turned to the others. "Leave us."

Chankah started to speak. "It's not safe—"

"Leave us," the woman repeated. Under the force of her stare they all retreated down the hall and out the door at its end, leaving the gaunt woman alone with Kelric.

"So." She walked into his cell. "You are Prince Kelricson."

It unsettled Kelric to hear his title in Coban. "Yes."

"I am Minister Karn."

Gods. Had they all come to see him die? "Is Ixpar with you?"

"Ixpar is not your concern."

"If she came—I don't want her to see the execution."

"You have contaminated her mind enough. I have no intention of letting you do so further."

"You came alone to witness it?"

"No." Jahlt regarded him with night-black eyes. "I came alone to meet the man who so affected my successor that she convinced me to grant him a stay of execution."

At first the words made no sense. He heard them but they were only sounds. Slowly they filtered into his mind and lodged there with a spark of hope. "A stay?"

"I stopped the execution," Jahlt said. "Your sentence is now a life term in the Haka prison."

II

Haka

10

Ruby Wedges

Set in motion by the wind, the desert rolled in from the horizon like an ocean of sand and broke in red waves against the Teotec Mountains. As the rider descended, Haka materialized out of the sandstorm, spread out on the desert floor and climbing into the Teotecs. Towers the hues of a pale sunset were carved out of the cliffs, with windows like square eyes. When the rider glided past them, Kelric could see people staring out at it.

He turned away and looked around the cabin. His guards filled eight of the seats, but they weren't who his gaze sought. Deha sat behind the pilot, with Chankah at her side. She was staring out the window, her face pensive.

The rider skimmed into the whirling sand and landed at the airfield. Deha disembarked first, followed by Chankah, both of them pulling their jacket hoods tight in protection against the blowing sand. Then the Dahl guards brought out Kelric.

An octet of Haka guards waited on the tarmac, eight giants in yellow uniforms and dusty boots, dark skinned and dark eyed, each with a tasseled scarf wrapped around her head as protection from the blowing sand. In addition to the usual stunners, they also carried daggers with blades as long as a forearm.

As the Haka guards closed around Kelric, Deha came over to him. Although it was impossible to hear her in the keening wind, he understood the words her lips formed: *Good-bye, my husband.*

Softly, Kelric said, "Good-bye, my wife."

Then the guards took him away, into the sandstorm.

Mountains rose from the desert in huge steps, dominating land and sky. At their feet, lesser peaks alternated with stretches of desert like rocks on a treacherous shoreline. Wind whipped the sand into plumes that sprayed against the crags.

Surrounded by guards, Kelric walked numbly, uncaring of the sand that scratched under his clothes, his hair, his armbands and manacles. A lifetime sentence, with no chance of parole. At least one ray of light eased his gloom: Deha was recovering. It meant more to him than he knew how to express, and it also gave him the illogical hope that he might find a way to escape this mess.

They took him to a small peak jutting up from the desert. A metal door in it opened into a tunnel with iron-gray walls. They followed the passage to a huge cavern partitioned into cubicles, with a ceiling so high it hid in shadow.

The guards took him to a cubicle where a clerk waited at a podium. "Sevtar Dahl?" she asked.

"That's right," the captain said. She pulled down the tasseled scarf that had protected her face in the sandstorm. "He's to go to Compound Four."

"Any valuables?" the clerk asked.

"Armbands," the captain said. "Ankle and wrist guards, too, but they're welded on."

"He's a *Calani*?" The clerk stared at Kelric, then remembered herself and looked at the captain. "He better leave the armbands here."

Kelric held up his wrists. After a guard removed his manacles, he gave his armbands to the clerk. She gently set them on her podium, then pulled out a gray uniform.

The captain took the uniform and turned to Kelric. "Take off your clothes."

He stood, looking at the guards. They just looked back. So. No privacy. Gritting his teeth, he undressed. The clerk and several guards averted their gaze, but the rest of the group watched. When he was done, he waited, sweat evaporating off his bare skin in the dry air.

The captain motioned to him. "Turn around and put your hands against the wall."

Kelric stared at her. Why a search? When he paused, balking, the guards dropped their hands to their dagger-swords. So he turned to the wall and put his palms against it. He didn't like what it said about the prison administration, that a guard could take such actions, apparently with no fear of reprisal.

The captain, a woman about his height, stood behind him and laid her hands on his shoulders. As she rubbed his skin with her fingertips, she murmured, "The gold really doesn't come off." She slid her hands down his back to his hips, speaking next to his ear in a low voice only he could overhear. "So this is how a Calani feels." Stroking his hips, she added, "What a waste, to put you in prison."

Clenching his teeth, Kelric said nothing, just stared at the wall, trying to imagine himself elsewhere. Anywhere else.

The captain spent a long time with her search, as if she could actually find something on bare skin. But finally she gave him the uniform and let him dress.

They led him back through the cavern to a new tunnel. After various turns and twists, it exited into the sandstorm. A clearing surrounded by crags stretched before them. Several buildings stood in its center, partially obscured by blowing sand; beyond them, mountains rose into the sky.

The guards took him to the fourth building. Inside, they followed a hall that ended at a massive portal. Opening it revealed a second portal. Only after they ushered him into the room between the doors and locked the first did they open the second. It was like going through a huge airlock.

The second door opened onto a hall lined with wide archways, with drifts of sand piled against the walls. The captain led him to the third cell. "This is it. Home."

Home? For the rest of his life? After the guards left, Kelric walked into the cell, a sandstone room about ten paces wide. A blanket lay on a pallet and sunlight slanted past the bars of a skylight in the ceiling. He went back into the hall. The rooms near the airlock showed signs of occupation: a shirt on a pallet, a dice pouch in the sand, a clay pot in a corner.

A large man with shoulder-length black curls and a thick beard appeared in the archway of a cell. "Got a bone for slithering snakes, heh, crooner?"

"What?" Kelric said.

"This one's slow in the upper level, heh? And the hum says

he's Calani." The man laughed. "Croon away, boy. Croon away." He came forward until his nose was a handspan from Kelric's face. "Your skin offends me."

"That's your problem," Kelric said.

"Think you're bigger than the wind, heh, boy?" The man snorted, deliberately turned his back, and walked away.

Kelric shook his head. Then he went to his cell and lay on the pallet. He slipped into a fitful doze, waking at every sound.

Toward evening footsteps entered his cell. When his visitor crouched by the pallet, Kelric snapped open his eyes and grabbed the wrist of a hand coming down at his head. Above him, silhouetted against the skylight, he saw the angelic face of a teenage boy.

The boy tugged at his wrist. "Let go. I only came to see what you was."

Kelric dropped his wrist and sat up. "Now you know."

The boy shrank away from him. "You're even bigger'n Zev."

"Who is Zev?"

"Zev Shazorla. He was here when the beaks brought you in." The boy made a face. "He's the one got everyone calling me Little Crooner. Kicks me off mad as a scowlbug for them to call me that, but seeing as they're big and I'm not, that's my name. But it used to be Ched. Ched Lasa Viasa."

It was the first triple name Kelric had heard. The boy must have been born in Lasa and later moved to Viasa. "Lasa is a Secondary Estate, isn't it?"

" 'Course it is." Ched squinted in the dim light. "You look like metal."

Kelric shrugged, tired of the comments on his coloring.

"You from Ahkah Estate?" Ched asked.

"Why would I be from Ahkah?"

"I heard they talk funny."

"My accent is Skolian."

"Sure." Ched laughed. "And I'm Manager of Haka." He settled by the pallet. "Where you from really?"

Kelric saw no point in arguing. "I was at Dahl."

"Haka's boss must be a happy clawcat tonight."

"Why should my sentence make Manager Haka happy?"

"You slow in the upper level or what?"

Kelric scowled. "Let's just say my upper level is empty. Fill it up."

Ched leaned forward. "Haka is a happy clawcat because what brews Dahl brews Karn and what brews Karn strokes Haka pink."

Dryly Kelric said, "That's clear." He wondered if anyone here spoke normal Teotecan.

"How long you here for?" Ched asked.

"Life."

The boy's smile vanished. The question *What did you do?* hung in the air. Then Ched's mouth fell open. "Hey! Where's your dice pouch?"

Crushed in a windrider crash, Kelric thought. He regretted losing Deha's gift. "I don't have one."

"Everyone's got one." Ched seemed more disturbed by his lack of dice than his life sentence. "And you told Zev you was a Calani. A Calani with no Quis dice. What a croon." He reached for Kelric's arm. "I can prove you're no Calani."

In reflex, Kelric knocked away the boy's hand. The motion pushed up his sleeve anyway, and his Calanya guard gleamed in the murky light.

"You got guards!" Ched said. "You steal 'em?"

"What would possess me to steal them?"

The boy peered at the gold. "Them's old. Ancient. Must be worth half an Estate." He looked up. "Got 'em on your ankles too?"

"Yes."

"Real gold and old as Haka. You better sleep with your eyes open."

"They're welded on. You can't get them off."

Ched shrugged. "All the gold on Coba won't do me no good in this place. But there's crooners here crazy enough to cut off your hands and feet for those things."

"Great," Kelric muttered. "Just great."

It was obvious to Deha Dahl that the Haka Manager had spared no effort to ensure her visitor received the finest treatment. They sat at a gleaming table, drank wine from crystal goblets, and dined on cream pheasant. A handsome youth stood ready to refresh their drinks. Rashiva Haka's intended message was also obvious: Haka had more wealth, more power, and more prestige than Dahl.

Despite the excellent meal, Deha only picked at the food. She felt too drained to eat, particularly when faced with the vibrant beauty of the woman across the table. Rashiva Haka was a desert goddess. She glowed with youth. Her hair glistened like black satin and her eyes slanted upward, black opals in a face as smooth and as dark as java-cream.

"Is the meal to your liking, Manager Dahl?" Rashiva asked.

"Excellent, Manager Haka," Deha said.

"I'm glad we had this chance to relax." Rashiva smiled. "Even Estate Managers need a rest sometimes."

"So they do." Deha remembered her first years as a Manager. "You will find, though, that the Managing becomes easier with time."

Rashiva's smile took on an edge. "I wasn't aware I found it difficult."

So much for polite conversation. Deha wished this ordeal were over.

"Would you like to take our drinks in the Kejroom?" Rashiva asked. "The tapestries there may amuse you."

Deha tried not to think about the doctors at Dahl and their adamant warnings to avoid liqueur. If she refused the customary jai rum, Rashiva would suspect the weakness of her health. She smiled pleasantly. "Yes, let us retire for our drinks."

Rashiva Haka, Manager of Haka Estate, felt like a misplaced dice cube. The Dahl Manager's imposing presence made her acutely aware of her inexperience. As she ushered Deha into the Kejroom, she looked around at the tapestries on the walls, rich with scenes from the Old Age: warriors aloft on giant althawks, Calanya ceremonies, battle scenes. Rashiva wished she could soak up the ferocity of those ancient warriors to help her deal with Dahl's formidable queen.

Deha walked about looking at the tapestries. "These are beautiful."

"They were a gift from Kej Estate," Rashiva said. "A Kej

Manager gave them to Haka over a thousand years ago, when the two Estates joined forces during the Desert Wars."

"Such detailed work." Deha studied a piece woven in gold, red, and blue thread. "It's a pity Kej didn't survive the Wars."

Rashiva stiffened, wondering if Deha meant to belittle Haka's alliance with Kej. To hide her reaction, she turned to a com on the wall and flipped the switch. "Nida?"

Her aide's voice floated into the air. "Here, ma'am."

"Manager Dahl and I will take our jai in the Kejroom."

"I'll send someone up right away," Nida said.

Deha smiled as Rashiva clicked off the com. "Shall we sit down?" The impeccable courtesy of her voice made her host seem inestimably rude to leave her standing.

"Most certainly," Rashiva said. "Let us be seated."

So they sat facing off in armchairs until a youth arrived with the liqueur. He poured two glasses of jai rum, then set the decanter on the table between them and withdrew from the room.

Deha picked up her glass. "Well." She glanced at the Quis pouch on Rashiva's belt. "Shall we roll a game of dice?"

Game? Rashiva thought. When two Managers sat at dice it was no game. Deha Dahl's mastery over the Quis was infamous. She would wipe the floor with Haka's young Manager.

"Perhaps another time," Rashiva said.

Deha nodded. "Another time, then. When you are ready."

When she was ready. The barb stung. Rashiva forced herself to relax. "How are the renovations going at Dahl?"

"Very well." Deha settled in her chair. "If Minister Karn pardons Sevtar, I will reopen the Akasi suite."

Rashiva nearly spluttered rum all over the table. *Pardoned?* Was Deha mad?

When she regained her equilibrium, she spoke in a mild voice that hinted at skepticism. "Why would he be pardoned?"

"He no more belongs in prison than I do."

She wondered what Deha was up to. Jahlt Karn would never pardon Sevtar. Rashiva tried a discreet probe. "Prison does seem inappropriate for a Calani. A waste of his talent."

"So it is." Deha sipped her jai. "After all, he mastered Outsider Quis in only a season."

Rashiva almost snorted. Did Deha think her a fool? "One rarely hears of such talent."

"True. But then, such talent rarely exists."

If ever. Yet it was an odd boast to make. What advantage lay in it? If it were true, Sevtar was a genius who now belonged to Haka. Why would Deha want her to know that?

Of course the "genius" was also a killer. Deha would be delighted if Haka rehabilitated Sevtar, taught him Haka Quis, and then sent him back to Dahl. No better way existed for one Manager to gain power over another than by obtaining a Calani versed in her Quis. The question was academic, though. Sevtar was as likely to get a pardon as the desert was to get up and walk away.

But . . . the documents specified only that he serve his sentence at Haka. They didn't dictate where at Haka. No stipulation said he *couldn't* go into the Calanya.

Rashiva considered the thought. To acquire a Calani from another Estate, a Manager paid a stratospheric price for his contract. But suppose she agreed to take Sevtar into her Calanya and teach him Quis for as long as he was in prison? She would pay *nothing* for his Dahl contract. Of course, were he ever pardoned, he would return to Dahl without Deha having to pay for his Haka contract. Considering the nonexistent chance of a pardon, Haka could only benefit from such an agreement.

She chose her words with care. "It is unfortunate Sevtar never had a chance to realize his potential."

Deha regarded her. "So it is."

"One could always hypothesize alternatives."

"I'm not sure I follow you, Manager Haka."

Rashiva sipped her rum. "Suppose a man is temporarily sworn to a Calanya. Say for the duration of his visit somewhere." She paused. "Perhaps a visit to prison. Assuming he can be rehabilitated."

"Go on."

"When his prison term ends he is released from his temporary Oath."

Dryly Deha said, "Not much of a bargain, if his term is life.

The original Manager is handing a genius to her adversary for nothing."

"True," Rashiva said. "But were he ever pardoned, the original Manager would get a Calani from her adversary for nothing. It would be a gamble for both parties."

For a long moment the Dahl Manager was silent. Rashiva couldn't tell if Deha was studying her, thinking, or simply pausing for effect. When she finally spoke, her voice was unexpectedly soft. "A worthy gamble, I would say, if it will free him from prison."

Rashiva stared at her. She hadn't seriously expected Deha to consider the proposal. It was too obviously weighted in Haka's favor. So. Dahl's formidable queen had a weakness. Sevtar. Deha must love him a great deal if, to get him out of prison, she would consider letting one of her greatest adversaries take him into her Calanya.

Rashiva set down her rum. "Perhaps we can discuss this hypothesis in more specific terms."

"Perhaps we can," Deha said.

They penned and signed the documents that night, an agreement that in all respects favored Haka. Yet when it was done and finished, Rashiva had an odd feeling, as if she had been outmaneuvered.

Kelric awoke into darkness as someone flipped him onto his stomach. Hands pinned down his limbs and a knife touched his throat. Fingers fumbled at his Calanya guards.

"You jus' lie still," Zev said. "Cooperate and you won't get hurt." He laughed. "At least not hurt as much as if you fight."

Kelric's reflexes took control. Even without full support from his damaged enhancements, his combat techniques were far superior to the methods used by his attackers. He knocked out two of the three immediately, then flipped Zev onto his back and knelt on his chest with his fist raised.

"I didn't mean nothing," Zev gasped. "Nothing. I swear."

"Ever touch me again," Kelric said, "and I'll smash your goddamned head open." Then he sent the Shazorla man into oblivion.

An arm flickered in an archway. By the time Kelric realized it was only Ched, he had already caught the boy.

"Lemme go," Ched warned. "Or I'll yell so loud everyone in Haka'll hear."

Kelric released him. "I'm not going to hurt you."

"Sure. I saw what you did to them." He peered right and left, then slipped into his cell and knelt by his pallet. A spark jumped in the air and then he held up a lit candle.

Kelric stood in the cell's entrance. "Where did you get the candle?"

"From Bonni." Chad retreated, going to sit against the back wall. "She's a guard. But she's all right. Not like Zev an' them."

"They come after you, don't they?"

"None of your business."

"I'm making it my business."

Ched hugged his knees to his chest. "What am I supposed to do? I'm no giant like you and I don't know nothing about fighting."

"Can't you protest to the authorities? File a complaint?"

"File a complaint," Ched mimicked. "Sure."

"If you've never tried, how do you know it won't work?"

"I did try. I won't do nothing that stupid again."

"Why?"

Ched scowled. "You ask too much."

"Why are you afraid to answer?"

"I'm not afraid of nothing." Ched curled his fist around the candle. "After my first night here, I told the guards I wanted to talk to our warden. They said 'He's busy' and left. Then one time the top warden came here for inspection. Zecha Haka. Keyclinker for the whole place. When I told her about Zev and them, you know what she said? That I must've asked for trouble and me being who I was I deserved it."

Kelric stared at him. "You deserved it? That's sick."

Ched shrugged. "Zev knew I talked. When they was done with me, I was two days in the Med House. They told the guards I fell in the quarry. So don't tell me to file a complaint."

"If you were beaten that badly, it should have been obvious you didn't fall."

"That's what the meds told Zecha. You think she cares? She hates me. And I got bad news for you, metal man. She hates Calani too."

"Can't you talk to Manager Haka?" Kelric asked. "If she's anything like Deha Dahl, she would be outraged by what you just told me."

Ched snorted. "Sure. We talk to the Manager all the time. Besides, the last Manager never came round at all. I don't know about the new one."

Kelric didn't like the sound of it. The more he saw of Haka, the worse it looked.

"You know," Chad said, "I never saw anyone put out a body fast as you put out Zev and them. Whoosh." He grinned. "Just like that, they was out flat."

"I've been trained to defend myself in virtually any circumstance."

"Virchilly. Sir-stance." Ched laughed. "If your words was pictures you could sell 'em for a lot of money. Real Calani, heh? But you got trouble. One night here and already Zev don't like you."

"I'll manage."

"Listen," Ched said. "What you need is a friend. Someone to let you know how things are here."

"That someone being you, I take it."

"I could do it."

"What is it you want in return?"

"Keep them away from me. Be my protection."

Deal or no deal, Kelric had no intention of standing by while the others took out their frustrations on the boy. "All right."

Ched smiled. "You're not so bad. You get cooped for what somebody else pulled?"

"No. I did it."

Ched made a show of looking nonchalant. "Did what?"

"Killed a guard on my Calanya escort."

The light vanished as Ched dropped his candle. "Winds," he muttered. "Where did that flint go?"

"You left it under your pallet."

"That's right." His voice shook. "Pretty slow of me, heh?"

"Ched, it was ruled accidental manslaughter."

"You just remember I'm with you. All right?" The boy relit his candle. In its dusky glow he looked scared and vulnerable.

"You're so young," Kelric said. "This is no place for a child."

"Don't go calling me a child."

"Why are you here?"

"Why? Because I'm a crooner. That's why."

Kelric crossed his arms. "I protect, you talk. So talk."

"Heh. Don't get mad." Ched retreated to sit against the wall again. "I was a tavern kinsa in Viasa. That was after I left Lasa."

"Kinsa? What's that?"

"You really must be from outer space."

"Ched."

"I got paid for making the customers happy."

"Happy how?"

"I was real nice to the women. In private." Ched squinted at him. "You know."

"You were sent here just for solicitation?"

"No. I'm here because of a scumrat." Ched leaned forward. "See, things was finally going better for me. Feni, she hired me out of the tavern. Took care of me." He scowled. "Then she went prowling after that scum. When he came to live with us, he treated me like mold in the pipes. Things got worse an' worse. So one night I put my hands around his scrawny neck and squeezed till he turned purple. If people hadn't heard him yelping I woulda squeezed off his head."

It made no sense to Kelric. He was generally a good judge of people and Ched hardly struck him as a murderer. "Couldn't you just leave Feni? Ixpar told me most city Houses will give someone a meal and a bed in return for chores."

"Well, it don't always work that way. How would this Ixpar Pixpar know anyway?"

"Her name is Karn."

Ched snorted. "Sure. Successor Karn herself. Winds, but you can croon."

Sand scattered as Kelric walked across the cell. He crouched in front of the boy. "I don't like being called a liar. Understand?"

Ched flattened himself against the wall. "Y-yes."

"Good." Kelric stood up. "Come on."

Ched scrambled to his feet. "Where are we going?"

"There's some garbage in my cell. I'm going to put it where it belongs. You better stay with me, in case they wake up."

After they carried the unconscious men back to their rooms, Ched settled down on the other side of Kelric's cell. Within moments he was asleep.

Kelric lay down on his pallet. *Bolt?* he thought.

No response.

He tried various resets, but none worked. His enhanced reflexes had tried to kick in during the fight, so he knew Bolt still functioned. His bio-electrodes must have stopped working, preventing him from contacting the node. He hoped the system could manage at least a partial repair. He had developed a symbiosis with Bolt over the past fourteen years.

To be without it was like losing part of himself.

11

Rock's Well

Zecha Haka, head warden at the Haka prison, sat tensed at her desk. The last person she had expected to show up in her office was the Haka Manager. Rashiva's doddering predecessor had never come to the compounds.

"The prisoner from Dahl." Rashiva was sitting across the desk from her. "Sevtar."

"I sent him out with a quarry crew this morning," Zecha said.

"You put a Calani on a quarry crew?"

"He's a convict now, ma'am."

Rashiva leaned forward. "I want him made into more. Rehabilitate him. And give him Quis instruction."

Bones and bugs, Zecha thought. "In cases like his, rehabilitation rarely works."

Rashiva stood. "I have faith in your abilities, Warden."

After Rashiva left, Zecha swore. Calani, heh? Lazy dice players who lived in luxury with everything given to them for nothing. She, Zecha, had worked for her position, starting as a nobody. Her mother was a disgrace, a losing dice player who gambled away everything she owned. Her father had been a Lasa kinsa like that boy in Compound Four. But none of that stopped Zecha. She had worked at her Quis until she became a power to be reckoned with. Why should she give favors to a Calani?

"Think the wind only blows for them, don't they?" she muttered. "We'll see about that."

The line of prisoners and guards wound into the cliffs, sweltering in the heat of a sun barely risen above the mountains. Kelric trudged up the path with Ched, holding the hood of his jacket tight against the blowing sand.

Ched grinned. "Like our weather?" When Kelric glowered at him, the boy smirked. "You see Zev this morning? Got him an ugly eye. Black as tar." His smile vanished. "You better watch yourself today." He hesitated. "Both ourselves. That's the deal, isn't it?"

"Yes."

"Yiss. Yish." Ched grinned as he imitated Kelric's accent. "I'm ready to keep my side of our deal. So. What you want me to tell you?"

Kelric considered. To make escape plans, he had to know what he faced. "About Haka. Is it like Dahl?"

"No way. Haka is home of the Scowl Laws."

"Scowl Laws? What are those?"

"They're old as the mountains. They say a man can't smile at a woman unless she's his wife. Smile at a Haka woman and she thinks you're a whore."

"That's crazy."

"That's Haka, metal man. Haka men can't go outside without an escort neither, and if they do go out they have to wear robes that cover them from head to foot, and these woven scarves that hide their faces, except their eyes." Ched snorted. "It's them Haka women. They spend half their time figuring ways to protect their men's honor and the other half trying to compromise it."

"But I've seen male guards here."

"They aren't from Haka." Ched nodded at a guard on the trail above them. "Like him. He has yellow hair. Hakaborn have black hair and black eyes."

"What about the prisoners in the other compounds?"

"They're from all over." Ched flipped his hand in dismissal. "They're in for little stuff. Four is where they put real trouble-makers. There's eleven crooners in the Compound Four women's coop." He grimaced. "Those are some big clawcats. Men's coop has Zev, Gossi, Ikav, and us. Zev killed a Scribe in Shazorla and Gossi blew up a Cooperative at Ahkah."

"Gods," Kelric muttered.

"I don't like them neither," Ched said. "They're in for life."

"What about Ikav?"

"He stole some dice. Got ten years."

"For stealing *dice*?"

"Calanya dice. He's lucky that's all he got."

Kelric fell silent, turning the information over in his mind. At the top of the trail, they came out onto a plateau. The line of prisoners stretched across it, almost lost in the whirling sandstorm. When they reached the far edge, Kelric saw it formed the top of a staircase that descended into a quarry. Sand cliffs loomed on all sides, jutting into the sky like red fingers. Eons of wind had eroded the cliffs until they were riddled with holes that bore an eerie resemblance to windows. Gales moaned through the cliffs like a chorus of ghosts.

As they descended the steps, Ched muttered, "This place gives me nightmares."

"I'm not surprised," Kelric said.

At the bottom, a massive man about Kelric's height stood checking off prisoners. A rough scarf with black tassels hung around his neck. He glanced at Kelric. "Sevtar Dahl?"

"Yes?" Kelric asked.

"What was that?" the man asked.

"Say *sir*," Ched whispered. "Yhee, *sir*."

"Yhee, sir," Kelric said.

The man made a check on his clipboard. "You'll work on the rim crew."

As Kelric and Ched hiked across the quarry with their guards, the boy said, "That was Torv Haka. Compound Four men's warden. You call all them keyclinkers 'ma'am' and 'sir.' " Ched raised his hand as if to strike Kelric. "If you forget they remind you."

"I thought Haka men had to wear robes."

"Can't have our warden running around in robes. How would he keep control over scum like us?"

Kelric grimaced. But the warden was his least worry. He felt an all-too-familiar nausea. "Ched—if a prisoner needed a special diet, would he get it?"

"You got to be joking. This isn't a Calanya, you know."

Kelric blew out a gust of air. "No, it certainly isn't."

Zecha stood with Rashiva at the rim viewing station. She indicated a distant line of prisoners winding across the quarry floor. "Down there. The big one with the odd coloring."

Rashiva looked. Sevtar Dahl stood out like gold among pewter. But what caught her attention more was the quarry. She saw no windbreaks to protect crews from the sandstorms, and the water system looked defunct. "What's wrong with the aqueducts?"

"The sand erodes them," Zecha said. "The system kept breaking down, so I quit using it. A team of carriers brings water up from the compounds instead."

Rashiva frowned. "Why hasn't this been reported?"

"I wasn't aware a report was required."

Rashiva considered her. The arrangement that gave full authority over the prison to the head warden made sense; a Manager didn't have time to run the prison as well as the Estate and city. And Zecha had an impressive record. Rashiva doubted the grizzled warden appreciated being questioned on it. Still, she had no intention of ignoring the prison as her predecessor had done.

"I want to see a report each quarter," Rashiva said. She nodded at the quarry. "Have the water ducts repaired and more windbreaks installed."

Zecha kept her voice neutral. "Yhee, ma'am."

"And Warden."

"Yes."

"Keep me posted on your progress with Sevtar."

Zecha regarded her with an inscrutable expression. "Of course, ma'am."

A guard issued Kelric a pickaxe, a sentry directed him to a workstation, and a captain warned him about the consequences of trying to use his pick on people instead of rock. Another guard assigned him a trundle in a train of cars that ran through the quarry. His job was simple: cut rock and fill his trundle.

Normally Kelric wouldn't have minded the work. It was hard but reasonable, at least for someone with his strength. But not today. The first spasm hit him while he was carrying a block of stone. As his stomach lurched, his grip on the block slipped and it crashed to the ground. He fell to his knees, wrapping his arms around his waist.

"Hey!" Ched ran over to him. "You don't got to lift such big—winds, what's *wrong*?"

Leaning over, Kelric vomited behind the block. When the spasm eased he spoke in a rasp. "Can you get me water?"

"They don't give us hardly none," Ched said. "The pipes broke."

Footsteps sounded behind them. Ched spun around, then relaxed. "He's sick, Bonni. Can he have some water?"

A guard knelt next to Kelric, a tall woman with the dark coloring of the Hakaborn. She brushed her hand across his forehead. "You're burning up."

"Today's his first day," Ched said. "He used to be a Calani."

She smiled. "A Calani? I heard rumors, but I thought that was just a story."

"It's true." Ched pushed back Kelric's sleeve, uncovering the gold.

"Cuaz above." Bonni looked at Kelric. "What are you doing here?"

A shadow fell across him. "Trouble, Bonni?" Torv Haka stood over them, a truncheon in his hand.

Bonni stood up. "This man is sick."

"He's from Compound Four," Torv said. "They'll give you any story."

Kelric stood slowly, watching the warden. Torv regarded him like a fumigator who had found a bug. "If you think you'll get high-level treatment because of that gold on your wrists, you're wrong."

Kelric gritted his teeth. "Yes. Sir."

Torv's voice hardened. "I don't like your tone, Calani."

"So choke on it," Kelric said.

"Cuaz me," Ched muttered.

Torv smiled. Then he whipped his club through the air. Kelric caught the pole, stopping it with enough force to knock Torv off his feet. As the warden fell, other guards in the area ran over. They grabbed Kelric while Torv climbed to his feet. With his face contorted in fury, the warden fired his stunner until Kelric collapsed, blackness closing around him.

Kelric came to in a pocket hidden from the quarry by crags of rock. He was kneeling in front of a boulder with his arms pulled around it and his wrists bound to a ring embedded in the stone.

"So," a voice said. "You woke up."

He looked around to see Torv Haka holding a thick belt. "Thought you'd knock me around, heh, crooner?" Torv grabbed Kelric's shirt and ripped it off his back. "You'll think differently soon."

12

Reopen

Kelric lay on his stomach on the pallet in his cell. In the starlight, he could just make out the jug of water Ched was setting next to him. The boy tore a rag from the remains of Kelric's shirt and dunked it in the pot. Then he went to work cleaning the welts and cuts on Kelric's back.

" 'Choke on it.' " Ched shook his head. "What gets into you, talking to the warden that way?"

"I'm not accustomed to being spoken to like that," Kelric said.

"I think maybe you got too much pride for your own good." Ched's frown shifted into a grin. "You got guts, though. It flew round the quarry faster than wind, about you knocking him down. One day here and already you're famous." With a smirk, he added, "And guess what? Torv put Zev and them on third shift at the quarry. Seems they didn't feel so good today. All they was doing was complaining." His smile faded. "Starting tomorrow you're on three shifts a day, too, for a tenday. You gonna be all right? You was pretty sick today."

"I need to boil my water," Kelric said.

"There's nothing here to make a fire."

Halfheartedly, Kelric thought, *Bolt?*

&$unct** degrad$#

He tensed, elated by the response. *Bolt, what's with my nanomeds? Can't they help make the water drinkable?*

Series J has suffered severe depleti^^#

Bolt?

No response.

Kelric exhaled. Series J included the nanomeds best equipped to deal with the bacteria in the Coban water, so its depletion explained his increased problems. However, as far as he could tell, the meds that repaired his cells, retarding his aging process, still worked. So if he survived, he faced the unpalatable prospect of several centuries at Haka.

"You don't look so happy," Ched said.

"Has anyone ever escaped from here?"

"It's a dumb idea, metal man. Even if you got out, which is almost impossible, the only place to go is the city. They'd catch you in no time. The next closest place is the starport and that's way out in the desert." Ched finished cleaning a cut on Kelric's shoulder. "When I first heard about Skolians I thought it was a big croon. Then Minister Karn said it was real. People from above the sky. Thing is, they won't even let us into their port." He went to work on Kelric's arm. "Maybe it really is a croon. I never seen no Skolian."

"Yes you have."

"I have?"

"Me." Kelric smiled. "If I tell you who I am, you'll really think I'm crazy."

Ched's interest perked up. "This sounds like a good croon."

"My brother commands Imperial Space Command. I'm one of his heirs. Just think, Ched. You're talking to the future Imperator of the Skolian empire."

The boy chuckled. "If you plan to take over the universe, you better get some rest. You're a mess."

Kelric laughed. "All right." He closed his eyes.

Sometime later a sound scraped by the pallet. He looked to see Ched kneeling down with a clay flask.

"I boiled some water," the boy said. "With my candles."

Sitting up, Kelric took the jug the boy offered and gulped the water, slowing down only when the last welcome runnels of warm liquid ran down his throat. Then he lowered the jug. "Thanks. I know what those candles mean to you."

"Heh. Well." Ched shrugged. "It's not like I'm scared of the dark or nothing."

"I know." It hadn't taken Kelric long to realize the night terrified Ched. "But I thank you anyway."

Night lamps threw a glare over the quarry, cutting the dark with shears of light. Kelric's pick caught glitters of light as it arced through the air. Where the tip hit stone, sparks jumped and chips swirled in the wind. Swing. Impact. Swing. Impact. His fatigue blended with the monotony, numbing his mind.

"Sevtar."

Kelric jumped. The guard Bonni stood nearby. As he stared at her, trying to focus his thoughts, her hand went to the javelin slung across her back. That was when he realized he still had his axe raised in the air. When he lowered it, Bonni considered him, then came over and handed him a foil package.

Opening the foil, he uncovered slices of meat and spice-bread. Dumbfounded, he looked at her. "Why?"

"Ched told me the food in Four makes you sick. He said you could eat this." Her voice softened. "You're a miracle for that boy. Without protection, he'd be dead within a year. It's wrong. He shouldn't be here."

The same thought had occurred to Kelric. "It's hard to believe he tried to commit murder."

"He talks tough. But he's no killer. Get under his armor and you'll see."

"All right." He lifted the package. "And thanks."

Bonni nodded. After she left, Kelric ate some of the food, then slipped the package into his waistband under his shirt. He hefted up a block and headed to his trundle car, hiking past sandblasted water pipes.

As he reached the trundle, a woman called out, "Hey, Goldy. You that color all over?"

He squinted into the wind. On a ledge a few hundred paces away, the Compound Four women's crew stood watching him. Clumped in a pack, they stood as tall or even taller than him, their hair hanging in greasy tangles around their massive shoulders.

Kelric grimaced. Then he headed back to his workstation.

On his next trip, one of the biggest women was hoisting a block into his car. "Well, looky that," she said. "Goldy."

He dumped his blocks in the trundle.

"Where's the Little Crooner?" she asked.

"His name is Ched."

"Not on third shift, heh?" She scratched the huge expanse of her stomach. "Too bad. He's near as good to look at as you."

"So look somewhere else."

She laughed, showing a row of gaps and rotted teeth. "I just watch the scenery. I don't much care whether or not it takes to being watched."

Kelric shook his head and headed back to his workstation, his shoulders twitching under her stare. It felt like her eyes were burning holes in his clothes.

Bonni was waiting for him. "If that bunch gives you trouble, let me know."

"It's no problem." He smiled. "But thanks."

She flushed and averted her eyes. It wasn't until after she left that he figured out why. She was Hakaborn. She probably never saw any man smile except her husband.

The night wore on interminably. When the shout for shift's end came, Kelric was moving in a haze. Three shifts were more than his recently healed legs could handle. He limped after the other prisoners, thinking of sleep. The climb out of the quarry dragged on forever, each flight seeming steeper than the last.

At the top, an unfamiliar octet of guards stopped their crew. The captain came over to Kelric. "Sevtar Dahl?"

It took a moment for the name to register through his daze. "Yes?"

"Come with us."

Gods, he thought. Now what? They took him down the mountain and past the compounds. By the time they reached the gatehouse, dawn was tinging the sky. Inside the gatehouse it was dark, but an office glowed with light at the back. A woman there was pouring herself a steaming mug of Tanghi tea. She was tall, with a lean build and dark red hair wound in a braid on her head. Sun and wind had weathered her face until she looked like a rusted pole.

As the guards brought Kelric into the office, the unfamiliar woman turned to the captain. "He make trouble today?"

"None," the captain said. "Filled his quota and then some."

The rusted woman nodded at a pouch on the desk next to Kelric. "Quis dice. For you. Take it."

As he picked up the pouch, the woman spoke to his guards. "You can take him back to the quarry."

The captain stared at her. "But he's done *three* shifts today."

"And you just have time to get him back for a fourth."

"No," Kelric said.

The rusted woman turned to him. "I hear a lot about you being a troublemaker, Calani." She took a swallow of her Tanghi. "I don't like troublemakers."

Kelric knew there had to be regulations against working prisoners until they dropped. "I want to talk to the head warden. Zecha Haka."

"You are." Zecha turned to the captain. "That will be all."

Kelric gritted his teeth, knowing further protests would get him nothing more than retaliation, probably in the form of more extra shifts. Clenching his fist on the pouch, he went with his guards.

Outside the building, he fumbled with the pouch, trying to tie it onto his belt. It slipped from his fingers and thudded into the sand.

The captain knelt down and scooped up the pouch. "Sevtar, I'm sorry." Standing, she tied it on his belt. "About the shifts."

He swallowed. "So am I."

As they climbed back into the cliffs, he wondered what he was supposed to do with a pouch of dice.

13

Continuity

<You'll die here,> the voice said. *Everywhere Kelric turned, monoliths blocked his escape. No light, no food, no water, water, water, water . . .*

"Winds above, wake up." Ched shook him. "Come on. I got you water."

Kelric sat bolt upright in the darkness, knocking down the boy. "What?"

"You don't got to push me over." Ched sat back up. "You

were thrashing around, moaning for water. So I boiled some."

Kelric practically yanked the flask out of Ched's hand. He swallowed its contents in huge gulps, nearly choking as the water quenched his parched thirst.

"You feel better?" Ched asked.

Kelric lowered the now empty flask, feeling a bit sheepish. "Yes. Much better."

The boy leaned back on his hands. "Had me a big surprise today. I met my quota."

"That quota is absurd." Kelric lay down again, his surge of nightmare-produced adrenaline subsiding. "I don't see how you ever meet it."

"I never do."

"You just said you did."

"I should maybe put it different. My trundles was filled when the captain came round to check. But it wasn't me who cut half them blocks."

"You probably just lost track."

Ched leaned forward. "So how come you didn't meet your quota? You cut more than you needed."

"You must have misjudged the amount."

"You been filling my cars. Winds know, I appreciate it, metal man. But I want you to stop."

"Stop what?"

"Cuaz me." Ched threw up his hands. "You're impossible."

Kelric smiled.

"Well," Ched said. "I'll just thank you for filling my cars you didn't fill and let you sleep."

Kelric thought of his nightmare. "Don't go."

"Bad dream, heh?" Ched nodded. "I get 'em too." He frowned. "We could play Quis, 'cept you left your dice pouch lying around and Ikav pixed it. You got to be more careful."

"He can have it." Kelric closed his eyes. "I'd rather sleep."

"Now, maybe. But we'll be off late shift in a few days. You'll see how boring it gets."

Kelric opened his eyes. "We?"

"I asked for a third shift." Ched laughed. "Now the guards really think I'm crazy."

"So do I. Why did you do it?"

"To get ahead on my quota so you'll quit killing yourself to fill my cars. Besides, Zev and them are off late shift tomorrow. I don't want to be here when they are and you aren't."

The same thought had occurred to Kelric. What would happen to Ched if he escaped? He could try to break out the boy, too, but he doubted Ched would last long on his own. And when faced with Ched's vulnerability it was too easy to forget he was in prison for a reason.

"Why are you looking at me like that?" Ched said.

"I was wondering about the man you tried to kill."

Ched tensed. "What about him?"

"Why did you try to strangle him?"

"What do you mean, why? He was sewer scum. He deserved to have his head popped off."

Kelric could imagine the effect Ched's language made at his Tribunal. "What did he do?"

"He didn't do nothing. Never. Except put drink inside himself." The boy flinched. "That's when he decided I needed lessons." Ched made a fist. "That."

"He hit you?"

"He said I made him do it. That last time he was trying to kill me." Ched swallowed. "Seems I fight real good when I'm scared outta my head."

Kelric stared at him. "Couldn't you get help anywhere?"

"Right. A kinsa. They would've laughed in my face."

"You have as much right to civil protection as anyone else."

"The right to get cooped in a city jail."

"What about the Children's Cooperative?"

"What about it?"

"Couldn't you go there?"

"No."

"Why not?"

"None of your business why not."

Kelric considered him. "Is there any way you can serve your sentence in a less severe compound?"

"You mean transfer?" Ched laughed. "If I kept ahead of my quotas, if Torv put in a word for me, if Zecha was in a good mood—not a chance."

"Bonni would put in a word for you."

Ched blinked. "You know, she might."

A clang rang through the hall, the sound of the security doors opening. Ched jumped to his feet and ran to the archway of Kelric's cell. "It's guards. Bundles of 'em."

Kelric joined him. Four guards were striding down the hall, the blades of their swords glinting in the starlight. More guards stood at the doors, keeping watch as Zev and the others appeared in the archways of their cells.

The captain halted in front of Kelric. "Turn around."

Disconcerted, Kelric turned. Someone locked his wrist guards behind his back—and then tied a blindfold over his eyes.

"Leave him alone," Ched protested. "He hasn't done nothing."

"Heh," Zev called. "Torv planning to work him over again?"

Gossi laughed. "Glad it's you, Calani, and not me."

Kelric tensed, disoriented by the blindfold. A guard slipped a hand under his elbow and guided him forward in the darkness. They took him out of the corridor and through the building, leading him by touch. Then they were outside, in the stinging sandstorm where the wind blasted unseen grit at him. He forced himself to put one foot in front of the other, having to trust their guidance.

Eventually they entered a protected space, walking down an incline. After a short time they stopped and a door clanged shut. Someone freed his hands and removed his blindfold. When his eyes adjusted to the light, he saw a room paneled with glossy amberwood and carpeted by a lush gold rug.

In the center of the room, Zecha sat at a Quis table.

She motioned to an armchair across the table. "Sit down."

Kelric stared at her, then settled into the chair.

Zecha glanced at the captain. "Where are his Quis dice?"

"Ikav had them." The captain pulled the pouch out of her jacket and set it on the table.

Kelric blinked at the warden. "You brought me here to play dice?"

"We'll wager work shifts." She took out her own pouch. "For each game you lose, you work one extra shift."

I don't believe this, Kelric thought. "What if I win?"

"Then you don't have to work the shift."

"That's not much of a bet." He pushed at the thick curls spilling down his neck. "How about a haircut for a win? A shave for a second win."

Zecha shrugged. "Whatever." She set a blue cube on the table. "Your move."

It was hard to change mental gears to Quis. He felt too tired. But the prospect of more shifts or being beaten again by Torv was worse. So he poured out his dice and set a blue cube on top of Zecha's die. She added a red cube to the stack.

"You can't do that," he said.

"Why not?"

"Red can't go on blue."

She snorted. "I thought you knew how to play Quis."

Bolt, he thought.

SDFJ$(

Bolt, come on. Can you access my files on Quis rules?

FD5A87+++++

Kelric gave up and fell back on intuition, placing a rod on the table to pull Zecha's play away from the cube stack. She set a sphere near the rod, and he added a rosewood arch between the sphere and stack.

Zecha laughed. "My game."

"Your game?" He looked at her. "It's not your game."

"You made a bridge. Both ends touch my pieces. A baby knows better than that."

Damn. He hadn't even noticed his arch touched her sphere. By bridging it to the stack, he had formed a structure. The combined rank of Zecha's pieces in it easily surpassed his, so she could claim it for the win if she wanted.

The warden cleared the playing area and set down a dodecahedron. Kelric put a blue triangle on top of it.

Zecha smirked. "Extra shift number two."

"I lost?"

"Miserably."

"Why?"

"My dodecahedron has black edges."

"So what?"

"So you can only play black on it." Zecha flipped his triangle back to him and left her dodecahedron. "New game. Your move."

Kelric rubbed his eyes, trying to stay awake. He set a heptahedron on the table.

Zecha laughed. "Shift three for you."

For pugging sake, he thought.

"I thought he was a Calani," a guard muttered.

"If you can't give me the reason why you lost," Zecha added, "you get a fourth shift."

Kelric wondered what possessed the head warden of the entire prison to drag him blindfolded across Haka in the middle of the night for a Quis lesson. "It's a continuity law," he said. But which one? Color? Shape? Dimension. That was it. Dimension.

"I lost on the first move of the last game," he said. "You opened this new game with the dodecahedron you played before. So continuity holds. I had to fix my losing move from the previous game by properly placing a piece with the same dimension as the one I misplayed before. Which means a flat piece. Two dimensions. But I instead played a three-dimension piece."

"Fourth shift," Zecha said smugly.

He gritted his teeth. "What for?"

"Your piece also had to supersede my dodecahedron."

"Nothing supersedes a dodecahedron."

"That's right." She took away his die and left the dodecahedron. "Your move."

Kelric scowled. The more sides on a polyhedron, the higher its rank. In Quis, no polyhedron had more than a dodecahedron's twelve sides and in the current structure no other shape would outrank a polyhedron. She had him trapped in an infinite loop of losses.

"Looks like another shift," Zecha commented.

Behind Kelric, the door opened. A girl came over and spoke to the warden in a low voice. Zecha frowned and nodded.

After the girl left, Kelric balanced an ebony ball on the dodecahedron.

"I'm sorry," Zecha said. "But that move is illegal."

His mouth almost fell open. It was the first civil phrase she had ever uttered to him. When he recovered from the shock, he said, "It's legal. I misplayed a three-dimension piece the last game and a ball is a three-dimensional piece."

"True," she agreed. "But it doesn't supersede a dodecahedron."

"Yes it does."

Her polite veneer cracked. "Don't contradict me. You need a piece with more than twelve sides. You don't have one."

He grinned. "A ball has an infinite number of sides. It's the limit of letting the number of sides on a polyhedron go to infinity."

With a scowl, Zecha knocked his ball off her die. Then she took her dodecahedron out of the playing area. "Well? You won. So open."

Kelric resisted the urge to laugh. He put down a pyramid and the game took off, rapidly evolving into a complicated series of structures. After a while something began to tug at him. What . . . ? Yes, there. Zecha had built a convoluted snake of green dice and was trying to close the coil.

She drummed her fingers on the table. "Are you going to take forever?"

"No." He played a blue pyramid.

She shoved a green pyramid into a structure. "Your move."

He smiled. "My game."

"It's not your game. Make your move."

Kelric tapped his finger along a line of pyramids winding through the structures. "Black, brown, red, orange, gold, yellow, green, blue, purple, violet, black. All mine except for the red and green." He laughed. "Grand augmented spectrum, my advantage. You owe me a shave and a haircut, Warden."

Zecha glared at him. Then she turned to the octet. "You can take him back now."

When he stood up, they locked his wrists, then blindfolded him and led him away.

Zecha leaned against the table in the Interstice room that connected the Estate to the underground tunnels of Haka. It irked her that Rashiva insisted she hold her Quis sessions with

Sevtar here, where a window of one-way glass allowed the Manager to watch unobserved. Spying, that's what Rashiva was doing. Smart idea to put that girl on lookout, to warn her if the Manager showed up.

Across the room, the door opened and Rashiva Haka entered.

Zecha bowed. "Manager Haka."

"Morning, Warden." Rashiva chuckled. "He caught you with the infinite-sided polyhedron, heh, Zecha? And that spectrum was a beauty."

"You missed his first games. He played like a child."

Rashiva stretched her arms. "Why did you schedule the session before dawn? If my aide hadn't seen you come in, I would have slept right through it."

Zecha had intended to be done with the "lesson" before the early-rising Manager awoke. "I didn't want to bother you, ma'am."

"It's no bother." Rashiva leaned against the table. "Do you need to blindfold and restrain him that way? It must be unpleasant for him."

"If we don't blindfold him, he'll learn the route here from the prison. Without restraints, he could break into the Estate." Maybe she ought to let him loose. If Sevtar knocked around Rashiva's staff, it might cure the Manager of this rehabilitation nonsense.

"He doesn't act dangerous," Rashiva said. "He seems a pleasant fellow."

"That 'pleasant fellow' killed Llaach Dahl."

Rashiva exhaled. "Yes. He did." She thought for a moment. "Let him off quarry crew today. He's obviously exhausted. And give him that shave he wanted. Just trim his hair, though. It's too gorgeous to cut off."

Bones and bugs. Rashiva expected her to manicure crooners? "It could be dangerous to let him near a razor. He might go for the blade."

"Take whatever precautions you think necessary."

"Yhee, ma'am."

After Rashiva left, Zecha brooded. So she was supposed to coddle Sevtar, heh? No chance. Maybe he expected his beauty to get him special treatment. She'd seen his smiles. His seductive behavior might blind Managers but it wouldn't work on Haka's warden.

But Sevtar got to her in another way. Somehow he crept into her brain. It had been years since she suffered nightmares of people talking in her head. Back then, she had feared she was going insane, until finally she stopped it by putting up an emotional wall that shut everyone out. It made her lonelier than a kinsa lost in the desert, but it kept her from hearing other people's thoughts.

Now Sevtar came, eating away at her fortifications.

Zecha gritted her teeth. This Sevtar business had gone too far. She had to get rid of him.

When Ched entered the cell, Kelric was holding himself up by the skylight, peering out at the blue sky.

"Cuaz and Khozaar me," Ched said.

Kelric looked down. "What does that mean anyway?"

"It's just something people say. Cuaz and Khozaar are wind gods, Akasi to the sungoddess Savina." Ched frowned at him. "You can't break the skylight bars, metal man. We've all tried."

Kelric dropped to the floor. "Want to play Quis?"

"No. You always beat me." Ched flopped down on the pallet. "Know what I'd like? A big feast, with lots of wine. Afterward, two beautiful warrior women carry us off and have their way with us."

Kelric smiled. "Sounds interesting."

"You ever been in love?"

"Twice." Kelric sat by the wall. "The first time I was younger than you. Fourteen. Shaliece used to sneak up and watch me swim in the river. One day I saw her. I was so mortified that after I got my pants back on, I chased her all over the woods."

"What happened when you caught her?"

Kelric laughed. "That, young man, is private."

Ched grinned. "She got you in trouble, heh? Happened to me too." His smile faded. "I was thrown out of the Children's Cooperative in Lasa 'cause of it."

"Thrown out? Why?"

"I let this girl talk me into stuff." Ched sat up. "Next morning she wouldn't have nothing to do with me. But she talked. Pretty soon all them girls was telling stories about me. It was all lies. I wouldn't touch those clawcats. I only liked that one but she wanted someone else. And you know what? She got him in trouble. To protect him she said I was the father. With all those stories about me everyone believed her." He swept his hand across the floor and sent sand flying. "So the Cooperative guardians kicked me out."

Kelric frowned. "They had no business turning you out."

"That's why I went to Viasa. No Lasa House would take me. People called me trash." He shrugged. "Guess they was right."

"They weren't, Ched. Never believe that about yourself."

The boy hesitated. "You think maybe different?"

"Absolutely. You've a lot of potential. You just need a chance to develop it."

"Heh. Well." Ched gave him an embarrassed smile. "You know, you're all right."

Rashiva paced across Zecha's office. "He looks so vulnerable."

Zecha sat back in her chair. "Don't let Ched's innocent face fool you."

"Bonni says he's a model prisoner." Rashiva stopped pacing. "She suggested transferring him out of Four."

Model prisoner? Zecha almost snorted. She knew his kind, how they manipulated women. Her father had been Ched's age when he propositioned her mother. Maybe her mother had been happy with the unexpected result of that night's pleasure, but Zecha still burned from the childhood taunts: *kinsaborn. Whore-baby.*

"Ched's always been a problem," she said. "He's kept ahead of his quotas lately, but I doubt it will last."

Rashiva frowned. "What quotas?"

Bones and bugs. Didn't Rashiva ever miss anything? "It's a reward system. If prisoners meet certain quotas they get privileges." As soon as Zecha had realized Rashiva didn't intend to doze her way through her reign like her doddering predecessor, she had cleaned out her files. Certain records could have been misinterpreted, particularly those detailing how she routed profits from the extra quarry shifts to her own accounts. So she got rid of them. Her files were pristine now. "I can show you the records."

"All right," Rashiva said. "And go ahead with Ched's transfer. Put him on another crew. Maintenance maybe. He doesn't look strong enough to work in a quarry."

Zecha stiffened. Who was warden here? Still, better to win Rashiva's confidence on a trivial matter like this. It would give her a stronger bargaining position on critical issues.

"I can send him to Compound Two," Zecha said. "They do maintenance."

"Good." Rashiva resumed pacing. "How is Sevtar coming along?"

"He isn't. You've seen his record. He started a fight his first night here and attacked Torv Haka his first day in the quarry."

"Perhaps you should separate him from the others." Rashiva considered. "Let him concentrate more on Quis. Working in a quarry is a waste of his talent anyway."

A plan was forming in Zecha's mind. "I think that's a good idea." Yes, an excellent idea.

She might never have to worry about the Sevtar problem again.

Sand stung Kelric's face as his guards led him through the sandstorm. They stopped at an isolated storehouse far from the compounds. When he saw Zecha waiting at the building's metal door, his unease grew. She heaved open the heavy portal, revealing both it and the storehouse walls to be over six handspans thick.

His guards prodded him forward with their swords, honed points nicking his skin as they pierced the cloth of his uniform. Inside the storehouse, he found a single large room with a pallet and a blanket. A row of barred windows stretched the length of one wall, set so high he doubted he could see out of them even if he jumped. Puzzled, he turned to Zecha.

"You're being separated from the other prisoners," she said.

"For how long?" he asked.

Her eyes glinted. "Forever."

Kelric lunged for the door, but the guards were already heaving it into place. As the portal slammed shut, he smashed into the metal. "No!" He pounded his fists on the door. "NO!"

No sound came from beyond the storehouse.

14

Rock's Chute

In the beginning Kelric raged, smashing his bulk against the walls that confined him. Each time his fury spent itself, he collapsed to the floor, his shoulders heaving as he gasped in air.

His jailors had converted one of the storeroom closets into a bathroom. The other closet held a blanket, a jug of liquid soap, and cleaning rags. Each morning his food appeared in a narrow tunnel cut through the bottom of the storehouse door. After he finished his meals, he shoved the empty bowls and plates back into the tunnel. When he heard someone removing them, he tried to grab their arm, but he couldn't reach far enough into the tunnel.

He refused to eat, hoping a hunger strike would force them to release him. After several days, when his jailers showed no reaction to his untouched meals in the tunnel, he wondered if Zecha wanted him to die by self-induced starvation.

He quit the strike that night.

Eventually he developed a routine. In the morning he exercised, and for the rest of the day he played Quis solitaire. When the light faded into night he escaped into sleep and when dawn trickled in the windows he awoke, every morning of every day, until the days became seasons.

Autumn cooled into winter, with rains that trickled in the windows, saturating his world with dampness. Once he caught a fever, becoming so sick he could barely move. In his lucid moments he wondered how anyone would know if he died.

After he recovered, he made a cloak out of his blanket, using a shard of rock to cut armholes and fashion a hood. He pushed the remaining scraps of cloth into the tunnel, and the next morning a new blanket came with his food.

Winter warmed into spring. His hair grew into a shaggy mane and his beard curled in a red-gold mat on his chest. In summer, he lay sweltering in the heat. Sand blew in on the hot wind and settled over his body.

At night, dreams from his home world of Lyshriol haunted his sleep. He saw its plains of silvery grass and the ancient dappled forests where he had played as a child. In other dreams he held a lover, often Deha, sometimes his first wife, more rarely other women he had known. It felt so real that when he awoke he wanted to beat the walls in protest of the empty spaces that greeted him.

He had always been an introvert, recharged by time alone, but this was beyond all reason. When he became depressed, Bolt released chemicals in his brain, powering up an endorphin high. It helped his mood but didn't counteract the loneliness, and it strained the already damaged computer, until finally, after several seasons, he lost contact with it. Bolt's silence saddened him; he no longer had even the voice in his head to converse with.

So he talked to the sand, the floor, the food. He named the insects that hummed in the windows. When he found himself giving a funeral to a dead airbug, he knew he had to find a distraction from the loneliness.

Quis became his existence. He covered the floor with structures and made extra dice with cement he chipped off the walls. When the rules grew constraining he added new ones. The Quis he played was his and his alone, with no influence, no history, no cultural memories, no input from any other player. The simple patterns he had learned at Dahl seemed laughable now. He wove his perceptions of Haka, of Coba, of the Imperialate, of the universe, into his Quis. The patterns evolved, illuminating the past, predicting the future, revealing hidden mazes in the subconscious corridors of his mind.

His dice took on personalities. Ched was the silver cube.

Every pattern he built of the boy's life in Compound Four evolved into death. He tried to find patterns of hope, but the dice refused to lie. He often found somber dice of mourning around the silver cube.

The obsidian decahedron was Zecha. Sometimes he trapped it in torturously convoluted structures, destroying its rank. Other times he built pattern after pattern, trying to understand why she loathed him. She remained an enigma. For some reason, even thinking about her here, alone in his cell, drove him to barrier his mind. She crept into his brain, negating him like an anti-empath.

Gradually his dice took on more complex aspects. Equations evolved in his patterns: complex variables, differential equations, topology, catastrophe theory, Selenian mystimatics. He created new theorems, becoming so absorbed in his life-long passion for abstract math that at times he even forgot the weight of his solitude. In his sleep he dreamt Quis equations.

Then the dice turned introspective, forcing him to relive the scorn of his half brother, Kurj, the Imperator: *Mathematics, Kelric? Why frustrate yourself in a pursuit beyond your ability?* The Quis showed what he had never understood: his brother's contempt masked fear.

It would have made no difference what dreams Kelric pursued, his brother would have crushed his confidence, tearing Kelric down to protect against what he, the Imperator, perceived as a threat to his power. Kurj saw only himself when he looked at Kelric, and having gained his title through violence and death he would never trust his own heir.

That was when Kelric smashed his hand through the dice, throwing them across his cell.

After that he sought fonder memories. He wove patterns of his father, a farmer bemused by the glittering technology of his wife's universe, a loving man who doted on his family, never dreaming he would someday become an interstellar potentate. The patterns of his mother were warmth and a shimmering gold beauty so great a galaxy bowed before it. She was the sun of home, the warmth of the hearth—and a political pundit who walked the halls of Imperial power.

Through his dice Kelric grieved for the loss of his home, his family, his hopes, his future. He lived among the structures, balanced on the edge of madness, unable to remember how it felt to touch another human being, until he wondered if his memories were no more than the dreams of an insane man.

15

Desert Tower

The Topazwalk spanned the top level of Haka Estate like a tawny corridor of light. Made from tinted glass, it looked out over a sea of sand. Two figures walked together along the corridor, bathed in its ruddy light.

"I'm sorry to be blunt," Zecha said. "But bring Sevtar onto the Estate and you will regret it."

"Your reports make his progress sound excellent," Rashiva said.

Zecha knew she had trouble. It had taken time and work to win Rashiva's confidence, and part of that success came from her encouraging reports about Sevtar. In truth, she had paid little attention to what he was doing this past year. Who could have known the Manager meant to take him into her *Calanya*? It was insane.

"It's true, he's made progress in a controlled environment," Zecha said. He had, after all, done nothing but play Quis. If he hadn't learned anything by now, he never would. "But I have grave doubts about his mental stability. There's no telling what might make him snap."

Rashiva nodded. "He will be kept separate from the others until we know if he's stable."

So. The Manager had her doubts. Zecha took stock of the situation. If he told tales of solitary, would anyone believe him? That Rashiva paid much closer attention to the prison than her predecessor would help here. The Manager knew about the delusions suffered by the prisoners in Four, and whatever marginal sanity Sevtar had possessed prior to his solitude was certainly gone now. Given his weak mind, he was probably raving mad. She could have her prison doctors certify him as insane, a madness that subsided only under their expert care.

Sevtar would soon be back in prison.

The grate of metal scraping on stone woke Kelric. He raised his head and peered into the predawn darkness.

The door of his cell moved.

The portal slowly swung open, revealing an octet of guards. They entered the cell like wraiths, shadowy and gray in the dim light. Kelric rose to his feet, unable to speak, surrounded by the Quis structures he had built. Seven of the guards took up a shadowed formation around him and the eighth gathered up his dice.

Stop, he thought. They were destroying patterns he had worked on for days. But he stood frozen, afraid if he moved the dream figures would vanish.

They gave him his pouch, the small sack bulging with dice. Then the captain raised her arm toward the door in a ghostly invitation. He looked from her to the other guards, still unable to absorb their presence.

Then he walked out of the storehouse.

They made their way through a daze of swirling, whirling sand, until they reached one of the lesser peaks with a door embedded in it. They entered the crag and followed a maze of tunnels that sloped down under the desert. Kelric's sense of direction soon failed him in the sameness of the passages and their turns. He didn't bother asking Bolt where they were; the node had long ago stopped responding.

At the junction of two corridors, his guards took him into an office. The captain removed some clothes from the desk: suede pants with sewn seams, a laced white shirt with Quis designs embroidered on its cuffs, knee boots the color of sand, and a robe made from lightweight russet cloth. She gave him a woven scarf as long as he was tall, made from white yarn with black tassels all around its borders. Quis designs adorned it, sewn in metallic yarns that glittered even in the room's cold light.

After the guards withdrew, locking the door behind them, Kelric stood holding the clothes. He couldn't comprehend them. For a year he had worn the same gray uniform, washed and rewashed by himself until it drooped with holes.

Eventually he changed into the new clothes. The robe covered him from neck to foot, with loose sleeves that came to his wrists. He had no idea what to do with the scarf, so he draped it around his neck and let it hang down his chest. Then he waited.

A knock sounded on the door, followed by a pause. The captain came inside and walked over to him, then bowed from the waist. She lifted the scarf and wound it loosely around his head, covering his neck and face, except for his eyes. She finished by raising the hood of his robe, hiding all of him but his eyes.

The octet took him back into the tunnels and escorted him deeper into the maze. At a rotunda that looked down onto a lower floor, they rendezvoused with another octet, one whose bearing and manner he recognized.

Calanya guards.

Finally Kelric understood. Hallucination. Loneliness had driven him to create these bizarre scenes.

The Calanya escort led him farther into the maze, climbing upward now, until he was sure they were above the desert again. The stone under his feet changed into glazed tiles and the tunnels expanded into halls with arabesques sculpted on the walls. Mosaics graced the corridors in geometric designs, with intricate borders around arches, niches, and column capitals.

He devised Quis rules to describe the patterns.

They came out into a painfully bright corridor where sunshine poured through floor-to-ceiling windows. It nearly blinded him. By squinting, he could make out the desert far below, sweeping to the horizon.

The doorway at the end of the hall looked like the keyhole for a giant skeleton key, with a stained-glass window in the upper circular portion. It had Quis designs carved around its edges and the Haka symbol of a rising sun at its apex.

Beyond the door was a suite. Spice rooms. Colors. Kelric could barely absorb it; his last year had been spent in shades of gray. These walls blended from cinnamon near the floor into gold and then cream at the top. Plants with saffron blossoms stood in vases and spheres of glass painted with flowers hung from the ceiling on gold chains.

They showed him through room after room of luxury, until finally it became too much. Kelric balked at an arbitrary archway when the captain pulled aside its curtain of reeds.

She smiled at him. "Go on in. It's yours, after all."

His? He walked into the room beyond the reeds. Larger than the entire Compound Four men's wing, it was only a bath chamber. A pool fed by fountains filled over half of it.

"Manager Haka had purifiers installed in the wells that serve the pool," the captain said. "So you won't get sick if you swallow any water."

A fountain in the shape of a flower stood at one edge of the pool. Kelric sat on the ledge of its basin and looked into the water-filled bowl inlaid by green and blue tiles. He traced his hand through the water and it swirled in Quis patterns.

The captain spoke again. "I am Khaaj. My octet will be Outside your suite. If you need anything, open the Outside door and we will summon the Calanya Speaker."

Speaker? He only knew how to speak to himself.

"A barber is waiting to give you a shave and a haircut," Khaaj added. "The metalworker will be here later this afternoon to change your Calanya guards."

Kelric stared into the pool, devising Quis equations to describe its ripples. He didn't turn around as his escort left, he just continued to watch his hallucination of a fountain.

It had finally happened. He had gone insane.

Fresh from his bath, dressed in his new clothes, with his hair cut and his face shaved, Kelric sat on cushions in his suite and stared at his wrist guards. The only symbol he recognized was the Haka rising sun. Why Haka guards? If his deranged mind needed to create an illusion, why not Dahl guards? His only good memories of Coba came from Dahl.

"Sevtar?" Captain Khaaj pulled aside the reeds in an archway across the room and bowed to him. "You have a visitor, with Speaker's Privilege." She withdrew and a new hallucination appeared.

Kelric stared at it. When the silence became strained, the hallucination spoke. "I know I'm under your level now, metal man. But couldn't you talk to me just this once? Manager Haka gave permission."

For the first time in a year Kelric spoke to another human being. "Ched Viasa is dead."

Ched grinned at him. "I guess nobody let me know." He walked across the room. "I've never seen a place this nice. Manager Haka takes good care of you, heh?"

Kelric tried to absorb his presence. "Compound Four—?"

"Bonni helped me get transferred, just like you said. I went to Compound Two." Ched laughed. "You know what I've been doing? Laundry. I haven't seen that hole in the cliffs for a year."

"Laundry." Kelric's voice shook.

Ched came over to him. "You all right?"

"No." He fought the tears but they came anyway, running down his face. He wasn't sure why he cried, whether it was Ched, the suite, the sound of a human voice, or his insane hope it was all real.

As Ched sat next to him on the plush rug, Kelric wiped his cheeks. "Not much of a metal man after all, am I?"

Ched smiled. "Well, you know what they say. 'Never iron cold is the touch of gold.' It's a saying more about people than metal."

Kelric smiled. "I'm glad to see you."

"They let me come because of your being sworn tonight." Ched hesitated. "Manager Haka talked to the warden—not Zecha, thank Cuaz, but the one over in Two. The warden knew Bonni knew you, so she talked to Bonni and Bonni talked to me and I said, yhee, if it was all right with you, so Bonni told the warden—"

"Ched, wait." Kelric almost laughed. "I lost track about when the warden talked to Bonni."

"I just don't want you to think I'm pushing where I have no right to push."

"Why would I think that?"

"Because you're supposed to ask."

"Ask what?"

Ched averted his eyes. "Me to be your Oath Brother."

Oath? As in Calanya Oath? That made no sense. But he valued Ched's offer of friendship more than he knew how to say. "Will you?"

"Sure." Ched relaxed and grinned at him. "I've sure missed you."

"Do they treat you well in Two?"

"It's all right. I get to take lessons from a Scribe, reading, writing, stuff like that. To make me smart, for when I get out." He glanced at Kelric's robe. "Can I look at your Talha? I've never seen one up close before."

Kelric offered him the robe, but Ched took only the scarf on top of it. "It's rolled right sharp, metal man."

"It's what?"

"You don't recognize it, do you?" When Kelric shook his head, Ched said, "Haka men have to wear Talha scarves in public. It's part of the Propriety Laws."

"Propriety Laws?"

"Scowl Laws." Ched brushed his fingers over the scarf. "Don't you remember? Warden Torv wore a Talha up at the quarry."

Kelric dredged up his memory of the Compound Four men's warden. "I thought it was to protect him from the sandstorms."

"That too. A lot of women wear them for the same reason." Ched gave him back the Talha. "Theirs are just plain, though. The ones like yours are for high-level men." He nodded. "Manager Haka means you great honor."

Kelric regarded the scarf, with its gleaming designs and ornate tassels. If Manager Haka meant him so much honor, why had he just spent a year in hell?

The Sunset Hall glowed beneath the colors of a true sunset. Stained-glass windows surrounded the hall, their lower edges flush with the floor and the tips of their onion-shaped crowns touching the high ceiling. Dark red curtains hung on the walls between windows and glazed bowls sat on tiled pedestals. Tendrils of smoke curled up from the bowls, scenting the air with incense. No furniture intruded; the highborn of Haka sat on the floor, among embroidered cushions with tassels at each corner, the women in jackets and trousers of brocaded silk, and the men in robes and Talha scarves.

Bathed in fiery light, and dressed in robes and Talhas, Kelric stood with Ched in the sunken hollow of a circle. A rail made from gold wood encircled them.

Cymbals chimed in soft rhythm, followed by the compelling beat of a drum and a pipe's haunting melody. Then a man's voice soared into the music. He sang in an unfamiliar language, one with an ancient sound, evoking images of Estates burnished like gold in the desert. The music swirled in the sunset, then faded into silence like a sun vanishing behind the horizon.

A woman's dusky voice coalesced out of the air. "Ched Lasa Viasa, do you stand as Oath Brother to Sevtar?"

"I do," Ched said.

"What do you speak for him?"

Ched took a breath. "Sevtar was a better friend to me than anyone else I ever knew. He stood by me no matter what. And he believed in me." He glanced at Kelric. "Knowing him made me a better person. I can't think of anyone more worthy for your Calanya."

Kelric touched Ched's arm in thanks, and the youth's face gentled.

A young girl spoke. "Your words are heard and recorded, Ched of Viasa."

Ched bowed, then stepped out of the Circle and withdrew to sit with his guards.

Cymbals chimed again. Then the woman with the dusky voice spoke. "For Haka and for Coba, do you, Sevtar, come to the Circle to give your Oath?"

Was this the price of freedom? His betrayal of Deha? Kelric stood mute, his silence stretching out in the gilded topaz light. As murmurs came from the watchers, the curtains at the end of the hall rustled.

Then a woman appeared.

No. Kelric clenched the rail, trying to anchor himself in its reality. Only in a hallucination would he see, on Coba, the fertility goddess Viana from the mythology of his home world Lyshriol. She wore a long white robe that clung to her voluptuous body like fluid rippling in a stream. Graced with creamy dark skin, her face had a mesmerizing beauty. Black lashes fringed her large eyes, and a braid of glossy black hair as thick as a fist fell over her shoulder to her hip. Rubies in her necklace glittered against her skin.

She came to stand before him. "Do you refuse Haka your Oath?"

Kelric pulled down his Talha, uncovering his face. "Are you the Haka Manager?"

"Yes. I am Rashiva Haka."

"Dahl already has my Oath."

"Manager Dahl has relinquished your vow."

"I don't believe you."

"Why would I lie?"

Why indeed. What possessed his fevered mind to create this mocking hallucination? He liked Deha. Why imagine she rejected him? For that matter, he couldn't see why he would imagine an Estate where a man had so little choice in the matter of his Oath that its Manager didn't bother to explain the situation before the ceremony. Rashiva acted as if it had never occurred to her that he might not obey. Why would he hallucinate this? Hell, he didn't know. He was insane anyway.

Rashiva spoke quietly. "I can offer you a better life than you will ever have in prison. But I won't force you to deny Dahl. If it is your wish to return to the compounds rather than enter my Calanya, I won't make you stay here."

A vision of his isolation rose in his mind like a nightmare. "How did you force Manager Dahl to allow this?"

"I forced no one. It was her idea."

He refused to believe Deha had thrown him away the moment he became a liability. This was a delusion created by a man driven mad with loneliness. But a delusion of solitude would be as crushing as the reality.

In a flat voice he said, "Then take my Oath."

Rashiva's voice took on the quality of a ritual. "Hear my words, Sevtar. But before you give them back to me as Oath know that your life is bound by them."

After a moment he realized she was waiting for a response. "All right," he said.

Softly she said, "You answer 'I hear and understand.' "

"I hear and understand."

"For Haka and for Coba," she said, "do you enter the Circle to give your Oath?"

"Yes."

"Do you swear you will hold my Estate above all else, as you hold in your hands and your mind the future of Haka?"

"Yes."

She watched him with night-dark eyes. "Do you swear to keep forever the discipline of the Calanya? To never again read or write? To never again speak in the presence of those who are not of the Calanya?"

"Yes." It made no sense to him, but he would have agreed to stand on his head if it kept him out of the storehouse.

"Do you swear—on penalty of your life—that your loyalty is to Haka, only to Haka, and completely to Haka?"

"If you want," he said.

" 'I swear,' " she murmured. " 'With my life.' "

She waited, watching him with her unsettling gaze. So he said, "I swear. With my life."

Rashiva raised her hand and the sound of a gong vibrated in the air. The colors in the hall were deepening into crimson shadows. "In return for your Oath," she said, "I vow that for the rest of your life you will be provided for as befits a Calani."

What did that mean? Deha had told him the same thing.

Rashiva reached into the folds of her robe and withdrew four armbands. She first slid on his Dahl bands, white gold engraved with the suntree symbol and other hieroglyphics, including just about the only written Teotecan he understood, his Coban name, Sevtar Dahl, the first word depicted by the glyph of a man striding across the sky, the second by the suntree glyph. The next pair of armbands she slid on him were a darker gold. He saw his Dahl name followed by a third symbol, the Haka rising sun. *Sevtar Dahl Haka.*

One other symbol on the Haka bands was familiar, a man with a mane of shoulder-length curls, his head turned to the right and his arm raised, bent at the elbow, with the palm at shoulder height and turned to face the ceiling. Kelric knew its meaning. The turned head symbolized fertility, the long hair denoted desirability, the raised palm acceptance. Husband. These were Akasi bands.

His anger stirred. For a year he had lived in a hell of solitude. Now this siren appeared out of nowhere and lured him with an alien vow of love.

Triumph flickered in her eyes. "Sevtar Dahl Haka, you are now a Second Level Calani of Haka."

16

Hawk's Fire

The audiocom refused to stop its insistent buzz. Chankah Dahl, the Dahl Successor, rolled over in bed and fumbled for the switch. "Who is this?" she grumbled.

Senior Physician Rohka's voice snapped out of the com. "You have to come to Deha's suite. Hurry. She's had another heart attack."

Chankah ran barefoot through the halls, her robe flying out behind her. Inside Deha's suite, she found the doctor Dabbiv pacing in the living room. Grief etched lines in his face.

"Why is she so rock-headed?" he demanded. "Why does she insist on working all night? We warned her, Chankah. Over and over. We *warned* her."

Chankah stared at him. Before she could respond, Deha's son appeared in an inner archway and beckoned to her.

She found the Manager lying in bed, her face pale. Chankah leaned over her. "Deha?"

The answering voice was faint. "I can't see you."

Chankah turned up the lamp on the nightstand. "Is that better?"

"A little." Deha watched her with faded eyes. "Remember all I have taught you. You carry much responsibility now. You are a power among the Estates second only to Karn."

Chankah swallowed. "Don't talk that way. You'll be up sooner than you can whistle."

"Not this time. Ah—Chani."

"I'm here. Right here."

"You must take care of him."

"Him?"

"Kelric. Get him a pardon. Promise."

Chankah would have sworn to deliver the wind if it eased her mentor's dying. "I promise. I swear it."

Deha's voice faded. "Don't mourn . . . My life has been rich . . . Good-bye . . ."

"No. Come back!" Chankah clenched the bedpost. "Deha? *Deha.*"

No life showed in the eyes of Dahl's queen.

Rashiva stood at the end of the Topazwalk, watching an octet come down the tunnel of light. The elderly Calani they escorted was distinguished, with silver hair and gray eyes. His escort towered around him like refugees from a world less serene than the one he inhabited. Saje Viasa Varz Haka was the elite of an elite, a Third Level Calani, one of the few among the Twelve Estates.

When Saje reached her, Rashiva smiled. "You look well today."

He nodded his greeting.

She turned to the escort. "You may wait Outside the Hyella Chamber."

After the guards withdrew, Rashiva moved aside to let Saje enter the tinted sphere of glass that ended the Topazwalk. Named for the translucent orbs that floated on the tips of hyella reeds, the chamber sat poised at the top of a tower, overlooking the desert. A glass bench ran around its interior wall and a glass Quis table stood in its center.

As they sat at the table, Saje studied her face. "The man from the prison troubles you."

"I played Quis with him this morning," Rashiva said.

"And?"

"Deha Dahl was wrong. Sevtar isn't talented."

Regret showed in Saje's eyes. "You are certain?"

She took a breath. "*Talent* comes nowhere near to describing his gift with the dice. It's like defining the desert as a grain of sand. Sevtar isn't a grain. He's an ocean."

"Such a gift should please you."

"Every pattern he makes is sorrow, Saje. He weeps with his dice."

The Third Level sighed. "Well, Manager Dahl is dead."

"He doesn't know. I don't know how to tell him." She paused. "He is her Akasi, after all."

"Was. He is yours now."

In name only, Rashiva thought. Sevtar was a stranger she saw only during their Quis sessions. "I'm concerned about how he will react. Warden Haka thinks he is dangerous. Her doctors say he is insane."

"What do you think?"

"I don't know. He's like the blank face of a cliff. I need your advice."

"To give you counsel," Saje said, "I must know him. To know him, I must sit at Quis with him."

Rashiva stiffened. "No."

Saje waited.

"It isn't safe," she said.

He continued to wait.

"I can't risk your life," she said.

"If you believed him to be that dangerous," Saje said, "he wouldn't be here on the Estate."

Rashiva looked out at the desert where sand swirled in patterns impossible to fathom. Like Sevtar. Saje was right. It was time Sevtar sat at Quis with a true Calani.

When Captain Khaaj and the escort came for him, Kelric balked. He had been alone in his suite for the past ten days, since his Oath ceremony. The only person he had seen besides his guards was Rashiva, three times, when she came to play Quis. They never spoke during the games. Apparently she hadn't found whatever she sought in his dice and now had sent his guards to take him back to prison and isolation.

He refused to leave the suite. No one forced him; the octet simply waited.

After an hour, Kelric began to wonder if he were wrong. He walked over to the octet. Khaaj bowed, then lifted her hand, offering to escort him out of the suite. He considered her. Then he finally went with them.

They followed graceful halls, climbed the spiral stairs of a tower, and came out in a corridor of glass. The walkway ended at a spherical chamber where an elderly man sat playing Quis solitaire. He wore three bands on each arm, over his sleeves rather than under them, as Kelric wore his. Kelric's guards took up positions with the Calanya escort already waiting outside the chamber, standing beyond the range of conversation but close enough to reach it in seconds. Kelric suspected their concern was for the elderly gentleman rather than him.

As Kelric entered, the man looked up. "Ah. Sevtar. My greetings." He indicated a chair across the table. "Please. Be comfortable."

Kelric sat down, watching him.

"I am Saje." He set a velvet pouch on the table. "Manager Haka wishes to give you this."

Kelric made no move to take the pouch. "I have Quis dice."

Saje slid the pouch over to him. "These are Calanya dice."

Kelric turned the bag over several times. Then he nudged out the dice. Not only did the pouch contain a full dice set, it also included unusual shapes, such as stars, eggs, and boxes with hinged lids. And they were real. The gold ball was just that—solid gold. White pieces were diamond, blue sapphire, red ruby. Some of the gems, like the opals, gave mixtures of colors that sparked ideas in his mind for manipulating color rank within dice structures.

Saje rolled out his own dice gems. "Shall we begin?"

"I can't." These new dice were strangers.

Saje didn't look surprised. "Use your other set today. In time you will feel comfortable with the new one."

Kelric refilled the new pouch. He tied it onto his belt, then took off his ragged bag and rolled out his dice.

"Stop hovering over me, Rashiva." Saje eased down among the cushions on the lush carpet in the sitting room behind Rashiva's office. "I'm not a blown-glass Quis die."

She sat next to him, as tense as a mountain climber's rope. "How did your session go?"

"Your Sevtar is a remarkable young man." Saje paused. "But strange. He has no sense of his own genius. He never analyzes. He does it by instinct. We give him dice so he plays Quis."

Rashiva nodded. "Yes, I thought so too. And his dice have almost no patterns of the prison. Just loneliness and solitude. If I hadn't known he's been down in the compounds, I would never have guessed it from his Quis. He plays as if he taught himself, with no input from anyone else."

Saje nodded. "I detected a faint reference to the prison. But it was very old." He spread his hands. "Perhaps it is the conditions under which he has played dice. He needs to sit at Quis with other Calani. He should live in the Calanya."

"It's too dangerous. Warden Haka thinks he's mentally ill."

Saje spoke quietly. "His only illness is loneliness. He needs company."

Rashiva had no answer for that. How could she risk her Calanya with him when she wouldn't risk herself?

The days blended together, each a repetition of the last. Kelric played Quis with gems now instead of rocks, and his guards brought his meals on silver trays instead of shoving them through the door, but the rhythm of his life was otherwise unchanged from his time in solitude. He lived in a trance.

One break existed in the pattern; each day either Rashiva or Saje sat at dice with him, in sessions so intense that conversation was an intrusion. As he learned Saje's Quis he came to know the man, his wisdom and gentle humor, better than had they exchanged words instead of dice. His sessions with the Third Level were an oasis in his loneliness.

Rashiva remained an enigma, craved but denied. He

watched her from the fortress of his mind, hungering to touch her, hating her for tormenting him.

His dreams jumbled in confused images. Sometimes he was a Jagernaut, fighting endless battles with no reprieve. Other times he saw Deha lying in death, her heart stopped. He relived Llaach's death again and again. In some nightmares he forced Rashiva to give him what he craved, with a brutality that left him stunned when he awoke. Or else ghosts entered his dreams, soldiers he had killed in battle. Each time he bolted awake, his mouth working to release a scream that never came.

Gradually an obsession took hold, a desire to go out into the desert, as if its endless space could release him from this agony of solitude, parch him dry until he no longer hurt. A thought worried at his mind like a dog with a bone: he would shatter a window and jump out. He tried with his fists, pounding the glass, but he nearly fractured his hand and still the thick glass remained solid. Another night he used a chair. It broke into pieces long before the window weakened, and the noise brought his guards running into the room.

After that, Saje no longer came to visit.

He changed his approach, using his Quis to deceive Rashiva. Like everyone else he had met on Coba, including Saje and Deha, she had no idea how to play dice. He hadn't realized it at Dahl. They were all children with Quis, blind to its intricacies. Rashiva never knew how his dice lied. He wanted her to suffer for what she let Haka do to him; his Quis told her that he was content, adjusting well to his new life.

On a night when clouds massed around the cliffs and lightning clawed the desert, an unfamiliar octet came for him. They took him through corridors emptied by the late hour, their boots echoing on the floors. With a numbness born from too long dreading this journey, he waited for the halls to become tunnels that ended at a barren gray cell.

They stopped in an alcove lit only by a torch in a claw on the wall. An ancient door faced them. The captain pushed it open, revealing a tower with spiral stairs. They climbed up and around, up and around, up and around . . .

A door at the top opened into a suite that made his own quarters look meager. Chandeliers hung from the ceiling, sparkling with colored crystals. Then he realized the "crystals" were gems: diamonds, rubies, topazes. The furniture was made from a lustrous black wood with red overtones, and upholstered in dark brocades. Urns as tall as his shoulder stood in corners, glazed with intricate Quis designs, and tapestries on the walls showed desert scenes. No windows softened the suite, only heavy drapes and walls paneled in rosewood.

After the escort left, shoving bolts into place and locking the door, Kelric wandered through the rooms. In one he found a bed covered in gold brocade, with darkwood posters at its corners and a canopy of red velvet. He took a blown-glass vase off the nightstand and turned it over in his hand. Why this new prison, this cage within a cage? At least his old suite had windows that let him see the world. Had they moved him here so he couldn't try breaking the glass? The walls pressed in, confining, suffocating—

The vase snapped in his clenched hand. Its body fell to the floor and shattered on the darkwood parquetry, leaving him holding a shard of glass. He stared at it. Then, slowly, he pressed its jagged edge against his wrist.

Soon he would be free.

In another room, a clock chimed. Sometime later it chimed again.

Kelric dropped the shard. Then he gathered up the pieces of glass and arranged them on the nightstand, taking care to place each shard in its proper place.

Finally he lay on the bed.

"Sevtar?"

Kelric hid in the gray world between sleep and waking.

"Sevtar?"

He doesn't exist, Kelric thought.

Fingers brushed his cheek. Opening his eyes, he saw Rashiva kneeling on the bed next to him. She was wearing a red lace robe that came to her thighs and she had freed her hair, letting it pour in lustrous waves over her body.

She watched him with her dark gaze. "The vase— Why?"

"It fell."

Her voice caught. "Into Quis patterns of death?"

Instead of answering, he put his arm around her waist and pulled her down on the bed. When she resisted, he held her down and rolled on top of her. Taking huge handfuls of her hair, he clenched his fists in the hollows where her shoulders met her neck.

"Sevtar, stop." She pushed against his shoulders. "It hurts."

He moved one hand to her breast and dug in his fingers. "Isn't this what you came for?"

"Not like this. Not in anger." Fear made her voice dusky. "This wasn't in your Quis."

"It was easy to fool you. You play Quis like a child." He watched her face. "You never asked if I wanted a wife. I don't. I already have one."

As soon as she tensed, he knew something was wrong. "What is it?" he demanded. When she didn't answer, he gripped her shoulders. "Answer me!"

She stared at him, still silent, but it didn't matter. Her reaction was so strong that even his injured Kyle centers picked it up.

Dead. Deha was dead.

He suddenly heard a rushing noise, one in his head rather than his ears. His voice came through the tumult. "How did she die?"

"Why makes you think—"

"Don't *lie* to me."

Softly she said, "Deha died of the heart sickness. Last season."

Last season? When was she going to tell him? Next year? Next century? A red haze blurred his vision. Had Rashiva gloated over Deha's death? Had she sat smug in her power over him while he rotted in solitude? He wanted to hurt her so much it burned in his mind. *Burned.*

He lay poised on the edge of brutality, a heartbeat away from violence. Except he couldn't do it. He couldn't inflict that harm on another person.

Kelric let out a long breath. Then he rolled off her, onto his back.

Hearing the covers rustle, he looked to see her kneeling at the edge of the bed, her hand resting on the nightstand's com switch. But she didn't call for help. Instead she spoke quietly. "I'm sorry. I should have told you. I didn't know how."

"I don't want you," he lied. If he lay with her now, he knew he would hurt her.

"Then what do you want?"

What indeed? He rolled onto his side and pushed up on his elbow. "To play Quis. Put me in your Calanya."

She gave him an incredulous look. "After what happened here tonight?"

His fist clenched in the velvet covers. "If you expect me to use sexual favors to get what I want, you can wait until the end of time."

"Why do you say such a thing?"

"It's what you expect, isn't it?"

Softly she said, "I would like you to behave more like a Haka man. Is that so outrageous? I am a Haka woman."

"I'm not a Haka man." He reached out and pulled her sash, loosening it until her robe slid off her shoulders, revealing her body underneath, her skin creamy dark against the rich red silk. "You better leave, Rashiva. If you don't, you'll get what you came for. But you won't like how it comes."

Watching him, she swallowed. She slid off the bed and put on a long robe she had draped over a chair. Then she left the room, her bare feet padding on the floor.

17

Multiple Builders

"A child." Rashiva stood in the Hyella Chamber looking out at the desert. "He thinks I play Quis like a *child*."

"He only understands Quis solitaire," Saje said. "He is right about the Calanya. He should be in it."

She turned to face the Third Level, who was standing by the Quis table. "I can't."

"You keep saying this. *I can't.* Why not? What has he done to warrant this distrust? Tried to break a window? Is this truly so dire?"

If only you knew, Rashiva thought. But her night with Sevtar would always remain private. What would she have done if he had raped her? Sent him back to prison, an admission of her weakness? No. Never would she let such humiliation become public. She would find other ways to deal with this. And she *would* deal with it.

The intensity of her reaction gave her pause. Despite how he had obviously wanted to hurt her, he had held back. So why did she want to punish him?

Because he had deceived her with Quis. He rejected her. If she did nothing, it would always be there between them, this imbalance that undermined her authority. It would eat away at her self-confidence, make her less of a woman, less in command at Haka.

No. Rashiva took a breath. She couldn't let this ruin her confidence. Nor could she let it interfere with her ability to run Haka. She had to make her decisions based on what was best for her Estate, not her pride.

Comfortable on cushions, four men were sitting on the carpeted floor around a low Quis table, too intent on their game to notice Kelric and Rashiva, who stood watching from across the room. The room was large, octagonal in shape, with walls painted in desert hues.

Rashiva spoke in a low voice. "This is the main common room." She indicated an arch in another wall. "Smaller common rooms are through there, and an exit to the parks."

He tried to absorb it. People. "How many Calani live here?"

"Seventeen." She raised her voice slightly. "Adaar?"

A Calani lifted his head, blinking like a diver coming to the surface of a lake. As the others looked up, Adaar rose to his feet and walked over to Rashiva.

She smiled. "Adaar, this is Sevtar."

Adaar bowed to him. "Welcome to Haka."

Kelric nodded.

"Do you know where the others are?" Rashiva asked Adaar.

"In the gardens, I think. I can get them."

"Yes. Thank you."

As Adaar left, Rashiva drew Kelric over to the table, where the other players were getting to their feet. She introduced him to all three, including Raaj, a First Level with the handsome features of a desert prince. His dark stare grazed Kelric like sandpaper.

A ripple of conversation spilled into the room, followed by more Calani. As they gathered around, talking at him, Kelric felt as if he were suffocating. He had thought he wanted this, but being plunged among humans so suddenly was too much.

Finally Rashiva said, "You can talk to him more later. I'm going to show him his suite."

More nods, more words, and then he and Rashiva escaped into a private suite. Except for its entrance into the main common room, it was otherwise much like his spice suite.

"This is where you will live." Rashiva spoke with awkward formality. "The common rooms are open to all, but no one can come in here unless you invite them."

"Does that include you?" he asked.

She stiffened. "No."

Kelric hadn't meant it to sound so hostile. He felt as if he had been suffering a fever, not in his body but in his mind, one he hadn't realized was burning until it began to ease. Like a distant voice nearly lost in a cave where no light had shone for years, thoughts were stirring, awakening from their slumber, trying to bring him coolness and health.

Rashiva pushed her fingers through her hair, tousling her normally perfect braid. "I will leave you to rest now." Her brocade trousers rustled as she exited the room.

He wandered through the suite for a while and eventually stopped in the bedroom. For a long time he stood at a window gazing at the desert. He tried to think about Dahl, but he couldn't imagine it without Deha. Tears ran down his face. He didn't move or make a sound, he just kept watching the desert while he cried. For Deha.

It wasn't until later that afternoon that he returned to the archway that opened into the common room. When he pushed aside the screen, he saw Saje in a nearby alcove talking to Adaar.

"Ah. Sevtar." The Third Level nodded to him. "Will you join us at Quis?"

Kelric returned the nod, trying to relax. Quis he could do.

With Adaar's assistance, Saje walked stiffly to a table where several Calani had been analyzing a Quis game. The players all rose, standing until Saje had settled into his cushions. After everyone was seated, Saje nodded to Raaj, the Hakaborn prince. "Will you begin? We will work on the Miesa Plateau."

Kelric rolled out his dice, wondering what a plateau in Miesa had to do with Quis. Raaj set a gold dodecahedron on the table and the session took off. At first Kelric had trouble following a game with so many players, but gradually the patterns became clear. The structures described an Estate. Miesa? Its Manager was young. Gold. Sun. It came up again and again.

"Savina," Kelric suddenly said. "The sungoddess."

Heads jerked up. Raaj scowled and Adaar dropped a cone, knocking over a structure.

"Yes," Saje said. "Savina is the name of the Miesa Manager. Please do not disrupt the session again."

Kelric winced. But as soon as the game resumed, he became absorbed in the patterns. It was as if he circled over Miesa, dropping nearer. It nestled in a valley where the mountains met a plateau that boasted a wealth of mineral deposits. The Manager who controlled the Miesa Plateau controlled the mineral markets of the Twelve Estates and so wielded great power. But Varz Estate rather than Miesa dominated the patterns. The once-wealthy Miesa had declined; until now it depended heavily on Varz.

After the picture was complete, the players projected various futures for Miesa into the structures. If a pattern formed with the Karn Ministry dominant, they destroyed it the same way an Outsider playing dice for money sought to destroy an opponent's advantage.

New patterns developed with Varz ascendent.

As they played, Kelric finally began to understand what the Calani did cloistered in their Calanya. They were shaping the future of their world.

* * *

Saje ushered Kelric into a private alcove in the Third Level's suite. They sat among cushions on a carpet so thick that Kelric's toes sank into the pile.

"Tomorrow," Saje continued, "I will sit at Quis with Rashiva and build her patterns of the work we did today."

Kelric was beginning to understand what Ixpar had meant, that Calani advised the Manager. "What happens then?"

"She plays Quis with selected aides. They play with others. Her input soon creates powerful ripples in the Quis net that spreads across the Twelve Estates." He slid a cushion under his legs. "It works both ways. She interacts with many high-level players, including other Managers, and then inputs her knowledge into our Quis by playing dice with us. We use the information to find advantage for Haka."

"But everyone plays Quis."

"Yes. Every woman, man, and child in the Twelve Estates." Saje paused. "It is one game. We have been playing it for a thousand years."

A new pattern was unveiling itself in Kelric's mind. Quis was the Coban equivalent of the star-spanning computer networks that tied together the Imperialate, the regular electrooptical webs and also the psiberspace webs only Kyle operators could access. Quis was a third type of web, one the Cobans "accessed" every time they played dice. This was a subjective net, depending on fluxes of personality and dice expertise rather than electricity or quantum physics. Its "memory" was the social, cultural, and racial memory of a people.

"Consider the situation at Miesa," Saje said. "We must help Varz stop the Ministry from taking control of the Plateau."

"Why?"

Saje snorted. "I should think this is obvious. If the Ministry controls the Plateau, it will give Jahlt Karn more power. She already has too much."

"She's the Minister," Kelric said.

"Varz challenges that claim." Saje settled his legs more comfortably on the pillow. "During the Old Age Varz and Karn often went to war. Now they battle with Quis."

"I take it Haka is an ally of Varz."

"Of course." Saje tilted his head toward the common room. "At the center of the ripples are the Calani. The more powerful a Calanya, the stronger its waves. But without a strong Manager, a Calanya is powerless."

"Why not just send Calani out into the network?"

Saje gave him a look that Kelric suspected he reserved for the dullest of the dull-witted. "We never speak with, read about, write to, or receive input from Outsiders. They are in no way allowed to contaminate the Calanya. If Outsiders can get to our Quis, they can manipulate it to their advantage. This would weaken Haka at its core."

The idea of protected nodes in a web intrigued Kelric. "Doesn't Third Level mean you lived on two other Estates before you came here?"

Saje nodded. "I was hardly more than a boy when I did my First Level at Viasa. I went to Varz soon after and stayed many years. Then I came here."

"Won't your knowledge of Varz and Viasa affect Haka?"

"Ah." Saje smiled as if he and Kelric were conspirators. "What better way to learn the inner working of another Estate than to obtain one of its Calani?" Quietly he added, "This is why we swear, on penalty of our lives, that our loyalty is to the Estate where we are Calani. It is also why the higher Levels are so rare. And so sought after. To bring me here, Rashiva's predecessor put Haka into debt for years."

"They *buy* us?"

Saje shrugged. "It is a matter of negotiation. I wished to come to Haka, Haka wished to have me. So. A trade was arranged." He shifted the pillow under his legs. "The desert climate eases my joints. I doubt I would leave Haka even if I were offered a Fourth Level."

"I had the impression Fourth Levels were nonexistent."

"Almost. Only one has existed in the last century." Saje leaned forward. "Mentar. He is at Karn. Akasi to the Minister. Mentar doesn't make ripples with his Quis. He makes tidal waves."

Kelric's mind created a Quis pattern of waves. "Has there ever been a Fifth Level?"

Saje thought for a moment. "In this millennium I believe records exist of two. Legends from the Old Age claim another.

But the cost of a Fifth Level settlement is prohibitive to the point of impossibility."

"What about a Sixth?"

Saje laughed. "A Sixth Level could never exist." His smile faded. "It is fortunate. The power of his dice would be beyond comprehension."

18

Toppled Chute

"Ixpar." Jahlt Karn, the Minister of Coba, looked up as the young woman strode into her office. "I didn't expect you back from Bahvla Estate until tonight."

"We left early. The pilot was worried about the weather." Ixpar dropped into an armchair and stretched her legs out to their full length, seeming to cover half the room. Strands of hair had escaped her braid and were curling in fiery tendrils around her face. "Manager Bahvla sends her greetings."

"And how is Henta?"

With a grimace, Ixpar said, "Nosier than ever."

Jahlt smiled. Henta Bahvla's penchant for gossip was well-known. "Did your visit go well?"

Ixpar leaned forward. "Henta supports a Ministry Wardship of the Miesa mines. I didn't even need to ask. She told me herself she thinks Varz holds too much control over the Plateau."

"Good. I'm also fairly certain of Shazorla Estate."

Her successor got up and paced to the bookshelf. "Henta has heard rumors that Ahkah will side with Varz."

"That would be unfortunate."

Ixpar paced to the window. "There's still Viasa."

"I wouldn't roll dice on it." The feud between Bahvla and Viasa was so old, Jahlt doubted anyone even knew its cause anymore. "Viasa almost always votes against Bahvla. So if Bahvla goes with us, Viasa will go with Varz."

"There's the new Manager at Viasa, though." Ixpar sat on the windowsill. "Even Henta doesn't know much about her." She got up and started pacing again.

Jahlt watched her successor, hiding her smile. Ixpar was as restless as a caged clawcat. "Perhaps it's time I sent an ambassador to Viasa, to give my regards to its new Manager."

Ixpar stopped pacing and squinted at her. "This ambassador wouldn't happen to have red hair, would she?"

"Manager Viasa is only a few years older than you. The two of you should have a lot in common."

"What about my visit to Dahl?"

"Dahl." Jahlt exhaled. "A difficult situation. It is best we postpone your trip there."

"I thought Chankah's support was solid."

"It is. This is another matter." Jahlt disliked bringing up the subject. It remained Ixpar's one weakness. "An offworld matter."

"Kelric."

"Chankah wants me to pardon him. It was Deha's dying request. I must tell her no."

"Why?"

Jahlt injected a coldness into her voice she rarely used with her successor. "I am surprised you need ask."

"You know," Ixpar said. "When one spends time with Henta one hears many rumors."

"Such as?"

"Such as, Dahl and Haka made an arrangement years ago."

Jahlt frowned. "I was not aware of any agreements between Dahl and Haka."

Ixpar walked over to her desk. "It was about Kelric. He's a Haka Calani now."

"Deha would never have consented to such an arrangement."

"Henta seemed sure of her sources."

Jahlt didn't like the sound of it. Not at all.

After the formalities were done, the Estate dinner eaten and the speeches given, Jahlt and Chankah withdrew to Chankah's private study. The new Dahl Manager poured out two glasses of jai rum and gave one to the Minister. "Deha would appreciate your visit."

"She was a fine friend and ally." Jahlt lifted her rum. "To Deha."

Chankah raised her glass. "To Deha."

"Well. Now we must decide what to do with this problem she left us." Jahlt settled back in her armchair. "What exactly is this contract she and Rashiva thought up?"

"Basically this." Chankah swirled her rum. "If a time ever came when Rashiva deemed it safe, she could take Sevtar into her Calanya. If he's ever pardoned, his Oath to Haka becomes void and he returns to Dahl."

Jahlt scowled. "Deha actually signed that?"

"I have an original of the document."

It made no sense to Jahlt. Deha knew the Ministry would deny such a pardon. Yet even so she gave her own Akasi to Haka. Why?

Since Kelric's entry into the Calanya, Haka's power in the Quis had surged more than could be accounted for by the usual fluctuations among Estates. Even more serious, an unpredictable factor had entered the Haka Quis, an influence like none Jahlt had seen before, as if it evolved independent of known constraints—which made it all the more dangerous. Kelric? He had been in the Haka Calanya only a short time. If he had already made such a marked difference, who knew what heights his dice might reach?

It was unacceptable, totally unacceptable that Haka should gain such an advantage.

Jahlt silently swore. Oh yes, Deha had known exactly what she was doing. The late Dahl Manager had outplayed them all.

"So." The Minister set down her rum. "It is time, Chankah, that we consider how to solve this problem Deha left us."

Columns pressed in on him. Gray columns. He would never escape, never find his way out, never be free, never touch another human being . . .

Kelric opened his eyes to see the exotic furnishings of an unfamiliar room. As his nightmare-driven surge of adrenaline calmed, he realized he was on a sofa with a plush blanket laid over his body. Across the room, Rashiva stood looking out a window, her body silhouetted against the dawn. She was wearing day clothes, trousers and a jacket, both made with soft brocade in amber hues.

Confused, Kelric rubbed his eyes. The last he remembered, his escort had brought him to Rashiva's personal suite the previous night. They hadn't told him why. He must have fallen asleep while waiting for her. As he sat up, rustling the blanket, Rashiva turned.

"Sevtar." She spoke awkwardly. "My greetings."

Kelric pushed his hand through his tousled curls. "My greetings." After an uncomfortable silence, he said, "Did I sleep here all night?"

"Yes. You seemed so tired last night. I didn't want to disturb you."

"Why did you want to see me?"

"I had thought we might dine together." She came over and sat stiffly on the other end of the sofa. "So that we might start over. A Manager and a Calani should not—have antagonism. It doesn't do well for the Estate."

This didn't fit his negative picture of her. He wasn't sure about any of his impressions anymore, though. Since he had come to the Calanya, living a normal life, interacting with others, eating well and getting fresh air, he had begun to feel as if he were recovering from a long illness. And she was right; their stilted relationship was affecting their Quis.

He spoke carefully. "Perhaps we could start over."

A shy smile dawned on her face. "Well. Good." She stood up. "When I get back, shall we try with dinner again?"

"All right." He paused. "Where are you going?"

She fastened her jacket, winding the silk ties around hooks. "To see Zecha Haka. Then to Viasa for a few days."

Zecha. The name hit like ice water. Kelric stood up, rolling his stiff shoulders. "Would you call my escort?"

She stopped tying her jacket. "Is something wrong?"

"No." He went to the door. "I would like to return to the Calanya."

"Is it the prison? Zecha told me it would bother you to be reminded of it."

Kelric wondered how he could have conceived, even for a moment, that he might want to become closer to this woman. "How can you live with yourself?"

"Live with myself? I don't understand."

He just looked at her. If she felt what they had done with him was justified, he had nothing to say.

But something was wrong. He had an odd sense about Rashiva, like the shifting of an optical illusion. Suddenly she wasn't the hardened seductress playing with him after subjecting him to a year of painful solitude. Instead, she just seemed young and puzzled, a good Manager but inexperienced compared to someone like Deha Dahl.

"Sevtar?" She was still watching him. "Your face changes so fast sometimes, it's hard to follow."

He spoke quietly. "You don't have any idea what Zecha does down there, do you?"

"It is natural you resent her. Hate her even. She was your jailor, after all."

"You see only what she wants you to see."

Rashiva stiffened. "Do you suggest that you, my Akasi, know more about what goes on in Haka than I?"

Kelric wanted to block out his memories of the prison. Nor did he think it likely Rashiva would listen to a convicted killer with a supposed history of mental instability over a high-ranking figure like Zecha, particularly if believing him meant Rashiva had to admit she had been duped.

But he had opened a dam and it refused to close. Although he spoke calmly, the words flooded out. "We worked double, even triple shifts in the quarry. No breaks, no helmets, no goggles, no scarves, no nothing. We weren't even allowed a drink of water. Guards had free rein to beat prisoners. Big convicts abused smaller ones, physically and sexually. Anyone who complained was punished."

"I've been to the compounds. I know what you describe doesn't happen."

He wondered if he would ever be able to speak of his time in solitary. "You live in a world where Quis dice are made from diamonds. It blinds you to Zecha's world."

She just looked at him. As the moment stretched out, he began to regret even mentioning the prison.

When she finally spoke, all she said was, "I'll use the smelter's door."

Kelric walked alone through the Calanya parks. The late-afternoon sky made a wash of blue and shadows dappled under the trees, but the day's tranquility was lost on him. In the three days since his talk with Rashiva, memories of the prison had plagued his thoughts and dreams.

Sand rustled behind him and he turned to see Captain Khaaj. Her presence jarred. Technically he was still an inmate, which meant he had guards assigned to him at all times. But usually they were so discreet he barely noticed them.

"I'm sorry to disturb you," Khaaj said. "But it's important."

Kelric waited. His year in solitary had reinforced his tendency toward reticence, and his Calanya Oath made his silences acceptable and expected.

"Have you seen Manager Haka since you dined at her suite?" Khaaj asked.

He shook his head no.

"I brought the Speaker with me," Khaaj said. "Will you talk to her?"

He considered, then nodded yes.

Ekoe Haka, Speaker for the Haka Calanya, was waiting in the main common room. Khaaj escorted Ekoe and Kelric to the Alcove of Words, a small room set apart from the common rooms. She stopped outside, leaving them in privacy as they sat opposite each other at the alcove's Quis table.

Ekoe spoke the formal words. "Manager Haka permits me to be your voice in times of crisis, when it is vital your words be known to Outsiders. Will you Speak to me?"

"Yes," Kelric said.

"You were the last person to see Manager Haka," Ekoe said. "Do you know where she is?"

Last person? "She said she was going to Viasa."

Ekoe shook her head. "A windrider came in from Viasa today. They wanted to know what happened. She never showed up. She also had a meeting with Warden Haka and she never showed up for that. No one has seen her for three days."

Kelric thought back to his conversation with Rashiva. "Just before she left for her meeting, she said something about a smelter's door."

"Smelter? What do you mean?"

"The back door," Khaaj blurted out.

Ekoe turned to the captain, who was supposed to be out of earshot, and raised her eyebrows.

Khaaj reddened. "Forgive my interruption. But Manager Haka says she's going in the smelter's door when she plans to use a back entrance. It's because smelters deliver their ingots to the back of an ore shop."

Suddenly it became clear for Kelric. He didn't want to believe it, but the pattern refused denial.

"The back entrance of what?" Ekoe asked.

"Compound Four," Kelric said.

Ekoe stared at him. "The *prison*?"

"Yes." He swallowed. "She's sent herself to prison."

The only sound in the common room came from the click of dice. Kelric paced past the table where Saje and the others sat playing Quis. He wished someone would laugh. Or yell. Anything to break the evening's tension.

The fourth time he crossed the room, Saje came over to him. "Why don't you sit with us for a while?"

"No."

"Rashiva will be fine."

Kelric scowled. "I'm not worried about Rashiva."

"Of course not." Saje drew him over to the table. "Play Quis. It will calm you."

"I am calm."

"Of course." Saje nudged him down into the cushions.

Kelric tried to concentrate on the session. Somber dice predominated: ebony octagons, purple balls, cobalt blocks. It looked like a study of relations between Varz and Karn. When his turn came, he pushed his Ixpar die against a dome Raaj used to denote the Varz Successor.

Raaj glanced at him with an expression close to hatred.

Then he played a black onyx die on top of Kelric's piece. As the game progressed the patterns became more and more muddled, disintegrating into a morass of hostility. Had it been an actual battle, deaths would have littered the field.

Finally Saje rose stiffly to his feet. "I'm afraid I tire more easily than you young people." He turned to Kelric. "Will you assist me?"

Kelric stood up, relieved to escape the session, and put out his arm. Saje leaned on him, limping as they crossed the common room. The moment they were within Saje's suite, he herded Kelric to an alcove. "Please be seated," he said, easing himself down among several cushions.

Kelric dropped down to sit against the wall, with his legs stretched in front of him. "I thought you were tired."

Saje scowled at him. "You must learn better control over your dice. Jumbled schemes, conflict between you and Raaj, patterns of Rashiva everywhere—it was a mess."

"My mind wasn't in it."

"You should never have Spoken to Ekoe this afternoon. It disrupted the Quis."

"I had to talk to her. As for Raaj—" Kelric shrugged. "The conflict is always there. He just plain doesn't like me."

Sage sighed. "I must admit, it is hard to believe you and he are so close in age. You seem much more mature."

At thirty-six, Kelric knew he had sixteen years on Raaj. But rather than trying to explain molecular cell repair, all he said was, "I am older. My people age more slowly than yours."

"You are fortunate." Saje rubbed his legs. "I age more every day. I should take myself to bed."

After helping Saje to his room, Kelric returned to his own suite. But he couldn't sleep. At Night's Midhour, he went back into the common room and sat at a table playing solitaire. When he heard footsteps, he turned, looking for Khaaj—but it was only Raaj, coming through an archway across the room. The youth saw him and stopped, standing like the statue of an ancient prince, tall and unsmiling. Then he left.

The doors of the common room suddenly swung open and Khaaj strode into the room. "She's here," the captain said.

Kelric jumped to his feet. As soon as he stepped outside, his guards closed around him and they headed for Rashiva's suite. He found her seated on a sofa in her living room, wincing while a doctor treated a bruise on her face. She wore a ripped gray uniform with the Compound Four label stitched into the arm.

Kelric crossed to her, started to speak, then remembered the others in the room and scowled.

"Doctor," Rashiva said.

The doctor straightened up. "I'll check on you later, ma'am." Then she and the others left.

When she and Kelric were alone, Rashiva drew him down on the sofa. "Don't frown so."

He wanted to shake her. "Are you insane? What were you doing down there?"

"You sound like my CityGuard chief." Rashiva rubbed her temple. "She almost had heart failure when I told her to give me a fake name and send me to prison."

"She should have told someone where you were."

"I ordered her not to. I didn't want to risk warning the prison authorities."

He looked at the bruise on her face. "Who hit you?"

Rashiva winced. "That one is from the Compound Four women's warden."

"Didn't she recognize you?"

"Only a few of the prison staff know me in person." Dryly she added, "One guard did tell me I looked like Rashiva Haka." She pushed back her disarrayed hair, which was unbraided and tangled. "Torv Haka knows me by sight. I had intended to find him when I left the quarry in the evening, so I could get out."

"Why didn't you?"

"He was gone. A prisoner knifed him and he's in the Med House."

So someone had finally gotten Torv. Kelric felt little sympathy for the brutal warden. "Couldn't you tell anyone else?"

"I did." She spread her hands. "Apparently I'm not the first prisoner to claim she's me. So after my two shifts in the quarry I got to see Compound Four firsthand."

He remembered the women's crew, could imagine all too

well how they responded to Rashiva. Beautiful and vulnerable, with no street knowledge at all, she would have been in an even worse position than Ched in the men's compound. He discovered that the thought dismayed him.

Kelric lifted a tangle of her hair, wondering who had undone her braid. He saw more bruises on her neck and the part of her shoulder visible through the tear in her uniform.

"Are you all right?" he asked.

She stared down at her hands. "I am—fine."

He felt her emotions roiling: anger, shame, pain. He also felt the lock she put on them and knew she would never speak of the experience.

Rashiva looked up at him. "It didn't take me long to find out no one had seen you for a long time. After my people got me out of the compound, I demanded to see where you had been. Khaaj finally found a guard who knew." Her voice caught. "Sevtar—so long—in that *tomb*—"

Don't ask me to remember, he thought. *Don't ask.*

She reached forward and switched on a com in the table. A sleepy voice floated into the air. "Nida here."

"Nida, this is Manager Haka. I want you to begin preparations for an Estate Tribunal."

The voice snapped into alertness. "A Tribunal, ma'am?"

"Yes. Notify Warden Haka." In a quiet voice, Rashiva said, "She stands accused."

Although it was almost dawn when Kelric returned to the Calanya, he found Raaj waiting. The First Level looked as if he hadn't slept the entire night. He strode over to Kelric. "Captain Khaaj said Rashiva is back."

As Kelric nodded, a few pieces of a puzzle fell into place. No wonder Raaj resented him. The Hakaborn prince loved Rashiva.

"Is she hurt?" Raaj asked.

"Some bruises." As fast as it had coalesced, the puzzle fragmented. Hadn't Saje told him Raaj was someone's kasi? That wouldn't necessarily stop him from loving the Manager, particularly considering how much attention she paid to him, but it was odd he would be this blatant about it.

His *sister.* Of course. Rashiva was his sister. He should have seen it before. They looked so natural together.

But then, why did Raaj's wife never visit him?

The puzzle suddenly snapped together. Kelric looked at Raaj's armbands and saw the symbols which, had he ever let himself notice before, he would have recognized as identical to his own. Not a kasi. Akasi.

"Sevtar," Raaj said. "Why do you stare at me this way?"

Kelric just kept looking at him. Then he walked past the Haka born prince and kept going, out into the parks and the predawn darkness. When a gazebo appeared in front of him, he went in and sat on a bench.

Sometime later Saje came to sit with him. "Raaj is in my suite. He thinks you only realized this morning that he is also Rashiva's husband."

"He's right." Kelric stared out at the darkness. So much made sense now. "This shouldn't have happened."

Saje sighed. "So goes the problem of all ages."

Kelric glanced at him. "What problem?"

"Man has always yielded to woman's nature." Saje nodded. "Woman is strength and man is passion. He sees with his heart and she with her mind. Woman leads, protects, innovates, builds, creates life. Man fathers children. So a powerful woman will gather her mates around her. And so the men she chooses must learn to deal with it."

Kelric snorted. "You actually believe all that?"

"Yes."

"Why?"

"It is what I have seen all my life." Saje paused. "The young now, they talk of a new way for woman and man. Perhaps they will find it. But I think they try to change a fundamental nature of that which cannot be altered." He watched Kelric's face. "In time you will come to terms with your life here."

"That isn't the problem, Saje. I can accept the Calanya. Hell, I like it, living like a king and playing Quis all day."

But sharing Rashiva was a different story. Each time he began to think he might want to know her better, something happened that made it impossible.

All he said was, "Raaj loves her. Having me here is killing him."

Saje exhaled. "Yes. It is."

Kelric looked out at the line of dawn on the horizon. The barriers between him and Rashiva were wider than he knew how to cross.

In the Haka Tribunal Hall, the Elder Judge stood behind the high bench. "The accused shall rise."

Zecha stood up within the Square of Decision. Tall and unflinching, she faced her accusers. She would show no weakness, never, no matter how many betrayals they committed against her. And the betrayals had been many. Witnesses from her staff had come forward, their words halting at first, full of fear, then condemning with more force. But more damning than a thousand traitors had been the Calanya Speaker as she gave Sevtar's statement, first of the compound, then of his time in solitude. Zecha could still see the horror on the judges' faces, still see Rashiva sitting with her head in her hands.

Her rage flared. *Did they expect a prison to be pretty?* For years she had faced what the rest of Coba wanted to forget. For years she had dealt with the ugliness the world dredged up from its sewers. The constant influx of thoughts from the basest element of the Twelve Estates had forced her to barrier her mind, condemning her to loneliness. Why? So the rest of them could live in blissful ignorance. This was her reward.

The Elder spoke. "The Haka Bench finds the accused guilty."

Betrayal, Zecha thought.

"From this day forward," the Elder said, "the convicted no longer bears the Haka name. All will forbid her work. All Houses will turn her from their door. All citizens will refuse her haven. She is Shunned."

Shunned. It was even worse than Zecha had expected. She had no home. No place. No kin. She was no one.

This was Sevtar's doing. She would remember this evil he had caused her.

She would remember.

19

Ruby Fire

Summer blossoms scented the Calanya parks, clusters of red-gold flowers blooming on the jahalla trees. Iridescent insects hummed through their branches, giving the desert a trilling voice. Kelric walked with Rashiva along a gravel path, past tiled pools filled with water that, in the desert, was worth as much as the gold around his wrists.

"We changed almost a third of the prison administration," Rashiva said. "It's one reason the Tribunal lasted two full seasons." She shook her head. "Zecha baffles me. She truly believes she did what was right."

She's gone, Kelric thought. That was all that mattered. Giving the Calanya Speaker his testimony had torn apart the equanimity he managed to regain after coming to Rashiva's Calanya. But it had been worth it to see justice done.

He knew Rashiva better now after two seasons, had come to see her as a dedicated and soft-spoken Manager. Although they remained formal with each other, their marriage unconsummated, the tension in their conversations had eased. Hate no longer drove the desire she provoked in him.

When she took his hand with unexpected shyness, Kelric smiled down at her. She squeezed his hand. "You've a beautiful smile, my husband. I've wondered how it looked."

That caught him by surprise. Had he never smiled at her before? It wasn't the Propriety Laws; unlike most Haka men, they weren't habit for him. Within the Calanya he had no reason to think about them, except around his guards, whom he never felt much inclined to smile at anyway.

Holding his hand, Rashiva led him through the trees along a hidden path that took them far from the Calanya buildings. Irrigation kept the parks blooming all year, including these forests of gnarled jahallas with leaves and limbs plumped full of water. In a private clearing deep within a jahalla grove, they sat together on the soft decade-grass, which took its name from its ability to lie dormant for decades in the desert and come back to life when given water. Golden flies with gauzy black wings flitted around them.

With a touch of blush reddening her cheeks, Rashiva cupped his face with her hands and drew him into a kiss. Her mouth was full. Soft. The fragrance of spice-soap scented her hair. He wrapped his arms around her and savored the sense of discovery he always felt the first time he kissed a woman.

When they paused, she brushed her hand across his trousers. "You will get grass stains on these handsome clothes."

He slid his hand up her leg. "You also."

"Perhaps we should find a way to avoid this problem."

Kelric smiled, this time using it with full knowledge of the effect it would produce. "Perhaps we should."

So they undressed each other, each exploring the other's body as they shed their layers of clothes. His mind responded to their intimacy like a jahalla to water, swelling to fullness. He felt swirls and eddies of her emotions, more than he had picked up in a long time.

Lying next to him, bare skin against bare skin, she touched the hair at his pelvis, rubbing a curl between her fingers. "It looks even more like metal than the hair on your head. It even feels like soft metal."

Kelric tightened his embrace around her. "All my hair is an organometallic alloy."

"Hmmm." She moved her hand, distracting their thoughts from metallurgy to biology.

At first Kelric kept his caresses reserved, assuming that in love she would be even more traditional than Deha. But eventually he rolled on top of her. She felt fine, her body firm beneath him, breasts plump and hips curved out from a small waist.

Instead of cooling off when he became more aggressive, she pulled him into another kiss, hungry for his mouth. Her thoughts brushed his mind; she *expected* him to be passionate, out of control. She took it as a sign of virility. It was one reason Haka women had created the Propriety Laws; Haka culture claimed men were impassioned vessels of love with no restraint over their desires. Without restrictions, they would drive women to distraction with their unbridled sexuality.

Kelric lifted his head and laughed softly. "Rashiva, you are such a sexist."

She blinked at him, her face flushed with arousal. "What?" Without waiting for an answer, she pulled him back down and sought out his mouth, kissing him deeply.

Secluded among the jahallas, they came to their lovemaking with an intensity made all the more urgent by the long wait, both choosing to forget, for one afternoon, the reasons for their prolonged restraint. Kelric stroked her hips and breasts, tasted the honey between her thighs. For all her arousal, her caresses were shy. He suspected she had never lain with any other man but Raaj, though he doubted she would admit to such inexperience. The longer they played with each other, the more her guileless curiosity aroused him.

Finally, as they lay side by side on the soft grass, he entered her. They rolled over, Rashiva on top, then he, then Rashiva, then he. He thrust deeply and she held on to him as they moved together. So they went, until she cried out and stiffened in his arms. He relaxed his control then, losing himself in the consuming release of an intense climax.

Afterward Kelric floated in a pleasant daze. It wasn't until Rashiva pushed his shoulder that he realized he had let his weight sink onto her. He rolled onto his back and she rolled with him, coming to rest against his side, her leg thrown over his, her head on his shoulder. As the sun descended below the trees, veiling the clearing in shadow, they lay in each other's arms, sated and content.

After a while Rashiva said, "Perhaps we will make a child."

He opened his eyes. *Child?*

"I know I can," she added sleepily. "My daughter is almost six."

Unwelcome thoughts of Raaj invaded Kelric's good mood. The Haka prince was twenty years old, ten years Rashiva's junior. If he and Rashiva had a six-year-old daughter, Raaj must have been a child groom, probably not even a Calani yet. Given the seclusion boys training for the Calanya lived in, Rashiva was probably one of the only women he had ever seen, let alone spoken to. Kelric needed no telepathy to realize what it would do to Raaj if she bore another man's child.

"You and I come from different worlds," he said. "We can't have children."

"Your parents did."

"How did you know that?"

"You are a Ruby Dynasty prince, yes? Isn't it true your mother comes from one world, your father from another? I have heard this."

Although he knew the ISC Public Affairs people might have included information about his family in their discussions with Minister Karn, it surprised him that Rashiva knew. Then again, Quis was the ultimate gossip mill.

"My parents have the same ancestry," he said. "My mother's lineage goes back to Raylicon, the home world of the people who colonized my father's planet."

"Ralkon is no world," Rashiva murmured. "She is a spirit of wisdom."

Kelric knew the similarity was more than coincidence. Six thousand years ago, an unknown race had moved a population of humans from Earth to the planet Raylicon and then vanished with no explanation. All they left behind were their spacecraft. As time passed, the stranded humans reproduced the technology and went searching for their lost home. They never found Earth, but they established a number of colonies, what historians now called the Ruby Empire. It collapsed after a few centuries, isolating the Raylicans on their world and cutting the colonies off from their mother planet.

So the Raylicans began a long slide into extinction. After four millennia, desperate for an influx of fresh genes to replenish their shrinking pool, they redeveloped space travel and went out to reclaim the lost colonies. Two factions formed: the Traders, who took the slave trade that had always tainted Raylican culture and turned it into an economy of mind-numbing brutality; and the Imperialate, an attempt by the free worlds to stay that way, or as free as possible in a civilization founded on the need for an indefatigable military machine that grew ever more powerful.

Less than two hundred years ago, in Earth's twenty-first century, her people had finally made their way to the stars—and found their siblings already there. Research soon showed that the Raylicans' ancestors came from Earth circa 4000 B.C. Yet no civilization from that period matched any remnant of ancient Raylican culture.

Some anthropologists postulated Egypt as their birthplace. But though ancient Raylicans built pyramids, they didn't look Egyptian. A few scholars believed they came from Meso-america, or perhaps both Mesoamerica and the Middle East or North Africa. Rare hints of Christianity and Greek myth-ology seemed to show up, yet all evidence indicated humans had been stranded on Raylicon four thousand years *before* the birth of Christ. One school of thought held that the abducted humans had been moved in time as well as space. Genetic drift, both natural and self-induced, added the final complication. It all added up to make the Raylicans' ancestry a mystery.

Kelric was certain the Twelve Estates descended from a lost Ruby colony. He saw many similarities between the Twelve Estates and the primary culture of ancient Raylicon, especially the hieroglyphic language and the Cobans' love of ball courts. But the lesser known side of Raylican culture also showed up, most notably in the architecture and names of Haka. He sus-pected scholars would find Haka a gold mine, a living remnant of a subculture that had vanished on Raylicon after the fall of the Ruby Empire.

He rubbed a strand of Rashiva's hair between his fingers. "My ancestors had black hair and eyes, and dark skin."

She opened her eyes. "Hakaborn."

"Like Hakaborn."

"But you need only find a mirror to see that you are no Haka-born man."

"I look like my grandfather." He paused, at a loss to explain the genetic engineering that altered his grandfather's people. Then he thought of Shaliece, his childhood love. "Even if you did conceive, the baby might not survive. The mother of the only child I've ever fathered had so much difficulty with her pregnancy that she miscarried."

Rashiva curled her fingers around his. "I'm sorry. I never knew you shared bands with another woman besides Deha Dahl."

"Once. But not with the girl who miscarried." He still remembered Shaliece's stunned look when he had offered to marry her. They were only fifteen. He pressed too hard and she fled, frightened by his Ruby Dynasty titles. Perhaps eventually he would have won her over, had she not miscarried. After a suitable amount of time, to let he and Shaliece mourn, Kelric's parents sent him offworld to the Deishan Military Academy. A few years later Shaliece wed another youth.

Rashiva was watching him with an inscrutable expression. "This woman named you as the father of her child but offered you no kasi bands?"

He brought his thoughts back to the present. "That wasn't our custom. I offered to her."

"*You* offered?"

"Yes."

She looked as if he had hit her in the stomach. "Was this the only time you offered to—to be free with—"

He stiffened. "With what?"

"Yourself."

How could she, who had two husbands, condemn him for past lovers? "No."

Rashiva drew away from him. "We should get back. I have matters to attend to on the Estate."

They dressed in silence. Although they headed into the forest together, Kelric soon stopped. He didn't want a day of such contentment to end in this stiff and silent walk. Better to let Rashiva go on alone.

She stopped and glanced back. For a moment he thought she would finally speak. Then she turned and went on, disappearing into the trees.

The screen in the archway of Kelric's suite rustled. "Sevtar?"

Kelric put down his dice. "Come."

Saje came in and eased himself down on the other side of

the Quis table where Kelric had been playing solitaire. "When you didn't show for dinner I worried you weren't feeling well."

"I'm fine," Kelric said.

Saje glanced at the structures on the table. "Red blocks. Red balls. Red bars."

"I wasn't paying attention to the colors."

"Red is often used in patterns of anger."

Kelric collected the dice and put them in his pouch.

"You came back from the parks alone," Saje said.

"Rashiva had business on the Estate." Kelric considered the Third Level. "Saje, do you have children?"

He smiled. "Two, born at Varz. They're adults now. They visit me whenever they come to Haka." Softly he added, "Their mother passed away a few years before I came here."

"I'm sorry."

"We had many good years."

"What would she have done if you had fathered a child who wasn't hers?"

Saje's gentle expression vanished. "I forgive such a question, Sevtar, because I know you have no idea of the insult you give."

Kelric winced. "I meant no offense. I just—" Just what? Need Rashiva? No. "I guess I'm tired. I should go to bed."

With a nod, Saje tried to rise, giving Kelric an apologetic look. "Could you assist me back to my suite? My bones grow less cooperative each day."

"Of course." Kelric stood and offered his arm. He walked slowly with Saje out into the common room. He suspected the Third Level suffered from advanced arthritis with spinal complications.

"Can your doctors help your joint stiffness at all?" he asked.

"Nothing much seems to work," Saje said. "But I don't tell them that. One doctor massages my spine and I don't want her to stop." He gave Kelric a conspiratorial grin. "She is very beautiful."

Kelric laughed, his tension easing. "Ah. I see."

They had just reached the screened archway of Saje's suite when the Outside doors across the room swung open and Captain Khaaj strode Inside.

Saje chuckled. "My thanks for your aid, Sevtar. I can make it from here."

Kelric nodded, his attention on the captain. Instead of going to his suite, she went to another and tapped on the screen. After a moment Raaj appeared, rubbing sleep out of his eyes.

Khaaj spoke—and Raaj smiled, his perfect teeth flashing white. Then the smile vanished, doused as the Propriety Laws reasserted their hold. He nodded to the captain and withdrew into his suite.

"Sevtar, you're breaking my door," Saje said.

"What—?" Kelric turned. Saje was trying to pry his fingers off the screen of his suite.

"You should come in." Saje lowered his voice. "I have some contraband. You can help me dispose of it."

"Contraband?" Kelric turned back in time to see Raaj reappear. The youth had changed into a black velvet shirt with its laces left loose enough to reveal his muscular chest. His Calanya guards gleamed under his cuffs and his hair glistened the way Rashiva's did after she brushed it. A Talha scarf hung around his neck. As Khaaj escorted him to the Outside doors, he put on the robe he was carrying and hid his face with the Talha.

"Contraband," Saje repeated. He pulled Kelric into his suite. "Come. I will show you."

Kelric forced his attention back to him. "What?"

Saje pushed him into the usual alcove. "Be comfortable." Before Kelric could object, the Third Level disappeared into an inner room.

Kelric scowled, but he did sit down. Saje reappeared with a decanter of gold liquid and two crystal goblets. He settled onto his customary cushion, then poured two drinks and gave one to Kelric.

"What is it?" Kelric tilted the glass, watching the glimmering liquid slosh around.

"We call it baiz."

He took a swallow. The baiz glided past his lips, eased down his throat, and detonated when it hit bottom.

"Gods," he muttered. He finished the rest in one swallow.

"You mustn't tell anyone I have it," Saje said. "If my

doctors knew they would take it away." He refilled Kelric's glass. "It settles well, yes?"

"That it does."

After his second drink Kelric lost track of how many times Saje refilled his glass. He leaned back in a pile of cushions and watched patterns swirl in his baiz. "Too bad you can't import this stuff. You'd make a fortune."

"It does have a calming effect," Saje said.

"I don't need calming."

"Whatever happened between you and Rashiva will mend."

"Beautiful Rashiva." Kelric shook the baiz patterns, destroying them. "Beautiful intolerant Rashiva."

"Sevtar—"

"My name is Kelric."

"Kelric?"

He looked up at Saje. "Jagernaut Tertiary Kelricson Garlin Valdoria kya Skolia."

"An unusual name."

"Maybe. But it's mine."

"You are the son of someone named Kelric?"

"No. Someone named Eldrinson." He took a swallow of baiz. "My parents named my oldest brother Eldrin. Guess they figured Eldrinsonson was overdoing it."

Saje smiled. "Who is Kelric?"

"Lyshriol spirit of youth." The room seemed to be tilting around him. "They named me that because I was their last child. Littlest Rhon child."

"Little," Saje said, "is hardly how I would describe you."

Kelric stretched out on his back, sprawled on the silk cushions. He tried to drink more baiz and discovered his goblet was empty. "I'll tell you something, Saje." He pushed up on his elbow and poured another drink. "My mother had a son long before she met my father."

"You have a half brother?"

"That's right. The Imperator. Military dictator of the universe. I'm his heir."

"This is a joke, yes?"

"No."

Saje took a swallow of the drink he had hardly touched.

"My infamous brother." Kelric finished his baiz. "But I'm not his heir anymore, am I? Now I'm a Calani in a cage."

"Sevtar—"

"I told you not to call me that."

"Perhaps you should have another drink."

"I don't like being in a cage."

Saje poured him a drink.

"You ever seen a Eubian, Saje?"

"Is that an animal?"

"That's right." Kelric downed his drink. "We call them Traders. Once one of their cruisers ambushed our squad and we crashed near their base." He tried to pour more baiz, but the decanter was empty. "My commander died." He stared into his glass. "In my arms."

"I'm sorry."

"Two of us made it out alive. Two. Out of fourteen. Afterward, I got drunk."

"Their deaths weren't your fault."

"I got drunk and went to where the tuners sing."

"Tuners?"

"Whores," Kelric said. "What our oh-so-charming Manager practically called me today. I sang all night with a tuner and she helped me forget." His voice cracked. "My brother told me I was too stupid to think. But I'm not too stupid to kill, am I?"

"People die in wars."

"Is that supposed to make it all right?" The decanter slid out of his hand and thudded onto the floor. "Maybe I should just shut up."

"Talk if it helps."

"Nothing helps." Closing his eyes, Kelric lay back and gave in to his exhaustion.

Several moments later he felt Saje laying a quilt over him. "Try to sleep," the Third Level said softly. "Try to forget. It is all you can do now."

20

Queen's Coup

Autumn winds keened around Haka, audible even deep within the Estate. As Rashiva entered her office, her aide Nida followed, reading from a scroll. "After you see the Modernists' delegation this morning, you have a Quis session with Adaar. Then Midday meal, then your meeting at the Children's Cooperative."

"Have the Cooperative files ready for me to read over lunch." Rashiva lifted her jacket off a rack made from hyella reeds. "And add my dinner with the delegation from Shazorla to the schedule."

A boy entered the office. "Mail, Manager Haka." He dropped a bundle on her desk, parchment scrolls wrapped in protective cloth. "There's a letter from the Ministry."

Just what I need, Rashiva thought. More veiled threats from Jahlt Karn about the Miesa Plateau.

Ekoe Haka, the Calanya Speaker, appeared behind the boy. "Manager Haka, do you have a moment?"

Rashiva pulled on her brocaded jacket. "Not now."

"It's the Calani Saje," Ekoe said. "He wishes to see you."

Ai. She could hardly refuse the Third Level. She pushed her hand through her hair. "I'll meet with him in the Hyella Chamber." That meant she would miss her meeting with the Modernists. Lunch was her only other free time and she could think of no better way to lose her appetite than by listening to Modernist tirades about sexual oppression. But if she put them off they might make trouble again, sending unescorted groups of men out in public without Talha scarves and robes. They had done it once before and nearly caused a riot.

"Tell the Modernists I'll see them during lunch," she told

Nida. She stuffed the letter from Karn into her jacket and sped out of her office.

"I realize it is personal," Saje said. "But it affects the Quis. His anger is in every pattern he builds."

Rashiva stood by the wall of the Hyella Chamber, watching the desert. "I regret what happened. But that changes nothing. I made a mistake when I gave Sevtar Akasi bands."

"That he was in prison for murder—this you could accept. Yet now you spurn him as if he committed an unspeakable crime."

She turned to face the Third Level, who stood by the Quis table. "It's personal, Saje."

"He trusted you. After all he has suffered, both on our world and before, he is not one who trusts easily." Saje spread his hands. "I've watched him heal, Rashiva. I've seen a man paralyzed by loneliness come alive again. Don't turn from him now."

"It isn't that easy."

"What has he done that is so terrible?"

"If you were Hakaborn you would understand."

"He cares for you and you for him. What more is there to understand?"

Quietly Rashiva said, "No woman but my mother ever touched my father. No other woman even saw him smile. Now the Modernists want me to abolish the Propriety Laws and I can't help but believe they seek to destroy the foundation of all that is right." She exhaled. "I wish what happened with Sevtar didn't matter. But it does. I can't bend that far, Saje. I just can't do it."

"Then I am sorry," he said. "Both for his sake and for yours."

When the day finally ground to an end, Rashiva escaped to her suite and crawled into bed. Within moments after she called for a doctor, an aide ushered Senior Physician Jy into the room. The longer Jy examined her, the more she frowned.

"You work too hard," Jy said.

Rashiva pulled the blankets up under her chin. "I just need one of your potions to settle my stomach."

"What you need is rest." Jy closed her bag. "When was your last cycle?"

Rashiva sat up. "You think I'm pregnant?"

Jy scowled. "Lie down."

"For wind's sake." Rashiva lay down. "You're as ornery as a desert crab."

"I did a pregnancy test. We will know the results tomorrow. Right now I want you to sleep."

"Pah," Rashiva grumbled. "Just who is Manager here?"

Jy smiled and picked up the jacket Rashiva had thrown across the bed. "Did you know there's a letter in your pocket with the Ministry seal on it?"

"Oh. Yes." Rashiva reached for the scroll Jy held out to her. "What do you think Jahlt is scheming about this time? The Miesa Plateau no doubt." Unrolling the scroll, she peered at its gilded hieroglyphs.

And sat up to read it again.

"What's wrong?" Jy asked.

"No." Rashiva stared at the parchment. "She can't do this. She *can't*."

"Can't what?"

Rashiva dropped onto her back and threw an arm over her eyes, crumpling the letter in her fist. "Jahlt Karn has gone insane."

. . . *boy was dying in his mother's womb. Kelric reached out, to help, to heal* . . .

Kelric turned over in bed. "He's sick. I have to help." He opened his eyes into darkness, his head throbbing. "Rashiva?" Closing his eyes, he slipped back into sleep.

The next morning only a trace of the dream lingered. After breakfast, Kelric's guards took him to a library where tapestries hung on the wall. He sat in an armchair until he grew bored, then got up and wandered around looking at the books. He pulled out one that caught his interest and settled back in his chair.

Although he had never formally learned written Teotecan, he had picked up a little in Dahl. He puzzled out the title's hieroglyphs: *Early Desert Games*. A few minutes of paging through the book revealed it was a text on differential equations. The authors treated the subject like a game, with no indication they realized it had practical applications.

Then it hit him: the book was about *Quis*. It was all there, in the dice: theories of mathematics, physics, even philosophy.

Like many of the stranded colonies, the one on Coba had apparently slid into barbarism after the Ruby Empire collapsed. But unlike the others, which continued to backslide, Coba had rebounded. The same innovative streak that sparked the creation of Quis also led them to recover lost technology. In recent decades they had even regained air travel and electricity, though Kelric suspected they didn't fully understand the science involved in either.

Given the way Quis tapped every facet of their lives, it didn't surprise him to find their lost sciences buried within the dice game, like old files hidden in an ancient computer network, available only to those who knew where to look. Sooner or later someone would find the link. What a day that would be for Coba. Her people could go from windriders to star travel overnight.

"What are you doing?" Rashiva said.

He looked up to see her standing in the door arch, holding a sheaf of papers. "When did you come in?"

"Just now." She closed the door and came over to him. "You are reading?"

He showed her the book. "Pattern games."

"What about your Oath?"

His voice cooled. "I wasn't aware it mattered to you anymore."

Rashiva exhaled. "At the moment I'm inclined to let you contaminate your Quis however you wish." She gave him the papers. "If you want to read, read this."

The glyphs on the document were too complex for him to decipher well. All he could make out was that the papers referred to a property settlement between Dahl and Haka.

Then it hit him; *he* was the property.

Ice came into his voice. "So that's what you consider me." He thrust the document at her. "Negotiable goods."

She took the papers. "It refers to your Calanya contract."

"What's the difference? Why did you tell me this?"

At first it seemed as if she wouldn't—or couldn't—answer. When she finally did respond, she sounded numb. "Minister Karn granted you a pardon."

He stared at her. "She what?"

"Minister Karn pardoned you."

It rolled around his thoughts, looking for a place to stop and unable to find it. "Why?"

Her fist clenched around the papers. "With the pardon, your Calanya contract reverts to Dahl. Deha *knew.* She knew what you could become and she knew the Ministry would never tolerate my Estate winning such advantage."

He had no idea how to respond. He couldn't absorb it. Go to Dahl? With Deha gone, nothing remained for him there but the memory of Llaach's death.

Kelric got up and went to a window. The city stretched out below in a jumble of desert colors, with onion towers gracing its architecture. Did he want to leave? He liked the desert, liked Haka, liked the Calanya, liked the exotic life. The Propriety Laws would have been a nuisance had he lived Outside, but they made little difference Inside the Calanya.

But nothing would ever change the millennia-old Haka customs. Rashiva was compelling, yes. But the longer he knew her, the more insurmountable the barriers between them seemed.

She spoke behind him. "Sevtar?"

Tell me you want me to stay, he thought. We'll find a way to understand each other. But you have to bend, Rashiva. I won't beg for your love.

The silence lengthened. Finally he said, "I take it Raaj is the father of your baby."

"How did you know I'm pregnant?"

Kelric turned around. Until he spoke, he hadn't realized he knew. She showed no outward sign of it. But all he could think to say was, "You've started to show."

Softly she said, "Yes. Raaj is the father."

* * *

On the dawn of an autumn morning, before the reddened disk of the sun raised its rim over the horizon, Kelric left Haka. Surrounded by guards, he walked with Rashiva to the airfield. With their retinue waiting beyond the range of hearing, he and Rashiva stood together, as if isolated in a bubble of desert air that shimmered with heat at its edges.

When she looked up at him, Kelric swallowed. He thought he saw tears in her eyes, but if they were there, the wind whipped them away before they fell.

III

Bahvla

21

Pause

Autumn in Dahl turned the suntrees into a splendor of gilt foliage. Kelric sat in the shade with his back against a tree whose branches bowed under the weight of their gold fruit. He picked up a succulent orb that had fallen and bit into it. Sweet juice ran down his throat.

At the bottom of the lawn that sloped away from his feet, he saw Chankah Dahl climbing toward him. When she reached the top, she flopped down next to him in the shade. "Heh. What a hike."

He swallowed a bite of sunfruit. "It's good for you."

"Probably." Her smile faded. "Kelric—we need to talk. About Jevi."

So. He had known this was coming. He still remembered the petition at his Tribunal from Llaach's widower: *The Calani Jevi asks that Sevtar never be allowed to live in the Dahl Calanya. If this is unacceptable, Jevi requests to leave Dahl* . . . Llaach's widower had eventually remarried, but every time the young man looked at him, Kelric knew he remembered.

"Jevi has his life here," Kelric said. "I should be the one who goes."

"I think it's for the best," Chankah said.

"So what do I do? Apply to another Calanya?"

"You won't need to. Six Estates have made offers for your contract."

"*Six?* What for?"

She smiled. "You really have no idea how well you play Quis. And you've been in two of the most powerful Calanya on Coba."

"Which means I know the Quis on both sides."

"Yes. It is unusual. Valuable."

"What offer will you take?"

"The choice is yours."

Kelric thought of Ixpar. "What about Karn?"

"The Ministry isn't interested," she said. "Neither Miesa nor any Secondary Estates made offers either, probably because they don't have the finances to consider a Third Level."

"I don't know any other Estate. I wouldn't know how to choose."

"Haka made an offer." Chankah paused. "A large one."

As much as he wanted to forget Rashiva, Kelric's pulse quickened. "Why? I'd only be Second Level there."

She pulled up a blade of grass and studied it. "Perhaps her reasons have nothing to do with Level."

Kelric doubted he and Rashiva could ever come to terms with their differences. Even if they did, Raaj would always be there. With difficulty, he said, "I prefer not to go to Haka."

Her tension eased. "All right."

"Do you have any suggestions?"

"I thought Bahvla," Chankah said. "Its Manager usually allies with Karn despite her friendship with the Miesa Manager."

Kelric remembered Miesa and its rich mineral plateau from his dice sessions at Haka, but he didn't recall much about Bahvla. "Does Manager Bahvla want an Akasi?" He had no intention of getting caught in that emotional war zone again.

"No, I don't think so."

"Do her Calani play Quis well?"

"Not as well as you. But few people do." She tilted her head. "In terms of Quis, I would rate Bahvla in the tier just below the four strongest Estates: Karn, Varz, Dahl, and Haka."

"Did Varz make an offer?"

She scowled.

Kelric smiled slightly. "I take it that means yes. And you have no intention of considering it."

"It would utterly defeat the purpose of getting you out of Haka."

He shrugged. "Then Bahvla is fine."

She nodded with satisfaction. "I will contact Manager Bahvla."

22

SunSky Bridge

Bahvla Estate nestled high in the mountains, in a misty valley at a much greater elevation than Dahl. Its Manager was Henta, a plump woman with graying hair whom Kelric liked immediately. She laughed often and loved to talk. Her husband was the Akasi Tevon, a male version of herself. Manager and Akasi often sat together in the common room, clucking over their latest gossip.

The Estate had twelve Calani. Just as Saje had been the only Third Level at Haka, so Kelric found himself the only Third at Bahvla. There were three Second Levels, including Yevris Tehnsa Bahvla. Dark and lean, with brown eyes flecked by green, Yevris reminded Kelric of a gnarled tree limb, one well flexed in exercise. He and Yevris often jogged together across the parks at daybreak or swam in the chill water of the Calanya lakes.

One morning Yevris decided they should climb the sculpted windbreak surrounding the parks.

"Won't my escort stop us?" Kelric asked. His pardon came with a stipulation, that he be guarded at all times. His escort was discreet, blending so well with the background that he often forgot they were there. It reminded him of being with his parents, who were required by the Imperialate Assembly to have bodyguards.

"Why stop us?" Yevris said. "I know. Because we're stupid enough to fall over the top and plummet to untimely deaths."

Kelric smiled. "You plummet. I'll climb."

Yevris grinned and took off. With his lighter build he outran Kelric, who made no attempt to engage his damaged hydraulics, but at the wall Kelric's greater strength got him to the top first. He climbed over the edge, stood up—and froze.

The outer side of the windbreak plunged down in a sheer,

unscalable cliff. Far, far below, forested mountains stretched out in slope after magnificent slope. A white mist hung over the world and for once the wind held still. The panorama swept out as far as he could see, a mystical land that faded into fog.

Yevris's head poked above the wall, followed by the rest of Yevris. He climbed up next to Kelric. "It's powerful, yes?"

"Yes," Kelric said.

"I thought you'd like it. It reminds me of you."

"Me? Why?"

"It's hard to explain. I'll build you a Quis pattern for it sometime." Dryly he added, "Better that than gamble with you."

"Why do you say that?"

"Because you pulverize me every time."

Kelric laughed. "We're Calani. We don't need to gamble. We have better things to do with our dice."

Yevris smiled. "I don't think I've ever met anyone who likes Quis as much as you."

That caught Kelric by surprise. But it was true; Quis fascinated him.

Turning around, he looked out across Bahvla to the mountains that rose up in the north, thrusting into an overcast sky. High in the northeast, a cluster of towers stood wreathed in mist. He indicated the distant hamlet. "What's that?"

Yevris followed his gaze. "Viasa Estate. Tehnsa is up there too."

"You grew up in Tehnsa, didn't you?"

"Yip." Yevris was in motion again, ambling backward along the wall. "It's not really an Estate, though. It's Secondary to Viasa."

Kelric followed him. "How is that different from an Estate?"

"Smaller. A Secondary can't survive independent of its main Estate." Yevris stopped and cocked his head. "The way Miesa is going, it'll be Secondary to Varz soon."

Varz. The infamous Ministry foe. "Can you see Varz or Miesa from here?"

"Too far. But you'll meet Manager Miesa. She and Henta are friends." He grinned. "Savina Miesa."

Kelric laughed. "I detect more than a casual interest here, Yevris."

"Heh. I've no wish to be number ninety-nine. Not that she ever showed any interest in making me ninety-nine."

"Manager Miesa has ninety-eight Akasi?"

"Well," Yevris amended. "Maybe I exaggerate. The last I heard she had four. But you see my point."

"That I do."

"Besides," Yevris said. "There is Rohka."

"Who?"

"Rohka." Yevris rocked on his heels. "You've met her. She comes to see me all the time."

"Oh. You mean your girlfriend."

"Who did you think I meant?"

Kelric shook his head.

Yevris scowled. "You always do that."

"Do what?"

"Close up like a treeclam in the rain."

"It's just that my mother's name is Roca." Although much of the Imperialate knew her as Cya Liessa, which was the name his mother used as a ballerina, her true name was Roca Skolia, with all of the Ruby dynastical titles that went with it.

Yevris let himself down over the inner edge of the wall. "No way is my Rohka your mother."

Kelric climbed down after him. As they walked back to the Calanya, Yevris swept his arm up at the sky. "It's hard to believe people live out there. Very strange, offworlders."

Kelric laughed. "So my father tells my mother."

A First Level appeared around a curve in the path. "Sevtar. Henta sent me to find you."

Yevris grinned at Kelric. "Maybe you have another suitor."

Kelric hoped not. First it had been a woman on the Estate staff. Then a Calanya guard. Then others. It baffled him why they kept coming to court him. He rebuffed all their advances.

In his suite, he bathed and dressed, then went to the common room where his guards waited. They took him through the Estate to an alcove high in a tower. Inside, Henta and her Akasi Tevon sat at a Quis table.

Henta clucked at his damp hair. "You're wet."

"You'll catch a fever," Tevon admonished.

Kelric smiled. "My greetings."

Henta chuckled. "And ours to you. Come sit with us." As Kelric settled into a chair at the round table, she said, "We've an important matter to consider. The Council of Estates meets at Karn in a few days. It is a crucial session."

"The vote on the Wardship of the Miesa Plateau comes up again," Tevon said.

Henta leaned forward. "How that vote goes, Sevtar, could depend on you."

"Me? Why?"

"It's been deadlocked," Henta answered. "Last year Dahl, Bahvla, Shazorla, and Eviza voted with Karn. Haka, Ahkah, Lasa, and Miesa went with Varz. So we had an even split."

"That's only ten Estates," Kelric said.

"Viasa abstained," Tevon said. "So its Secondary, Tehnsa Estate, did as well."

Henta nodded. "Usually Viasa votes with Varz. But Manager Viasa and Ixpar Karn, the Ministry Successor, seem on good terms these days."

"It sounds like it depends on Manager Viasa, then," Kelric said.

"It isn't so simple," Henta said. "I may abstain this year."

"I thought you supported a Ministry Wardship of the Plateau."

"It's Savina Miesa." Henta picked up a gold dodecahedron from a pile of dice, then set it down as if she didn't know what to do with it. "How can I vote to strip her of the Plateau? She may act daft, but she's *not*. I believe she can pull Miesa out of its mire without Karn taking over the Wardship. The problem is that Savina lets Avtac Varz intimidate her."

Kelric thought back to his work at Haka. "Without Varz's help, Miesa would have collapsed years ago."

Tevon snorted. "Varz saves Miesa from a crisis Varz created."

Kelric considered them. "If Manager Miesa is in so much trouble, why is everyone who claims to be her friend trying to take away the mines that support her Estate?"

"If the Wardship goes to Karn, the mines will still support

Miesa," Henta replied. "Minister Karn will simply control that support."

"That doesn't sound any different from the way it is now," Kelric said. "Except it will be Jahlt Karn who takes from Miesa instead of Avtac Varz."

"Karn is not Varz," Tevon said.

"Jahlt I trust," Henta said. "Avtac I don't."

Tevon set a ruby ball in front of Kelric. "You know Haka better than any Karn ally." He added an opal to the structure. "You also know Dahl. You have the tools to determine why past strategies of Dahl against Haka have succeeded or failed."

Henta placed a gold ball by the opal. "With your help, I may be able to neutralize Haka in Council, perhaps even swing Viasa to our side."

An unbidden memory rose in Kelric's mind: Rashiva's face lighting up as he entered the room. "Suppose I don't want to give you advantage over Haka?"

Henta and Tevon exchanged glances.

"Chankah told me it was your choice to come here," Henta said.

Kelric exhaled. "Yes. It was."

She spoke gently. "We wish no harm to Rashiva Haka. We seek only to protect Miesa. You will understand better after you play Quis with Savina."

Quis with another Manager? "Aren't you worried about giving her advantage over your Estate?"

"Yes," Henta said. "But I must make her see. Avtac Varz is destroying Miesa and Savina won't admit it."

"Why have me sit with her?" Kelric glanced at Tevon. "Why not someone who better understands your motivations?"

Tevon spoke. "Because no one else at Bahvla comes close to your expertise at Quis."

Henta nodded. "Maybe you can help me make some sense out of Savina." She sighed. "That is no easy task, I tell you. Winds only know what goes on in her mind."

Among all Estates, Varz stood highest in the Teotecs. It crowned the apex of Mount Skywalk, its towers shearing stark lines against a sky that was forever cobalt-blue. The cliffs around it dropped straight down until they disappeared into clouds massed below the fortress.

A windrider knifed toward the Estate, piloted by a grizzled woman from Lasa Estate. Her craft carried only one passenger and that passenger carried only one name.

Zecha.

A trio of Varz riders shot out of the cliff. Painted black, with carnelian eyes, they bore the Varz clawcat emblem on their wings. They came around and escorted the Lasa craft to the cliff. The pilot's eyes darted back and forth as she took her rider into a tunnel in that massive wall of rock. Only the lamps in the eyes of the windriders lit the cold shadows.

They soared out of the tunnel above an airfield and landed on the icy tarmac. As Zecha disembarked, Varz guards jumped down from the other riders.

A captain strode over to her. "Follow me."

Zecha nodded, acutely aware of what the request lacked. No *follow me, please, Warden Haka.* There was no warden and no Haka, neither now nor ever again.

The captain took her to an alcove on the Estate and left her there.

Zecha waited.

An aide appeared and took her to another alcove.

Zecha waited.

The next aide took her to an office. It was a sparse room, long and narrow. A window dominated the far wall, and beyond it the night loomed in a harsh canopy of stars on a black backdrop. A desk stood in front of the window.

Avtac Varz, the Manager of Varz, sat at the desk.

The cold light edged the planes of Avtac's face, delineating the hollows of her eyes and the bones of her cheeks. Her gaze riveted. It was as if a miner had dug two chunks of iron from the ground, shaped them into orbs, and set them in the sockets of her face. She spoke in a shadowed voice. "My greetings."

Zecha bowed. "My greetings, Manager Varz."

Avtac lifted a narrow hand and indicated a chair by the wall. "Be seated."

Zecha sat.

"You come from Lasa?" Avtac asked.

"I work on the CityGuard there," Zecha said.

Avtac lifted a scroll from her desk. "Then why does this letter say you seek employment?"

"My abilities are wasted as a Lasa guard."

"I have heard much about you, former warden." Avtac set down the scroll. "Perhaps the authorities at Lasa also had ears and this is why you seek new employment."

Zecha had her answer ready. "Your Estate is known for many things, Manager Varz. Strength. Wealth. Power." She paused. "One thing it isn't known for is weakness."

"Meaning?"

"Meaning the weak may shun the strong because of fear."

Avtac steepled her fingers. "Even my closest ally?"

"Young Managers make mistakes."

"Perhaps." Avtac picked up a stylus and tapped it against her fingers. "The captain of my hunting unit grows older. She expects to retire soon."

Zecha tensed. Did Avtac offer her a chance at the position? Varz might well starve if it wasn't for its renowned hunting unit that brought in game from the lower elevations and protected the city from marauding clawcats. Famous for their fierce expertise, the Varz Hunters were both admired and feared throughout the Twelve Estates. Captain of their unit was a position of tremendous prestige.

Zecha spoke carefully. "Many must hope to fill the vacancy."

"So they do." Avtac put down her stylus. "A slot is available on my CityGuard. You will start tomorrow." She paused. "When the captain retires—we will see how matters stand."

The touch brushed Kelric's mind like a caress. It was the first time in his three years on Coba that he had felt another telepath.

Yevris laughed. "She affects one that way, heh?"

Kelric focused his attention outward, on Yevris, who stood with him in an alcove off the main common room. "What?"

"Manager Miesa." Yevris tilted his head toward the common room. "That's who you were staring at."

Kelric looked and saw a petite woman watching a Quis game in the common room. Savina Miesa? No wonder people used gold dice in Miesa patterns. Glossy gold tresses cascaded over her shoulders, spilled down her back, floated around her waist and hips. Curls drifted about an angelic face as innocent as a child's. The cut of her blouse drew his eyes as it swelled out to her ample breasts, plunged in to a tiny waist, curved out again at her hips. Gold lace blouse, gold satin trousers, gold suede boots. Golden sungoddess.

"Saints almighty," Kelric said.

Yevris grinned. "Artwork, yes?"

Kelric thought of Rashiva. "It's just artwork. Nothing more."

Yevris leaned against the wall. "What is it with you? 'Just artwork. Nothing more.' And you ignore every woman who comes to call on you. Is it that you prefer men?"

Kelric scowled. "Of course not."

"Why else would a healthy—"

Kelric advanced toward him. "I told you I didn't."

"There's no reason to get hostile."

"Where I grew up a question like that got your head cracked open."

"I don't see why." Yevris shrugged. "It is a tradition dating from the Old Age."

"Why was it more common then?"

Dryly Yevris said, "Our foremothers were too busy killing each other. So there were many more of us than them. It's why they often took more than one husband." He rocked on his heels. "Eventually they quit lopping each other to pieces on the battlefield. Then there were more of them, which meant if one woman had many kasi, many women had none. So the Managers got together and made a law. Only Managers can have more than one husband."

Kelric snorted. "That figures."

Yevris smiled. "Yes. It does. But you avoid the question, my friend. Why do you ignore all these women who come hoping to make you their only one?"

Kelric crossed his arms. "I prefer not to discuss it."

"You always say that." Yevris crossed his arms in imitation of Kelric. " 'I prefer not to discuss it.' Maybe if you discussed more you would brood less."

Henta appeared in the archway and smiled. "Manager Miesa is here, Sevtar."

Kelric glared at her.

"Ah—hmmm." Henta glanced from him to Yevris. "Maybe I should come back later."

Kelric uncrossed his arms. "No. Now is fine."

As he and Henta walked into the common room, Savina Miesa looked up and gave him a cursory glance. Then she did a double take and stared. Her mental touch brushed his mind like a kiss, stopping him cold in the center of the room.

Savina came over and bowed, her tousled hair making her look like an imp. "Sevtar Bahvla? I am honored."

Kelric nodded, silent and unsmiling.

An octet escorted them to a private alcove in an isolated tower. The guards took up posts Outside while he and Savina sat at the Quis table. She untied her pouch, glanced at him, and promptly spilled dice all over the table.

"Did you know you're a psion?" Kelric asked.

Savina reddened. "Hush. The escort will hear. I'm not supposed to talk to you."

"They can't hear. They're Outside."

She tried to make a neat pile out of her dice, but the stack kept falling over. Finally she thunked a ruby cube in the center of the table. "Your move."

"Did you know?" he asked.

"Know what?"

"That you're a psion."

"A sigh-on?"

"A telepath."

"Are you making a joke?"

"No."

Savina smiled. "You think I can hear your thoughts?"

"No. You don't have the training. But you are a psion."

Her look turned mischievous. "Do you sigh-on, Sevtar?"

"I lost most of it." He hesitated. "But when I felt your touch—maybe it's not gone."

Her face went crimson. "Felt my touch? You know what I'm thinking?"

"No."

"Oh." She relaxed. "Well. I don't know what you're thinking either. So we better play." She grinned. "Play Quis, that is."

Kelric set a topaz by her cube and the game took off. For some reason, she played almost exclusively with rubies and sapphires.

"You know," she said. "Blue is a special color."

He glanced at her. "It is?"

She nodded. "Blue sky. Blue water. Blue."

"Oh." He played an emerald disk. "Your move."

"Pah," Savina muttered.

Yevris handed Kelric a glass of wine. "Blue? She could have meant a lot of things. Were you making water patterns?"

"No," Kelric said. "It was about her Estate."

"Maybe she meant the sapphire mine."

"I don't think so."

Yevris smiled. "Blue is also the color of love."

"I thought that was red." Kelric reviewed the game in his mind. "She used a lot of rubies."

Yevris laughed. "Red, my friend, is for lust."

"For pugging sake," Kelric said. "If that's what it was, the interest isn't mutual."

"Sure. And I'm an offworlder."

Kelric glowered. "You have a perfect word for that. Pah."

Wreathed in mist, Henta and Savina strolled past the old battlements of Bahvla Estate. "I leave tonight for Council," Henta said. "I want to get to Karn early."

Savina pulled her fur-lined jacket tighter around her body. "I have to go to Miesa first. But I'll be at Karn in time for the opening session."

Henta laughed. "You'll dash in ten seconds before it starts."

"I will not."

"You always do."

"Not this time." Savina paused. "Are you bringing any Calani?"

"I might."

"Which ones?"

Henta recognized the too-casual tone of her voice. "I don't know, Savina. Who do you think I should bring?"

"Well, there's that fellow I played Quis with—what is his name? The gold one. He seems quite skilled. At dice, I mean."

"You know perfectly well what his name is."

"Sigh-on."

"What?"

"Sigh-on." Mischief danced across Savina's face. "He thinks if he sighs enough he can read minds."

"Yes? And just where did you get this gem of information?"

"He told—oh." Savina's hand flew over her mouth. "Uh. Hmmmm."

Henta scowled. "What were you doing, talking to my Calani?"

"Sorry."

"Sorry, pah. You ought to know better."

"Well, how was I supposed to concentrate on dice with that glorious specimen of manhood sitting across the table from me? Winds, Henta, how could you not make him your Akasi?"

"I don't want another husband. Besides, Sevtar doesn't want to be an Akasi."

"Does he belong to anyone?"

"Yes. Himself. You'll get nowhere with that one. He's not interested."

Savina spoke in a dramatic voice. "It's his Haka mystique. I can't resist it."

"What Haka mystique? He's an offworlder."

"But he acts like a Haka man. They drive me crazy." Savina's face reddened. "The way they go around all covered up except for their eyes. It gets me hot just thinking about what's under there. And even if they do let you see their faces they never smile. *Never.* Do you know what it does to me when Sevtar acts that way? Just one smile out of him and I'll lose control. One smile. You'll need an octet to hold me back."

Henta sighed. "Did it ever occur to you that he doesn't smile at you because he's not interested?"

Savina scowled. "You're a cranky old clawcat, you know that?"

23

Queen's Spectrum

The Hall of Teotec at Karn Estate seated hundreds when its galleries and balconies were full. Today only Managers and their retinues were present, gathered around the oval-shaped Opal Table that dominated the lower floor, the edges of its amberwood surface inlaid with opals, rainbow ivory, and snowstones.

When Henta entered the Hall, she found many of the Estate Chairs already occupied. In the Haka Chair, Rashiva sat heavy with pregnancy. The desert queen's luster had dimmed into pallor, and fatigue creased her face. An aide spoke to her in a low voice, obviously urging her to retire from the session, but the Manager shook her head.

Henta settled into the Bahvla Chair, her retinue taking seats behind and around her. Her Senior Aide leaned over to her. "Do you want a last look at the files?"

Henta shook her head. "I'm as prepared as I'm going to be." But she had a feeling the Council might not be prepared for Bahvla this year.

The great double doors behind the Ministry Chair swung open and the aide at the entrance announced, "Ixpar Karn, Ministry Successor."

Henta found it hard to believe that the striking young woman who strode into the room was the same gangly child she had known a few years ago. Ixpar brought to mind a painting Henta had once seen, an Old Age warrior queen in bronze and leather armor standing with her long legs planted on a cliff, holding a spear aloft in one hand and a shield in the other, her hip-length hair whipping out behind her body, turned into fire by the sunset.

As Ixpar took her seat next to the Ministry Chair, a flurry of noise came from the entrance, followed by the announcement, "Savina Miesa, Manager of Miesa Estate." Savina sped into the Hall, conferring with a bevy of aides, and ran smack into the Varz Chair. She reddened, looking around, then made her way over to her own Chair next to Bahvla.

As Savina sat down, Henta smiled. "A dignified entrance."

Savina caught her breath. "I thought we'd never make it."

The doors of the Hall opened. "Avtac Varz," the aide said. "Manager of Varz."

Silence fell over the room. A tall woman entered, steel-gray and rigid: gray eyes, gray braid, gray vest, gray shirt, gray trousers and boots. At her left walked a woman with hair the color of rust.

Henta leaned toward Savina. "Who is that with Avtac?"

"Her name is Zecha," Savina said. "She'll be replacing the captain of the Varz Hunters soon."

"Rashiva doesn't look pleased to see her."

The aide at the entrance cleared her throat. "Jahlt Karn." She paused. "Minister of Coba."

Henta rose with the other Managers and their retinues as Jahlt entered. A single figure dressed in black, Jahlt needed no retinue. Her presence filled the Hall. She went to stand before her Chair and spoke in a gravely voice. "The Sixty-sixth Council of the Ninth Century of the Modern Age is now met."

A rustle sounded as, all around the Opal Table, Managers settled into their Chairs and brought out their pouches.

The Minister placed the first die. So began the Council Quis of Coba.

Avtac paced the living room of the Varz guest suite. Zecha waited by the door and several aides hovered in the doorway to an inner room. Stahna, the Varz Successor, stood by the bookshelf.

Avtac stopped in front of Stahna. "Incredible." She started pacing again.

"It was luck," Stahna said. "Henta Bahvla has never dominated the Quis like that before."

"What luck?" Avtac demanded. "Bahvla has a Haka Calani."

Stahna spoke with distaste. "An offworlder."

Like a bite of sour fruit, Avtac thought. It made Bahvla unclean and tainted Haka as well. "Rashiva's Quis was abominable today."

"She's too ill to be at Council," Stahna said.

"If pregnancy makes a Manager too weak to sit in Council she shouldn't be a Manager." Avtac turned to a secretary waiting in the doorway. "Go tell Manager Haka I want to see her." As the young man sped off, Avtac resumed pacing. "Henta has Savina so confused, Savina doesn't know a cube from a disk. If this continues, she will vote to give away her own mines."

"I'll get her into a Quis session tonight," Stahna said. "Maybe I can undo some of Bahvla's damage."

"A good idea." Avtac went over to Zecha. "This man Sevtar. Can he affect the dice the way we saw today?"

"It's possible," Zecha said. "There was a definite change at Haka after he went into the Calanya."

Avtac frowned. "I fail to understand how Rashiva let herself be duped into that arrangement with Dahl."

"My recommendation was to leave him in prison," Zecha said.

"It would have avoided a lot of trouble." Avtac saw the boy she had sent for Rashiva coming back alone. "Where is Manager Haka?"

He stopped in the archway. "Her aides said she can't go anywhere tonight."

"So." Avtac turned to Zecha. "We will see for ourselves."

In the antechamber of the Haka guest suite, they found a cluster of aides playing Quis. As Avtac entered with Zecha, the group hastened to its feet. An older woman bowed to her. "Our greetings, Manager Varz."

"I've come to see Manager Haka," Avtac said.

"I'm sorry, ma'am. She can't have visitors now."

Avtac considered the woman. "What's your name?"

"Chal Haka, ma'am."

"Well, Chal, I suggest you let Manager Haka make her own decisions as to who she will and will not see."

Chal flushed, then bowed and withdrew from the chamber.

"May we get you anything, Manager Varz?" another aide asked. "Some Tanghi? Jai rum?"

"No," Avtac said.

Chal reappeared. "Manager Haka bids you welcome, Manager Varz. She will see you now."

Rashiva was sitting up in bed when Avtac and Zecha entered the inner chambers of the Haka guest suite. A handsome youth wearing the bands of a Haka Akasi stood by the nightstand, straightening up as if he had just slid off the bed. From his dark beauty, Avtac guessed he was one of the Haka highborn. In the privacy of Rashiva's chambers he was barefoot, wearing only his trousers and shirt, but his robe lay on a nearby divan and a Talha scarf hung around his neck. Although he regarded her with no smile, Avtac knew he made suggestive invitations with his dark eyes. Haka men were all the same. It was no wonder their women had to keep such close watch on them.

"My greetings, Avtac." Rashiva touched the boy's arm. "This is Raaj."

Avtac bowed to the Calani. "My honor at your presence, Raaj."

He nodded, still without the forbidden smile, but Avtac recognized the falseness of his modesty by the way his clothes molded to his well-built body.

Rashiva curled her fingers around Raaj's hand and kissed his knuckles. He squeezed her hand, then took his robe and left with his guards.

Avtac frowned at the Haka Manager. "You and I have business to discuss."

Rashiva glanced at Zecha, then back at Avtac. "The affairs of Haka are not the affairs of one Shunned by Haka."

"The affairs of Haka are a mess," Avtac said. "You let Henta dice you into corners today. How is it that an offworlder gives Bahvla advantage over you?"

"You never sat at the Quis table with him," Rashiva said. "Don't underestimate him."

"If his Quis is so strong you should never have let him leave Haka." Avtac thought for a moment. "Perhaps we can still get him out of Bahvla. My Estate can back your offer. For a high enough price I'm sure even Henta will sell him."

Rashiva shifted the cushions behind her back. "He doesn't want to come to Haka."

Avtac leaned over her. "A strong Manager takes a firm hand with her Calani. You would do well to remember that. Let the wishes of an Akasi become prominent in your life and he weakens both you and your Estate."

"Avtac, it's late," Rashiva said. "This pregnancy doesn't go well. I will see you tomorrow."

Offworlder contamination? Avtac straightened up. "Is it the Skolian's child you carry?"

"No."

"That beautiful boy's? Raaj?"

"I think so."

"You think?" Avtac frowned. "Stop brooding over that offworld Calani, Rashiva. Put the pieces of Haka back in their proper patterns and start acting like a Manager."

Chal Haka breathed in relief when the Varz visitors finally went on their way. Her good spirits vanished when she returned to the bedroom and found Rashiva pulling herself out of bed.

"Manager Haka." Chal strode over to her. "You mustn't get up."

Rashiva leaned on the bedpost. "I'm tired of Avtac's attitude, that anyone who isn't her isn't worth a wooden die."

"Please." Chal took her arm. "Go back to bed. Think about the child."

"I will be fine. I attended Council while I was carrying my daughter and had no problems." She let go of the post. "See? Why don't you fix me a mug of Tanghi? I will take it in my study."

Chal knew arguing would only annoy the Manager. Besides, the Tanghi might make her sleepy enough so she would go back to bed.

As Chal left, she glanced back. Rashiva was sitting on the bed with her head bowed, her skin so pale she looked like a ghost.

* * *

Ixpar downed the rest of her cooling Tanghi in one swallow. "That was a long session today."

"But productive." Folding her hands around her glass of jai rum, Jahlt relaxed in an armchair in her study. It was an advantage of being Minister; the Council met at her Estate, which meant at night she retired to familiar rooms.

"Who would have thought Bahvla could come through so well?" Jahlt said. "Or Haka so weak? Perhaps we will take the Plateau vote this year."

Ixpar clunked her mug down on the table. "Only Haka and Miesa stand firm behind Varz." She got up and paced across the room, stretching her arms. "Near the end of the session I even started to wonder about Miesa."

"Henta has done good work," Jahlt said. "But she worries me."

Ixpar lowered her arms. "You think she means to abstain?"

Jahlt nodded, gratified Ixpar had caught that subtle trend in the Bahvla patterns. "If her Quis stays as sharp as today, though, we could still get a majority."

"I hope so." Ixpar rubbed her neck. "That session lasted forever. I get stiff just thinking about it." She grinned. "What do you say, Jahlt? How about a jog around Karn?"

Jahlt snorted. "You will send me to my grave with your ideas." But she was not displeased. Ixpar's vibrant health strengthened the Ministry. In the Old Age, Ixpar would have turned her energy to the battlefield, no doubt maturing to become a legend among warrior queens. Now, however, no wars existed to calm her young successor's raging energy and hormones.

"Henta was amazing today." Ixpar started pacing again. "She obviously has a strong Calanya behind her."

" 'A strong Calanya.' " Jahlt snorted. "I am not fooled by these attempts of yours to disguise references to Kelricson Valdoria by including large numbers of people in comments about him."

Ixpar turned to face her. "If I want to praise him, I won't disguise it. Why should I? Didn't you see anything of the man he is that night you talked to him in Dahl?"

Jahlt got up and went over to her. "I saw a man who could become legend."

"Then why do you so dislike him?"

"It is not dislike." Jahlt spoke quietly. "With his dice, he is like a sorcerer given a power he doesn't understand. What will his Quis do to Coba?" She walked to the mantel and stared into the fire. "I cannot answer that question, Ixpar. None of us can." She looked up at her successor. "That is why I fear it."

The only sound in the Hall of Teotec came from the clink of dice. Managers sat arrayed about the Opal Table, intent on their Quis. Their successors leaned forward to see better, and behind them the ranks of aides watched.

Ixpar observed from her seat by the Ministry Chair. The Managers looked like a queen's spectrum, the power of each symbolized by the braid hanging down her back. Youngest of all was Khal Viasa, whose auburn braid had yet to reach her waist. Manager Shazorla's braid was black sprinkled with gray, Manager Ahkah's gray sprinkled with brown. Savina Miesa's hair escaped in a disarray of curls that floated around her face.

The Ahkah Manager let out a breath and leaned back in her seat. It started a rustle of motion: people shifted position, sipped from mugs, rearranged piles of dice.

Jahlt spoke. "Perhaps we should take a recess."

A murmur of agreement answered her. Managers pushed away from the table and conversation trickled among the observers.

Outside the hall, Jahlt joined Ixpar for a walk. "What do you think of the session?"

"Rashiva's patterns are stronger," Ixpar said. "She must have worked on strategies all night."

Jahlt nodded. "Miesa may go with Varz after all." She frowned. "We need this vote. Every year Varz succeeds in blocking us, Avtac gains more control over Miesa."

A shout came from behind them. Ixpar turned to see an aide running up the hall. The woman stopped in front of Jahlt. "It's Manager Haka." She gasped for breath. "She was getting up— from her Chair. She collapsed."

Jahlt strode back toward the Hall, with Ixpar and the aide at her side. "Has Med been summoned?"

"I sent for the Karn Senior Physician," the aide said. "A Haka aide went for the Haka doctor and Manager Dahl sent for a doctor who came with the Dahl retinue."

Inside the Council Hall a knot of people were kneeling near the Haka Chair. Rashiva lay on the floor, her face the color of old ashes. Jahlt stepped past the others and knelt by the crumpled form. "Rashiva?"

"Ah . . ." The Haka queen's lashes stirred. "My baby . . ."

A doctor strode into the room, the Med patch blazoned on the shoulder of her tunic showing the Haka emblem of a rising sun. Behind her came the Karn Senior Physician, and behind her a man with the Dahl suntree emblem on his shoulder.

An aide cleared the Hall. Only Jahlt remained, with Ixpar and Avtac Varz. They moved back, waiting while the doctors examined Rashiva.

Jahlt indicated the man from Dahl. "He looks familiar."

"That's Dabbiv," Ixpar said. "He was Kelric's physician at Dahl."

Avtac frowned. "Dabbiv Dahl? It may be unwise to let him in here. His ideas about medicine are questionable."

"Manager Dahl thinks highly of him," Ixpar said.

Shallina Karn, the gray-haired Karn Senior Physician, came over to them. "We're going to take Manager Haka down to Med."

"Will she be all right?" Jahlt asked.

"We'll know by tonight. The child is coming."

Ixpar stared at Shallina. "But it's too soon."

"Her baby," Shallina said, "doesn't plan to wait."

. . . across the village, Shaliece cried. Kelric ran out of his father's house and through the cobbled streets of Dalvador. At the turreted house where Shaliece lived, a midwife stopped him. His son was gone. Miscarriage. Dead . . .

. . . Far across a world, Rashiva called to him . . .

Kelric bolted awake, sitting up in bed. He stared into the dark, fragments of a dream lingering in his mind. Sweat soaked his shirt. He took the water flask off the nightstand and drank deeply. Then he went into his living room.

When he opened the balcony doors and stepped outside,

wind heavy with moisture rushed in at him. His balcony was at the top of a tower, the trellised veranda reinforced with struts. Far below, the Teotecs spread out to the edge of the world, where a line of light hinted dawn might come despite the rain. Sporadic thunder rumbled across the mountains and wind whipped back his hair. A wildness saturated the air, ancient and free.

But even the untamed night couldn't wipe away the traces of his dream. He went back inside and wandered out of his suite, into the main common room. It was dark, except for an oil lamp burning in one corner.

Kelric opened the Outside doors. Taul, the captain of his Calanya escort, sat Outside with his other guards, dozing by a Quis table. Kelric left the Calanya and walked down the hall.

"Heh!" Running boots sounded behind him and then he was surrounded by guards. Captain Taul drew him to a stop. "You can't come out here."

Kelric had no idea what he was doing, he only knew a buried instinct was pushing him. "I need to go to the Observatory."

As Taul's mouth fell open, several guards drew in breaths. Taul's turmoil showed on her face, and Kelric sensed her reaction: should she pretend she hadn't heard the forbidden words? Would it affect his Quis if she denied a request so urgent he broke his Oath for it? Would he fight, forcing them to mishandle a Third Level? Would they have to shoot? If she woke someone in authority, would she lose ranking, prestige, honor?

After a long moment, Taul came to a decision. "We will escort you to the Observatory. But please—don't talk anymore."

Kelric nodded. He set off again, surrounded by the escort.

When they reached the Observatory, he still had no idea why he needed to go there. All he could think of was that it faced Karn. With his guards, he went out on the high balcony that circled the building. Memories flooded him; Shaliece, her eyes huge and violet, running across the plains of Dalvador with her skirt whipping around her legs, laughing as he caught her and they tumbled into the grass. Shaliece, crying for the death of their child.

Why now? Why did the pain of his son's death come back to him now, after it had rested for so many years?

In the muted hours before dawn, Ixpar woke from her sitting-up doze on the couch. She looked around the alcove. Jahlt stood by the entrance, in conversation with an aide, and Avtac Varz was sitting on a couch, leaning back with her eyes closed. Across the room, Henta snored in an armchair.

Jahlt came over to her. "It's late. You should get some rest."

"You too," Ixpar said.

"Heh." She sat on the couch. "Women have been having babies since time started. Rashiva will be fine."

"It's taking too long."

Jahlt exhaled. "Yes. It is."

Shallina, the Karn Senior Physician, appeared in the alcove entrance. Dark circles rimmed her eyes and her gray hair was pulled from its braid, curling in tendrils around her face. She said, simply, "It's done."

Across the room, Avtac Varz rose to her feet. "Manager Haka?"

"She sleeps now," Shallina said.

"What about the child?" Ixpar asked.

Shallina pushed back her hair. "A boy."

"Mother and son are all right?" Jahlt asked.

"Manager Haka is exhausted," Shallina said. "But she will be fine. The baby, however, is too weak." She spoke quietly. "He won't live more than a few days."

A shadow appeared behind Shallina, solidifying into Dabbiv Dahl as he came into the archway. "Minister Karn, I've seen symptoms like Manager Haka's before. So for her son—"

"We don't try untested procedures on an infant, young man," Shallina said.

"It's tested," Dabbiv said. "We can use the diet that—"

Avtac interrupted him. "You want to experiment on Manager Haka's son?"

Dabbiv shook his head. "It's not—"

"We've already discussed this," Shallina said. "Getting emotional serves no purpose for anyone."

Dabbiv made a frustrated noise. "I'm not getting em—"

"Young man," Avtac said. "Perhaps you should leave these matters to those with the experience to deal with them."

"Dabbiv is right," Ixpar said.

Everyone turned to her.

"I should have seen it before," Ixpar told them. "Manager Haka's symptoms in Council were just like the ones Kelric had at Dahl before we changed his diet."

Relief filled Dabbiv's face. "Yes. That's what I've been saying. If we can find a formula based on that diet, it might increase the baby's chances of survival. While Manager Haka nurses him, we should keep her on the same diet—"

"The Haka Senior Physician," Shallina said, "suggests we give the boy mineral baths and bubble water for his stomach." She regarded Jahlt. "Besides, the baby's father is not this man Kelric, or Sevtar, or whatever his name is."

"Kelric was also a Haka Akasi," Ixpar pointed out.

"We will follow both plans," Jahlt said. She considered Dabbiv. "Can you see to the diet?"

"I'll be glad to," he said.

Jahlt turned to Shallina. "Keep working with the Haka doctor. Do whatever you can for the boy."

"All right." Shallina glanced around at all of them. "We also need a Plan Three."

"Plan Three?" Avtac asked.

Shallina scowled. "Plan Three is that you all go to bed before you pass out."

Jahlt smiled. "Very well, Doctor."

So they woke up Henta, and then they all dispersed to their various suites.

Late-morning light poured into the Hall of Teotec through its arched windows. Jahlt looked out over the Managers arrayed around the Opal Table. "Based on the Council recommendations, it is my decision to impose no new tariffs on the Shazorla wines."

No surprise there, Ixpar thought. As Minister, Jahlt could have vetoed the tariff vote, but she let it stand. The next vote was different; a motion concerned with the support of an entire Estate could neither be overridden by Jahlt nor passed without a majority.

"We now address the Wardship of the Miesa Plateau," Jahlt said. "Placing a diamond cube is a vote of *yea* to moving the title of Ward from Miesa to Karn. The obsidian cube is a vote of *nay* and the crystal ring is an abstain." She turned to Ixpar. "Proceed."

Ixpar poised her quill over her scroll. "Tehnsa?"

Instead of placing a vote, the Tehnsa Manager said, "Tehnsa will follow its Primary of Viasa." When Ixpar called the other two Secondary Estates, Evisa and Lasa, they also deferred to their Primaries.

Ixpar turned to Savina. "Miesa?"

Savina lifted her hand. For an incredible instant it hovered over the crystal ring. Then she picked up the obsidian cube and set it in the center of the table.

No Miesa surprises after all, Ixpar thought, hiding her disappointment as she noted Savina's move on her scroll. "Viasa?"

Khal Viasa set a crystal ring by the Miesa cube. "Viasa abstains."

The Tehnsa Manager placed her ring. "Tehnsa follows Viasa."

Another disappointment. At least Viasa hadn't voted with Varz. "Ahkah?" Ixpar asked.

The Ahkah Manager placed an obsidian cube. "Nay."

The Lasa Manager placed her black cube. "Lasa follows its Primary."

Ixpar was growing worried. If Henta Bahvla abstained, Karn would lose the vote. "Bahvla?"

Henta gave Savina a look of apology. Then she placed a diamond cube on the Table. "Bahvla votes yea."

Dahl voted with the Ministry, as did Shazorla and its Secondary Eviza. Rashiva's successor, an adolescent girl, placed the black cube for Haka. After Varz and Karn played their dice, the vote was done; five diamond cubes, five obsidian cubes, and two crystal rings sat on the table.

Jahlt spoke. "The pattern is clear. The vote remains deadlocked."

Avtac Varz smiled.

24

The Tower of Odana

When Kelric first heard the clank of metal hitting stone, he thought the wind had dislodged the trellis on his balcony and sent it clattering down the tower. But when he pulled aside the curtains everything looked normal.

A large metal hook trailing a rope arced into the air and caught on the trellis.

"What the—?" Kelric went out and looked over the balcony. The rope stretched down from the hook to a window far below his suite. Knots appeared at intervals along the cable—and Savina Miesa was hanging on to its end.

"Hey!" Kelric called. "What are you doing?"

She stood balanced on the windowsill with one arm hooked around the leg of a gargoyle while she pulled on a pair of gloves. Looking up at him, she grinned. "Throwing my hook."

"You can't come up here."

Mischief showed on her face. "Why not?"

"Because I don't want you to."

"Then I'll hang out here bemoaning my unrequited love until I fall off and smash to an untimely death."

"For pugging sake," Kelric said.

Savina yanked on the rope, testing it, and then started to climb. Wind and momentum immediately took over, swinging her out over the abyss of air. She swung back in, scrambling for a grip on the wall, and found a foothold. Then she walked up the tower, holding on to the rope.

When she reached the top, Kelric scowled at her. "Are you crazy or what?"

She vaulted over the trellis onto the balcony. "Crazy with

love. You better offer me a good strong drink to calm me down."

"You look perfectly calm to me."

She walked past the glazed balcony doors into his living room. "If you're worried about Henta, she's down in the city at a meeting."

Kelric followed her inside. "I want you to leave."

"I just got here." Savina dropped onto the divan, her hair spilling in a gold waterfall everywhere. She was all hourglass curves, full and firm in a snug blue jumpsuit, more like an erotic holomovie goddess than a Manager. Kelric stared at her, tried not to stare, cleared his throat, then crossed to the rosewood cabinet and pulled out the first flask his hand touched. He took two tumblers and went over to Savina.

"One drink," he said. "That's all."

"Baiz." Her smile dazzled. "A good choice."

He looked at the flask. "You want something else?"

Savina pulled him down on the divan. "Baiz is perfect." She filled one glass brimful and handed it to him. "Just perfect."

Kelric downed his drink in one swallow. "Why did you pull that stunt?"

"I wanted to talk to you." She trailed her fingers along his neck. "You're the only offworlder I've ever met."

"I don't talk to Outsiders."

"I'm not really an Outsider." She refilled his glass. "Tell me about the Imperialate. Do Skolians have Akasi?"

"No."

Her fingers explored the sensitive skin around his ear, then slid down to pull on the ties of his shirt. "What do Managers do for love?"

He finished off his baiz in one swallow. "We don't have Managers."

"You were telling me about sigh-ons." She poured him another drink. "Do Skolian men really sigh so much?"

"I'm going to get the escort."

She leaned close to him, brushing her fingers across his lips while her plump breasts pressed against him. "You don't really want to do that."

He stared at her angelic face. Then he drained his glass.

"You know, you don't look so steady." Savina pushed him onto his back on the divan. "I think you need to lie down."

He tried to sit back up. "I feel fine."

"No, you look terribly pale." She shoved him back down, leaning over him. Somehow she had undone his shirt and was stroking his chest. "Smile for me, beautiful Calani."

It was too much. Kelric pulled her down on top of him, filling his arms with soft, supple Savina and his senses with musky Savina scent. "You should watch where you prowl, Manager Miesa," he growled. "You don't know what you'll find."

A tap sounded at the screen. "Sevtar?" Henta called.

Savina's mouth opened in a big O. She tried to scramble off the divan but Kelric refused to let her go, too drunk and too aroused now to care about Henta.

"Sevtar?" Henta repeated. "Are you all right?"

Savina managed to twist out of his arms. She jumped off the sofa and ran into an inner room. As Kelric sat up, fumbling with the thongs on his shirt, the screen of his suite moved aside and Henta looked in at him.

"I thought you were at a meeting," he said.

"It finished early." Her gaze traveled over the baiz flask, the two glasses, the disarrayed divan. Then she watched him trying to put his shirt back together. "Sevtar."

He gave up on his shirt. "Yes?"

"Can't Savina use the front door like a normal person?"

"Cuaz me," a voice said from the inner room.

"OUT," Henta said.

An abashed Savina appeared. "My greetings, Henta."

"What do you think you're doing, climbing up towers and getting my Calani drunk?"

"Well—I—uh—how did you know I was here?"

"I'm asking the questions, Manager Miesa."

Savina looked like a child caught with her hand full of stolen candy. "I came to see Sevtar."

Henta scowled. "You came to see Sevtar. How nice. How many laws do you think you broke here?"

"Wait." Kelric stood up. "Don't call a Tribunal."

"I ought to," Henta said.

"She'll do something worse," Savina said. "She'll lecture me."

"Out," Henta said.

Savina retreated out of the suite, followed by the glowering Bahvla Manager.

"No." As far as Henta was concerned, that concluded the conversation. She turned to watch a group of children splash in a fountain on the other side of the plaza where she and Savina had ended up after their walk through Bahvla.

"Why not?" Savina said.

"He is Calani," Henta said.

"Since when can't Calani have visitors?" Savina demanded.

"You aren't a visitor. You're an Estate Manager. Besides, what makes you think Sevtar wants you to visit him?"

"He does. He just doesn't know it yet."

The children suddenly realized who shared the plaza with them. They stopped playing and gaped at the two Managers.

Henta smiled. "Apparently we're more interesting than a fountain."

"They probably see Managers about as often as they see Calani," Savina fumed. "Not that there is any harm in someone seeing a Calani every now and then."

"I told you no."

"Why not? You think big brutal me will commit nefarious acts against helpless Sevtar?"

Henta turned to her. "There are many ways a man can be hurt. Leave him alone."

Savina swept out her arms. "You're denying the expression of true love."

"Pah."

"Pah yourself." Savina put her hands on her hips. "How do you know I'm not in love with him?"

"You're always in love. Aren't four husbands enough? You need a fifth?"

"You know Miesa could never afford a Fourth Level."

"I see. You just want to use my Calani and then leave him unhappy."

"I do not."

"Pah."

"I really wish you would stop saying that," Savina grumbled.

With a wild rush of air, the rider skimmed over Kelric and Yevris a second time. As they sprinted for the cover of a snow-fir grove, the craft descended, flattening grass and whipping tree branches into a frenzy.

Kelric skidded to a stop under a tree. "It's landing."

"In a Calanya park?" Yevris lifted his arm to shield his face from the wake of air. "I can't think of anything more illegal."

The rider set down on a nearby lawn. Its hatch swung open and the pilot jumped out onto the grass.

"Cuaz and Khozaar," Yevris said.

Kelric laughed. "No, not the Akasi. What we have here is the sungoddess."

Savina Miesa walked toward them, a stunner in her hand.

"Let's leave," Yevris said.

"Why don't we see what she wants?" Kelric said. *Better yet, steal her rider and go to the starport.*

"It's you she wants." Yevris tugged his arm. "Come on. You don't have to take this insult."

"You can let him go, Yevris." Savina stopped in front of them. "He's not going with you."

Kelric regarded her with curiosity. "Why not?"

"You and I are taking a trip," she said.

"You can't kidnap me."

Savina drew her stunner. "Want to roll dice on that?"

Kelric knew the gun was a bluff. If she stunned him, she could never drag him to the rider and lift him into its cabin. She only stood as tall as his chest and he was more than twice her weight. Stealing her rider would be easier than playing Quis with a baby.

He glanced at Yevris. "Well, I don't want to get shot. I better do what she wants." Across the parks, he saw his guards running toward them.

Savina followed his gaze. "Hurry up, Sevtar."

As Kelric headed for the rider, he heard Savina behind him.

He reached for the hatch—and spun around to grab her gun. She had no time to react after he lunged. Yet before he even finished turning, she had already pumped five stun shots into him. The only way she could have done it was by shooting *before* he made his move. He collapsed onto the grass, barely conscious, unable to move or speak.

She dropped next to him. "I'm really sorry I had to do that." Suddenly she looked up and fired the stunner again. He heard Yevris swear, followed by the thud of a body hitting the ground.

Savina disappeared. An instant later the grind of a grain-loading machine started in the rider. She reappeared and pushed a sled under his body, working with frantic speed as she secured him onto it with ropes. With Savina pushing and the grain-loader pulling, Kelric found himself being hoisted into the rider.

As soon as she had him inside, she slammed the hatch shut and spun around to the copilot's seat. She had rigged the chair so it tipped down to the deck. As she untied Kelric and struggled to slide him into the seat, his head rolled to the side. Through the window, he saw Yevris picking himself up from the ground. Behind the Second Level, guards were closing on the snowfir grove.

Savina grunted. "Winds, you're heavy." She shoved Kelric upright in the chair and turned it around to face the rider's windshield. Next she bound his arms to the armrests and his ankles to a bar on the deck. Then she slid into the pilot's seat. As his escort reached the grove, she taxied across the lawn. She soared up into the sky and the guards stared up after them, disbelief on their faces.

"It worked!" she exulted. "It actually worked."

I don't believe this, Kelric thought.

As the stun shots wore off, he worked his mouth to loosen the muscles. Then he said, "Do you always go around kidnapping people?"

Savina glanced at him. "I'm sorry about tying you up."

He scowled.

"Well, you're a lot bigger than me," she said. "I knew you might go for the rider. It wouldn't have done any good, though.

I only put in enough fuel to get where we're going. If you had tried for the starport you would never have made it."

"Then you can't reach Miesa either."

"We're not going to Miesa. It's the first place Henta will check." She navigated through a bank of clouds. "Besides, if I show up with a Bahvla Calani, my staff will have collective heart failure."

"So where are you taking me?"

"A fortress higher in the mountains. A Tehnsa Manager built it during the Old Age to hide an Akasi she stole from Viasa." Savina grinned. "Appropriate, heh?"

"You can't keep me locked up in a fortress forever."

"I probably can't keep you more than a few days. Henta will be furious."

"Then why are you doing this?"

Mischief danced in her eyes. "I'm powerless to resist you."

"For pugging sake," he said.

It was past sunset when they reached the fortress. As the rider descended, eroded towers and crumbling battlements took form out of the shadows. Savina landed behind the remains of a parapet. When she cut the engines, it left a sudden silence filled only by the moan of the wind in the mountains. Somewhere an animal howled.

"Charming place," Kelric muttered.

Savina got out of her seat. "I fixed up a room inside. It's not so bad." She came over to untie him, but then stopped, an impish smile spreading across her face. Leaning forward, she kissed him instead.

Kelric pulled his head away. "Stop it."

"Come on," she coaxed. "Smile for me."

He glared at her.

"Come on." She kissed him again. "One little smile."

I don't want to like you, he thought. *It's not safe.*

Savina played with the laces on his shirt, then slid her hand along his arm. When he tried to lean away from her, she caught his chin in her hand and kissed him a third time.

Kelric jerked away his chin and yanked against the ropes that bound his arms to the chair. "Untie me, damn it."

"Oh, but I can't." She stepped between his knees and sat on

his leg, sliding her arms around his neck. As she kissed his ear, her breasts rubbed against him.

"Cut it out," he said, with less conviction than before. He tried to pull his arms free, telling himself he intended to push her away rather than embrace her. The golden waterfall of her hair poured over his arms. Many Coban women had beautiful hair, but Savina beat them all, with curling tresses so thick, soft, and glistening he would never have believed it was real if he hadn't felt it himself.

Savina sighed. Raising her head, she gave him a guilty look, her eyes glossy with desire. "I am a beast. But ai, Sevtar, it is so difficult to hold back when faced with—" She smiled. "With you." Taking a breath, she stood up, which left his leg feeling cold. She loosened the ropes on his arms, then backed up into the cabin. "You better get the rest. I don't trust myself."

After Kelric worked his arms free, he untied his feet. When he stood up, his returning circulation felt like pins poking his limbs. He turned to see Savina aiming a stunner at him. She threw him a jacket and motioned toward the hatch.

The gales that hit him as he jumped out of the rider were even stronger than those at Bahvla. Mountains loomed above the fortress in a stark landscape of snow and bare rock. Even with supplies and climbing equipment he doubted anyone could survive for long this high in the Teotecs. It was no wonder the Cobans invented the windrider ahead of its time. Between Estates, it was the only survivable mode of travel and communication.

Savina jumped down next to him. When she spoke the wind whipped away her words. He shook his head, so she motioned to the turret of a nearby tower with a jagged hole in its side. He ran over to it with her and ducked his head to climb through. It was quieter inside, but pitch-dark. He stumbled over a clutter of debris.

"Wait," Savina said. "I have a lamp." A sphere of light appeared around her, revealing the remains of a staircase spiraling down the tower. "It's safe," she said. "I've already tested it."

Their trek through the ruins took them down crumbling stairs and along collapsed halls, most of it barely visible in her lamp's lonely radiance. Finally they came to a room that had been restored, with oil lamps glowing in readiness for their visit. Cleaned tapestries hung on the walls and a canopied bed made with silk and velvet stood on a dais at one end. The rosewood Quis table in the center of the room had a candle on it and a decanter of rosewine with two crystal goblets.

"It's not so bad, is it?" Savina said.

"It's beautiful." The restoration astounded Kelric, revealing an unexpected side of the Miesa Manager. The work must have taken her many tendays of painstaking labor. He ran his hand over the carved rosewood flowers on the edge of a chair. "I'm surprised no one has taken this furniture away. It's gorgeous."

"Nobody comes up here. I doubt even Manager Tehnsa knows about it."

"How do you?"

"I used to take a rider and go exploring when I was young." She indicated a stack of logs by the fireplace. "There's a flint in the little bureau by the bed and supplies for you in the cupboards."

"You're leaving?" It disappointed Kelric more than he wanted to admit.

She nodded. "I left just enough fuel here for a return trip to Bahvla."

Kelric regarded her uneasily. Without Savina, he would be stranded in the ruins with no supplies. He could easily overcome her and make her tell him where she hid the fuel, but even if he had been willing to cause her harm, which he wasn't, what good would it do? His lack of experience in a rider made his flying erratic, a problem the ripping gales of upper ranges would exacerbate. He would use up the fuel long before he reached Bahvla. At best, it would strand him in the mountains; at worst, he would crash.

Savina had chosen this site well. He was beginning to understand what Henta had said, that the Miesa Manager was far more savvy than most people realized.

She was watching his face. "I know how all this looks. But I really do intend right by you. Henta just wouldn't listen to civilized arguments."

"Right by me? What do you mean?"

"About Rashiva—"

He stiffened. "I don't recall mentioning Rashiva."

"I just wanted to say—I don't know why she turned away from you but I can guess. It was 'honor,' yes? Well, it doesn't matter to me if offworld ways are different. I respect your honor."

That's a cultural minefield, Kelric thought. He didn't want to get blown up again.

She hesitated. "Will you have a glass of wine with me before I go?"

His face relaxed into a smile. "All right."

"Ai. So beautiful." She sighed. "It lights up your whole face."

"It?"

"Your smile." She came over and put her arms around his waist. "Your beautiful smile."

Don't do it, Kelric warned his arms. Hold her now and I'm lost. His arms ignored him and wrapped around her.

"Ummm." She closed her eyes and rubbed her cheek against the curling hair on his chest. "Shall I make a fire?"

"All right."

While she worked at the fireplace, Kelric sat down and poured the wine. "What will happen when you get back to Bahvla?"

Savina came to the table. "Henta will threaten and rage and swear." She sat across from him. "But she won't call a Tribunal. Summoning one against an Estate Manager is too serious a matter."

"You kidnapped me just to make her mad?"

"No. I hope to make her understand." She hesitated. "Maybe I've been a fool. I don't even know—if you . . ."

He smiled. "Yes. I want you to visit me."

"Ai." She sighed. "Sevtar. God of the dawn. It fits you. I can almost believe what I heard, that you are Rhon."

"I am."

Her eyes widened. "You don't act it."

"How does Rhon act?"

"I just imagined they were—different."

Kelric recognized her reaction. "Cruel? Arrogant?"

"That was before I knew you." She paused. "I once heard a Skolian saying: 'Across the stars the Rhon may trod, but still the gods of Kyle are flawed.' "

"We aren't gods. We're people."

"Not normal people."

He reached over and took her hand. "To be an empath—it means we absorb it all: people's hopes, fears, dreams, hates. In love it's a gift. But in so much else it's a nightmare. A barrage. We build barriers to shut it all out." For some reason an image of Zecha came into his mind. Then he thought of his half brother, the Imperator. "Some cut it off so completely that they smother part of what makes them human."

Savina curled her fingers around his. "A barrage. I feel that way sometimes."

"I'll bet you also have a remarkable memory for conversations."

"How did you know? It makes Avtac crazy. She says I 'conveniently' remember whatever fits my needs."

"Empaths remember conversations well because we recall the feelings as well as the words." He stroked her knuckle with his thumb. "I'll bet you almost always know when someone is lying."

"I never told anyone about that."

"But it's true, isn't it?"

"Even if it is, that still doesn't mean I hear thoughts."

He tried to think of an example she would accept. "Why did you shoot me in the Calanya park?"

"I really am sorry about that. But you were about to hit me over the head and steal my rider."

"How did you know?"

"How? You went after me."

"You fired before I did anything."

It was a moment before she answered. "There are times when—well, it does seem I feel what others feel. Avtac says I'm oversensitive."

"Maybe it's Avtac who lacks sensitivity."

"I don't want to be Rhon."

"You aren't. You are a Kyle operator, though." Kelric took out his dice and made two parallel lines of cubes on the table.

"Kyle traits come from mutated genes. Recessive genes. Unless you get them from both parents, the traits don't manifest." With a sweep of his hand, he whisked away one line. "A person can carry all the genes unpaired and never show a single trait." He removed parts of the remaining line, then put down dice to pair several cubes still on the table. "Someone like you only carries a few Kyle genes, but with pairings, so you show some Kyle ability. The Rhon—my family—carry every one of the genes paired. That's why our Kyle abilities are so strong."

Savina picked up a cube. "It sounds like those strange ideas the scientists at Varz have about blue eyes being weaker than black."

"They probably mean blue is recessive to black."

"Avtac supports the research because she wants something to turn up and give her advantage over Karn." She shrugged. "But really, it's all games."

Kelric lifted a lock of her hair. "What color hair did your parents have?"

"Yellow."

"What about their eyes?"

"Gray. Both my mother and father."

"You think it's coincidence you have yellow hair and gray eyes?"

"Well, no." She put down the cube. "A lot of people look like their parents. But not everyone."

"The genes are still there."

"Not always."

He smiled. "Always. Really."

She started to answer, then stopped.

"What is it?" he asked.

"I—it's about Rashiva."

His smile vanished. "What does Rashiva have to do with it?"

"Her baby."

Don't ask, he thought. But the question came anyway. "How is he?" *He?* Why he?

"Jimorla nearly died at birth," she said. "But he's much better now. He's a beautiful child, as dark as any Hakaborn. But he has violet eyes. That never came from Rashiva or Raaj."

The spell of firelight shattered around Kelric. At first he just stared at her. Then he stood up and walked to the fireplace.

Savina came over to him. "Sevtar? What is it?"

A spark flew up from the fire and winked out, leaving an ember to drift onto his hand. "It's late, Rashiva. Maybe you should go."

She spoke quietly. "My name is Savina."

Kelric exhaled. "I'm sorry."

Silence stretched between them. Finally she said, "You should be safe here. This wing of the fortress is sound. It's probably wise not to leave it, though."

"All right."

"Well." She hesitated. "I guess I'll go." She lingered a moment longer. When he made no response, she left.

Kelric continued to watch the fire, but instead of flames, images of his boyhood flickered in his mind. He kept seeing his father, a well-built man with large eyes.

Violet eyes.

Violet. Like the eyes of all Lyshrioli natives.

My son, Kelric thought. Rashiva, he is my son.

25

Rumrunner's Gamble

When Henta disembarked from the rider and saw her aides waiting on the airfield, her hope surged. She hurried over, puffing from exertion. "The other search party found him?"

"I'm afraid not," her Senior Aide said. "But guess who's in your office? Manager Miesa."

Henta scowled. "How nice of her to visit."

"I have guards ready to take her to jail."

"Good." Henta headed for the Estate. She posted the octet at her office outside and then stalked into the room.

Savina was standing by the window. "My greetings, Henta."

"I can't believe you had the audacity to show up alone."
Henta slammed the door. "Where is he?"

"Safe."

"Safe? With you? A false friend who abuses my trust?"

"You wouldn't listen to civilized arguments."

"Civilized," Henta sputtered. "I don't know where you get
the gall to talk about civilized after you steal my Calani."

"I only—"

"No excuses. I want him back. Now."

"Not unless you agree to let me visit him."

"You really are crazy." Henta waved her arms at the Miesa
Manager. "You want to be stripped of your name? Shunned?
Sent to prison? What has blown into your head to make you act
this way?"

Savina swallowed. "A Calani blew in. I can't get him out."

Henta wanted to shake her. "All you think about is yourself.
What about him? Or maybe you don't care how he feels."

"I love him."

Henta snorted. "You love him. Don't make me laugh. He
deserves better than your infatuation with his physical beauty."

"It's not infatuation." She pushed her hands through her hair.
"Maybe it was at first. Or maybe it was the challenge of him.
But it's gone beyond that. He's in my head and I can't get him
out."

"You hardly know him."

"Visitation. That's all I ask."

"And what will you 'ask' after that? No. Bring him back or
I'll call a Tribunal."

"I know you won't."

"You're wrong. You've gone too far this time." Henta
opened the door and spoke to the guards. "Take Manager
Miesa into custody."

"Wait," Savina said.

"Put her in jail," Henta told the guards.

"Henta, stop," Savina said. "Listen to what I have to say."

As the guards surrounded Savina, Henta held up her hand.
When the captain tilted her head, Henta said, "Wait outside."

After the octet withdrew, Henta shut the door and crossed
her arms. "This better be good."

"What do you want for Sevtar's Calanya contract?"

Henta closed her eyes. When she opened them, Savina was still standing there with a perfectly serious expression on her face.

"You're being irrational," Henta said.

"That's not an answer."

"Miesa could never afford a Fourth Level. Especially one like Sevtar."

"Just answer the question."

"The question is demented."

"How *much*?"

"Ten million denai, five First Level Calani, and two Second Levels."

Savina gaped at her. "That's absurd."

"It's very reasonable. The only ludicrous proposition here is yours."

"Miesa doesn't have two Second Levels."

Henta went over to her. "Neither does Miesa have anything close to ten million denai in assets. And I hardly think seven of your Calani want to leave. You only have nine, for wind's sake. Have you forgotten four of them are Akasi? Not to mention that you only made two of them Calani because you couldn't marry them otherwise. They can't play Quis worth spit. Whatever possessed you to think Sevtar has any desire to be husband number five? Are you crazy or what?"

"I don't want to hurt my Akasi. But you don't understand. You think I glut myself on love but you're wrong." Savina spoke awkwardly. "They aren't happy with me. Winds, Henta, they would be glad to leave Miesa, to find a woman who loves them. No matter how much I try, no matter how much they try to love me, I need something they can't give. All my life I've looked for it and I don't even know what it is." She swallowed. "Now I've found it. It's in Sevtar, in his mind somehow, in his heart."

"I'm sorry. But it's impossible."

"What if I gave you a trade equal to the Second Levels?"

"You don't have anything worth two Second Levels."

"I do." Savina took a breath. "The Wardship of the Miesa Plateau."

In the stillness that followed the words, a rush of images jumbled in Henta's mind: Bahvla victorious over mighty Karn and Varz, Bahvla alive with new vigor, Bahvla flushed with the power and wealth of the Plateau.

Then the images faded, replaced by memories of her friendship with Savina. "I can't let you cripple Miesa."

Savina grimaced. "I'd rather you had the Plateau than Karn or Varz. Your Estate has the assets and experience to manage it, so they won't have grounds anymore to take it. And Henta—I'll have a Fourth Level who's a true genius."

"He doesn't want to be your Akasi."

"What if he does?"

What then? Henta blew out a gust of air. "If *Sevtar* asks to go to Miesa, then—and only then—will I consider the trade."

Kelric spent the morning wandering through the fortress, thinking about Rashiva's son. His son. He tried to stop brooding. He wished he could forget Rashiva had ever existed.

Eventually he returned to his room and sat on the bed. He built a Quis structure of the fortress, then transferred its layers onto the quilt and studied the architecture. He became so absorbed in the patterns he barely noticed when day faded into night. This castle had stories buried in the arch of its flying buttresses, the placement of its crenellations, the sweep of its staircases. It told him about the ancient queen who ruled from this keep, an atavistic warrior who bequeathed to her descendants a ferocity that still lurked beneath the civilized façade of the Modern Age.

"I've never seen structures like that," Savina said.

With a start, Kelric looked up to see her in the doorway. "How long have you been there?"

"A few minutes. You were concentrating so hard, I didn't want to disturb you."

"Did you talk to Henta?"

Savina walked to the bed. "My plan backfired." She winced. "I'm lucky Henta didn't throw me in jail. She said absolutely no visitation. If you aren't back in Bahvla by morning she will call a Tribunal against me."

Her news punctured the sense of well-being he had built

while playing Quis. She had breached the battlements guarding his heart and now she came to tell him it was all a mistake, that she had no way to follow through on her promises of love.

No. He didn't care. He wouldn't be hurt again. "When do we leave?"

"Sevtar—"

"What?"

"You aren't sorry it turned out this way?"

He gathered up his dice. "I didn't ask you to drag me up here."

"But last night—I thought—"

"Are you going to take me back or not?"

"You were so warm last night. Now you're like stone."

Stone never cries, he thought. "Why did you bother with a kidnapping? Why not just buy me from Henta? That's the way it's done with Calani, isn't it?"

She paled. "Don't say that."

Kelric knew if he stayed any longer his painfully built defenses would collapse. Ignoring Savina, he got off the bed and strode out of the room, into the night-black corridor. Debris rattled at his feet.

His only warning, as he stalked down the hall, was the groan of cracking stone—and then the floor collapsed. He hurtled downward with a shower of debris and dust, landing on a pile of rubble. He wasn't sure if a rock hit his temple or if he hit his head, but he felt blood run down his face, tasted it on his lip. He lurched to his feet and took off again, limping through the dark ruins.

Several times he heard Savina calling his name. He evaded her voice as he would evade an enemy soldier, until the calls faded in the distance.

It was the air, or lack of it, that finally forced him to stop. The atmosphere was too thin. In a room where wind whistled through broken walls, he sagged against a pile of rubble and slid to the floor, hugging his knees to his chest as he heaved in labored breaths.

A furry body scuttled across his feet. Outside the castle a prowler howled.

Sometime later more rustles came from across the room.

Whatever approached loomed much larger than the previous rodent. Kelric tensed, preparing to defend himself.

The prowler spoke. "Sevtar?" She sounded exhausted. "Are you here?"

She had called him stone. He would be stone.

Savina materialized out of the darkness. "Thank the winds." She knelt next to him. "I was afraid you were lost."

Stone . . .

"Sevtar—what you said about buying Calani—it isn't that way. It isn't."

He swallowed.

"Don't hate me," she said.

"Hate you?" It was impossible.

"I asked Henta if I could bring you to my Calanya. As my Akasi."

"For what price?"

"Your agreement."

"Just my agreement?"

She paused. "Also a settlement between Bahvla and Miesa."

"I'm not for sale."

Her eyes glistened in the starlight trickling through the ruined ceiling. "I would give all of Coba for you. If it took the stars I would pull them out of the sky. Is that so wrong?"

"To be only one of many—I can't love that way."

"You wouldn't be one of many." A tear ran down her cheek. "To bring you to Miesa would mean giving up my other Akasi."

"You would turn from them for me?"

"Yes."

Kelric felt his defenses crumbling. When Savina put her arms around him, he laid his head against hers. As she stroked his hair, her hand slid over the gash in his temple.

"You're hurt," she said.

"It's just a little cut."

"This is no little cut." She stood up. "I'll be right back." Then she disappeared into the shadows.

Kelric waited, too tired and too winded by the thin air to follow her. His shoulders felt cold without her arms.

She reappeared. "There's a place where you can lie down in the next room. I'll go upstairs and get the med supplies."

"I'm fine."

Her voice softened. "I know. But humor me."

She took him through the ruins to a bedroom with starlight and chill mountain air pouring through its collapsed roof. Sitting him down on the bed, she said, "I'll be back as soon as I can."

After she left, he lay on his back. Soon after he closed his eyes, he felt her cleaning the gash on his head.

"Full circle," he mumbled.

"Sevtar? You are awake?"

He looked up at her. "I must have made a full circle through the fortress."

"Why do you say that?"

"Aren't we under my room?"

"We're on the other side of the Estate."

"But you just left."

She started bandaging his wound. "It only seems that way because you fainted."

"Jagernauts don't faint."

"What do they do?"

"Pass out."

Savina smiled. "Then you passed out."

She finished with the bandage. Then she stretched out next to him, her hair spilling over his body. Kelric put his arms around her and they lay together in the predawn dimness. She smelled of soap and a musky Savina fragrance that needed no help from any perfume.

Pressing against him, she rubbed his chest, banishing the chill in the air. She kissed his Adam's apple, then his chest, then his stomach. Then she undid the laces on his pants and went lower. Kelric lay with his eyes closed, savoring the feel of her lips on him and her silken hair brushing his thighs.

Eventually she eased off his clothes. He sat up and pulled her close, between his legs, his erection rubbing the velvet cloth of her blouse. As he undressed her, he stroked her body. Even with his large grip he couldn't hold all of her breast, but when he put his hands around her waist his fingers met on her back. The curling hair below her belly was softer than he expected, and as gold as the curls that floated around her face. Her face was even more beautiful in the predawn light.

He touched her cheek. "How can you look so angelic and be so devilish?"

Savina laughed softly. "I'm incorrigible." She didn't sound incorrigible, though. She had a voice like dark honey.

When she nudged him down on his back, he pulled her with him. Rolling over on top of her, he watched her face, trying to gauge her reaction.

She looked up at him. "What's wrong?"

"You don't mind this?"

"Why would I mind it?"

He thought of Deha and Rashiva. "I'm holding you down, on top of you. Isn't that taboo here?"

Savina sighed. "So many rules. Women do this, men do that. I don't care." She pulled him down and kissed his ear. "I just want to feel you inside."

So he nudged apart her thighs and accommodated her wishes. She molded to him as if they were two parts designed to fit together. They made love in the rosy dawn filtering through the ruins, teasing each other almost to a peak and then pulling back at the last minute, again and again, in a tantalizing play of love.

When the crest finally pulled them over the top, he wasn't sure if the orgasm he felt was his, or both of theirs together, for in those few moments their minds merged.

Savina brought the rider down onto the Bahvla airfield in the day's blazing light. Guards were running across the tarmac. She tried not to look at the copilot's seat where Sevtar sat staring out the window. He had given her no sign, no hope he would come to Miesa. He hadn't even spoken.

What had possessed her to make love to him? It was like torture, to have him for one morning and then lose him forever.

Then they were down on the airfield, with ranks of guards converging on the rider.

Sevtar suddenly turned to her. "Yes."

She almost jumped. "Yes?"

"Yes. I want to go to Miesa."

The hatch burst open and guards erupted into the rider. As

they dragged Savina out of the cabin, she looked back at Sevtar—and his smile blazed like the dawn.

Sun poured through the large window behind the desk. Savina squinted into the glare, barely able to distinguish the woman sitting there.

"Ten million denai," Avtac Varz said. "You ask a lot."

"I can raise a part of it," Savina said.

"How much?"

It unnerved Savina to talk to someone she could barely see. "Maybe one million."

"One million." Avtac leaned back in her chair. "And you think my Estate has nine million just lying around for you?"

Savina twisted the edges of her belt. "There must be an arrangement we can make."

"All for this Calani." Avtac shook her head. "Savina, you are a perfect example of how too much time with Akasi weakens the mind." She shifted a paper on her desk. "Why should I lend you more denai? Your Estate already owes mine so much it will be years before I see it again. If ever."

Savina stiffened. "I'll repay every tekal I owe you."

"So you claim. Yet your debts grow larger every year."

"Avtac, you're the only one I can turn to. Name whatever terms you want."

The Varz Manager picked up the paper lying on her desk. She glanced over it while Savina shifted her feet. "An arrangement may be possible. There is, however, the matter of collateral, now that the Wardship is no longer available."

"Anything you want," Savina said.

Avtac looked up at her. "Your Estate."

"What?"

"Your Estate and the city of Miesa."

Savina stared at her. "I can't agree to that."

"Very well." Avtac set the paper on her desk and folded her hands. "The matter is closed."

"There must be something else—"

"I said, the matter is closed."

"No. Wait." Savina went closer to the desk so she could see

Avtac better. "If I agree to your terms, how will they bind to my successors?"

"Your successors?" Avtac snorted. "And when will the loan be repaid? In a millennium? No. The term of the loan is your term as Manager. If at the time of your death the debt remains outstanding, Miesa becomes part of Varz."

"I can't gamble with an entire Estate and city."

"You are a young woman. You have decades to repay the debt."

Decades. Savina's thoughts circled around the proposal. A lifetime was a long time.

But. Her Estate already tottered on the rim of disaster. If she agreed to Avtac's terms, she put the literal existence of Miesa in jeopardy.

But. Miesa would have a Fourth Level. A brilliant Fourth Level, one unmatched anywhere among the Twelve Estates.

She took a breath. "I accept your terms."

Avtac slid the paper across the table. "Sign on the line under my name."

The Morning Hall sparkled like the interior of a lightbeam. Sunshine scintillated through the crystal dome, glistening on the Miesa dignitaries seated around the glimmering dais in the center of the Hall. Kelric felt their anticipation as he stepped with Yevris into the Circle of the Calanya. He saw Henta Bahvla with her retinue in a position of honor among the dignitaries. When he nodded, she smiled, the lines around her eyes crinkling in that way he had always liked.

Pipe music danced into the air. Three girls sat on the dais steps playing a set of reeds, their melody sparkling like sunshine.

A door opened at the end of the Hall and Savina entered, dressed in a long yellow robe that fluttered around her body. She walked to where Kelric waited in the Circle and looked up at him with mischief. "This is where I tell you, with great pomp and ceremony, to enter the Circle. Except you're already in it."

He grinned. "Your Miesa thugs brought me here."

Her laugh glistened. "I will tell my aides you called them thugs."

As he reached across the rail to take her into his arms, Yevris grabbed him. "For wind's sake," the Second Level said in a low voice. "Not here."

Savina smiled at them. Then she walked to a table on the dais and stood there with her Senior Aide. She spoke—and her voice resonated, deep and full, carrying to every edge of the Hall. "Sevtar Bahvla, you come today to the Circle of Miesa."

The power of her voice stunned Kelric. Suddenly she was no longer a tousled-haired imp, but the Manager of an ancient and once-powerful Estate.

"Is there one here who stands as Oath brother to Sevtar?" she asked.

"I stand for him," Yevris said.

"What are your words?"

"I have been honored to know Sevtar," he said. "There are none other like him. If you look at stars in our sky, you will see a hint of him. He is dreams and light, the glory of dawn's first fire, and he will honor your Calanya."

Kelric blinked. Poetry, from Yevris? The Second Level grinned at him.

Savina's Senior Aide spoke. "Your words are heard and recorded, Yevris of Bahvla."

Quietly Savina added, "And Miesa is honored by the Speech of a Bahvla Calani."

Yevris bowed, then stepped out of the Circle and left the dais.

In the luminous light of the Morning Hall, Savina gave Kelric the Oath, and for the first time the words had meaning to him. With the ceremony came a sense of closure. On a world that had saved his life and then taken his freedom, he had unexpectedly found, in Savina and the Quis, the dreams denied him as a Jagernaut. Savina had nearly crippled her Estate to bring him to Miesa, an enormous gamble with sobering stakes. But Kelric saw what others missed, that her beauty and unimposing manner masked a dynamic intellect. All Coba underestimated Miesa's Manager.

It baffled Kelric that Coba's people, even its powerful

queens, understood so little of the Quis. But he saw. With the knowledge of four Estates, from both sides of the political hierarchy in the Twelve Estates, he would handle the dice as never before. The challenge exhilarated him. Together he and the woman he loved would reshape the future of Miesa.

When the Oath was done, she came to the Circle. Looking up at him, she said, "The bands I offer you are those of an Akasi. Will you accept?"

He smiled. "Yes."

She slipped the circlets on his arms, making them the fourth pair he wore. "Sevtar Dahl Haka Bahvla Miesa, you are now a Fourth Level Calani of Miesa."

This time when Kelric reached across the rail, no Yevris was there to stop him. He held Savina, her lips meeting his as he bent his head. Ignoring the shocked murmurs in the Hall, they embraced, bathed in the streaming sunlight of a new beginning.

BOOK TWO

Years 971–976 of the Modern Age

IV

Miesa

26

Endgame

Lightning stabbed the thunderclouds with brilliance. The night closed around again and thunder came with it, booming through the windrider. Neither person in the small cabin spoke as the pilot fought her grim battle with the storm.

The woman in the copilot's seat gripped the armrests. *I refuse to die*, Jahlt Karn thought. *There is too much I have yet to do with my life.*

The Elders of an Estate sat high in its hierarchy of power. As the senior advisers to the Manager, they followed only the Estate Successor and Senior Aide in rank. Highest of all the Elders on Coba were the Seven of Karn.

They found the woman they sought in an alcove. She stood with her back to them looking out over the city, her fiery hair held in a thick braid that fell down her back to her waist. At twenty-six years of age she already carried an aura of authority, a self-assurance that hinted at future greatness.

Elder Solan, First among the Seven, spoke. "Ixpar."

The woman turned, her face lighting with welcome. "My greetings." She looked at the array of Elders. "Is Jahlt back from Shazorla already?"

Solan went to stand with her in the afternoon's waning light. "Jahlt will not be returning."

Ixpar smiled. "So she decided to stay for that wine festival after all, heh?"

"No." It seemed to Solan that someone far away spoke with her voice. "She left Shazorla this morning."

Ixpar's smile faded. "I don't understand."

"There was a storm. They had no warning."

Ixpar froze. "And?"

"The rider crashed in the mountains." Solan stopped, deserted by the words she needed. Outside the window a small althawk glided by, its shadow wheeling across the alcove.

"Solan," Ixpar said. "Go on."

"A Viasa logging crew found their remains this morning."

"No." Ixpar stared at her. "It can't be."

The Elder shook her head. She knew nothing else to say. The shock went too deep.

Ixpar turned away, looking out at the city. For a long time she stood motionless. Finally she spoke. "A funeral must be arranged." She turned to face the Elders. "All of Coba will know how we honor the memory of Jahlt Karn."

Solan bowed and spoke words she had not thought she would say to this woman for many years yet. "As you wish, Minister Karn, so we shall do."

27

Alchemist's Gamble

"I can't tell you," Savina said. "Then it wouldn't be a surprise."

After seven years of living with Savina, Kelric had given up trying to outguess her. "So where is this mystery hidden?"

She pulled him through her suite and into a study she used for storage. The boxes and old furniture had vanished. Fresh paint brightened the walls, shading from sun-yellow at the floor into white at the top. A sun peeked out from behind puffs of cloud on the ceiling and a rainbow arched across one wall. Lacy curtains billowed about the windows, revealing glimpses of the mountains.

Kelric looked around the room. "If this is for me, it, uh, well, it isn't a paint job I would have chosen."

Savina laughed. "It isn't for you, dummy. It's for the surprise."

"Dummy?" Kelric pinned her against the wall and kissed her nose. "Don't you call me dummy."

She dimpled. "Have you figured out the surprise?"

"You found a ton of paint and threw it at the walls."

"No. This surprise we both made."

He brushed his lips over her hair. "I don't remember making anything."

"We made love. Then the surprise came."

He stopped kissing her. "You're *pregnant*?"

"Surprise."

"Are you sure?" It was too much to believe. They had been trying for seven years to have a child.

"Positive, certain—*heh,* what are you doing?" Savina laughed as he swung her around in a circle. "What would you like? A girl or a boy?"

He set her on her feet. "Either. Any. Both."

"Twins. A little you and a little me in the Cooperative."

Cooperative. It hit him like cold water. "If she goes to live in the Cooperative, how will I see her?"

Savina sighed. "It is the difficulty for Calani, yes? But she can visit the Calanya."

"It's not the same. I lived with my parents when I was a boy."

"To isolate her from the other children—it is not our way. What do we say when she asks why she is being kept apart?"

Kelric absorbed the words. His child was Coban. She would probably see separation from the other children as a punishment. Unlike other Coban parents, however, he couldn't choose to live in the Cooperative.

"She can stay here for the first few years," Savina said. "When she does leave we will work it out. You will see her as much as you want. I promise."

"Even so." Many adults he didn't know were going to have a hand in bringing up his child. "I want to see the Cooperative, the grounds, the guardians, the tutors, all of it."

She looked as if he had just asked her to eat Quis dice. "Visit the Cooperative?"

"Yes."

"It would be an anomalous thing for a Calani to do."

He smiled. "I'm an anomalous Calani."

"I had better send an aide to warn them. Our visit will create a stir."

By Midday they were ready to leave. As they walked through the city, the wind fanned his Calanya robe out behind him. He had brought the Talha scarf he still sometimes wore, but he let it hang around his neck, enjoying the crisp breezes on his face.

I have an update, Bolt thought.

What's up? Kelric asked.

Nanomed series J just reached critical population. It is no longer in danger of becoming extinct.

Good work, Kelric thought. It had taken seven years to reestablish the series, but Bolt had done it. He glanced at Savina, watching the wind play with her curls. Since coming to Miesa, he had gradually been healing over the years, his depleted meds given a chance to renew by his improved lifestyle, which demanded less of their services. The same was true for his biomech web and Kyle senses. The gentle touch of Savina's mind was a balm bringing him health. He had no doubt that a scientific reason existed for her effect on him, a combination of the positive influences happiness was known to have on health and sympathetic resonances between his neural activity and hers. But he didn't care about reasons. All he knew was that he loved her.

An octet accompanied them on their walk; Savina obeyed to the letter the condition of his pardon, taking no chances that she would lose him back to prison. Miesa's citizens fell silent when he passed and children stopped their games to stare. Each person he looked at bowed to him.

"The city will hum with news tonight," Savina said as they crossed a plaza. "People will say, 'I *saw* him. The Fourth Level!' They will remember it for the rest of their lives."

"Not much to remember," he said.

She smiled. "To you, maybe not. To everyone else, it is."

The Cooperative was a circle of whitewashed houses facing on a courtyard. The cluster of women and men waiting for them in the yard looked like a handful of sky brought to the ground; all wore white shirts and blue vests, with darker trousers tucked into sky-blue boots.

A statuesque woman with a braid of auburn hair came forward. "My greetings, Manager Miesa."

"It's good to see you, Jasina." Savina presented the woman to Kelric. "This is Jasina, Senior Guardian of the Children's House." She indicated the others. "And her staff."

They all bowed deeply to him. Jasina said, "You do us great honor with your presence."

Kelric nodded, silent.

They visited the parks first. Toys clustered everywhere: sculpted boulders, giant Quis structures to climb on, huts tucked away in the trees. As they walked along the shore of a lake, Jasina indicated a large building across the water, hidden among trees, a house with a peaked roof and blue shutters. "That's the Parents' House. Parents may choose to live there, in a suite in the Cooperative, or in a Common House in the city." She spoke to Savina, respecting the custom that set Calani apart, but Kelric knew her words were meant for him. Savina needed no introduction to the Miesa Cooperative. She had lived in it.

"Parents who stay in the city are still expected to visit the Cooperative at least twice a day," Jasina said, "for their children and for their work detail." She glanced at Kelric. "Except for Calani, of course."

He wondered what she would think if she knew how much he wanted to forgo that exception.

The Children's House was a low building with many windows and playrooms, designed on the same plan as a Calanya, with suites arranged around common rooms. The younger children lived in skyrooms or sunrooms, but the older ones decorated their rooms themselves, with a wide range of styles, particularly for the teenagers. Although the Cooperative was large enough so every child could have a private suite, many chose to share with friends or kin. Interspersed with the children's rooms were suites occupied by parents or Cooperative guardians.

In a playroom filled with toddlers and sunshine, Jasina

paused to describe how the children were supervised. A boy toddled over and peered up at Kelric. After considering the matter in great depth, he sat next to Kelric's foot and proceeded to unload dice from his toy cart onto Kelric's shoe.

Jasina's face blazed red. When she reached for the child, Kelric touched her shoulder and the guardian straightened up with a snap, as if his touch had sent a shock through her body.

Kelric picked up the boy himself, feeling awkward, worried that his huge grasp might frighten the toddler. The child nestled comfortably in his arms. "Lani?" the boy asked.

Savina spoke gently to the boy. "Yes. Calani."

He wiggled in Kelric's arms. "Dow."

Smiling, Kelric set him on the ground. The boy reloaded his cart, companionably patted Kelric's shoe, and then ambled away, pulling his cart behind him.

A spurt of angry voices erupted in the hall. Two teenage girls stalked into the room, their clothes muddied and their hair disheveled. The bigger one waved her fists at the smaller one. "I *saw* you change that dice stru—"

"Call me a cheater again," the second girl yelled, "and I'll—ai!" Her mouth dropped open as she saw Kelric. Both girls gaped until Jasina cleared her throat. Then the brawlers remembered themselves and bowed, bumping into each other in the process.

Savina's mouth twitched upward. "Our greetings."

The duo stammered in unison. "We are honored, Manager Miesa."

Jasina spoke. "Perhaps you two can settle your quarrels in a more civilized manner than using your fists?"

"Yhee, ma'am," they answered.

Kelric grinned at Savina. As Jasina ushered the girls to the door, he spoke to the Manager in a low voice. "Do they remind you of someone?"

She glared at him. "I never got into fights."

Jasina came back over. "Would you like to finish the tour privately, Manager Miesa?"

At first the question puzzled Kelric. Then he realized Jasina was offering to withdraw so he and Savina could talk if they wished.

Savina nodded. "My thanks, Jasina. We appreciate the time you gave us."

· "It is our pleasure, ma'am."

So Savina took Kelric on her own tour, his guards walking far enough away so he could converse with her. They strolled through the sunlight that slanted through the windows, talking about their childhoods. Eventually they came to a foyer where a youth sat reading a book.

He looked up. "Manager Miesa. We've been expecting you." He opened a door in the inner wall of the foyer. "She's in the dayroom."

The room beyond was filled with plants and sun. An old woman sat by the window, dozing in a wicker chair. Savina bent down and kissed the woman's cheek. "My greetings, Nonni."

Nonni opened her eyes, blinking. "Little Vina?"

"I brought Sevtar to see you." Savina smiled at Kelric. "Nonni was my nurse when I lived here."

The wrinkles around Nonni's eyes crinkled as she looked up at him. "Such a big fellow." She peered at Savina, then Kelric. "You have to watch that one," she told him. "Wild clawcat, she was. Always getting into fights."

Savina turned red. "Winds above."

"You keep her behaved," the nurse told Kelric.

Kelric smiled. "I'll do my best."

The nurse's eyes widened. "He spoke to me, Vina."

"I heard," Savina said.

Nonni patted his hand. "A Fourth Level at Miesa. There hasn't been one for over a century." She nodded her head. "The last would have been Mevryn Miesa. He died before I was born."

They stayed with Nonni until the sun dipped behind the roofs outside the window. When they finally headed back to the Estate, evening had brought a chill down from the mountains. People thronged the streets as day shifts came home and night crews left for work. Kelric didn't know if it was the cold or the crowds that bothered him, but he felt ill at ease until he fastened his robe and wound the scarf around his head. So they passed through Miesa, a shield of guards around a tall figure hidden in robe and Talha.

At the Estate, an aide hurried out to give Savina a letter. "A rider came in with this, ma'am. The pilot said it was urgent."

Savina waited until she and Kelric were in the privacy of her suite before she read the scroll. When she finished, she went to a window and stared out at Miesa, her brightness muted, her smile gone.

"What is it?" Kelric asked.

She turned to him. "Jahlt Karn is dead."

Rashiva Haka sat on the carpet in her suite, playing Quis with Jimorla, her seven-year-old son. The Akasi Raaj lay next to them, studying the dice. When Raaj set a truncated cone into one structure, Jimorla looked up in bafflement, blinking his violet eyes. Rashiva smiled and kissed his forehead, evoking an embarrassed blush from the boy, and Raaj tousled his hair.

A knock sounded on the door.

Rashiva sighed. Not now. She treasured these moments with her family. But as Manager, she had no choice. She went to the door.

A guard waited Outside. "I'm sorry to disturb you, ma'am. But this came in by rider." She handed Rashiva an envelope. "The messenger said it was urgent."

"Very well." Rashiva nodded to her. "You may go."

After the guard left, Rashiva read the letter. Then she exhaled, her hand dropping by her side.

Raaj came over to her. "What's wrong?"

"Jahlt Karn." Quietly she said, "She's dead."

Avtac Varz despised her seasonal tour of the research facility. Boring people, messy labs. *They waste my funds,* she thought. *If they don't produce results soon I will put them on maintenance crews.*

Today she visited the chemists. When her retinue arrived, Avtac saw Iva and her assistant Senti leaning over some contraption on a table. Avtac stopped in the entrance, regarding the room with distaste. Bottles crammed the shelves. A hood overhung a ledge along one wall and air hissed from a hose by the sink.

When Avtac's aide knocked on the door, Iva looked up. "Manager Varz." She hurried over. "My greetings, ma'am."

"I understand you have a demonstration for me," Avtac said.

"That I do. I'm working on a synthesis. We've just set up the distillation." Iva handed her a pair of safety glasses and ushered her over to the contraption. Avtac listened while the chemist explained her work. It sounded like she was just boiling dirty water. Games. All games. Useless. She should put them both on maintenance.

Mercifully, the demonstration soon ended. With relief, Avtac took her leave of the chemist and her dull assistant.

"Thank Khozaar that's over with." Senti settled onto a stool by the distillation apparatus. "We won't have to see that old pod-bag for another season."

"Senti," Iva admonished.

"Do you want me to keep labeling these bottles?"

"Yes." Iva frowned as oil sputtered in the pan on a hot plate under the distillation apparatus. A clamp held a round flask partially suspended in the oil.

"Where is the thermometer?" Iva asked. "This oil bath looks too hot."

Senti glanced up, a bottle of white crystals in one hand and a label in the other. "It's on your desk." She held up the bottle. "What's this?"

"Potassium nitrate." Iva turned down the hot plate, then went over to her desk. "There's no thermometer here."

"It's on the shel—ai!"

A crash punctuated Senti's cry and Iva looked in time to see the nitrate bottle Senti had dropped smash into a bottle of sulphur on the lab table. Brilliant yellow powder flew across the nitrate while the broken bottles spun in circles. As Iva ran across the room, squeezing between the lab benches, one bottle crashed into the hot plate and knocked over the pan, sending hot oil flying over the mess.

"Senti," Iva shouted. *"Get away from there."*

Flames erupted in the oil, tongues of fire that ate away the supports of a shelf above the table. An edge of the shelf slipped and bottles of charcoal absorbent toppled, raining dark powder everywhere. Just as Iva reached Senti, the entire shelf collapsed, slamming into the fiery chaos, confining it under pressure—and the table exploded with a force that hurtled them into the wall.

Zecha Varz, Captain of the Varz Hunters, found Avtac taking a glass of jai rum in the library. The Manager was reading, as she often did in the evening. The text surprised Zecha. Chemistry? The subject bored Avtac stiff. All it seemed good for was causing lab accidents. Iva and her assistant were lucky they survived that explosion with treatable injuries. Now here was Avtac, reading about potassium nitrate, of all things.

Avtac glanced up at her. "Yes?"

Zecha handed her the letter. "This came in by rider."

After Avtac read the scroll, she leaned back in her chair, a thoughtful expression on her angular face. "So. Untried youth replaces experience."

"Untried youth?" Zecha asked.

Avtac smiled. "Jahlt Karn is dead."

28

The Column of Time

Torch in hand, Elder Solan led Ixpar through the maze of catacombs beneath Karn, until they reached a dead end where engravings covered the stone wall. Solan pressed the engravings in a complex pattern and the clink of cold stone tapping stone answered her. When she leaned her weight into the wall, a tall block slid inward and scraped to the side, revealing a cubical chamber that brought to mind a hollow Quis die.

The Elder turned to Ixpar. "Jahlt told me about this room as a precaution." She paused. "In case anything happened before she brought you here herself."

Ixpar nodded, trying to keep her face composed. For two tendays now, since Jahlt's death, she had held on to her grief, afraid that if she let go, its immensity would overwhelm her. She lifted her torch, peering into the cubicle. "What is it?"

"All I know is this: Jahlt taught you a rhyme when you were a child, one about a hawk—I don't know the words. Do you remember it?"

"I think so."

"Then you know how to open the door." Solan bowed and then left, her robes whispering as she disappeared into the catacombs.

Ixpar walked into the cube. Directly across from her, a portal of old iron stood embedded in the far wall, like an ancient sentinel. Feeling rather foolish, she went to the portal and said the nursery rhyme:

> *From desert to peak,*
> *The great hawk did fly,*
> *For came he to seek*
> *A war queen on high.*

Not surprisingly, nothing happened. She peered at the door. Although engravings covered it, none showed a desert, peak, hawk, or anything vaguely resembling a war queen.

From desert to peak. What did it mean? Haka to Varz? Haka hadn't existed when these catacombs were built. From Kej to Varz, then. So. Why would a hawk seek a war queen? Presumably because of the bond that formed between bird and human. *On high* probably referred to warriors riding hawks through the skies.

Ixpar studied the engravings. Squares. Circles. Lines. A dot above a circle, two slashes over a rectangle. The marks were *accents*, symbols from the ancient language Ucatan, sometimes called Tozil, which predated even Old Script. Originally Ucatan had been purely hieroglyphic, but over the centuries the glyphs had become stylized, breaking into two parts, a

Quis shape and an accent. Jahlt had insisted she learn Ucatan even though almost no writings survived in it.

Dot. It meant blue. Slash indicated higher dimension. Dot and slash over circle could be the lapis lazuli ring of a seeker. The engravings were Quis patterns, cruder than modern glyphs but readable. She saw the topaz octahedron of Kej and the obsidian of Varz. From Kej to Varz. The room itself, the oversized cube, symbolized the word *great*. It was all there, the entire rhyme depicted in Quis symbols.

Except nothing denoted a war queen. Maybe the portal was the final symbol, standing to protect whatever lay beyond. Ixpar pressed the engravings, using the pattern outlined by the rhyme. A series of clicks rewarded her efforts, but when she pushed the door nothing happened.

She studied the symbols. One looked like a forest, another like a mountain. Or a mountain cat—

Clawcat. Of course. The ancient warriors fought with the ferocity of those huge mountain beasts. She pressed the cat pattern and heard the clink of stone hitting metal. This time the portal slid inward under her push, with a grating protest, and then creaked to the side. As a gust of stale air assaulted her nose, she walked into a round room.

Ixpar looked around. The curved walls were made from white marble veined with black, and black and white tiles shaped like diamonds covered the floor. Had Jahlt left a message here for her? The thought made her eyes burn with unshed tears. If only she could have said good-bye to Jahlt, perhaps her grief would be bearable.

She searched the room but found no hidden niches or other exits. Finally she sat cross-legged on the floor and rested her chin on her hand, trying to fathom the purpose of a room made like a hollow cylinder. Cylinder on flat tiles; it was a Quis structure for the passage of time, the past portrayed by the flat base and time's passing by a column reaching up to the future.

Ixpar looked up.

Far above her head the ceiling vaulted to a point. Black and white tiles shaped like althawks were inlaid in it, with a gray hawk in the apex. The tiles made interlocking circles around the center; as she looked away from the apex she saw widening circles of smaller and smaller hawks, until at the edge where the ceiling met the walls the birds were no more than dots.

Hawks. She tried to imagine the ancient architect who built the room. What had hawks meant to her? The future. Travel in the Teotecs was difficult on foot, both now and in the Old Age. Without the giant althawks, the ancient warriors would have been confined to the Estates. Their way of life would have died.

As it did. When the althawks became extinct the wars ended. Peace endured in this era of windriders because centuries of isolation had established Quis as the dominant means of conflict. Before invention of the rider, the Estates had learned to fight with Quis, which could be sent through treacherous mountains far more easily than conventional warfare. It only took one person and a pouch of dice.

She ran her hand over the floor. Why diamonds for the past? Was it their shape? Perhaps it meant the crystal itself, hardest of all substances, enduring for all ages, as the past endured regardless of the future. But why black and white? White, as the mixture of all light, and black, as its absence both ranked high in the color hierarchy of Quis. Entirety and absence. Past and future? Without one, the other had no meaning.

Our ancestral memories live in Quis, Ixpar thought. And Quis is our future. Coba was a dice game, always evolving from what came before. She smiled. Maybe this room was meant to remind Ministers they were just Quis players with a fancy title.

She considered the gray althawk in the ceiling. Gray: a blending of black and white. The present, where the past blended with the future? But if the floor was the past, the walls the passage of time, and the ceiling the future, the present should have been down here, where the floor met the walls.

Ixpar studied the diamonds under her, rubbing her hands over them—

The tile directly below the ceiling's gray hawk moved.

She pushed harder and the tile slid into the floor. Across the room, a clink came from the cube chamber, followed by the grinding noise of old gears. Startled, she jumped to her feet and ran to the door.

Her knee hit its lower edge.

Ixpar tensed. When she had entered this cylinder room, the door had been flush with the ground. Now, while she watched, the floor was sinking away from it.

As Ixpar lifted her foot, intending to climb into the cube room, a grate of stone on stone came from inside that chamber. Then, across the cube from her, the door where she had first entered the chamber crashed shut, leaving a blank wall. Beneath her, the floor of the cylinder room continued to sink.

"Winds *above*." Ixpar dropped her torch and grabbed the bottom edge of the door. The floor dropped out from under her and then she was hanging with her feet dangling in the air.

Now what? If she let go, she would fall into a slick well of marble with unscalable sides. If she climbed into the cube, she was putting herself in a sealed box with smooth walls. What if it didn't open from inside? She saw no air vents in the chamber and Solan was the only one who knew she was here. She could suffocate long before the Elder came looking for her.

Several clicks came from inside the door, followed by the ominous grind of gears. Then, with Ixpar hanging from it, the portal began to swing closed. She braced her legs on the wall, straining to hold the portal open, but she couldn't stop its inexorable motion.

She had to decide what to do—and fast.

With a deep breath, Ixpar let go of the door. She plummeted through the air and hit the floor with a jarring impact. The torch rolled away from her, down the slanted floor of the chute.

Slanted?

A clang vibrated through the tiles and the floor hit bottom, throwing Ixpar forward as if she were a wayward Quis die. Flailing for a handhold, she tumbled down the slanted surface to its lowest point, which had ended up flush with a Minister-sized hole. The torch slid under her body, scorching her back until her weight smothered the flame. She hurtled through the hole and into darkness.

The walls around her drew in closer, slowing her passage, until she feared she would wedge to a stop, neither able to climb up the glassy chute nor continue to its end. Then she shot out over a ledge and flew into space. An instant later she hit bottom, her head banging on stone.

Her last thought was that she had no successor to take her place.

Intent on their dice session, Miesa's nine Calani sat at a table in the main common room. To aid their study on lowering Miesa maintenance costs, Kelric built patterns for other Estates: Bahvla insulation, Haka aqueducts, Dahl oil lamps. Miesa history also molded the patterns, as they searched out flaws in past methods of running the Estate.

The longer they worked, the more the session foundered, until finally Kelric pushed back from the table. The others stirred, looking around, clothes rustling, chair legs scraping the floor.

"I'm a bit tired," Kelric said. When they nodded to him, he left the table and headed for the parks, to think.

When Kelric had first come to Miesa, he had been one of only five Calani. He had expected they would immediately delve into studies on how to improve Miesa's position among the Twelve Estates. Instead, the others sought his advice. It fast became clear why Miesa was in trouble; her Calani had no idea how to play Quis. Awkward with the role of mentor they cast him in, but confident in his dice, he taught them Quis as he knew it, at the highest level he had mastered, from every Estate where he had lived.

Eventually the Calanya had formed a coherent unit with him as its focal point. Then they began to reach out, seeking to act as well as learn. How much difference they had so far made for Miesa, Kelric wasn't sure, but he had noticed a change for the better in the patterns Savina brought back from Outside.

Yet for all that work, he had become more and more aware over the past year that something was hampering their efforts. At first he couldn't define it, but as it grew more prominent it became clear.

The problem was him.

The pad of feet sounded in the hall behind him. He turned to see Hayl, a thirteen-year-old boy who had been in the Calanya for less than a season.

"I was tired too," Hayl said. "Can I walk with you?"

Kelric nodded his assent. It was odd to see the boy without Revi, his constant companion. Revi was huskier than Hayl and five years older, but the two boys were otherwise like brothers, with the gold hair, gray eyes, and angelic looks common among Miesans.

Outside in the parks, rain drizzled from a gray sky, saturating the parks with a hint of wildness. They followed a path overhung by vines that protected them from the weather. It wasn't until a fat drop rolled off a leaf and splattered on his nose that Kelric realized he hadn't even spoken to Hayl.

He looked down at the boy. "How's Revi?"

"He's fine." Hayl took a deep breath. "Sevtar—what is it? What did we do?"

"Do?"

"To make you angry."

"I'm not angry."

"Is it that you dislike us?"

Kelric smiled. "Of course not. Why do you think that?"

"Lately you hardly talk to anyone. And you just walked out on a Quis session." Hayl hesitated. "Revi says it's because we're such a minor Calanya. I know we're not good enough for a Fourth Level, especially one like you, but we're trying."

"Hayl, no. I left the session because I was making a mess of it." Kelric considered the boy. "When you were in the Preparatory House, you studied subjects like Miesa history as well as Quis, yes?"

"Well, yes. Of course. Didn't you do that at Dahl?"

"No. I was never in a Preparatory House."

The boy gaped at him. *"Never?"*

"I taught myself Quis."

"Calanya Quis? I didn't think anyone could do that."

Kelric shrugged. The more he learned, the more he saw how little he knew. Years ago he had thought himself adept with the dice, but now he understood that he had barely begun to learn its potential.

"I'm glad you came to Miesa," Hayl said. "Otherwise I would never have met you." Swirls of admiration came from the boy. "Someday I'm going to play dice like you."

Kelric blinked. "Thank you." He tilted his head. "What made you decide to come here?"

"I never wanted to go anywhere else." Hayl raised his hands as if to say *But what do I know?* "My Quis mentors told me I should try for the big Estates, though, so I asked them to write Varz and Haka. Manager Varz said no. Manager Haka said I was too young, but to write again in a few years."

Kelric could understand why Rashiva thought the boy was too young. Eighteen was generally considered the minimum age for a Calani. "Why did you apply so soon?"

"Revi was ready to leave the House."

"And Savina took you both?"

Hayl nodded. "At first she just bid for my contract. After she met us, she decided to take Revi too. She said Miesa needed more Calani."

Kelric could imagine how the boys affected Savina. She could never have made herself split them up. But Miesa needed experienced players. Although Revi was competent and someday Hayl would be brilliant, at the moment neither were first-class players. Nor could they supply what the Miesa Calanya sorely lacked, knowledge of other Estates. With the exception of himself, every Calani here was First Level.

Kelric returned with Hayl to the common room, but instead of resuming the Quis session, he went over and heaved open the Outside doors. The Calanya escort sat Outside, playing Quis.

Captain Lesi looked up at him. "Do you want the Speaker?"

Kelric shook his head.

"Manager Miesa?" she asked.

He nodded.

Lesi got on the com to Savina, after which the escort took him up to her office. As soon as the guards left, Savina grasped his hands. "What's wrong? Lesi said you were upset."

"Not upset. Worried. I'm damaging your Estate."

"Winds, Sevtar, why do you say that? Don't you see the effect you're having?" She let go of his hands and spread her arms as if to encompass Coba. "Word spreads when the Quis of an Estate gains power. For the first time in decades skilled guildspeople are coming *to* Miesa instead of leaving. Merchants, weavers, metalworkers, all new in the city, first a trickle, now a steady flow." She radiated enthusiasm. "And Sevtar—I'm holding my own in Council now. Next year I'll dice those clawcats into corners. You and I—together we can do anything."

He couldn't help but smile. "If I were Coba, I would melt at your feet. But I doubt my Quis can have the effect you want. I lack too many of the basic tools other Calani get as children."

Her face gentled. "One tends to forget, when faced with your gift, that you haven't studied Calanya Quis all your life."

"I should go to the Preparatory House."

That stopped her cold. "What?"

He paced across the office, gesturing with his hands to accent his points. "More and more lately I've felt the lacks in my education. Any one of your First Levels could give you a far better picture of your Estate's history, character, and culture. I *need* that education." He came to a stop and turned to face her. "I have to go to the Preparatory House."

"A grown man? A *Fourth* Level?" She laughed. "If I sent you there, my Senior Aide would commit me to the setting-sun-asylum for the mentally diminished."

"Savina, I'm serious. My Quis dominates the Calanya, which means my deficiencies do as well. It didn't matter for the first few years because we had so much catching up to do. But we're ready for more sophisticated work now and I'm holding it back."

She considered him as if she were shifting his words back and forth in her mind. Finally she said, "I could bring mentors and teachers from the Preparatory House here to the Estate. For you."

He liked her solution better than his. It would save him a lot of embarrassment. "Yes. That would be good."

"So." She nodded to him. "Your Quis will become all the more formidable."

Ixpar awoke in darkness. When she moved, pain flared in her shoulder. She pushed onto her knees, trying to figure out where in a dice cheater's hell she had landed. She found the torch, but had no flint to light it. Further exploration revealed she was trapped in a round cavity. By standing and stretching up her arms, she could just reach into the chute above her head. Its edges and walls were like glass, unclimbable.

She was running her fingers along the wall at waist height when she touched an engraving. She spelled out the Ucatan glyphs by touch: *So to Karn comes the ward of lives.*

Ixpar scratched her chin. So to Karn comes the ward of lives: it was the oath that appeared on the Ministry seal. Just as a Manager swore to protect her Calanya, so the Minister swore to protect her people. She ran her fingers over the script again. Then she stopped and felt more carefully. It wasn't the Ministry Oath, at least not as she knew it. This read: *To you, Karn, comes the ward of lives.*

To *you?* Historians believed the name Karn derived from *carn-abi* in Old Script, which in turn probably derived from the even more ancient Ucatan language, the *chabi* glyph, which meant "to guard, care for, or watch over." Had Karn actually been a person, perhaps a Ucatan warrior who lived many millennia ago, in those shadowed years before the Old Age, a time of darkness and barbarism?

She wondered why the oath appeared in this cavity. Sphere: highest-ranking Quis die, symbol of continuity, the womb where life began, completion. Birth. Then again, death was the completion of life.

However, this wasn't a true sphere. It had a gap. She reached up and examined the opening above her head, this time feeling for any mark rather than just a handhold. At the edge where the cavity met the chute she found a line, hardly more than a scratch. She recognized the pattern from her childhood games in Karn's hidden tunnels. Scraping her fingernails into the line, she pushed its switch.

Old gears rumbled into action and an arc of metal slid out, nudging aside her hand. As she felt along the arc, she realized it was a lid, closing to complete the sphere. She grabbed the metal, intending to pull herself into the chute. Then she paused, straining to keep the lid open. If she hoisted herself out, where would she be after the lid closed? At the bottom of an unclimbable chute. Even if she did manage to make her way to its top, the cylinder was unclimbable. For that matter, its floor might have already risen back to its original position.

Ixpar let go of the lid, and with an ugly clang it hit the opposite side of the chute. The grate of the gears changed pitch, faltered, started again—and stopped. She stood in the darkness, breathing raggedly, waiting for something to happen.

Silence.

"No," Ixpar said. "You can't break down." The darkness felt heavy, claustrophobic. She banged on the lid, hoping to jar it into motion. Next she pounded the walls, methodically covering the entire sphere. Finally she dropped to the ground, knowing that the more she moved, the faster she used up her air.

Jahlt, why did you send me here? she thought. Is this a test I've failed? Or had the test itself failed, its machinery crumbling with the passing of time? Perhaps Jahlt had never meant for her to enter this ancient puzzle.

Suddenly the gears faltered into life again and the sphere rotated like a giant ball bearing, rolling her over in a somersault. When the cavity stopped, its lid had become the floor.

She waited, holding her breath.

When the lid began to retract, she grabbed its edge and lowered herself through the widening hole. She hung in the air, kicking out her legs, trying to find a foothold. Then the lid finished opening, taking away her handhold, and she dropped like a rock through cold darkness.

Ixpar hit a flat surface with a thud that shoved out her breath. As she groaned, the torch clattered down next to her. She climbed to her feet and took an exploratory step, waving her arms in front of her. Another step, another—and her foot hit a barrier. It felt like a table leg. A sweep of her hand across the table sent a small box clattering to the floor. She scrambled after it and her hand closed around a flint.

When Ixpar relit her torch, its dusky light showed her a small room. A row of torches hung along one wall and huge Ixpar shadows flickered on the stone. In the opposite wall, a closed door waited, bands of crumbling metal holding it together. The exit? She went over and opened it.

Then she simply stood, staring.

The room,beyond was as big as the Hall of Teotec. Her first impression was of shadows and *glitter.* As her eyes adjusted to the sight, she managed to absorb what was throwing back the light of her torch in such a multitude of gleams, glints, and flashes.

Boxes inlaid with glistening stones, stacks of vases, bolts of metallic cloth, chains of precious metals; the riches spilled everywhere. Finely tooled shields lined the walls; urns sparkled, heaped full with jewels; gilt chests overflowed with coins. Weapons lay in great stacks: swords, honed discuses, shotputs, jeweled daggers, marble bolos.

For a long time Ixpar simply looked, stunned by the scene's lustrous glory. When she finally walked into the hall, she saw a set of ruby-inlaid Calanya guards on a table by the door. She picked up one of the guards and ran her thumb over the althawk seal engraved on it, above the original Karn Oath, written in Ucatan; *To you, Karn, comes the ward of lives.*

On the table, an ancient parchment penned in Ucatan lay under a pane of modern glass. As Ixpar pieced out the glyphs, a chill ran up her back. It was as if she heard a warrior from before the Old Age, more than two thousand years in the past, an antediluvian queen with an articulate voice in an age when almost no one even knew what "written language" meant, let alone could write:

Mourn not my death, Karn. It is the honor of a warrior to die defending that which is hers. I leave here my legacy. Learn you well from these memories. See our triumphs and our failures.

This I bid you: choose from among our tribe's children she who is ablest, fiercest, most intelligent. Train her to succeed you as I taught you to follow me. As I have done for you, so must you someday leave for her those memories that best tell her what we have been and what we can become. Build our people into more than a wandering tribe that fights for personal gain. Let your battles be for the future, to give those of our blood more than barbarism for their legacy. Bring back the glory of the lost Raylikarns,

> *our Ruby ancestors who descended from the stars on pillars*
> *of fire.*
>   *Make us more than we are.*
>   *This is my dream, Karn. As I must die, I entrust it to you.*

The document was signed Avaza Teotec.

Ixpar swallowed. Avaza Teotec. Her life was lost in the mists of history, but the mightiest mountain range on known Coba bore her name. This parchment was the beginning, the birth of modern civilization, the dream of an ancient chieftain who envisioned far ahead of her time the world that was now Coba.

Ixpar turned over the wrist guard. It wasn't a Karn guard, it was *the* Karn guard; the first, made for the Akasi of a woman named Karn, who founded the first Estate on Coba. *Bring back the glory of the lost Raylikarns, our Ruby ancestors who descended from the stars on pillars of fire.* Incredible that a memory of the Ruby Empire remained alive here, in Karn, after five thousand years.

She wondered at the word *Raylikarns*. Had the name Karn derived not from Ucatan, but from this even older remnant of the Ruby Empire? She felt as if an ancient breeze had blown across her face, whispering secrets long vanished from the rest of Coba.

Near the Calanya guards, she found a box lined with velvet. Two armbands lay inside, engraved with the name Jimorla Karn. Next to them was a plaque with the likeness of a youth etched on it. The inscription read: *In honor of the Akasi Jimorla, freed by the tribe of Karn from the tribe of Kej in the Second Season of the Twelfth Year of the Reign of Karn.*

The Reign of Karn. Now they called it the Old Age. These armbands came from the twelfth year of an age that had lasted 1032 years.

Ixpar walked down the hall, awed by the heaped treasures, a wealth far more than just gold and jewels. Each Minister had left a legacy of her reign: scrolls and dice, texts and documents, the feather of a giant althawk embedded in glass. A Minister Shaba commissioned the construction of a miniature Estate and inscribed the rooms with phrases lauding the beauty of an Akasi named Kozar. Kozar? The mythology of Khozaar, most handsome of all gods, originated in the Old Age. Was this man its origin?

Like Kelric . . .

Stop it, Ixpar told herself. Why did she still think of him after so many years? It truly was an exercise in futility.

History unrolled before her as she continued down the hall. New Estates rose: Kej and Varz, Haka and Miesa, and more. Weapons became rarer and Quis more prominent. More and more scrolls mentioned the dice expertise of a Minister's Akasi. Gradually a new word came into use, the title Calani, given for a previously unheard of position, men in a Calanya who weren't Akasi, but gifted Quis players.

At the end of the room, an arch opened into a second hall. It was there Ixpar found the Oath of Olonton, the original parchment believed lost a thousand years ago. It lay preserved under modern glass, signed by the Managers of every Estate in existence on that First Day of the First Century of the Modern Age. Its message—short, simple, and visionary—set the pattern for modern Coba: *On this day let it be sworn; a new era is born, the Era of Olonton. Of the Heart. The Era of Quis. May bloodshed never again break the Oath we make here today.*

So the wars ended.

As she continued into the next hall, the centuries unrolled before her. Eventually she came to a model of the first windrider. Farther on she found armbands that had belonged to an Akasi of Jahlt's predecessor. Then she saw a document written in Jahlt's own hand; Council proceedings, with the last entry from the previous year. Next to the scroll lay the portrait of a child.

Ixpar picked up the picture. It was a drawing of herself as a child, done years ago by an artist from Shazorla. An inscription on the back read: *In honor of my Successor, Ixpar Karn. Signed, Jahlt Karn, Fifty-third Year of the Tenth Century of the Modern Age.*

Ixpar swallowed, struggling against a hotness in her eyes. She set the picture down by the model of a recording machine. Then she realized the recorder wasn't a model. She pressed its switch—and Jahlt's voice floated into the air:

"If you are listening to this, Ixpar, you must now be Minister. Yours is a unique destiny: to lead our people during the era when we must learn to coexist with those who came to us from the stars.

"In these two halls you will find an aid to that destiny: the Memory of Karn. Beyond the Memory is a chamber with no apparent exit. It is actually the end of an entry designed by an ancient chieftain to test her successor, Karn Teotec. Ministers in the Old Age used the entry to challenge the worthiness of a successor. In the drawer of this stand, you will find diagrams that describe its various rooms. I advise against trying the actual entry; the machinery is ancient and may fail."

So, Ixpar thought. Jahlt had indeed never meant for her to try the entry. These halls must have another entrance, one Jahlt had apparently not yet shown Solan. Or perhaps she had feared to reveal too much, lest Solan guess the existence of the Memory. How long had it been since anyone used the secret entry? Decades? *Centuries?*

Jahlt's voice continued. "Most people think of the Minister as she who makes laws. But two parts exist to our office, Ixpar, and the setting down of law is, to my mind, only our secondary function. We are first the primary builders of the Quis. The wealth of the Memory looks staggering, but its true value lies in its distillation of all that has formed our world. Learn it well. It will give you an understanding of the Quis shared by no other Manager."

Jahlt's voice softened. "If my Akasi Mentar outlives me, please give him the letter I have left in the drawer. When his time comes, I ask you to place his armbands and guards here with a plaque to honor his name."

And then: "You mean as much to me as a daughter, Ixpar. If the pattern of our lives continues after death, my love is with you even now."

Ixpar bent her head, as if that gesture could fend off the upwelling in her eyes. A drop of water fell on the recorder, then another, and another. The tears flowed with gathering force, her long pent-up grief finally given outlet.

After a time she straightened up and wiped her face. Softly she said, "Good-bye, Jahlt. Rest well."

She found the letter for Mentar next to a scroll with diagrams of the secret entry, along with interpretations of the Quis rooms by various Ministers, some similar to her own thoughts on the puzzle. As she replaced the scroll, a sparkle in the drawer caught her attention. She reached for it and pulled out a medallion. When she held it up, it dangled in the torchlight by its gold chain, a platinum triangle with an exploding star inscribed on it. She had seen it once before, the day the Imperialate delegation presented it to Jahlt as a gift.

Ixpar set down the medallion and looked around. At the end of the room she found a door that opened onto a spiral staircase. She climbed the stairs up and around, level after level, until she reached a landing with engravings on its wall. When she pressed in the sequence given by the ancient rhyme, a door opened in the stone.

Ixpar walked out into the private suite of her predecessor.

29

Toppled Queen's Spectrum

Starlight shone through the windows, pouring across Sevtar. Savina lay next to him, tracing a finger along his biceps.

"Hmmm." He stirred. "Thought you were asleep . . ."

"I'm thinking. About our baby. We need a name for her."

He opened his eyes. "How about Roca? It's my mother's name."

"Rohka Miesa." She tilted her head. "It has a good sound."

His eyes closed. "That it does."

"Sevtar?"

"Hmmm?"

"What was she like? Your mother, I mean."

"You look like her. Except she's much taller." He opened his eyes and smiled sleepily at her. "Actually, you look more like the native Lyshrioli girls on my father's world."

"Lyshriol." She rolled the word on her tongue. "A pretty name."

"For a pretty world." Rolling onto his side, he pushed up on his elbow, wide awake now. "I want to take you there."

That threw her like a tossed dice cube. "Take me off Coba?"

"Don't you ever wonder what's beyond your world?"

"It is forbidden to us."

"Not to me. And you are my wife."

She tried to imagine him as a Jagernaut, but the image was too foreign. He was Calani. Akasi.

Yet he had the mark of a warrior. When she touched the faint scar that cut across his shoulder, he said, "It's from a laser carbine."

"Lai Zher? Is that a place?"

"A gun." He paused. "I could have had the scar removed, but doing that seemed false somehow. As if I were hiding the scars inside."

She wished she knew how to soothe away whatever nightmares haunted him. A Calani shouldn't have such memories to darken his life.

Sevtar sat up, pressing his palms against his temples, as he did when his Kyle headaches came. Then he got up and left the room, pulling on his robe as he went. Puzzled, Savina threw on her own robe and followed. She found him standing by a window in her den.

"Sevtar." She went over to him. "What is it?"

"I'm not what you think I am."

"You are the Miesa Fourth." Her voice gentled. "My Akasi."

"You only see what you understand, Savina. The darker side won't go away just because I play Quis now instead of killing."

"That doesn't negate the side I see." Silently she thought, *I wish I knew how to ease your memories.*

He touched her cheek. "You ease them more than you know."

Anthoni Karn strode across the courtyard with Tal Karn, his hair tossing in the autumn wind. It was hard to believe a full season had already passed since the two of them won the coveted apprenticeships to the Ministry staff.

"I've never seen Elder Solan this worried," Tal continued. "Minister Karn missed all of her appointments yesterday. No one can find her." She hurried with Anthoni up the wide steps of the Estate. "I'm sure the Elder knows something. She keeps going down to the catacombs."

Anthoni slowed down as they entered the building. "I hope Minister Karn is all right."

Tal snorted. "I'll bet you do."

"Why do you say it like that?"

"It's the way you fawn all over her, displaying yourself. Just look at the way you dress."

Anthoni had given up discussing this with her. He acted and dressed like all the other aides. If Tal had a problem with the way he filled out his clothes, she could learn to deal with it. He had no intention of hiding himself in robes and Talha, like a Haka man.

When they reached the junction of a hall that led to the suite of the late Jahlt Karn, Tal suddenly froze, staring down the cross hall. A ghostly figure was coalescing out of its shadows, as if the dead Minister had returned to possess the Estate. The "ghost" came nearer, resolving into Ixpar Karn. Gashes caked with blood covered her arms and dirt smudged her face.

Anthoni bowed, followed by Tal. "Greetings, Minister Karn," he said.

Ixpar pushed a straggle of hair from her eyes. "Have either of you seen Elder Solan?"

"Yhee, ma'am," Tal said. "She's looking for you."

"Go tell her I will meet her in my office." The Minister turned to Anthoni. "I'd like you to have a crew prepare the Minister's suite. I want to move in as soon as possible."

"Right away," he said.

As Anthoni and Tal strode off, they exchanged glances. So. There had been those who said Ixpar Karn would never truly be Minister until she could bring herself to live in the Ministry suite, which had previously belonged to her predecessor.

Far out on the Miesa Plateau, the mineral flats baked under the sun. Hot springs released fumes into the late-afternoon haze and vapors blew across the ground in gritty streamers of yellow and purple. As the rider skimmed low over the flats, Avtac Varz stared out the window.

In the seat next to her, Zecha sat watching the flats unroll beneath them. "Ugly place," she commented.

Avtac scowled. "That ugly place is making Bahvla rich." Her expression became more thoughtful. "However, the sulphur down there is cheap."

Bones and bugs, Zecha thought. Why Avtac's sudden interest in chemicals? First it was potassium, then carbon, now sulphur. What was it about these substances that so fascinated Varz's formidible Manager?

The cluster of Miesa aides stood in the sitting room outside Savina's bedroom, talking in whispers and trying not to stare at the Fourth Level pacing on the other side of the room. Kelric ignored them, too worried to care if they gawked. His guards waited at their posts.

The inner door of the room opened, framing Behz, the Miesa Senior Physician, in its archway. The elderly doctor regarded them all with her faded blue eyes, then beckoned to Kelric.

Inside the darkened bedroom, he found Savina dozing under a mound of quilts. He sat on the bed and took her hand.

"Sevtar?" she murmured.

"How do you feel?"

"Better." She opened her eyes. "Avtac will despise me."

"Why do you say that?"

"She will think me weak to be so sick from carrying a child."

"What Avtac Varz thinks doesn't matter." He stroked her hair. "That you can have my child at all is a miracle."

"Rashiva did."

Kelric stiffened. How did she know Rashiva's son was his?

Savina curled her fingers around his hand. "She brought him to Council. Few people have ever seen you, so most don't realize the resemblance. And he has to stay on a special diet. Like yours." She closed her eyes. "Rashiva had trouble, but not like this."

Kelric thought of the primitive state of Coban medicine and the room seemed to darken around him. "I want to get you a better doctor."

"Behz is the best."

"For Coba, yes, Behz is good. There are better elsewhere."

Her eyes snapped open. "Go offworld?" She stiffened. "Your Rhon would take away my baby. They would say I am not good enough to be the mother of their grandchild."

"Savina, no. My parents would love you." He lifted her into his arms. "Come home with me."

She watched him with her large eyes. "If you left Coba you would no longer be Sevtar."

"I would love you no matter what my name."

"I couldn't bear it if you rejected your Oath." She touched the outline of his armbands under his shirt. "The highest love is that of a Manager for her Akasi."

"I don't have to be Calani to love you."

Softly she said, "I'm not sure I can say the reverse."

He didn't want to believe it. "I could make you happy."

"Your ISC would punish my people for making you stay here. They would occupy Coba. Take away our Restriction. Use our world. Disrupt the Quis."

After living on Coba for twelve years, Kelric had found much about its culture he valued, just as he loved Savina and Quis. He no more wished to see Coba's unique civilization disrupted by ISC occupation than did her own people. He wasn't sure he wanted his old life back, with its vicious political intrigue and harsh realities.

But these were extenuating circumstances. "I'm worried about the baby. And you."

"I can't risk my world for the lives of two people." Tears glistened in her eyes. "Not even for my own child and myself."

Rain drummed against Dahl Estate. The clock in Chankah's office chimed Morning's Second Hour, but still she sat at her desk absorbed in work. When a tap sounded at the door, she looked up with a start. She went to the door and found the doctor Dabbiv waiting outside, his face flushed from running.

"What's wrong?" Chankah asked.

"You've got to see—" He tugged her arm. "Come see."

He hurried her to his lab, where a solitary lamp burned in one corner. An odd device sat on a table there, a brass tube clamped to a mount that let the tube incline at an angle. When they reached the table, she saw a platform fastened below the tube, with a concave mirror under that. The setup reminded her of the lens toys hobbyists used to magnify insects and leaves. The toys were notoriously faulty, though, with lens aberrations that gave blurred or false images.

"What is it?" she asked.

"I'll show you." Dabbiv took a flask off the table. "This is a sample of the contaminated water you asked me to analyze."

"The plant engineers say it's not contaminated. They couldn't find anything in it."

Dabbiv waved the flask at her. "Nothing they could *see*." He dabbed water from the flask onto a square Quis die made from glass and set it front of her. "I've been working with an optician, minimizing lens aberrations." He handed her a magnifying glass. "Try this one."

Chankah peered through the glass at the water. A pink speck darted across her field of vision. "It moves too fast."

Dabbiv took a vial of slow-syrup and let a drop fall into the water. "Now try."

This time the speck drifted in a circle while a second one floated lazily into view. "There's something. It's hard to see."

"That's because a single lens doesn't magnify enough." Dabbiv tapped his brass tube. "So I put several lenses together, like in the toys skywatchers use to look at stars." He gestured with his hands. "You see, if you get the distances between lenses just right, the image from one forms an object for the next. It gives much better magnification."

"But aren't the images terrible?"

Dabbiv gave a wave of dismissal. "Lens toys make blurry images because glass bends the different colors in light by different amounts. But if your 'lens' is achromatic, that is, if it's really a series of lenses, you can compensate for the bending. It took me a long time to find the right shapes and the right glass. But I think I have it now. I call it a microscope." He set the Quis square on the platform below the tube and switched on a light in the mount. "Just look at it, Chankah."

She squinted into the eyepiece. "I see a black cord."

"A cord?" Dabbiv looked like a windrider that had just smacked into a cliff. "There shouldn't be a cord." Leaning over, he peered into the eyepiece. "Ah. So." He whisked a hair off the tube. "Now try."

Chankah squinted into the eyepiece and saw a clump of pink blobs. "It's blurry."

He touched the screw on the mount. "Use the fine-focus."

She turned the screw—and the blobs resolved into a cluster of translucent oval bags with hairs waving about their edges. Little rods darted through the cluster.

"Well, I'll be a Quis cube." Chankah looked up at him. "What are they?"

Dabbiv grinned. "Some kind of animal. I think there's a whole universe of small animals to see."

His success gratified Chankah. Once again he had proved wrong the many critics who insisted his ideas would never work.

Kastora Karn was a tall woman with a wealth of mahogany hair she wore swept into a roll on her head. Ixpar had known her since they were children in the Cooperative. Although Kastora was older, in their childhood she had followed Ixpar's lead in everything, from sports to boys to school. Ixpar valued her loyalty, her hard work, her keen intellect, and her good sense. So when she became Minister, she appointed Kastora as her Senior Aide.

Today they considered funding requests from Karn scholars. Kastora handed her a file. "These are from the science labs."

Ixpar recognized most of the proposals. But at the back of the folder she found a surprise. "Bahr Karn wants research funds? I thought she was a professional gambler."

Kastora chuckled. "With Bahr you never know. A few years ago she wanted to apply to the Calanya."

"I remember. To say it offended Jahlt is an understatement." Ixpar scanned the proposal. " 'Quis Models of Elemental Structure.' What do you suppose she's doing?"

Kastora shrugged. "Playing pattern games."

"This idea she describes, a Quis chart for chemical elements—I've heard something like it before. I can't remember where."

"Maybe she suggested it to Jahlt."

"No . . ." Ixpar finally caught the memory, recalling it from a time when she had been half her current age.

Periodic chart, Kelric had said. Atomic structure.

Quis Wizard Bahr sat on the cobblestones in the market, her low table set up on the flagstones, her dice out and ready for challengers. She leaned against the wall of the building behind her, soaking up sunshine. Stalls stood everywhere in the plaza and lengths of metal balls clinked and clanked on their roofs. People thronged the square, come to trade or watch the street artists.

A lyderharpist set up his stool by a nearby sausage stand and soon people were gathering to listen as he charmed lively notes from his handheld harp. Some of the listeners came to sit at Bahr's table and try their luck with a Quis Wizard. They were challengers in name only, but she let a few of them win anyway just to keep people coming back.

Not such a bad day after all, Bahr decided. She hadn't felt like setting up at market this morning, but she couldn't spend every day working on pattern games in her suite. After a while she started talking to the dice. Besides, she had to eat. Quis was her living and as Wizard of the Karn Quis she lived as good as the living came. It was no coincidence the former Minister (the goddess rest Jahlt's cast-iron soul) often asked her to the Estate for Quis. Bahr grinned at the memory. Those had been some games.

Her good mood dimmed. Too bad she threw it all to the wind, asking to apply to the Calanya. The look on Jahlt Karn's face had said, plain as dice, that a certain Bahr Karn overstepped the bounds of decency. After that, the Minister no longer sent her invitations for Quis.

Pah. She had just wanted to play dice. *Good* dice. Outsider Quis was too easy, as boring as filling out census forms. Still, she couldn't help but smile as a daydream formed; Bahr wakes up with half-dressed Calani all around her: tall ones, small ones, dark ones, sunny ones, big muscled ones, and lithe supple ones—

"Heh," a voice said. "You won't make a cental if you sleep all day."

Bahr opened her eyes and scowled. Rhab Karn was leaning his well-built self against the wall. "Go away," she said. "I'm not in the mood for Modernists today."

Rhab grinned, his teeth flashing white. It irked Bahr to no end. She had long ago decided Modernists were Modernists because they looked so ugly no woman would glance at them twice. Rhab's existence continually confounded her conclusion. It wasn't even that he was really *that* handsome, at least not in a classic sense. But something about him disrupted her equilibrium.

"Go sell your pots," she grumbled.

He sat next to her. "My apprentice is watching the stall."

"You come to preach to me again about melting down Calanya armbands? Having men Managers? It'll never happen, Rhab."

"Sure it will. Maybe not this year or the next. But it'll happen."

She leaned close to him. "You know what you need? Some Manager to put you in a Calanya and make you behave. Get all these ideas out of your head."

"You won't lock me up in Calanya guards."

"Nobody locks Calani anymore."

"Maybe not their wrists or ankles." Rhab tapped a finger against her temple. "But inside here we're all just as locked and guarded as in the Old Age."

"I'm not."

"I wasn't referring to you. Only to half of Coba. The male half."

"Pah."

"Pah yourself. Unlike you, not all of us want to be Calani."

Her face burned. "Where did you get the dumb idea I wanted to be a Calani?"

Rhab laughed. "Tell you what, Bahr. I'll give you wrist guards and you can be my Akasi."

"Khozaar above." She looked around, fast and furtive. "Don't talk so loud. Someone might hear."

Still grinning, he stretched out his legs, his tame brown boots nicely accenting the flaming red of hers. "Looks like you bought new boots."

"Sure did. Got 'em to match my hair." Bahr angled a look at him. "Got me new rooms in the Women's House too." Her mind made a fantasy of Rhab in her rooms; the sexy Modernist condemns her advances until she overcomes his resistance and he gives in to her. Then she had an odd thought; it would be nice to have Rhab's company even if he didn't succumb to her amorous overtures. "Maybe I'll bring you over and let you see them."

"Prowling after Modernists, heh?"

She reddened. "Prowling, pah. I'd rather go after off-worlders."

"I hear they're all Modernists. Matter of fact, I hear their Minister is a man."

"Just shows how gullible you are." But Bahr had caught wind of the same rumor. It was in the Quis. All sorts of news was there to read, from the growing legend of the Fourth Level at Miesa to the mysterious goings-on in the Varz labs. Strange undercurrents ran through the dice, offworlder ideas, subtle and confusing, detectable only to a Quis Wizard.

"Heh," Rhab said. "Look at that."

Bahr looked. A retinue had entered the market, rippling excitement through the crowd. "I wonder who it is," she said.

"The Ministry Senior Aide, looks like."

"Kastora? Cuaz me. It is."

"She's coming over here."

Bahr snorted, primarily to hide the fact that important people made her knees shake. But Rhab was right. Kastora was coming their way.

The Senior Aide stopped in front of Bahr's dice table. "Quis Wizard Bahr?"

Bahr scrambled to her feet, acutely aware of how Kastora towered over her. "Yhee, ma'am. I mean, that's me."

"Minister Karn sends her greetings." Kastora handed her a letter.

Bahr read the letter, then gaped at Kastora. A nudge from Rhab's foot started her tongue working again. "Uh—yes. Tell her I will. I mean, tell Minister Karn I will be honored to meet with her."

I've no reason to be intimidated, Bahr thought. Ixpar Karn was just a person, hardly older than Bahr herself. But she recognized the late Jahlt Karn in the woman who faced her from behind the large desk. Ixpar had that same aura of understated power. She also possessed a quality Bahr had never detected in Jahlt, a ferocity just below her civilized exterior.

I'm not intimidated, Bahr reminded herself.

"I wish to know more about the work you describe in your proposal," the Minister said.

Bahr rubbed her sweating palms on her trousers. "I want to understand elements. Chemical elements, I mean."

"Why?"

"Well—ah—" She had never thought about why. "It's interesting."

"I see."

Bahr knew she sounded like an idiot. But she couldn't quit now. She wanted the funds too much. Sure she boasted about her great life, rolling dice and making pots of coins. Truth was, she didn't like gambling. Nor was she a woman to parlay her skill with the dice into power and prestige. She didn't care about that. She just wanted to play Quis. Real Quis. Like a Calani. Like a man. She could hear the laughter; *not much of a woman, heh, Bahr?* Well, she would learn to take it. She had to. She needed support if she wanted to play pattern games full time and this was the only way to get it.

"I'm trying to find a Quis pattern that describes the elements," she said. "Actually, I already found one. But it has problems."

"Problems?" Ixpar asked.

"I think we're missing some elements. A lot of them." Her fascination with the project jumped in and kicked away her nervousness. "My pattern predicts periodicity in the elements. It all fits. It's beautiful. But some elements it predicts aren't in any chemistry scroll I've found. And a few elements listed in the scrolls don't fit my pattern."

"Which ones?" Ixpar asked.

"Water. And air." Bahr knew any respectable scientist would laugh her out of the room. But she had to see this through. "I don't believe water and air are really elements."

"I see." Ixpar picked up a folder on her desk. "These are your tutorial files from the Cooperative. You have an unusual record."

Bahr's face flamed. *Unusual* was a polite term for a truant who had been too busy playing dice to bother with lessons. The Minister's meaning was obvious; where did someone like Bahr get the wind to challenge the patterns of established science?

"It isn't exactly an impressive file," Ixpar said.

"No, ma'am, it isn't."

"Were you bored?"

The question threw Bahr. "Bored?"

"With your lessons."

Bahr had no idea how to answer. She had never paid enough attention to remember the lessons. "I don't know."

Ixpar considered her. "Atomic structure."

"I don't understand."

"Neither do I." Ixpar closed the folder. "A man once said those words to me while trying to explain the chemical elements."

"What does it mean?"

"That's what I want you to tell me." Ixpar tapped her stylus against her fingers. "You will have to move onto the Estate."

Bahr was getting confused. "Estate?"

Ixpar leaned forward. "Understand me, Quis Wizard. I would never let a woman loose in my Calanya nor tolerate the suggestion of such. But you will take the Oath and live as a Calani. Mentors from the Preparatory House will instruct you." She paused. "I assume you will put more effort into your studies now than you did as a child?"

The room whirled about Bahr. "Calani? Me?"

"I want you to study it all with your Quis: physics, chemistry, elements. Full time. I want you to tell me what is atomic structure."

Bahr gaped at her. "I'll be blown over a bubble."

"Are you interested?" the Minister asked.

"Yhee, ma'am," Bahr said. "That I surely am."

Kelric closed his eyes, trying to ease the throbbing in his head. It didn't even help that he was sitting in his favorite armchair in the main common room, as he always did after dinner. In a nearby alcove Hayl strummed a lyderharp and Revi lay next to him. As Hayl played, Kelric brooded. The question of taking Savina offworld had become moot; she was too sick to travel and too far into her pregnancy for him to bring back a doctor in time even if he could have gone for one. Their child's life was in the hands of the Coban doctors now.

Hayl began "Song of the Snowprince," a ballad about a Varz Akasi from the Old Age who died when he was caught in a blizzard as he fled from the stone-hearted Manager to the arms of the woman he loved. Although Kelric usually enjoyed Hayl's playing, tonight even the music couldn't soothe his headache.

In the seven years since he had come to Miesa, his brain damage had *gradually* been healing. Until now. Suddenly his Kyle centers were reactivating with a vengeance, an uneven resurgence that felt like shards of glass driving into his head. How could Savina's gentle touch evoke such an intense response? The KEB in her brain didn't have enough active sites to broadcast a signal this strong.

He closed his eyes and concentrated on the link he shared with her. With his Kyle senses so sensitized, he picked her up more easily than ever before. As her presence grew more distinct, it separated. One part remained a dim glow, warm and familiar. The other blazed like a blue giant star being born.

Being born.

Kelric jumped to his feet and strode past a startled Hayl to the Outside doors. Heaving them open, he looked out at the escort. "I have to see Savina."

Captain Lesi dropped her pouch, scattering dice across the floor. One of the guards jumped, knocking over a Quis structure, and another sputtered Tanghi tea across the table.

"For pugging sake," he said. "Do you think my vocal cords

have been cut?" He headed Out into the hall. If they were going to gawk, he would find Savina himself.

In seconds the guards had surrounded him, their stunners drawn. He forced himself to stop. Being knocked out would get him nowhere.

"Manager Miesa is sick," Captain Lesi said.

"I need to see her."

His voice shook them up more than anything else he could have done, short of jumping off a tower. Lesi motioned six of his guards into formation around him and sent the seventh running ahead.

Behz, the Miesa Senior Physician, was waiting for them at Savina's suite. Kelric walked straight past her. As he entered the darkened bedroom, he heard Lesi order someone to put down their gun. His back itched, waiting for a stun shot, but it never came. Inside the bedroom he paused, halted by the sight of Savina's small form curled under the quilts.

Behz came in and closed the door. Drawing him aside, she spoke in a low voice. "If she gets any worse she will lose the baby. Can't this wait?"

He shook his head no. She studied his face, as if searching for an answer. "You will take care with her, yes, Sevtar?" When he nodded, she bowed to him and withdrew from the room, leaving him alone with his wife.

Kelric sat on the bed and gently rested his hand on Savina's abdomen, so near now to full term.

"Is Avtac here . . . ?" she asked.

"It's me," he said.

Her eyes opened. "You look scared to death."

"Savina, it's about the baby. She's a more powerful psion than I realized."

"Psion?" She nestled against him, closing her eyes. "Sigh for me, Sevtar."

He didn't know how to describe for her the way the quantum wavefunctions of her brain and his coupled with each other and with that of the baby's developing brain. Through that three-way link, he and Savina already loved their child, on a level deeper than conscious thought. But a danger also existed. An infant had little or no control over its developing Kyle organs.

During the trauma of its birth, its mind would probably hit Savina with a neural overload. A Kyle birth usually gave the mother a headache or at worst caused a convulsion. It might have no effect if the mother knew how to release neurotransmitters that blocked receptor sites affected by the overload.

Except their child was no ordinary Kyle.

"The baby doesn't know she can hurt you," he said. "My mind is like hers. I can protect both you and her."

Drowsily she said, "You worry about the strangest things."

"I have to be with you when she's born. Right here. Kyle effects fall off roughly as the coulomb force, so the farther away I am from you, the weaker my interaction with the two of you."

She opened her eyes, her face gentling. "I would like for you to be here. I wanted to ask, but I wasn't sure how. Some men feel uncomfortable in the birthing room." She sighed. "Avtac will protest, of course."

"You mean Avtac Varz?"

"She comes to help Manage Miesa while I am sick."

"Can't your staff take care of it?"

"Yes. But not as well as Avtac. I appreciate her help."

"I don't trust her."

"You never met her."

"I don't like the Quis patterns I've seen of her."

"I know she intimidates people," Savina said. "But she has always been a friend to me. Harsh and demanding, but also steadfast."

The door opened, making a line of light in the dark. "Manager Miesa?" Captain Lesi asked. "Is everything all right?"

"Fine," Savina said.

After the captain withdrew, Savina smiled at Kelric. "You must have shaken them up."

"I wasn't exactly being a model Calani." He smoothed her hair. "They're right, though. I should let you rest."

She curled closer to him. "Don't leave. I feel better when you're here."

So he held her while she slept. His own thoughts refused to let him rest. How could he have known Savina carried the full set of Rhon genes, mostly unpaired, hidden and recessive? No wonder he loved her. Far down, in a place deeper than conscious thought, like had recognized like. Her unexpressed genes had paired up with his and produced a child of phenomenal strength.

Their daughter was Rhon.

Avtac Varz locked her valise and straightened up, fastening her jacket to ward off the predawn chill. She considered stopping by Hettav's apartment in the city to say good-bye before she left for Miesa, but decided against it. The time had come to end her arrangement with him. Young and handsome though he was, he had ceased to please her.

In fact, last night Avtac had found herself seeking out Garith, her only Akasi, the father of her five children. A tall man with a muscular build and eyes like the sky, his beauty had once been stunning. The decades had streaked his gold hair with gray and added lines around his eyes, but even after so many years she still enjoyed his company.

Besides, Hettav wanted too much. He should have realized she would never make him an Akasi. He gave away his virtue too easily, on top of which he was a terrible dice player.

An aide appeared in the archway, shivering in the cold. "The rider is ready, ma'am."

"Good." Avtac handed her the valise. "Take this out to the airfield." She headed to her office for a last—but most important—meeting. Zecha should be there by now.

Avtac knew there were those who criticized her decision to appoint Zecha as captain of her hunters. Before making the decision, she had gone over every detail of Zecha's methods at Haka. The former warden hadn't understood the subtleties of power and so abused it. But for a Manager who knew how to utilize her strengths and control her excesses, Zecha made an excellent, and loyal, officer.

It was also obvious why the Haka Bench reacted with such severity in Zecha's case. It involved a Calani. At times Avtac was convinced the sungoddess Savina had created men as punishment for some perceived misdeed of womankind. Either handsome and seductive, with few redeeming qualities aside from the obvious, or else plain and querulous, they forever caused trouble.

When she reached her office, she found Zecha waiting with the chemist Iva. Although Iva had recovered from the injuries she took during the lab accident, a scar marred her cheek. It struck Avtac as inappropriate that Iva wore the mark while the clumsy assistant who caused the accident went unscathed. The accident itself, however, intrigued Avtac.

Sulphur, nitrate, charcoal.

"I've read your research proposal." Avtac moved her hand in dismissal. "Pattern games."

Iva had her arguments prepared. "Working out Quis patterns of inorganic syntheses has great potential to improve our lives, Manager Varz. It could lead to uncountable new compounds."

"Whatever," Avtac said. "I'm giving you the funds."

A surprised smile jumped onto Iva's face. "You won't regret it, I assure—"

"With one stipulation," Avtac interrupted. "I want you to complete a project first." She took a folder from her desk and handed it to the chemist. "You will work with Captain Zecha and a crew of metal-shapers she selected."

Iva glanced through the file. "Metal Quis dice with chemicals in them?"

"That's right. Can you do it?"

"Well—yes, I think so." Iva looked up at Avtac. "I'm not sure they will have much use. But I can do it."

Papers, Savina thought. She listlessly regarded the piles stacked on the bed. How could a tree be left anywhere on Coba? They had all been cut down to make papers Savina Miesa must read.

At least since Avtac's arrival yesterday, Savina had found more time to rest. Except that Zecha had flown down from Varz today to report to Avtac. Although Savina found nothing specific about the captain she could point to and say "This bothers me," Zecha disquieted her, like a pressure against her mind.

Savina let the folder she held drop onto the bed. As she lay back, a cramp caught her like a vise. With a gasp, she reached out to the nightstand for the com. The added weight of her pregnancy gave her more momentum than she expected and her awkward size made it difficult to recover. Her body unbalanced and she rolled forward, off the bed, tumbling through the air. She landed on the floor with a thud.

"Ah—no . . ." Savina cried out as a full-blown contraction clenched her. "Behz! Someone!"

The door burst open and people ran into the bedroom. As Behz knelt next to her, another contraction hit Savina, shooting firebrands up her spine. She gazed up at the doctor, mutely imploring her to make the pain stop.

After a quick exam, Behz looked up at the nurses. "We will need clean sheets. And boil some water."

"No." Savina groaned as they lifted her onto the bed. "The baby hasn't even turned yet."

As much as Behz tried to hide her concern, it radiated off her like heat off an ingot. "That may be. But you're in labor. I can't stop it."

Avtac paced the living room outside Savina's bedroom while a cluster of aides spoke with hushed voices. Zecha waited by a window, staring out at the city, her face drawn as if she hadn't slept the entire night.

Suddenly the outer door of the suite swung open and Captain Lesi of the Calanya escort strode into the room.

"Is there a problem in the Calanya?" Avtac asked.

Lesi bowed to her. "The Calani Sevtar wishes to be with Manager Miesa."

Avtac could imagine the consequences of letting a high-strung Calani into the birthing room. "Tell him no."

"He's already here, ma'am. I could barely convince him to wait in the alcove."

The lack of discipline at Miesa appalled Avtac. Savina indulged this Fourth Level far too much. "Take him back."

The Miesa Senior Aide came over to them. "Savina wants him with her, ma'am."

That gave Avtac pause. "She spoke to you about this?"

"I think she and Sevtar just made the decision."

"But did she give orders?" Avtac said.

It was a moment before the Senior answered. "Not yet."

"Yet?" Avtac wished the woman would be more specific. "Then she told you she intended to give orders on the subject."

"No," the Senior admitted. "But she did intend to."

Avtac appraised the Senior. Was she operating on her own agenda or did she truly believe Savina wanted this excitable Calani hovering around while she labored? Avtac had never asked for Garith in the five times she had given birth. His presence would have been an intrusion.

A nurse opened the door of Savina's bedroom. "Manager Varz?"

Avtac went over to him. "How is Savina?"

"She's had several convulsions, we aren't sure why. And the baby is in the wrong position." Quietly he said, "Behz doesn't know if either she or the baby will live."

No, Avtac thought. Savina, be strong. "Has she asked for the baby's father?"

The nurse shook his head. "She sleeps between contractions and isn't coherent during them."

"Do you think it would help her to have him come in?"

The nurse spread his hands. "We don't know."

Avtac suspected that if Savina had said nothing about the matter this far into her pregnancy, she didn't want Sevtar in there. Unfortunately, with Savina it was difficult to tell; you could never be sure what was going on in her odd, albeit engaging, mind. Nor was promptness one of her strong points.

Avtac went to the window where Zecha stood. As the captain turned to her, Avtac was surprised by the extensive lines of fatigue on her face.

"You knew this man Sevtar at Haka," Avtac said.

"He isn't stable," Zecha said. "Let him in there and you could have a disaster."

Avtac motioned for the Calanya captain. When Lesi came over, Avtac said, "Do you believe Sevtar might lose control of himself in the birthing room?"

"Not at all," Lesi said.

"He never behaves in an erratic manner?"

The Miesa captain hesitated.

"Answer with care," Avtac said. "Your Manager's life could depend on what you say."

Lesi exhaled. "I can't guarantee he'll do nothing unexpected."

The Miesa Senior Aide joined them in time to hear Lesi's comment. "Sevtar is steadier than a rock," the Senior said.

A guard opened the outer door of the suite. "Captain Lesi? I don't know how much longer he's going to wait."

"Bring him," the Senior said.

Avtac spoke to the guard. "You will do nothing until you have my permission."

The guard hesitated, looking from Avtac to the Senior. Then she said, "Yhee, ma'am," to Avtac.

Zecha drew Avtac to one side. "I would think before you let him in there. It's well-known what you have to gain if Savina Miesa dies."

Avtac had no wish to see Savina die. The Miesa Manager was one of the few people she actually liked. Besides, if she appeared to seek Savina's death, the political ramifications would be ugly. On the other hand, if she refused the Fourth Level and it turned out Savina had actually wanted him there, the consequences could be just as serious.

A bead of sweat ran down the side of Zecha's face. She wiped it away with a distracted motion.

"Are you sick?" Avtac asked.

"It's the tension. Can't you feel it?" Zecha pressed the heels of her palms against her temples. "It's like being in a mulch compactor."

Avtac frowned. "What are you talking about?"

Zecha's face took on an odd expression, as if she had closed and shuttered herself. "It's nothing."

"Manager Varz." Captain Lesi stepped over to them. "We need to decide."

Avtac considered her, then turned to Zecha. "I need your best opinion, Captain. One untainted by anger."

Zecha stiffened and Avtac saw that her implication wasn't lost on the captain. If the wrong decision was made, it would reflect on Zecha now as well.

Zecha rubbed her temples, her face drawn. With complete certainty she said, "Manager Miesa wants him with her."

Kelric's awareness of the foyer faded as he concentrated on the force being born in the other room. His daughter reacted in instinct, innocent of the knowledge her miraculous power could kill. Kelric buffered Savina, easing the onslaught, but holding his link with her proved difficult from two rooms away.

The foyer door opened, framing Captain Lesi in its archway. She said, simply, "I will take you to Manager Miesa."

Somehow, through his tension, he managed to nod. He wound the Talha around his face and pulled up the cowl of his robe, secluding himself from watching eyes so the covetous reactions of people to his appearance wouldn't disrupt his concentration.

As soon as he was inside Savina's bedroom, he slipped off his robe and Talha and went to the bed, standing back from the gathered medics. Savina strained with another contraction and his mind reeled with the intensity of her effort. He deepened his concentration, spurring her brain to produce chemicals that blocked its pain receptors.

After the contraction finished, Savina dropped back on the bed. At first he thought she had passed out, but then she opened her eyes. "Sevtar," she whispered. "Come help. Please."

When Kelric started toward her, Behz laid her hand on his arm. "Be careful."

He swallowed and nodded. They helped him to kneel on the bed behind Savina and showed him how to support her during the contractions. He was so close to her now that both she and the baby glowed in his mind.

Again and again Savina strained in his arms, her body wrung with her exertions. The day ground into night, blending into a haze of exhaustion. As her strength ebbed, their child's mind began to fade. Kelric refused to admit what was happening, that his wife and daughter were dying in his arms. He poured his support into Savina, barely even realizing he was all now that kept her and their child alive. She had stopped thinking, giving all her remaining strength over to the agonized labor.

Suddenly Behz cried, "She's coming!"

Kelric heard through a daze. With his consciousness focused inward, the room had blurred around him and he could no longer see.

Suddenly Savina screamed, her body going rigid as if she were struggling back from the threshold of death for one final, gargantuan effort.

Then a baby wailed.

With a curiously gentle sigh, Savina sagged in his arms. Incredibly, for the first time in hours, perhaps even days, she looked up with recognition. Her voice was a whisper. "She lived because of you."

Tears ran down his face. "And you."

"I'm so tired . . ."

"Savina." He rasped her name. "Savina, don't."

She smiled, her face blurred in the room's dimmed light. "I love you, Sevtar."

Then her eyes closed.

30

The Tower of Souls

The torch on the wall flickered, gilding the corridor with antique light. Avtac walked in silence. At the end of the hall she stopped before an archway and stood with her palm resting against the door, the only concession to her crushing grief she would ever reveal. Then she unlocked the door and entered the room where a legend waited.

He was sitting in a window seat, staring out at Miesa far below the tower. Then he turned—and she saw that the legends of his beauty were indeed false. The reality of him was not less, as she had expected; it was more, far more. His flawless face, the symmetry of his form, the beauty of his skin: he was perfect. Utterly perfect.

Instead of the midnight-blue cloak of mourning, for some reason he wore black: boots, trousers, shirt, vest—all black. The only color came from the gold of his wrist guards glinting under the edge of his cuffs.

So. This was the man who had destroyed an Estate.

Sevtar turned away from her and stared out the window at Miesa again. No, not Miesa. Varz. It was hers now, all of it, and a Fifth Level as well. But it came at a bitter price.

Softly she said, "Your daughter survived, Sevtar."

He looked back at her, for the first time showing a spark of life. Avtac wondered at his reaction. Calani such as he were another species, erratic in emotion and thought. Still, perhaps it would be kind to let him see the infant.

Within moments after she sent for the child, a nurse appeared with a small bundle wrapped in blankets. When Avtac nodded, the youth approached Sevtar and bowed. Then he offered Sevtar the bundle.

The transformation that came over Sevtar astounded Avtac. He cradled the tiny infant in his massive hold with a tenderness incongruous to his reputation. Then he murmured a name.

The nurse jerked back and Avtac motioned for him to leave. Despite the jolt of hearing Sevtar break his Oath, Avtac understood his lapse. It wasn't his fault men of great beauty lacked moral strength. Today he needed to mourn. She would leave Calanya discipline for another time.

She wondered about the name he spoke. Rohka. Had he and Savina picked it for their daughter? She sat next to him and spoke gently. "Rohka will have the best care we can offer."

Sevtar looked as if he were trying to answer. But words failed him. Instead he bent his head over the child and repeated her name in his husky accent, making it sound like Roca. As a tear ran down his face, he added words that made no sense:

"No longer am I the littlest Rhon child."

Varz stood alone, high in the mountains, ancient and immutable, a solitary garrison with the grandeur of the Teotecs stretching away on all sides as far as a hawk could fly. The riders landed on the airfield in the icy shadows of dusk. Cowled and hidden in robes, surrounded by their escorts, Kelric and Hayl moved across the frozen tarmac like ghosts.

They gave their Oath at Night's Midhour in the Hall of Souls, a place of ebony and onyx spaces, hung with sable curtains. Kelric stood alone, encircled by an ebony rail on an obsidian dais, his heart as dark as the hall where he swore loyalty to Varz. The words were dust in his mouth.

After he gave his Oath, Avtac Varz appeared from behind a curtain, a tall woman in ash robes. He watched numbly, uncaring that in moments she would make history.

She asked no questions as she placed the Akasi bands on his arms. "Sevtar Dahl Haka Bahvla Miesa Varz," she said. "You are now a Fifth Level Calani of Varz."

V

Varz

31

Switch: Black Onyx

Ixpar slid open the stained-glass doors of her suite and walked onto the patio. In a distant garden she saw Bahr at a table, intent on her dice. The gambler looked like a wild gypsy: huge hoop earrings, yellow scarf tied in her red curls, blue trousers, yellow shirt, and those spectacular red boots of hers. Nearby, her friend Rhab was bent over a potter's wheel, hard at work.

Ixpar smiled. They made quite a picture: the Quis Wizard who lived as a Calani and her Modernist friend who came to pay suit the same way a woman would court a Calani, though neither of them would admit Rhab was courting anyone. Jahlt would have had a fit.

Ixpar sometimes wondered why she had done it. Supporting Bahr in the full style of a Calani was no meager investment. The arrangement drew constant criticism from the Elders. But the gambler's unusual mind, brimming with its plethora of odd ideas, fascinated her. She wanted Bahr to play Quis with her Calanya and for that stratospheric privilege, Bahr would have to keep the Oath for the rest of her life.

A man appeared in another garden, his brown hair whipping in the breeze as he strode down a path. When he neared, Ixpar recognized him as Anthoni, one of her more promising Estate aides. He came over and bowed to her. "I have a message."

"From whom?" Ixpar asked.

"Skybird."

Ixpar motioned him into her living room, then closed the doors and pulled the curtains. "Who gave you the message?"

"A pilot. The name on the delivery sheet was Levi Karn."

"This pilot asked for your name before she spoke to you? Twice?" When Anthoni nodded, Ixpar said, "Who else knows of this?"

"No one. I came straight here."

"Good. What did Levi tell you?"

"This: 'The skybird flew high and now roosts well. His nests are clean.' "

Skybird. It was the code name for her agent Jevrin. The message meant he had established himself at Varz with a position on the CityGuard. Given Avtac's views on the unsuitability of men for the Guard, Ixpar hadn't been sure he would make it this far. But Avtac's inflexibility worked to Ixpar's advantage; the iron-hard Varz Manager was less likely to suspect a man as a spy, given it required numerous traits she associated only with women, including that he be discreet enough to keep his true identity out of the dice.

A considerable portion of Jevrin's training had gone into Quis, to ensure he didn't reveal himself. But he couldn't use the dice to send messages to Karn; no matter how well he secured his work, a Quis Wizard might still pick up the patterns.

"Was there anything else?" Ixpar asked.

Anthoni nodded. " 'The sun is extinguished.' "

"What?"

"That was the message. 'The sun is extinguished.' "

"Are you certain? You didn't hear it wrong?"

"I'm sure."

She took a breath. "Thank you, Anthoni. You've done well."

After Anthoni left, Ixpar sank into a chair. How could it be? *The sun is extinguished.*

Savina Miesa is dead.

If that were true, then Varz now owned Miesa. Ixpar's fist clenched as she thought of what else belonged to Varz.

Kelric.

32

Ravaged Tower

The days passed Kelric like ghosts, ten and then twenty, in dark, silent procession. Winter's blizzards raged outside, but he barely noticed. He lived in a universe of numb silence.

In such a large Calanya he had company even tonight, when he wandered through the common rooms after most of Varz slept. Two men conversed at a Quis table and another sat absorbed in solitaire. As always, each person he passed stopped what he was doing and nodded to him, silent and deferential.

Fifth Level. He felt abnormal. The other Calani treated him the way Outsiders treated all Calani. No one intruded on his solitude and he talked to no one. Even Avtac had the decency to leave him alone, despite the Akasi bands. He had finally, today, changed from the black of mourning into normal clothes, but what he wore made no difference. The shadows inside him remained.

The main common room was dark, except for a night lamp in one corner. Kelric tapped at Hayl's screen, but no one answered. As he turned to leave he heard a faint noise within. Crying? He hesitated, reluctant to trespass, yet knowing that were Hayl his own son he would try to help.

The crying came again, almost inaudible. So he went in. He found Hayl in a darkened alcove, lying on the rug among several cushions. Like most Miesans, the boy had never grown very tall; hidden in shadows he looked even younger than his fourteen years.

"Are you all right?" Kelric asked.

Hayl looked around with a start and then sat up. "Sevtar?"

"I'm sorry—I didn't mean to intrude. But I thought I heard crying. Can I help?"

"No." Then Hayl said, "Sevtar, wait. Stay."

Kelric sat on the rug. He couldn't bring himself to mention Savina, so instead he said, "Is it Revi?"

Hayl nodded, wiping tears off his cheeks. "Do you know what my mother told me once? When I was a baby and Revi was five, I wouldn't go to sleep unless he carried me around the nursery in the Cooperative."

"Avtac probably didn't realize how close you two were."

"She knew. The Miesa Senior Aide told her." Hayl swallowed. "Manager Varz doesn't care. She just wanted the best of us and a good price for the rest." He wiped his palms on his trousers. "Someday I'll be a Third Level. At Haka. With Revi."

"Perhaps you will."

"You've been to Haka. Do you think Revi likes it there?"

"I did. The desert is beautiful."

"Tell me about it."

As they talked, Hayl's spirits recovered a bit. Although they skirted the subject of Savina's death, Kelric felt Hayl's grief and knew the boy understood his. It helped in some way, sharing their silences about her.

When Kelric eventually returned to the main common room, he saw Qahotra, the Calanya captain, waiting by his suite with his "valets," Tak, Thek, Netak, and Katak. The Taks, as he called them. With diplomacy, or perhaps duplicity, Avtac chose to call these four of his guards "servants in honor of his position." Given that all four men carried guns, were larger even than Kelric, and obviously had martial-arts training, they didn't make convincing valets.

When Kelric saw what Qahotra carried, his heart leapt and he forgot the Taks. He strode over and stopped in front of her, accepting the blanket-swathed bundle she offered him. He cradled his daughter in his arms, gazing at her beloved face as he swayed slightly from side to side, rocking her.

When he finally glanced up, he saw Qahotra watching him with a smile. Even the Taks looked like they might actually crack their wooden faces with a pleasant expression.

"We'll be back in an hour," Qahotra said.

After the captain left, the Taks sat around a Quis table and played dice. Kelric settled into an armchair across the room, enfolding Roca in his arms, and murmured nonsense words. She watched him with wide blue eyes that someday would turn gray, gold, green, or violet, he had no idea which. She felt so small, so vulnerable. He hadn't realized fatherhood would come with such an intensity of response on his part.

When he had told Avtac he wanted Roca to live with him in the Calanya, the Manager hadn't even responded, she had simply stared as if he were demented. The next day when he and Avtac sat in a private Quis session, he introduced patterns of Roca into his dice, trying to make Avtac see what his daughter meant to him. She said nothing then either, but the next day Qahotra brought Roca up from Miesa for her first visit. Since then he had seen her every one or two days.

The hour went by far too fast. Kelric wasn't sure how he looked when Qahotra returned, but she gave him another hour. When she finally took the baby, she spoke gently. "She'll be back for another visit soon. I'll see to it myself."

After the captain left, Kelric went to his suite and sat in his living room, struggling to make his mind blank. If he let his thoughts surface, they would turn to Savina, to a grief that went too deep and too far. If he let it pull him under now, he would drown. For Roca, he had to stay on top of his life. He would make the Varz Quis soar as it never had before, turn this Estate and its dependents into the gilded land, give Roca the best world it was within his power to create.

Several hours later a tap came at his screen. He found Qahotra outside again, this time with both the Taks and his Calanya escort.

They took him through the Estate, along ancient halls made empty by their isolated location and the late hour, and lit only by lamps shaped like clawcats. Eventually they ascended a tower, climbing its spiral staircase. This journey he recognized. He had taken it three times before, once in a drugged daze at Dahl, once in incomprehension at Haka, and once in joy at Miesa.

They left him locked in a suite that gave reality to the age and wealth of Varz. Chandeliers made from diamonds hung above rugs so thick his toes disappeared in the pile. The antique furniture looked priceless. Gold, ivory, ebony, silk; it was an Akasi suite unparalleled by any he had seen.

The living room had no windows. He wandered through the other windowless rooms, glad to discover none of them contained Avtac either. In the bathing room, he went for a swim in the pool. When he finished, he dried off with a towel someone had laid on a stone bench and he dressed in the robe he found there. Then he sat by a fountain, watching rainbows flicker in the cascade of water. When his eyes refused to stay open any longer he went to the bedroom and was relieved to find it still empty. Apparently unexpected business had kept Avtac away.

He folded his robe on a chair and went to bed. Within moments he was asleep.

A tiring job, this merger of two Estates, Avtac thought as she lit a lamp in the living room of the Akasi suite. But well worth the trouble; since absorbing Miesa, the power of Varz had surged. Perhaps she had judged too harshly Savina's decision to acquire Sevtar. The man was a remarkable Quis player. More than remarkable. Truly gifted. But neurotic. What bizarre notion had prompted him to dress in black for so long? It was hard to believe he mourned Savina. He hadn't shed a tear since her death.

At least he had finally changed into normal clothes. Whatever his capricious logic, it wouldn't have done for her to violate what looked like mourning. But the wait had made her impatient.

She found him in the main bedroom. Asleep, he was even more provocative than awake. Light crept in from the living room and curled glowing fingers around his body. He lay on his back with one arm thrown across the pillows behind his head and the other stretched out on the bare sheets, the fist clenched in the silk. The quilts had ended up on the floor and the sheet was bunched around his waist, leaving his bare chest in view.

She sat next to him and explored his chest, satisfying the curiosity that had tugged at her since he came to Varz. His skin felt like a metal alloy, warm and flexible.

His eyes opened and he grasped her hand. "Avtac. It's late."

"So it is."

"I'm tired."

His reluctance whetted her desire. When she tweaked away the sheet, uncovering his body, he avoided her gaze. Given his past, she doubted his modesty was real. But it was far more fitting behavior for an Akasi than that of the youth she kept in the city, who made no secret of how much he enjoyed her company.

She spoke gently. "Sevtar, turn over. I will help you relax."

He glanced at her, his face guarded. But he did roll onto his stomach, laying his head on a pillow and his arms by his sides.

Still fully dressed, Avtac straddled his hips and massaged his back, working deep into the stiff muscles. After a while, his eyes closed and he sighed, murmuring a sleepy thanks. She ran her hands along his arms, then lifted his wrists and brought them together.

With a click, she locked his Calanya guards behind his back.

Sevtar looked back at her, blinking sleep out of his eyes. "Why did you do that?"

"Shhh, sweet dawn god," she murmured. Sweet submission. He excited her even more than she had expected. She stretched out on top of him, caressing his sides with long strokes as she rubbed her pelvis against his buttocks. While she moved on him, he stared at the wall across the room, his expression numb. He was hers to own and enjoy.

Her pent-up desire and the friction of her motion made her rise happen so fast she could barely control it. When the release came, it was with a shuddering intensity.

After a while, when her breathing had calmed, she rolled off him and lay on her back with her eyes closed, one leg stretched out and the other bent.

"Are you done?" he asked.

Avtac looked at him, his perfect face, his long lashes, his gold curls. She traced her finger along his cheek. "You are a great beauty, Sevtar."

"I can't sleep with my arms like this."

In her youth, she might have spent the rest of the night with him, but she was too drowsy now. Come morning, all would be new again, a time for full lovemaking. She wanted him well rested.

As soon as she unlocked his wrists, he turned onto his back and stared at the ceiling. Avtac stretched her arms, then removed her clothes and set them in a neat pile on the nightstand.

Then she rolled over and went to sleep.

33

King's Spectrum

Kastora Karn, Senior Aide to the Minister, studied the metal dice on the table. They had an odd shape: cylindrical at one end, pointed at the other. She glanced at Ixpar. "These are for Quis?"

"It would seem not." The Minister put a packet of dark powder next to the dice.

Kastora poked at the packet. "What is it?"

"A mixture," Ixpar said. "Charcoal, sulphur, nitrate."

"What does it do?"

"Explode."

Kastora quickly withdrew her hand. "Is it for the quarries?"

Ixpar shook her head. "Jevrin, the agent I have at Varz, smuggled it to me. The powder goes in the dice."

"Rather odd dice. What does one do with them?"

"Apparently," Ixpar said, "one puts them in a rifle."

"A rifle?"

"A gun."

"Why put dice in a stunner?"

"A rifle is different than a stunner," Ixpar said. "It propels the dice out again."

"Whatever for?"

"To damage the target, I assume."

Kastora stared at her. "Why?"

"That," Ixpar said, "is what I would like to know."

* * *

"So you see," Bahr finished. "By putting the dice structure in a high level and controlling how it evolves to a low level, the pattern models a chemical that glows with a single color of light. Like red light."

Ixpar relaxed at the table where she and Bahr had been dining. Bahr's outrageous ideas never ceased to fascinate her. "What would one do with this red light?"

"You could use it in the Calanya fountains." Bahr took a spice muffin. "Thing is, I wouldn't know bread from cheese how to make a real device that does what my Quis pattern predicts."

"I can have the labs look into it." Ixpar sipped her wine. "What do you call this light-making pattern of yours?"

"I haven't decided." Bahr washed a bite of her muffin down with wine. "You see, what actually gives off the light are motes I call atoms. When a mote is in a high level, it wants to emit light by going to a low level. For the patterns I'm working on now, you have to kick the mote to make it relax to the lower level. So I was thinking of calling it a kicked-mote emitter."

Ixpar could imagine the reaction Bahr would get to a Quis structure called kicked-mote emitters. "What you're doing is modeling a system that amplifies light by stimulating the emission of radiance. Why don't you abbreviate that?"

"Albsteor?" Bahr grimaced. "It sounds like a rock."

"Maybe if you just used letters from the main words. Alser. Laser. Saler."

"Sailor? Sailing light." Bahr beamed. "Yes, that sounds better."

Ixpar laughed. "Sailing light? It doesn't make sense."

"Sure it does. The light sails out of the device."

"All right." Ixpar smiled. "I will see if the labs can make you a light-sailor."

"Come on," Hayl said. "Wake up. You said you would run with me this morning."

Kelric opened one eye. Through a window in his suite, he saw dawn tinging the sky. He closed his eye and pulled a pillow over his head.

"Sevtar." Hayl tugged away the pillow. "You promised."

Kelric grimaced. Most Cobans found the concept of jogging as strange as eating Quis dice, but in Miesa he had talked Hayl into running with him in the mornings. Now he wished the boy hadn't taken to it with such enthusiasm.

Waking up to run, though, was better than waking up to Avtac. Mercifully, she had been at Council the past few days. Otherwise she sent for him almost every night, for "love" making that left him feeling emotionally bruised.

The one facet of Avtac he missed was her Quis. No other person he had played on Coba could match her brilliance. If a man's love were measured by a desire for a woman's dice rather than for the woman, then instead of abhorring Avtac he would have loved her with a passion like none other.

Right now, his only passion was to sleep. But he had promised Hayl. He rolled out of bed and limped to the bureau where he kept his running clothes. After he dressed, they went into his living room and found the Taks were already there, lounging in chairs. The "valets" followed Hayl and Kelric out to the ice-covered parks and stood out of earshot, watching them warm up, their breath making clouds under a sky of leaden clouds.

"I know they're your servants and all," Hayl said. "But I wish they would go away."

"At least they quit trying to run with us."

Hayl smirked. "They're too lazy." He leaned forward and pulled a hair off Kelric's head.

"Why did you do that?" Kelric asked.

Hayl gave him the hair. "Your first gray one."

Kelric rolled it between his fingers, then let it float away on the wind.

"Don't look so depressed," Hayl said good-naturedly. "Everyone gets gray hair."

"Come on." Kelric stood up. "Let's go."

As they ran, taking a path down to the lakes, Kelric made a listless attempt to reach Bolt. The node remained silent, as it had since Savina's death. It didn't matter; he knew what was happening. His meds were no longer performing the cellular repairs needed to retard his aging. The trauma of Savina's death had sent his only partially healed biomech web into shock, and

his grief, combined with his life at Varz, only served to exacerbate his condition. That the primitive state of Coban medicine
left him with a limp—that he could live with. But having Varz
take a century off his life was another matter altogether.

When they returned to the Calanya, the common rooms
were filling up, as Calani trickled out from their suites looking
for food, conversation, or Quis. While the Taks sat down at a
table to eat, Kelric continued across the room with Hayl.

A Second Level named Jev intercepted them. "Some of us
are having Tanghi in Orttal's suite," he said. "We wondered if
the two of you would like to join us."

Kelric almost declined. Then he saw the anticipation on
Hayl's face. So instead he said, "Thanks. We'll be over as soon
as we clean up."

As he and Hayl continued on to their suites, Hayl smiled.
"Maybe we won't be so much like Outsiders here anymore."

"Maybe not," Kelric said.

"Sevtar—"

"Yes?"

"It might help if—well—they might like us better if you
were friendlier."

Kelric squinted at him. "Sorry. I'll try."

Inside his suite, he bathed and dressed. As he pulled on his
shirt, his wrist guard twisted and he winced. Neither of his
guards fit properly and both irritated his skin, but to get them
fixed meant going to Avtac. And he had no intention of being
put in the humiliating position of having to ask her for anything.

Rummaging through his bureau, he found an old cloth. He
ripped off a strip and worked it under his guard to protect his
skin from the metal. Then he left his suite.

Orttal answered when Kelric tapped at his screen. He was
the higher ranked of the two Third Levels at Varz, yet he
bowed as if he were an Outsider compared to his Fifth Level
guest. In the living room, Kelric saw Hayl sitting on a divan
talking to Mox, a First Level who moved with an agility that
made him look ready to burst into somersaults.

"It's a matter of timing," Mox was saying. He juggled three
Quis dice, then handed them to Hayl. "Go ahead. Try it."

When Kelric entered, all conversation stopped. Orttal ushered him to a Quis table, giving him the position of honor by the window, across from the Second Level Jev. Everyone was watching him except Hayl, who kept trying to juggle Mox's dice.

The gems clattered to the floor. "Pah," Hayl muttered.

Mox laughed and scooped up the dice. "Try with two first."

Conversation begin to flow again. The others tossed sentences back and forth with an ease that fascinated Kelric, who had never mastered the art of talking to people he didn't know well. Mox's energy and Jev's quiet confidence impressed him, but it was Orttal who commanded attention. A husky man with gray-streaked hair, the Third Level reminded Kelric of the contained power in a starship engine.

Jev was speaking. "You have to admit, Orttal, refusing to play Quis in order to make a point about Modernism is extreme."

Hayl stared at Orttal. "You're a *Modernist*?"

"Don't get him started," Mox warned.

Jev smiled. "He doesn't foam at the mouth, Mox."

"I just don't see why he joined a Calanya, that's all." Mox frowned at Orttal. "If you thought it was all so repressive you should have stayed Outside."

"People change," Orttal said. "The Oath, however, is for life."

"Why would you want to leave?" Hayl asked. "What more could you want than what we have here?"

"Just the freedom to control my life, that's all," Orttal said. "Look at the price we pay to use our intellects; submission to an Oath that binds us like chains."

"You don't need to read or write," Mox said. "You have Quis."

Orttal leaned toward him. "As usual, you miss my entire point."

"I thought Modernism was illegal," Hayl said.

"Why would it be illegal?" Jev asked.

"Because," Hayl said. "It isn't—I don't know. It's immoral."

"What's immoral about parity?" Orttal demanded.

"Modernists tear down people's values," Hayl said. "Like trying to convince kasi not to wear bands or Calani not to take Oaths. Modernists are frustrated because they can't be Calani and no woman wants them as her kasi."

Orttal raised his eyebrows. "Really?"

Hayl looked at the kasi inscriptions on Orttal's Calanya guards and reddened. "Well, I guess not all of them. But it's still wrong. Women and men are different. There's a natural way of things. You can't change it."

"Brainwashed," Orttal said.

"I am not," Hayl said.

Mox grinned at the boy. "How'd you like to have a Calanya? Ten female Akasi all to yourself."

"You don't have to be rude," Hayl said.

Mox laughed. "Avtac must love him."

"What Avtac loves," Orttal said, "is controlling people."

Mox smiled. "You ought to hear what she says about Modernists."

Orttal scowled. "I have."

Jev spoke. "She can't be that hostile toward you, Orttal, considering how much she paid for your contract."

The Third Level made a frustrated noise. "I'm a human being. Not a commodity."

"You're just talking into the wind," Mox said. "You've been a Calani all your life. How could you live on the Outside? It's easy to complain when you don't have to give this up."

"You haven't a clue what I'm talking about," Orttal said. "Tell me, what would you do if you were an Estate Manager?"

Mox grinned. "I'd get me a slew of gorgeous women Akasi and spend the rest of my days juggling."

"Seriously, Mox."

"Why would I want to manage an Estate? It would give me a headache."

Orttal glanced at Jev. "What about you?"

"I don't know," Jev said. "A Calani is all I've ever wanted to be."

"I think I could do a good job," Orttal said. "But that doesn't matter, does it? None of us will ever get the chance to manage anything."

"You wouldn't be happy if you did," Hayl said. "It's a woman's job. You can't change biology."

Orttal threw up his hands. "You are impossible."

Hayl turned red. "Why? Because I'm happy being what I am? I don't hate women."

"Neither do I," Orttal said. "What I hate is being told I'm inferior because I'm a man."

"If men were like women," Hayl said, "there would be men Managers. But there aren't. Because of biology."

Orttal scowled. "I'll tell you how biology comes into it. Patterns of reproductive dominance permeate our social structure."

Hayl blinked. "What?"

"He said women control sex," Mox said.

Hayl reddened. "Is that all you think about?"

"Why shouldn't he?" Orttal demanded. "I'll tell you why. Because we have something women want, something they can only get from us, and they don't like that. The more control we have over our own sexuality the more it threatens the Avtacs of Coba."

"So what would you do?" Hayl said. "Run around fathering children everywhere? And you claim Modernism isn't immoral."

Orttal regarded him with exasperation. "I never said that. How can you be so gifted at Quis and so blind when it comes to patterns preset for you by society?"

"They aren't preset," Hayl said. "It's the nature of womankind."

"Womankind?" Orttal snorted. "Is that supposed to include me or what?"

"You know it does." Mox juggled his dice. "Orttal, if we put you in charge of Varz, the Estate would fall apart. We'd be at war with Karn in a year." He waved his hand at Kelric without missing a single die. "Just ask him about the Imperialate. Wars, wars, wars, and their Imperator is a man."

"Actually," Kelric said, "the first Imperator was a woman."

Mox blinked and dropped his dice. Every head in the room turned to Kelric.

Orttal leaned forward. "But a significant fraction of the Imperial leaders are men, aren't they?"

"About half," Kelric said.

"Then what do you think?" Orttal said. "Could a man manage an Estate?"

They were all watching him as if they expected him to say something profound. Since Kelric had nothing profound to offer, he said, "Ideally, yes."

"Ideally?" Orttal looked ready for battle. "What does that mean?"

"As far as ability goes, yes, of course a man can manage an Estate," Kelric said.

"But?" Jev asked.

"A leader can only be effective if people are willing to follow him."

"And you don't think people in the Twelve Estates are," Orttal said.

Kelric considered the thought. "It depends where you are. In a place like Haka or Varz, no. But somewhere like Dahl, yes, I think so. Someday maybe even here, given enough time."

Hayl gaped at him. "You really think that?"

Orttal laughed. "Don't look so shocked."

A tap came at the screen. Orttal went over and pulled aside the reeds, revealing a guard. "Manager Varz is ready for the Quis session with you and Sevtar," the guard said.

Their escort took them through the Estate to a high chamber with arched windows that overlooked Varz. While the guards took up positions outside, Kelric sat with Orttal at the Quis table. A moment later Avtac strode into the room, flushed as if she had been outside in the wind. Kelric suspected she had just arrived back from Karn. She nodded to him, treating him as she always did in public, with an impersonal respect that acknowledged his Level.

As with every one of their sessions together, once they began he saw only her glorious dice. They worked on strategies for issues that had come up during Council, playing Quis at its highest level, a sophisticated weave of patterns designed to shift public opinion to favor Varz over Karn. It required a delicate balance: too obvious, and the patterns could backfire on Avtac when she introduced them into the public net; too modest and they would have little or no effect.

The longer the session progressed, the more Kelric detected a subtle perturbation the others seemed unaware of. He wasn't even sure how to define it. That afternoon, after he returned to the Calanya, he stayed in his suite studying structures from the session. Finally he set aside his dice and went to visit Orttal.

When he knocked, the Third Level called for him to enter. He found Orttal in the den of his suite, standing by an armchair. A cabinet stood next to the chair, its doors closed and locked.

Orttal motioned to another armchair. "Can I get you some Tanghi?"

"Thank you. But no." Kelric sat down, followed by Orttal. "I wanted to talk to you about this morning's session."

"An engrossing one, yes?"

"Yes. But wrong somehow." He searched for the words. "Like someone had been playing Quis with a Calani from the Old Age."

Orttal laughed. "I hope you don't think I sat at dice with a dead Calani."

"Not sat with one. Read about one." He nodded to the cabinet. "Is that where you keep your books?"

Orttal stiffened. "You seem to think Five Levels gives you the liberty to insult people."

"If I'm wrong, I apologize."

Orttal got up and walked to a window that stretched from the floor to the ceiling. He stood silhouetted against the skyscape, watching clouds drift past the glass. "Your Quis tells me much about you, Sevtar."

"Such as?"

Orttal turned. "Such as perhaps you understand me more than the others."

Kelric went to stand with him. "I've lived in a different culture. Several of them, in fact. I may see patterns that someone who grew up here misses."

"Yet you like being a Calani."

"In some ways." In Miesa he had liked it. In Quis terms, his situation at Varz was even better. But without Savina, it all felt like dust.

"And if you knew a Calani had broken his Oath?" Orttal asked. "You are Akasi."

"I won't tell Avtac, if that's what you mean."

Orttal considered him. Then he went to unlock the cabinet. He withdrew a book and brought it over to Kelric. "I was reading this when you knocked."

Kelric took the book. The title, stamped in gilded letters on a suede cover, read: *Legends from the Kej.* Gold edged the parchment pages and the hand-drawn hieroglyphics were artwork, especially the symbol that started each page, a large glyph drawn in gilt inks, with vines curling around it and intricate borders.

"It's gorgeous," Kelric said.

"My wife, Naja, smuggled it to me on her last visit. It's about the reign of the last Kej Queen." Orttal returned the book to the cabinet and locked it away. "I had thought I was keeping it out of the Quis. I should have realized one can hide little from a Fifth Level."

"Our Oath serves a purpose," Kelric said. "Outside influence contaminates the Quis."

Orttal snorted. "Maybe it should be contaminated."

Kelric wished he knew the words to make Orttal see. It mattered to him that the Quis favored Varz: if Avtac's Estate thrived, so did Miesa. Savina's legacy. His daughter. But against Orttal's honed verbal skills, he had no chance of convincing the Third Level.

He had, however, a more powerful tool. He indicated the table. "Will you join me at dice?"

"Of course."

Kelric began with structures of ancient Kej and Orttal responded with patterns of his book. They brought in a sense of the Old Age, how Kej would have solved the problems they had tackled that morning with Avtac. At first the ancient and modern patterns developed along similar lines; Varz was much closer in attitudes to the Old Age than any other Estate except Haka. Then Kelric extended the patterns, showing how ancient Kej solutions to modern Varz problems ultimately failed.

Finally Orttal set down his dice. "You need go no further. I understand what you're trying to tell me." He pushed his hand through his hair. "I've no desire to weaken Varz. But I am *starving*. I want to consume all the literature of the world yet I am forbidden even to read my own name."

Kelric surfaced from the Quis with the disorientation he often experienced after an intense session. "Perhaps if you asked to be released from your Oath—?"

"Few Managers would release even a First Level." Bitterness edged his voice. "But yes, I asked. Avtac refused. I asked to be traded. She refused. I saturated my Quis with Modernism hoping to make her want to be rid of me. It backfired. She retaliated."

"Retaliated? What do you mean?"

Orttal picked up an amber block he used to denote their guards. "She sent an octet for me at night. They moved me all over the Estate, never letting me sleep. Other times she refused to let me see Naja." He touched the opal ball he used for his wife. "This visitation marriage—I am no good at it. I want to live with Naja, see her every day, wake up with her in the morning. I hate it when I can't be with her."

"So you gave in to Avtac?"

"Yes," Orttal said. "I gave in."

"Your Modernism patterns may be more subtle now, but they're still there."

"We all put ourselves into the dice." He regarded Kelric steadily. "The more powerful the Calani, the more it happens."

34

Toppled Nested Tower

Winter blanketed Varz in meters of snow. Hayl looked out at drifts as high as his waist and wondered if Revi liked the desert. At least here he had Sevtar. Brilliant, strong, solid, respected by all Calani; the Fifth Level had no equal. Hayl had feared that once Sevtar began to assimilate into the Varz Calanya, he would tire of having a boy tag after him, preferring the sophisticated company of Orttal and the others. Yet despite his new friendships Sevtar remained steadfast to the old.

Today frost iced the parks. Hayl's breath made misty puffs as he and Sevtar sat on a bench, lacing up the soft shoes they used for running. When Sevtar rolled up his cuff, Hayl saw abrasions around his ankle guard.

"You should tell Avtac about that," Hayl said. "She can have your guards lined."

Sevtar shrugged. "It's nothing."

Hayl tied his other shoe. "At Miesa, my first set of wrist guards didn't fit. Savina had them fixed right away."

A snap broke the morning stillness, and Hayl looked up to see Sevtar holding a broken shoelace. The Fifth Level swore, then tied what was left of the lace and stood. "Let's go."

Hayl bit his lip. For a moment he had forgotten Savina was dead.

Although a crew had cleared snow from the path where they ran every morning, ice feathered the flagstones. Sevtar set a grueling pace and Hayl soon tired, leaving the Fifth Level to sprint up a hill alone. At the top, Sevtar skidded on the ice. He fell backward and rolled down a hill, somersaulting through the snow until he piled into a grove of icefirs and hit the trunk of a tree.

Hayl plowed his way uphill, through billows of snowy powder. He found Sevtar buried in a drift, breathing in labored gasps as if he couldn't pull in enough air. As Hayl knelt next to him, footsteps crunched behind them. He looked up to see the valets gathered around them, all wearing stiff meshes on their boots that let them walk on top of the snow.

Netak turned to the others. "Go get a tank of air." While they took off, Netak crouched down and dug Sevtar out of the snow. Sevtar tried to sit up, then fell back again, struggling to breathe.

Within moments a guard captain appeared, running toward them with an air tank. As she neared, Hayl recognized her as Zecha, captain of the Varz Hunters. Her presence in the

Calanya made him uneasy. Three times now she had come specifically to visit him, and the last time Avtac had given her Speaker's Privilege.

Zecha went to Netak and tilted her head toward the Calani gathering at the bottom of the hill. "Keep them away. But let Doctor Shyl through as soon as she gets here." She glanced at Hayl, her face gentling. "You go wait with the others."

He couldn't leave, not until he knew if Sevtar was all right. He retreated, but stopped when he moved out of Zecha's sight. He saw her put the air cup over Sevtar's mouth, but she didn't switch on the tank. Although Hayl had thought he was out of earshot, he clearly heard her speak.

"You need air?" she murmured. "Beg for it, crooner."

Sevtar swore and grabbed the tank, his fingers scraping across the metal. Dismayed, Hayl ran up the hill, his passage through the icefirs snapping off needles with loud cracks.

Zecha spun around. "I told you to keep away!" She switched on the tank so furtively that had he not known it was off he would never have noticed her turn it on.

Suddenly Doctor Shyl strode past him. As she knelt next to Sevtar, he lay back, drawing in huge lungfuls of air from the tank.

Zecha walked over to Hayl and spoke in a gentler voice. "I'm sorry I shouted at you." Looking down at him, she trailed her fingertips along his cheek. "You shouldn't surprise me that way."

Hayl regarded her uneasily, then backed away to watch the meds help Sevtar to his feet. He wished Zecha would leave him alone.

As soon as Avtac received the message, she strode to the Calanya. She found Sevtar sitting on the bed in his suite, still breathing from the tank but otherwise apparently all right. Hayl hovered nearby and Doctor Shyl stood at the foot of the bed conversing with the Speaker.

Avtac drew the doctor aside. "Why is he having trouble breathing?"

"There's nothing wrong with him," Shyl said. "He told the Speaker something about the air up here being too thin."

"Thin air?" Avtac asked. "As opposed to what? Fat air?"

Shyl smiled. "I didn't ask. I gave him a sleep potion. It should calm him."

Avtac nodded. Sevtar's eyelids were drooping already. She waited until he lay down, then dismissed everyone from the suite. When she was alone with Sevtar, she sat on the bed and watched him sleep. What possessed him to career across the ice with no care or caution? And why hadn't he told her about the problem with his Calanya guards? It was fortunate Shyl noticed it. Had he let it go much longer, the abrasions could have become infected.

She sighed. One never knew with Calani. Illogical behavior seemed innate to their nature. She touched his lips. So warm. The smell of him drew her, made her want to hold him, cradle his head in her lap, surrender to his masculine warmth.

No. Avtac stood up. Never would she let him make her weak. Never would she let him do to her what he had done to Savina.

The blizzard pounded the night like an enraged warlock. Hayl tossed in bed, unable to sleep. Bizarre fragments of nightmare flickered in his mind: desert landscapes, a quarry, Zecha in a warden's uniform. Outside the wind shrieked and battered sleet against the window. Lightning stabbed the room, followed by thunder loud enough to split Varz away from the mountain. He pulled the quilt over his head.

"Hayl?" a voice asked.

He almost jumped out of bed. Then he realized it was only Sevtar standing there in the dark. "Heh. Where did you come from?"

"I'm sorry about the nightmares," Sevtar said. "I didn't mean to keep you awake."

Keep him awake? His dreams weren't Sevtar's fault. "I can't sleep either with all that noise out there." Hayl lit the lamp on his nightstand. "Why don't you stay?"

"All right," Sevtar said. "I'll be right back."

It surprised him that Sevtar wasn't sleeping. The Fifth Level tired more easily now than he used to, why Hayl didn't know. Nor was the accident today the first time Hayl had seen him struggle for breath.

Sevtar returned with a decanter of baiz and sat in an arm-chair by the bed. He made them each a drink, baiz for himself and Tanghi laced with baiz and tawmilk for Hayl. While the wind roared Outside, they sat drinking and talking, covering everything from snow to politics to Quis to starships. By the time Hayl finished his drink he had forgotten the storm.

"Hmmm . . ." He peered into his tumbler. "Makes you float away. Wish I could do that to Zecha."

"You and me both."

"She asked Avtac to give me to her."

"Give you to her?" Sevtar blinked. "What do you mean?"

"Kasi." Hayl stretched out on his back. "They set the cere-mony for my fifteenth birthday."

"Saints *almighty,* Hayl." Sevtar stopped himself. "Unless—is that what you want?"

Hayl grimaced. "When I think about rolling the red die with her, I want a bath."

"Rolling the red die?"

"Mox's favorite subject. Sex."

Sevtar laughed. "Ah, yes." His smile faded. "I take it that means no, you don't want to marry her."

"I'd rather fall through the ice on a frozen lake."

"Tell Avtac how you feel."

"I tried. She never listens." Hayl hesitated. "Could you—I mean, with you being her Akasi—"

"Yes. I'll talk to her for you."

Relief swept over Hayl. "Thanks." He pushed up on his elbow. "Why is Zecha angry at you? Why wouldn't she turn on the air tank?"

Surprise flickered across Sevtar's face. "How did you know that?"

"I heard her."

"You were too far away."

"I know. But I heard her."

Sevtar considered him. "I've thought for a while that you show traces of Kyle reception."

"What is that?"

"It means you have a few Kyle genes paired." He paused, as if looking for the right words. "You're like a receiver. You can pick up a little of what others feel, especially when they're speaking or dreaming. They would have to be empaths, though, to make a signal strong enough for you to register." He tilted his head. "I'll bet Revi is an empath. It's probably why you two are so close. Kyle genes seem more common in pure Miesan stock."

Hayl sat up. "Does that mean Zecha is an empath?"

"Hardly."

"You said I could hear what empaths think. And I heard her. So she must be one."

Sevtar stared at him. "Gods. You're right."

Kastora pushed open the tavern door and walked inside with Ixpar. The hour was late and the youth who usually sang on the stage had gone home. Ixpar indicated a booth in one corner. After the waiter took their orders, she said, "Did you find anything?"

Kastora rested her arms on the wooden tabletop. "I dug up every record of a Fifth Level. In the entire Modern Age only two others besides Sevtar Varz have existed."

The waiter reappeared with their mugs of ale. Ixpar waited until he left, then said, "What were their contracts?"

"After the earthquake of 232 destroyed Hahvna Estate, the survivors went to Ahkah. So the Hahvna Fourth Level became an Ahkah Fifth." Kastora took a swallow of ale. "In 507 a Bahvla Manager fell in love with a Varz Fourth and brought him to Bahvla as a Fifth. The price of his contract was the Bahvla Calanya."

Ixpar's eyebrows went up. "She agreed to that?"

"And more. Varz took all profits from the Bahvla lumber industry for the next century."

Ixpar let out a whistle. "What about in the Old Age?"

"During the Desert Wars, Kej captured a Karn Third and held him prisoner as a Fourth. He escaped and received asylum from Dahl as a Fifth." Kastora set down her ale. "A few centuries later an Ahkah Manager kidnapped a Viasa Fourth and made him her Akasi."

Ixpar smiled. "I guess I could always resort to abduction."

"Are you really thinking of Fifth?"

"We have to do something. Varz is too strong now."

"The only living Fourth is Mentar," Kastora pointed out. "He's already in your Calanya. You would have to arrange for a Third to go to another Estate, stay there long enough to soak up its Quis, and then come here. Even that would do no good. The price of a Fifth Level would wipe out Karn."

"Varz is already wiping us out." Ixpar clenched her fist on the table. "It is unjust. Sevtar has reached the highest Level a Calani can attain, become a legend, had songs written about him, yet he is denied his happiness."

"His wife died. Of course he's unhappy."

"It's more than that."

"How can you know that?"

"It's in the Quis."

"You're the only one who sees it."

"It's there."

Kastora leaned forward. "You know what you need?"

"What?"

"An Akasi. Someone to keep your mind off Avtac's husbands." Kastora thought of the tavern singer. His voice stirred her heart and his slender physique stirred the rest of her. "A warm fellow to curl up with at night. It settles a woman."

Ixpar laughed. "You should see your face. Gone courting, heh?"

"Of course not." In truth, she hadn't yet summoned the courage to make her interest known to the singer. "A Minister, however, should have an Akasi."

Ixpar shrugged. "There is no Calani I wish to wed."

The ancient dilemma, Kastora thought. Law required Managers to declare vows only with a Calani, the higher the Level the better, particularly for the Minister. Most Ministers chose a Second or Third from another Estate, often arranging the marriage after seeing the man only once or twice.

"Jahlt probably felt the same way," Kastora said. "But look how well her arrangement with Mentar worked out."

"I'm not ready to take an Akasi. I'm only twenty-seven, for wind's sake."

Kastora downed her ale. "Well, someday."

"Someday," Ixpar said.

* * *

Standing in the snow-covered park under an icefir, Kelric watched Garith. The Second Level was about twenty meters away, sitting on a high-backed bench with his eyes closed and his face tipped back to savor the winter sun. A tall man, though not as tall as Avtac, he had classic features, with the blue eyes and yellow hair so rare and so prized among the northern Estates. Although Kelric knew he looked much younger than Garith, the two of them were actually the same age, in their late forties.

Kelric walked over to him. "May I join you?"

Garith opened his eyes. "No."

Although Kelric inwardly winced, he plowed ahead anyway. "Garith, we need to talk. This is affecting our Quis."

"Talk about what?" Garith stood up. "I never say a word about her boys in the city. What good would it do? When she brought that First Level here I kept my mouth shut. She got bored and traded him to Shazorla. Now you're here and you won't be leaving. So what do you expect me to say? That after all these years, I like being pushed aside like an old dice pouch?" He shook his head. "I have no wish to talk to you." Then he turned and walked away.

Gods, Kelric thought. So much for his diplomacy.

He went back to his suite and stood at a floor-to-ceiling window in his bedroom watching clouds nudge the glass. The thick pane was set into a cliff that plunged down until it disappeared in the mountains far below. If he could just step out . . .

Stop it, Kelric told himself. What would Roca do without her father? Her next visit wasn't until tomorrow and her absence left him empty and lonely.

Kelric settled into his favorite armchair and dozed, waking at intervals to look at the tall clock across the room with its swinging pendulum. The afternoon passed with numbing dullness.

Toward evening he heard someone push aside the screen of his suite. Then Hayl appeared in the door arch of the bedroom.

"Yes?" Kelric asked.

"I was worried when you missed dinner."

Kelric stayed slouched in his chair. "I wasn't hungry."

As silence stretched between them, Hayl looked around as

if searching for a way to cheer Kelric up. When he saw Kelric's boots by the window, he smiled. "I figured out how to open the cliff windows. Some of them have pattern locks worked into the carvings on their frames."

Kelric sat up straighter. "Hayl, it's not safe." Somehow the boy had picked up his interest in the windows. On some sides of the Estate, the outer walls were cut straight from a cliff and decorated with bas-relief. A person could conceivably climb out to a ledge and creep along the wall to the city using projections for handholds. Of course they could also fall, a drop of over a kilometer.

However, in the region of the Calanya, no decorations graced the sheer wall of stone that dropped into the clouds. Kelric had no doubt the reason was historical, dating from the Old Age when Calani were often held against their will. The architecture still served its purpose, trapping him here.

"I don't want you to open the windows," he said.

"Not even the ones in my suite?" Hayl asked. "They just open onto the parks."

"You figured those out too?"

"They were easy."

Hayl's knack with the locks amazed him. The mechanisms were designed from tiny bars and knobs that had to be pushed, pulled, and turned in patterns that seemed random to Kelric. Some quirk of Hayl's brain allowed him to solve the puzzle every time.

"Just be careful," Kelric said. The drop from Hayl's windows to the parks was only a few meters, but it could still cause injury. "Don't hang out of them."

"I won't," Hayl promised.

After the boy left, Kelric stared at the ceiling. It had been days since he talked to Avtac about Hayl's kasi ceremony, a resounding failure of an attempt. He had to give it at least one more try.

He went to find the Taks.

Avtac waited until the Taks withdrew from the den in her private suite. Then she said, "I hope this is important, Sevtar. I have a lot of work to do."

Kelric detested sparring with her, but he had made a promise to Hayl and he meant to keep it. He stood facing her across the expanse of the desk, where she sat in her big chair.

"It's Hayl," he said.

"This better not be about his kasi ceremony again. That matter is none of your affair."

He leaned forward, his hands braced on the desk. "Can't you see how he feels about it? You'll ruin his life."

Avtac took off her reading glasses. "I am tired of this vendetta you have against Captain Zecha. It is jealousy, yes? Right now you are the most important person to that boy. You don't want to lose him to Zecha."

"This has nothing to do with Zecha and me. Hayl doesn't love her. He doesn't even like her. And he's a child, for wind's sake. He's too young to be anyone's kasi."

Annoyance edged her voice. "Maybe if there weren't so many 'modern' men today, women wouldn't have to seek half-grown youths to find an unsullied mate." She considered him. "But then, I'm not telling you anything new."

"What is that supposed to mean?"

She put her glasses back on. "You should know. You've been with half the Managers on Coba."

He scowled. "So find yourself a 'cleaner' Akasi and leave me alone."

"You should be grateful I was willing to overlook your past." She got up and walked around the desk to him. "This isn't Miesa. Savina may have let you meddle in Estate business but I will tolerate no such interference."

Kelric felt as if she had kicked him in the stomach. "Let Savina be."

Avtac spoke in a gentler voice. "I don't mean to hurt you." She laid her hand on his arm. "I realize you cannot help your nature."

It was too much. Kelric snapped up his arm to throw off her hand. With no warning or reason, his enhanced strength kicked in and he literally flung her into a bookshelf. As the shelves toppled, she jumped away and smacked her palm against a com on the wall.

Gods no, Kelric thought. He stepped toward her. "Avtac, I didn't mean—"

She grabbed a beam from the fallen shelf. "Stay back."

Combat mode on, Bolt thought.

What the hell? *Mode off!* he thought.

He heard running feet and spun around to see his valets and Calanya escort. As Netak drew his stunner, Kelric struck the gun out of his hand, his speed enhanced by the malfunctioning Bolt, which for some bizarre reason had interpreted a domestic quarrel as a combat situation. Could he actually be that traumatized by his situation at Varz? The combination of his neurological damage with stress must have pushed his already erratic biomech systems even further out of kilter.

The escort tried to stun him, but despite the damage to his systems, his hydraulics kept him moving and his biomech web synthesized an antidote. Finally the Taks managed to pin him against the wall. While he struggled, Qahotra appeared with a straitjacket. They wrapped it around his torso and fastened him into it with his arms pulled across his chest.

"Take him into the bedroom," Avtac said. "But be careful. I don't want him hurt."

Combat mode off, Bolt thought.

No! Kelric thought. *Reactivate!* Now, when he needed Bolt's help, it had deserted him.

The Taks half carried, half dragged him into the bedroom. As they held him down on the bed, a nurse tried to force a pill down his throat. When he spat it out, Doctor Shyl bent over him with a syringe.

Avtac grabbed the doctor's arm. "What is that?"

Shyl showed her the syringe. "It injects the medicine into his blood. It's much faster than a potion."

"I won't have you experimenting on him."

"It's safe," Shyl assured her.

Kelric stared at the syringe, then redoubled his efforts to escape. With the Taks holding him down, Shyl administered the shot. Within moments, his muscles went lax and voices became muffled, as if he were underwater.

Avtac leaned over him. "He's calmer now."

Shyl's face appeared. "What set him off?"

"He's always been high-strung," Avtac said. The rest of her answer faded into blackness.

When Kelric awoke, groggy and disoriented, twilight filled the room. A blur sat on the bed and spoke with Avtac's voice. "Can I get you anything?"

He wet his lips. "Water."

Lifting his head, she tilted a glass to his mouth. "It will all be fine," she murmured. "The medicine will help you."

"Not sick," he mumbled. Then he passed out again.

The next time he awoke, sunlight was streaming through the windows. Someone had removed the straitjacket and bathed him. Turning his head, he saw an orderly sitting in a chair by the bed.

She looked up from her book and smiled. "Feeling better? I'll call Manager Varz."

Before Kelric could protest, the orderly was on the com to Avtac. The Manager appeared a few minutes later and dismissed the orderly, then sat on the bed and smiled at Kelric. "I'm glad you are feeling better."

Better from what? Her emotional abuse? Regardless of how he felt about Avtac, though, he hadn't meant to attack her. "Are you all right?"

She nodded. "We will speak no more about it."

Why the hell not? he thought. But he said nothing. Silence was his only defense against words that cut deeper than steel. Anger edged his thoughts, mixing with the Quis patterns in his mind. He tried to suppress it, lest it turn into a rage that could sear his dice, and through them Varz, Miesa, and the Twelve Estates.

It was only a glimpse, a flash of yellow hair on the icy windbreak. Kelric almost called Savina's name—but the distant figure was only one of his guards. He walked on through the snow-deep park, uncaring where he went.

". . . all right?" a voice said. "Sevtar, what is the matter?"

Kelric stopped. Orttal stood in front of him, silhouetted against an overcast sky. The Third Level started to speak, then stopped, looking past him. Turning, Kelric saw the juggler Mox running to where Qahotra stood in the next park. He skidded to a stop in front of the Calanya captain and waved his hands as he talked to her. She listened, then took off running back the way he had come.

Kelric and Orttal walked over to the juggler. "What's going on?" Orttal asked.

"It's Hayl," Mox said, breathing hard from his run. "I didn' even know he was playing with it—then he leaned out—to see a bird or something—I don't know what."

Not again, Kelric thought. Hayl's game with the windows in his suite had continued unabated. Even if Hayl had fallen, though, he couldn't be too badly hurt. Had the boy been in pain, Kelric knew he would have felt it.

"I told him to get back inside," Mox said. "*I told him.*"

"Mox, slow down," Orttal said. "What happened?"

"He fell. *Fell.*"

"Is he all right?" Kelric asked.

"In my suite—he figured it out—I don't know how. I didn' even know those cliff windows opened."

Kelric's sense of calm shattered. "The *what* windows?"

"The cliff." Mox's voice cracked. "He fell over the cliff."

No. It couldn't be true. If Hayl had died he would know. Kelric took off for the Calanya, his mind creating nightmare images of Hayl plummeting down the cliff, as if he saw his own son hurtling to his death.

When he reached Mox's suite, he pushed past the crowd in the door arch. Avtac was already inside the bedroom, and Zecha had gone to the floor-to-ceiling window that stood open like a door of glass. Chill wind whispered past it as a cloud seeped inside, curling tendrils of mist around her.

Kelric walked to the window, past even Zecha. He stood in the opening and looked at the cliff plunging down from his feet. Hayl, he thought. Come back. His mind conjured up unwanted scenes: Hayl skidding on the cliff, Hayl tearing through trees, Hayl caught in a cage of roots.

Zecha spoke in a low voice. "He told me yesterday he was going to impress you." Incredibly, tears showed on her face. "And now he's dead." She took his arm to draw him back into the room, but in the same moment that he pulled away from her, she let her hand drop, her face numb, as if she didn't care whether he fell or not. As a result, he gave his pull more momentum than he needed, lost his balance—and stumbled out the window.

"No!" Avtac shouted. "Stop him!"

The sky careened past Kelric as he toppled into the abyss of air. His biomech toggled on and he grabbed the sill as he dropped past it, yanking to an arm-wrenching halt. With hydraulic-driven strength, he vaulted back into the room.

Dimly he was aware of people shouting and pulling him away from the window. The shock of Hayl's death together with his biomech-enhanced drive of adrenaline was too much. He lashed out with his fists, catching a guard, then another, then Zecha. His escort kept firing their stunners, until he sank to his knees on the floor.

As his adrenaline calmed, Bolt took him out of combat mode. Kelric looked up to see aides and Calani staring at him in disbelief. He stared back, too stunned by his own reaction to move.

Night gathered in Avtac's office. She stood alone in the dark, gazing out a tall window at the stars.

How did it happen? So few cliff windows even opened and those that did locked with intricate patterns. Only a trained smith who knew the combination could release them. Hayl could never have solved a puzzle that would stymie even her, Manager of Varz. It was harsh, bitter luck. Somehow he'd stumbled on the sequence, a fluke that cost his life and almost took Sevtar's as well.

Why did Sevtar jump? Why did he change his mind? Why did he go berserk? She still felt the horror of seeing him lunge to his death, still felt that terrible sense of loss that hit her when she thought he was gone. After he vaulted back into the room she had wanted to sob with relief.

She was losing control.

It was unacceptable. Was Zecha right, that Sevtar destroyed everything he came near? Or was Doctor Shyl right, that he suffered from some traumatic stress disorder complicated by grief and loneliness? What trauma? He lived a life of luxury. He showed no signs of grief. And how could he be lonely? She spent almost every night with him.

Her desk com buzzed. Avtac flipped the switch. "Yes?"

"Captain Zecha is here, ma'am," an aide said.

Avtac turned on the lights, filling her office with harsh luminance. "Send her in."

It was a muted Zecha who entered and bowed to her. "My greetings."

"How are you?" Avtac asked.

"I'd like to return to duty."

Avtac knew work would heal Zecha better than sitting in Med. "All right."

The captain hesitated. "The searchers—have they—"

Avtac wished she knew words to console the captain for her loss. "They haven't found his body yet. But they will keep looking, even in the storm."

Zecha nodded. "And Sevtar?"

Avtac went to the window and stared out at the night. "Still in Med. Shyl felt it best to keep him sedated until we know how to treat him."

In a soft, ugly voice, Zecha said, "Is having him worth it, Avtac? Are his Five Levels worth the grief they've brought you?"

Avtac continued to stare out the window. She answered to no one and that included the captain of her Hunters. Was having Sevtar worth the grief of losing Savina and Hayl? Only she would ever know her answer to that.

Yes. He was worth it. Nothing would ever convince her to let him go.

Nothing.

In the freezing darkness, thick flakes of snow whirled about a gnarled tree that clung to the cliff face, its roots buckling out of cracks in the rock to form a basket. Hayl huddled within the basket's precarious embrace, shivering violently, starting a slide of pebbles that fell and fell and fell, their clatter fading in the wail of the blizzard. He listened to the wind shriek, knowing that at any moment his added weight on the tree could cause its roots to rip away from the cliff.

The search parties would look for his body at the base of the cliff. Not here. He had no food. No water. No protection. No chance of rescue.

He could only wait to die.

35

Queen's Gamble

Jevrin Karn, alias Jevrin Varz, flew his rider on instruments through the blizzard. The route he took down from Varz hugged perilously close to the cliff, hiding him from the other craft also out in the storm.

The limbs of a tree leapt into view, and he barely managed to yank on the wheel in time to sheer away from the branches. Incredibly, as the tree careened past the windshield he saw what looked like a boy clinging to its roots.

It was impossible, of course. But the image of the boy's terrified face stayed with him, until finally he circled back. By folding in the rider's wing slats, he managed to pull closer to the tree—and this time he distinctly saw a figure huddled within its roots.

Jevrin swore. How in a dice cheater's hell did a boy get there? More important, how did he get him out? Although the rider had extra airfoils to stabilize it in high winds, it was madness to put it on autopilot during a storm. But if he went back to Varz for a properly equipped rescue party, he would be caught flying a rider he had no business flying with a cargo he had no business carrying. He could reach Karn, but the boy would probably be torn away from the cliff long before he brought back help.

With a prayer to the wind gods, Jevrin locked in the autopilot, jumped out of his seat, and ran to the back of the cabin. As he grabbed a crane hook and rope from the locker, the rider pitched like a Lasa drunkard. He made it to the pilot's seat in time to steady the craft. He tied one end of the rope to the chair and the other to the hook, then headed back to the tree.

When Jevrin sighted the boy, he hit the autopilot and went to the hatch, playing out the rope so it pulled taut from his hand to his seat. As he heaved open the hatch, wind rushed at him, threatening to knock him over. Hanging on to the rope with one hand, he hurled the hook into the night.

The throw went wild, nowhere near the boy. Jevrin yanked the hook back in, then scrambled for the pilot's seat as the rider swerved and shuddered. Coming around for another try, he changed the camber of the airfoils and the arch of the wing slats, trying to stabilize the craft.

This time when he heaved out the hook, it flew through the blizzard and caught in the tree roots. The boy grabbed at it—

And the entire tree ripped away from the cliff.

A scream tore through the night. In the same instant, the rider bucked and Jevrin had to jump for the pilot's seat, leaving him no time to see if the boy was hanging on to the rope pulled taut out the hatch. As soon as he regained control of the craft, he spun around and hauled on the rope.

Miraculously, a wildly tousled crown of curls appeared in the hatch—and dropped from sight again. Jevrin swore and pulled harder, frantic now. No one could hold on for long while the rider pitched in the storm.

He kept pulling, struggling with no success to haul in the boy. The rope slipped in his hands and he almost lost control of it. With a gasp of desperation, he gave an extra hard yank—and heaved a body into the cabin. The boy sprawled across the floor, breathing in huge sobs. Just before Jevrin whirled back to the controls, he saw what gleamed on the boy's arms.

Calanya bands.

As Jevrin struggled to steady the rider, he heard the hatch slam closed, leaving an abrupt silence. Glancing over his shoulder, he saw the Calani huddled against the hull. With tears streaming down his face, the boy mouthed the words *Thank you.*

Jevrin nodded awkwardly, wondering if his guest would feel so grateful when he found out his situation. He couldn't take the Calani to Varz; the circumstances would incriminate him as a spy. He had no choice but to bring the youth with him, making the rescue into an abduction.

At Jevrin's invitation, the boy came over and sat in the copilot's seat. Jevrin peered at his armbands. "Hayl?"

The Calani nodded.

"How did you get out there, Hayl?"

When Hayl pantomimed a fall, Jevrin realized he must be the Calani rumored to have gone over the cliff this morning. Relief swept over him. No one would guess Hayl had been kidnapped; as far as anyone knew, the boy was dead.

Hayl pointed to the altimeter registering their drop in altitude, then gave Jevrin a puzzled look and motioned upward.

"We're not going to Varz," Jevrin said.

The boy touched the Varz insignia on his wrist guard.

"I know," Jevrin said. "I'm sorry, Hayl. But you aren't going back."

Hidden among jutting crags, a rider crouched under the stars in an abandoned quarry. The shadow of a second craft slipped through the night and settled next to it like a giant bird. Its hatch opened, letting Jevrin disembark. The hatch of the other rider opened and the ruler of Coba stepped out into the wind.

Jevrin bowed to her. "Minister Karn."

Ixpar nodded, concerned by his lateness. "Did you have trouble getting here?"

He told her about the Calani he had rescued. "I brought him with me."

They climbed inside the darkened cabin of his rider and he set screens over the windshield, then turned on the lights. The Calani sat in the copilot's seat watching them. Lithe and slender, with large eyes, he reminded Ixpar of a hazelle colt.

Jevrin presented her to the boy, respecting the custom that gave a Calani social rank above even a Minister. "Hayl, this is Ixpar Karn."

Hayl stared at her, then turned confused eyes to his rescuer.

"I'm from Karn," Jevrin said.

Hayl pointed to the Varz badge on Jevrin's uniform.

"I know," Jevrin said. "But I work for Karn."

The boy gave him a look that plainly said *traitor*. He turned away and stared straight ahead, gripping the arms of his seat.

Laying a hand on Jevrin's shoulder, Ixpar tilted her head toward the hatch. He switched off the lights and they stepped back out into the wind, where they could talk in private.

"You have news?" Ixpar asked.

He reached inside the hatch and took an object from where he had lashed it to a bulkhead. Ixpar recognized his cargo; her own newly formed ArmsGuild was also making rifles.

She tested the gun's balance. "What were you told was its purpose?"

"To hunt," he said. "It could be true. The winter this year was even worse than usual. Lack of game has been making the big cats desperate. They're even coming into the city."

The strain in his voice disturbed Ixpar. "Is Varz in danger?"

"No. I don't think so."

She watched his drawn face. "What is it?"

"There was trouble, something with the Fifth Level."

Ixpar tensed. "Go on."

"I'm not sure what happened, but he's in Med." Jevrin shook his head. "There have been rumors, Ixpar, ever since he came to Varz. It isn't pretty. And apparently now they're 'treating' him with electroshock therapy."

So. It was true, the subtle traces she picked up in the Quis that her advisers claimed she imagined. "Avtac has no right."

"Sevtar is her Akasi. She has every right."

Ixpar knew no Estate would support her if she challenged the Akasi Law of Ownership, which should have been banished to the history scrolls long ago. The Managers would never tolerate such an intrusion into their private lives.

Ixpar cocked the rifle and braced it against her shoulder.

"Raise arms against Varz over this," Jevrin said, "and every Estate on Coba will be set against you."

She sighted on a boulder. "Varz invented the rifle. Not Karn."

"If you kidnap Sevtar, the Council will hunt you down. You'll start a war."

Her grip on the rifle tightened. How could she, who presumed to lead a world, think to destroy a peace that had lasted a thousand years?

She lowered the gun. "No one on Coba will support me if I challenge Avtac over this. No trade exists for a Sixth Level. If I take him by force I start a war I can't win."

"I've tried to think of a solution." Jevrin spread his hands. "I don't see any."

"Do you know the third passage from Roaz?"

"Something about virtues, isn't it?"

" 'I seek three virtues,' " Ixpar said. " 'The strength to face my enemy, the courage to face my fears, and the wisdom to face my failures.' "

"Which do you seek now?"

She gave him the gun. "The one Roaz missed. The brains to find an answer."

Stahna Varz, Successor to the Varz Manager, set the letter on Avtac's desk. "This came today from Karn."

Avtac glanced up from her papers. The letter looked, from its thin size, like the usual request for verification of Varz attendance at Council. "You have authority to respond to Ministry communications."

Stahna spoke quietly. "Not this one."

Avtac picked up the letter. "What is it?"

"An offer for Sevtar's contract."

"Are you making a joke, Stahna?"

"No."

"Then Ixpar Karn is making a joke. A childish one." Avtac pushed the letter across the desk. "Throw it away."

"Perhaps you should read it first."

Avtac considered her. Then she opened the letter. The message consisted of one sentence.

She read it.

And read it again.

Avtac took up a quill and parchment. The note she wrote was brief. She rolled it into a scroll, tied it with a thong, sealed it in wax, and handed it to Stahna.

"Send this to Karn," she said.

All of Karn watched the flock of windriders land. People peered out of towers, climbed up on housetops, scaled every wall of every building in every section of the city. Like vines growing fresh on the roofs, heavy with fruit, spreading leaves in a profusion of life, the people crowded out to watch. After today, Coba would be changed forever.

A Sixth Level was coming to Karn.

Ixpar waited in the Hall of Teotec, watching from a window above the airfield as the Karn escort disembarked from the central rider. Then a tall figure, robed and cowled in black, stepped down. The escort walked with him across the tarmac and crossed the gardens outside the Estate. When they disappeared from view, she left the window and faced the great double doors of the Hall.

Moments later the doors swung open and a retinue swept in, followed by a double column of aides. The Calanya escort entered next, with the cowled man in its center.

Suddenly it seemed to Ixpar that the Hall would burst with people. With a motion of her raised hand, she dismissed everyone: retinues, aides, guards. They looked at her in consternation, but when she met their gazes with silence they left.

Then she stood alone, on the dais in the great Hall where the Council had convened for two millennia. At the end of the Hall the robed figure watched her. When he pushed back his cowl everything seemed to stop: the winds no longer blew, the dice no longer rolled, and her heart ceased its beat.

Incredibly, at first he looked no older than on that day his ship had made its flaming descent into the mountains above Dahl. Then she saw the gray in his hair, the dulled sheen of his skin.

But it was Kelric.

He walked down the Hall, his cloak billowing out behind him. As he drew near she drank in the sight of him, still so familiar after so many years. He climbed the dais and came to the Circle, never smiling, never taking his gaze from her face. When he stepped down into the Circle, his eyes were level with hers. The Oath waited for their voices to give it life, to raise it to a power greater than ever before known.

Ixpar spoke. "For Karn and for Coba, do you enter the Circle to give your Oath?"

"Yes." The burr of his accent was still strong.

A chill ran up her back. "Do you swear to keep forever the discipline of the Calanya? To hold my Estate above all else, as you hold in your hands and mind the future of Karn?"

"Yes."

"Do you swear, on penalty of your life, that your loyalty is to Karn and only to Karn?"

"Yes."

"In return for your Oath, I vow that for the rest of your life you will be provided for as befits a Calani." Silently, she added: *No one will ever hurt you again. On penalty of my life, I swear it.*

Then, finally, she spoke the question she had waited half her life to ask. "Will you accept the bands of an Akasi?"

When he said nothing, only looked at her, Ixpar died inside. Fumbling, she reached into her pocket for the other armbands, those with no Akasi inscription.

"Yes," Kelric said.

It was one word, one simple sound, but it had the power to change a world. She swallowed, then put back the armbands and took the pair out of her other pocket. The Akasi bands. She slid them onto his arms, making them the sixth pair he wore.

"Kelric Sevtar Karn," she said. "You are now a Sixth Level Calani of Karn."

For a long moment he looked at her. Then he spoke in a husky voice. "What price a Sixth Level?"

Silence echoed in the Hall. Her words fell into it like stones.

"The rule of a world."

VI

Karn

36

SunSky Bridge Denied

Ixpar drummed her fingers on her desk, wondering what demented ancient had thought up the custom that made a Manager wait half her wedding night before going to her Akasi. Did Kelric really need all that time to prepare? It seemed more likely he would get bored and go to bed.

She got up and paced around the office until she came to the mirror. She hardly recognized her reflection; the unfamiliar lace blouse and velvet pants were foreign to her usual plain trousers and shirt. She had freed her hair from its braid, letting it fall to her waist. Tendrils curled around her cheeks.

Would he think her attractive? Was she? All she saw in the mirror was Ixpar. She had no idea whether or not her appearance pleased. It had never occurred to her to worry about it before. Beauty wasn't on the list of qualifications for a Minister.

No, not Minister. Manager. All her life she had taken it for granted she would rule Coba. Now the title was gone, for her and all future generations of Karn. Would history curse her for what she gave to Varz? When she and Kelric were buried, what would it matter that a Sixth Level had existed?

It matters, Ixpar thought.

She had wrestled with her decision. Who truly ruled Coba: Minister or Quis? In the past those two choices had been the same. Now the patterns were in upheaval, re-formed in ways no one yet understood. The Quis of a Sixth Level combined with the hidden Memory of Karn; it would be a power never before known on Coba. Kelric's legacy would survive for millennia. But could it swamp even the might of a Varz Ministry?

Ixpar didn't know the answer. Faced with that uncertainty, with Kelric's situation at Varz, and with the danger of his growing rage to the Quis, she had made the best decision she could. Only history would know if it had been the right one.

She picked up an amberwood box from her desk and lifted its polished lid. A statue nestled inside, an althawk carved from wing-ivory. She had commissioned Karn's most renowned carver to make it ten days ago, when she learned Kelric would come to her Estate.

The clock on the wall chimed. Ixpar jumped, startled by its announcement that Night's Midhour had arrived. Then, gift in hand, she left the office and went to her groom.

The Akasi suite was dark. Kelric's dinner sat untouched in the dining room and the bed was empty. Ixpar wondered if the escort had somehow made the absurd mistake of taking him to the wrong suite. Then she saw a trickle of light in a hall. She followed it and found him sitting in a dimly lit alcove.

"Kelric?" she asked.

He didn't even look at her, he just stood up and walked past her into the bedroom. Sitting on the bed, he began to unlace his shirt.

She watched from the door arch. "You are so silent."

He looked up at her. "I wasn't under the impression talking was what you wanted."

No. This wasn't how it was supposed to happen. "Would you prefer to be alone?"

"Yes," he said.

She suddenly felt ludicrous, an ex-Minister dressed up in silly clothes. "I will call for the escort. They can show you to your Calanya suite."

For the first time a response flickered across his face. Relief.

"Before you go—" She swallowed. "Would you answer a question for me?"

He said nothing, just waited, and it made the asking all the more difficult. But she had to know. "Why did you accept my Akasi bands?"

He spoke in an emotionless voice. "You paid a high price for your Sixth Level. Obviously you expected more than Quis in return."

Ixpar inwardly reeled. Yet what else should she have expected? What made her think that after all he had suffered he would want to lie with a virtual stranger? Why should he? It was only she who had harbored a secret love for half her life.

After he was gone, she sat on the bed and buried her head in her hands.

Hayl set his octahedron next to Bahr's cube. "My game."

"Pah," the Quis Wizard grumbled. "Aren't you supposed to meet an escort?"

"Ai! I forgot." Hayl scooped up his dice and hurried to his suite entrance, trailed by Bahr. They found his guards Outside talking to the Karn Calanya escort.

Eb, the escort captain, bowed to Hayl. "Shall we go?"

He nodded uneasily and went with misgiving, unsure of their destination, leaving his own escort to return Bahr to her secluded suite. Although Bahr couldn't live within the Calanya, he feared Ixpar meant to put him in her Calanya as a prelude to forcing a Karn Oath on him.

When he first refused to play Quis at Karn, she seemed to understand. His Oath was to Varz. But he soon grew restless, until finally he agreed to sit at Outsider Quis with Bahr. The gambler just didn't seem like a real Calani. He wondered now if the games with Bahr had been meant to soften his resistance.

He tried to resent his abductors, but it became harder as time passed. He had never met anyone like Ixpar Karn, who had Avtac's power and Savina's humanity. If Avtac found out he was here, she would be within her rights to call a Council Tribunal. They would "rescue" him and punish Karn, probably with fines, tariffs, and embargoes. Worse, Karn would lose influence in the Quis. Despite his Varz Oath, he had no wish to see harm come to Karn. Besides, as long as he was "dead," Zecha couldn't touch him.

The escort led him through unfamiliar halls. When they stopped in front of two huge portals with gold handles, he knew they had reached the Calanya. As Eb opened the doors, he balked.

"It's all right," the captain said. "We're only visiting."

Hayl stayed put. He couldn't resist looking Inside, though. Light slanted through stained-glass windows, making patterns of color on the floor. The serenity drew him. When Eb opened the door wider, he ventured forward, and the escort came with him into the common room. Some of the Calani glanced up and nodded, then went back to their dice.

For some reason Eb urged him over to an archway, where she tapped at the screen. A moment later a man drew aside the screen—and Hayl's mouth fell open.

The man smiled, holding up his hand to invite Hayl into his suite. As soon as they were alone, Hayl said, "Sevtar! What are you doing here? Winds, you've got six bands. Six." He closed his mouth as the import of it hit him.

Six Levels.

"So it's true." Sevtar watched him with a gentle gaze. "You're alive."

"A tree caught me."

"Gods, Hayl." Sevtar's voice caught as they embraced. "It's good to see you." He set Hayl back from him and smiled, a drop of water glistening in the corner of his eye. Then he motioned at his Quis table. "Will you play dice with me?"

Almost giddy with seeing Sevtar again, Hayl pulled off his pouch.

It wasn't until long afterward that he realized just how thoroughly he had broken his Oath.

37

The Bridge of Olonton

Summer in Karn lasted longer than in the upper ranges. Autumn gusted with chill winds but the winter snows came gently, wafting from the sky. Spring unfurled in a multitude of lavender, pink, and blue blossoms on the plumberry vines. Kelric watched the seasons from his suite, where the interplay of sunshine and shadow in the rooms shifted with a grace that spoke eloquently of the architects who had built this, the first Estate.

On a morning in early spring, he walked across the parks to a secluded lake far from the Calanya. Sitting on a knoll that overlooked the water, he bowed his head. The tears came softly, running down his cheeks, silent in their release from the prison he had built around his heart in Varz and then slowly dismantled as the seasons in Karn passed. He made no sound, just sat by the lake and cried until his grief spent itself in the gilded afternoon.

Ixpar sat by a window in her study, warmed in a pool of sunlight. While she ate her Midday meal she went through the last of the Ministry documents still at Karn, filing them to send to Varz. It had taken well over a year to shift the Ministry, but soon the transition would be complete.

She lifted a page off the pile. This was the conclusion, the final document she had signed as Minister. It wasn't world-shaking, simply a pardon for a young man in the Haka prison, a bookkeeper in Compound Two. Ched Viasa. She wondered how he would feel if he knew he was the last person touched by the reign of Karn.

An aide tapped at the door arch. "Ma'am? Captain Eb would like to see you."

"Send her in." Ixpar blinked at the interruption. She had scheduled no Quis sessions today, feeling a need to be alone while she concluded her final acts as Minister.

Eb entered and bowed. "Sevtar wishes to see you, ma'am."

A ticklefly fluttered in Ixpar's stomach. "Very well."

While Eb went for him, Ixpar paced a bit, then stopped by a window and watched children playing in a courtyard below her suite. Why today? Kelric had never before sought her companionship. He sat at dice with her and played a miraculous Quis like none she had ever known, but that was their only contact. She felt no closer to him now than the day he had taken his Karn Oath.

"Ixpar?"

She turned with a start. He stood by the archway, glimmering in the sunlight like his Coban namesake, god of the dawn. Her voice tied itself into knots and left her mute. Watching him, she again felt the guilt that came every time she remembered how little success she had so far in gaining custody of his daughter for him from Varz.

Kelric came over to her. "I wanted to tell you."

"Tell me?"

He hesitated. "About that night—"

"Night?" So close to him now, she found herself incapable of coming up with intelligent responses.

"In the Akasi suite."

"The Akasi suite."

"About the—you see, what—ai, Ixpar, I don't know how to do this. I am no good with words."

She thought of her sparkling responses in the past minute. "Right now, neither am I."

He grinned. "The infamous Orator of Karn is tongue-tied?"

His expression caught her utterly off guard. It was a full smile, not his usual slight curve of the lips. His teeth flashed white, lighting his entire face. It made it even harder for her to say what had to be said. "It was wrong for me to push the Akasi bands on you. If you wish to be only Calani, I will release you from your Akasi vow."

"Ixpar, no. That wasn't what I meant." He took her hands. "You were so beautiful that night, a warrior goddess in velvet and lace."

A curious sense came over her then, as if she floated above their bodies looking down in the slanting rays of the sun at a private moment captured in amber. She stepped forward and Kelric came into her arms.

That afternoon, they joined together in the simplicity of her own rooms rather than the opulence of an Akasi suite. Afterward they lay in the rays of a setting sun that left a faint glow in the room. A hint of fiery light touched Ixpar's face as she drifted to sleep.

38

Multiple Phalanxes

"Karn cheated Varz." Avtac walked through the Estate gardens with her successor. "Ixpar lied."

"She signed the papers," Stahna said. "You are Minister."

Avtac opened her fist, revealing her Karn octahedron, a diamond that threw splinters of sunlight into her hand. "No one can touch her Quis. No one even comes close." She dropped the die and it thudded onto the dirt path. "With her Sixth Level she holds Coba in a stronger grip than when she was Minister."

"Does it matter?" Stahna retrieved the diamond for her. "Ixpar and Sevtar won't live forever. Varz will. And the Ministry with it."

Sevtar. During the tenday before he left for Karn, Avtac had wanted him constantly, knowing he would soon be gone. She could still see his golden body stretched across her bed, driving a hunger she never satisfied. She had thought sending him away would quench her desire, give her back control, but instead her craving grew worse. She hated herself for that weakness, tried to bury it with her work, with Quis, Garith, a new youth in the city. Nothing worked.

Sevtar was hers. He belonged to Varz.

Henta Bahvla sat glowering at her desk. Any aides who ventured into her office received a cold stare until they retreated.

"Why doesn't she just send copies?" Henta said to the empty room. "Why bother with a new letter every time?" Beneath the formal jargon, every one of Avtac's messages said the same thing: Miesa was now Varz and that included the Miesa Plateau.

Only in a dice cheater's hell, Henta thought. None of this rolled well with her. Ixpar had been a good Minister. More than good. Brilliant. Avtac was iron. The unrelenting power of Varz boded nothing but trouble.

"She'll not get the Plateau," Henta said. "Not if I can help it."

Rashiva always enjoyed her dinners with Jimorla. Tonight they celebrated. News had come this morning; ten-year-old Jimorla ranked well in his exams and was accepted to the Preparatory House.

He grew so fast, this son of hers, like a steeplestalk, with the creamy dark skin of the Hakaborn. Like Raaj. Only when the sun hit his skin just right did it reveal that telling gold shimmer.

Jimorla watched her from across the table. "Why are you so quiet?"

"I was thinking about Raaj. He's very proud of you."

His face brightened. "Father wants to come to the ceremony at the Preparatory House. Do you think he can?"

"Of course."

It pleased Rashiva that the bond between Raaj and Jimorla was so strong. Afraid to break that tie with the weight of a legend, she had never told her son that his father was the Karn Sixth Level.

Yezi Lasa, freight hauler extraordinary, or so she styled herself, jumped from her rider onto the Karn airfield and eyed the young man with the inventory sheets. Strange world it was nowadays, when they had boys out greeting the pilots.

"Well, looky you," Yezi said. "Manager Karn send you to make us pilots happy?"

He handed her the clipboard. "You can sign for your cargo here. A freight crew will load it."

Yezi peered at the board, looking for his name. "Heh. Anthoni." She angled a look at him. "What're you doing on the docks, Anthoni? Maybe looking for company, hmmm?"

"I'm an Estate aide," he said.

"My winds." Yezi signed the clipboard and handed it back to him. "An Estate aide."

"Your crew is on dock six," Anthoni said.

"Righto." Yezi wondered if the fellow was always so sullen. Least he could do was turn out a smile to please a tired pilot.

As Anthoni went to the next rider, a voice behind Yezi said, "You there."

Yezi turned to see a burly pilot who also flew the Varz/Karn route. "Heh, Ada."

Ada tilted her head at Anthoni. "Nice."

Yezi grimaced. "I think he's a Modernist."

Ada took out a tin of tas and rolled the leaves in a paper. "Modernists on the docks is nothing compared to what I've heard lately." She lit her tas stick. "Seems there's a rumor about a dead Calani that isn't dead."

"Sure, Ada."

"It's true." Ada blew out a stream of smoke. "Varz Calani. Boy fell over a cliff right into Ixpar Karn's lap."

"How would you know what goes on with high-level folk?"

"You want to check it, roll the dice." Ada puffed her tas. "It's in the Quis if you know how to read it."

Yezi snorted. But in truth the tale intrigued her. A right good story it was, like in the Old Age. Now *those* were days to be alive. No modern men back then. She smiled, imagining her circle of listeners. She had one gutsy tale to take to Varz.

Chankah Dahl stood in Dabbiv's lab, surrounded by his gadgets and scrolls. "You went to the *starport*? And no one stopped you?"

"There's no one there," Dabbiv said. "A robot told me to leave but it didn't do anything to me." He shrugged. "It's probably because the buildings all have locks. All I could do was walk around the streets." He gave her a guilty look. "I did find a few broken locks, though. So I went in and, uh—"

Chankah recognized that look. "Yes?"

"I filched some books." His face changed again, lighting up as fast as wind. "They're amazing! You can change the glyphs into any style you want and the books make three-dimensional pictures. They even *talk*."

She stared at him. "Are you mad? If you get caught, ISC will haul you off to prison."

"Am I supposed to pretend it isn't there? Think what we could *learn*."

Chankah could imagine how frustrating it was for a scientist with his vision to know such great knowledge lay so close, yet just beyond his grasp. "Were the books interesting?"

He grinned. "I can't tell you. It's Restricted." When she glowered at him, he laughed, then unlocked a drawer in his desk and pulled out a text with a metallic cover.

She peered at the title. "You can read that?"

"I taught myself Skolian."

"What does it say?"

" 'Proceedings of the Eighty-sixth Conference on Circulatory Pathology.' It's a collection of papers given at a meeting of Imperialate doctors."

"Do you understand it?"

"Not yet," he said. "But I'm learning."

Hayl strolled to the entrance of his suite, trying to look nonchalant as he watched his escort gambling Outside. Nesina, the youngest guard, looked up at him and smiled. She was twenty-three, eight years older than him, with dark eyes and hair.

Somewhere within the suite, a pot banged on glass. Hayl followed the noise to his sunroom, where a breeze gusted through an open window, ruffling his hair and jostling a hanging plant by the curtains.

How was the window open?

It wasn't until the wall blocked his view that he realized he was backing out of the room. He made himself stop, reminded himself he could step out the window and reach the ground with his feet while he straddled the sill.

It had been worse when Ixpar first brought him to Karn. She imprisoned him in the logical place to hold a captive: the top of a tower. He hid his fear, never speaking of the nightmares that splintered his sleep, but somehow Ixpar guessed. Soon she moved him to this suite on the ground level, where he could fall no more than the length of his own body.

Bracing himself, Hayl walked to the window and reached out to close it.

Hands grabbed him so fast he barely realized it had happened before he was thrown into the wall. Spinning around, he saw a bulky figure vault over the sill. He lunged back to the window, but by the time he looked out, the courtyard Outside was empty.

Hayl scowled. Then he returned to the entrance of his suite. When the captain of his escort looked up, he pointed toward the sunroom and mimed a person climbing in the window. As the other guards went to investigate, Nesina came over to him.

"You look upset," she said.

He shrugged. Compared to his fall over the cliff, a peeper in his suite wasn't much to get excited about.

She took his arm. "You should lie down."

He didn't feel like lying down. But she was pulling him toward the bedroom, so he went with her. Inside, she paused in front of the mirror over his bureau. Standing behind him, taller than him, she looked over his shoulder at their reflection. Then she slid her hand through his hair. "You've beautiful curls."

Hayl reddened. No woman had ever touched him in such a familiar manner.

Nesina pushed him over to the bed. "You lie down. I'll get something to calm your nerves."

His nerves were fine. But he lay down anyway, too intrigued to object. Nesina disappeared and returned with a decanter of wine.

By the time they had finished the wine, he felt remarkably calm. So calm, in fact, that he had a hard time remembering why he was lying on his bed in a locked room with a guard sitting next to him. And Nesina *had* locked the door. Even from across the room, he could see the bolt pushed in place.

"You look pale," Nesina said, her voice a little slurred. "We should make you more comfortable." She unlaced his shirt and pulled it off his shoulders.

Hayl tried to sit up and she pushed him back down. "Relax," she said. "Try to forget what happened."

Nothing had happened. In fact, the only "happening" was here, as Nesina slid her hand along his leg. He tried to roll away, afraid she would see his erection, but she held him in place.

"I won't tell, Hayl," she coaxed. "You're ready, a man now. I won't feel any differently about you tomorrow."

While he fumbled with his thoughts, Nesina fumbled with the flaps on his pants. He tried to marshal arguments about why she should stop, but it was more interesting to feel her take off his clothes. She undressed herself next, giving the word "interesting" whole new shades of meaning. When she stretched out on top of him, he slid his arms around her waist, unsure how to proceed.

Nesina kissed him, first gently and then with more passion. She guided him with her hand, her touch so arousing that almost as soon as he was inside her, he reached his peak. As his breathing calmed, he realized she had just started and he had already finished.

Hayl flushed. "I'm sorry."

"You shouldn't be." Nesina lifted her head. "Your voice is beautiful."

Winds above. What was wrong with him, getting drunk, making love to his guard, and breaking his Oath? He ought to be appalled with himself. Actually, though, he was rather pleased.

Nesina slid off and stretched out against his side. After they had dozed in each other's arms for a while, he started to explore her body. As she opened her eyes, he said, "This time I'll hold on longer."

She smiled, then nudged him onto his back, rolling with him. Pushing up on her elbows, she looked down at him. "It was your first time, yes?"

He nodded.

"I'm glad you let it be with me, Hayl."

He pulled her down on top of him. "Me too."

Seven women and one dark-haired man made up the Varz octet. They stood side by side, each with a rifle over her shoulder. As Avtac walked along the line, Zecha called out orders and the guards obeyed in unison: right, left, poise, aim, relax.

Avtac stopped in front of the man. "What's your name?"

"Jevrin Miesa Varz, ma'am."

"Think you could shoot a clawcat, Jevrin?"

"I have, during city patrol last winter."

Avtac glanced at Zecha and the captain nodded.

After Zecha dismissed the guards, Avtac frowned at her. "A unit of elite hunters is no place for a man."

"He's a good marksman," Zecha said.

"I do recall a boy in the Miesa Cooperative named Jevrin. He would be about this man's age now." Avtac paused. "He had yellow hair."

"I can run another check," Zecha said.

"Do it." The Minister walked to a rack on the wall and lifted out a rifle. "I want no leaks. If any have opened, plug them." She sighted along the gun barrel. "Permanently."

"We searched the entire Estate." Senior Aide Kastora walked with Ixpar along a cobbled street that crooked between two buildings. "Whoever broke into Hayl's suite got away."

"Was anything stolen?" Ixpar asked.

Kastora shook her head. "His guards think it was a peeper trying to see a Calani."

"I hope that's all." Ixpar grimaced. "If she came from Varz, we're in trouble."

They turned into a lane that ended at a building dating from the Old Age, its turrets and spires silhouetted against a blue sky puffed with clouds. The sign read THE KARN INSTITUTE.

They found Ekina bent over a clutter of equipment in her lab. The physicist straightened up, smoothing out her smock. "Minister Karn. I wasn't expecting you."

"Manager Karn," Ixpar said.

Ekina reddened. "My apologies, ma'am."

Ixpar nodded, wondering if the title "Manager" would ever feel right. "Bahr is curious to know how your work on her light-sailor is going."

"Not so well." Ekina nodded at an apparatus on the table, a helical tube wrapped around a red stone. "I'm using a ruby crystal. I managed to get a light pulse, but when I try to pump out a steady beam of light I overheat the ruby." She shook her head. "Every time I solve one glitch, I run into another."

"Suppose I put my Calanya on it?" Ixpar asked. "They're amazing with these pattern games of Bahr's. Maybe they can help figure out what you need here."

From Ekina's look, Ixpar might have suggested she stand on her head and eat Quis dice. "Calani help with equipment?"

"Let's see what they do with it," Ixpar said.

The escort left Bahr alone in the Coral Chamber. She sat at the Quis table reminding herself she wasn't nervous. She *wasn't*. Every time she heard a sound she jumped like a shylark.

Then the door opened and a man walked into the room.

Bahr nearly fell off her chair. "Winds above."

Sevtar smiled and sat across the table from her, glimmering gold. "My greetings."

Ai! What a voice. He was a prince of Calani, no doubt about that. For days she had been preparing for this first session of hers with the Sixth and now she would make a fool of herself.

Once they got started, though, Bahr forgot everything except the dice. Sevtar *knew*. He understood her patterns. His Quis exhilarated, challenged, was a true matching of wits. She barely noticed when a guard slipped in and lit the hawk-shaped lamps.

Eventually Sevtar pushed back from the table. "Perhaps we should take a break."

She blinked. "Heh?"

"A break. We've been here all day."

Bahr peered out a window. "Well, I'll be a pog on a pole." It was dark outside. Stretching out her legs, she discovered that her feet, encased in their fine red boots for this special occasion, had gone to sleep. She got up and hobbled around the room, grumbling as her circulation returned.

When Sevtar laughed, Bahr squinted at him. "What's so funny?"

"You're just not how I imagined Coba's leading theoretical physicist."

"Physicist? I'm a Quis Wizard."

"That you are. Your Quis is brilliant."

Bahr smiled. "Heh. Well. You too."

That night after Bahr returned to her suite, she sat down to review her session with Sevtar. He understood her new pattern, the one she called a hot-light sailor.

"Quis Wizard?" a voice said.

Bahr jumped. A guard was standing in the door arch. She almost told the woman to go away, but remembered her Oath in time.

"You have a visitor," the guard said. "Shall I bring him?"

Him? Maybe it was Rhab. Bahr nodded and stood up.

The guard reappeared with the potter Rhab. She said, "Manager Karn grants this visitor Suitor's Privilege," and then closed the door, leaving Bahr and Rhab alone together.

"*Suitor's* Privilege," Bahr sputtered.

"It means I can talk to you," Rhab said.

"You *always* talk to me."

"Apparently I've always been your suitor."

"Like grub you have."

"It's true. Manager Karn told me tonight that Suitor's Privilege is the only way a woman in my position would be allowed to visit a man who is a Calani."

"She never told me that."

Rhab came over to her. "She waited because she thought we needed a while to adjust to the, uh, unusual circumstances."

Bahr squinted at him. Sure there were times when she fantasized that a sexy fellow like Rhab reversed the roles and pursued her. But in real life she didn't feel comfortable with it. If courting was going on, she should be doing it. Just how she would manage that, though, was a mystery. She couldn't even leave her room without an escort.

She regarded the Modernist warily. "You come to pay me suit, Rhab?"

"I don't know." He grinned. "Is it safe?"

"Probably not."

He took her hands. "I'm willing to risk it."

His forwardness flustered her. She tried to think of something to say. "I played Quis with the Sixth Level today."

He looked suitably impressed. "What was it like?"

"Rhab, it's like *flying*. He helped me with a new idea I have for my light-sailor. I'll bet we could make one that gives off enough energy to burn a hole in wood."

"Why would you want to do that?"

Bahr blinked. She hadn't thought about that. "Campers could start campfires with it."

"Seems to me it would be easier to use a flint."

"Probably," she admitted. "But I'll tell Ixpar about it anyway."

It was late when Ixpar left her office, numbers from freight inventories still reeling off in her head. She took the long way to her suite, through the Atrium, an airy hall two stories high, filled by plants, its walls and dome made from tinted glass. A staircase swept up from the floor to an indoor balcony. Halfway up the stairs, she lingered, watching a winter storm lash the glass, knowing an empty bed waited for her. Kelric had an early Quis session in the morning and had slept in the Calanya.

When she reached her suite, though, a line of light under the door greeted her. In the bedroom a lamp glowed on the nightstand, and a fully dressed Sixth Level lay fast asleep on the bed.

She sat next to him. "Kelric?"

He stirred. "Hmmm . . . ?"

"I thought you were sleeping in the Calanya."

"Axis," he mumbled.

"Do you know where you are?"

"On the Z-axis."

Ixpar smiled. She undressed him and herself, then slipped into bed. As she reached for the lamp, he walked his fingers across her outstretched body. "Have you had dinner yet?"

"Dinner?" She dimmed the lamp, then slid into his arms. "A long time ago."

"What time is it?"

"Morning's Second Hour."

"Second Hour? I must have fallen asleep." He motioned at a strange dice structure on the nightstand. "I was working on an equation for Bahr. I guess I fell asleep."

It took Ixpar a moment to isolate why his response seemed odd. He had repeated himself. Not that repetition was all that unusual; he just never did it. "You sound tired."

He smiled sleepily. "Not that tired." Then he pulled her into his arms.

In the morning, he missed his Quis session because she

couldn't wake him up. She almost called for the doctor, but when he finally did get up, he seemed fine.

In her excitement, Zecha strode straight into Avtac's library. The Minister stood by a bookcase, intent on a book she was reading.

"The rumors are true," Zecha said. "My agent saw the whole setup. Hayl is at Karn! He's been there the whole two years he's been gone. Jevrin kidnapped him."

Avtac raised her eyebrows at the interruption. "And have you found Jevrin?"

"Not yet." The Karn spy had disappeared the night after Avtac inspected the hunting unit, just hours before Zecha's people broke his cover. Even knowing she had incurred Avtac's displeasure didn't dim Zecha's mood. Hayl was *alive*. Besides, she knew what bothered Avtac most about Jevrin; he had been clever enough to figure out the Manager was suspicious.

"What about the other hunters?" Avtac asked.

"I ran checks and double checks," Zecha said. "There are no more spies."

"There had better not be." Avtac closed her book. "So. Ixpar Karn adds thievery of Calani to her list of crimes."

"What will you do?"

"A good question."

Zecha waited, knowing Avtac would speak when she came to a decision. One fact was obvious: the longer Hayl stayed at Karn, the more chance Sevtar had to contaminate the boy's Quis. They locked her out, the way they shared that quality, that *sameness* of their minds.

No. She gritted her teeth. They shared nothing. Comparing Hayl to Sevtar was like comparing fresh linen to soiled laundry. Yet the innocence Sevtar lacked and Hayl possessed— was it more than sexual? Whenever Sevtar had looked at her, both here and at Haka, he had seemed to say: *I know you*.

Avtac slid her book onto the shelf, revealing the title on its spine: *Strategic Pattern Games of the Old Age*. She turned to Zecha. "Ixpar Karn may have defrauded me out of a Fifth

Level, but she dressed it up in documents to make it look legal." In a deceptively soft voice she said, "Now she has given me justifiable cause for action."

Kelric awoke with a sense of lethargy. He had fallen asleep sitting up in a window seat of his suite. Rays of afternoon sun slanted across his body and traces of a dream lingered in his mind, an impression of Zecha like a sour aftertaste.

With the clarity of hindsight, he understood her now. As with many empaths, the same genes that gave rise to Zecha's Kyle abilities had probably hurt her. It was the main reason Kyles were so rare; most mutations associated with the genes were harmful. Only in rare cases such as Kelric's family did the Kyle genes produce a viable human.

Zecha's trouble was subtle, but devastating. He suspected her brain couldn't produce sufficient concentrations of kylatine, a chemical that blocked receptors in the neural structures that interpreted signals she picked up from other people. In other words, she couldn't block out emotions. Most empaths learned to produce kylatine blockers at least on a subconscious level, and Jagernauts could even order their biomech webs to make it.

Genetic therapy could repair defective kylatine genes, but it also reduced the empath's Kyle abilities. Most people either took the treatment or else withdrew from human contact. Neither choice had been available for Zecha. Worse, as warden of Coba's only prison, she had lived with the ugliest side of human nature her world had to offer. Without protection from that onslaught, it was no wonder her mind had warped.

Nor was it any wonder she loved Hayl. He was her opposite, sheltered all his life from the dark side of humanity. He must have soothed her like water in a desert.

Avtac was another story. Kelric doubted she even understood the concept of empathy. What malediction had the power to describe his last days at Varz? She never told him why his doctors stopped the electroshock therapy that was supposed to "cure" him. Instead she let him believe that only as long as he pleased her would he be free of it. Until the moment he left her Estate, he hadn't known he was going to Karn.

You dwell too much on the past, he thought. He looked for a better memory and eventually found one: the jeweled world of his childhood. It glistened like a bubble isolated in encroaching darkness.

39

Hawk's Claw

It was a spring morning of the new year when Ixpar found Kastora on the outside balcony that circled the Observatory. Mild breezes blew back the Senior's hair as she considered the polished box she held in her hands, with its two jeweled dice.

"Those look like Suitor's Dice," Ixpar said.

Kastora looked up with a start. "What gave you that idea?"

Ixpar chuckled. "Does he have a name?"

The Senior simultaneously reddened and smiled. "You know the singer in the tavern where we go—" She paused, her gaze shifting to the sky. "Look at that."

Ixpar looked to see a pair of windriders above the northern mountains. As they drew nearer she made out the black Varz clawcat on their wings. "They're going to miss the airfield."

"There's nowhere to land in the direction they're going," Kastora said.

"Yes there is." Ixpar scowled. "The Calanya parks." She spun around and strode to the stairs, looking back at Kastora. "Send two octets to the Calanya. And stay on com." Then she took off.

At the Calanya, Ixpar found most of her Calani absorbed in a dice session. The Fourth Level Mentar left the table and came over to her. Gray-haired and gray-eyed, he reminded her of the Scribe who had been her father.

"You look concerned," he said.

"Varz riders are headed for the parks," she said.

"Why?"

"I wish I knew. Where is Sevtar?"

"He sleeps in his suite."

That surprised Ixpar. "Is he sick?"

"I don't believe so. Just tired."

Eb, captain of the Calanya escort, appeared at Ixpar's side. "Two octets from the CityGuard are Outside."

"Post one in Sevtar's suite," Ixpar said. "We'll take the second out to meet the riders."

She found the two craft crouched in a sculpture garden they had wrecked when they landed. A trio of Varz guards disembarked and bowed to Ixpar. "Manager Karn," a thin woman said. "I am Ahva Varz."

Ixpar frowned. "Trespassing on Calanya grounds is illegal, Ahva Varz."

"I apologize, ma'am. But we bring a message from the Minister."

"If Avtac has something to tell me, she can do it without breaking the law."

"It seems a difficulty exists." Ahva took a scroll from another guard and handed it to her. "I believe this explains the problem."

The message made no sense; written in legal jargon, it just restated the contract she and Avtac had signed when Karn relinquished the Ministry.

I will put these people in jail, Ixpar thought. Did Avtac actually expect her to let such an intrusion pass? Of course she would protect her Calanya.

Ixpar froze. Of course. *Of course.* She thrust the scroll at Captain Eb. "Lock up these people." Then she took off running across the parks.

When she reached a com Outside the Calanya, she banged her hand against the com. "Kastora!"

A voice snapped out of the speaker. "Kastora here."

"Get as many octets as you can to Hayl's suite," Ixpar said. "Get him out of there!" Then she set off running again.

Ixpar reached the gardens around Hayl's suite in time to see three Varz riders descending, the rumble of their engines swelling into a roar as they landed on the lawns, tearing up grass and destroying fountains. As she raced toward Hayl's patio, Varz guards burst out of the craft—all armed with rifles.

Hands yanked Ixpar to a stop. Twisting around, she found herself staring up at Borj, a gigantic captain on her CityGuard. She had to shout to be heard over the noise. "Let go of me!"

The rumble of engines drowned out Borj's answer, but her grip stayed firm. Ixpar struggled with the massive captain, then gave up and wrenched around in Borj's arms in time to see the rest of the captain's octet converge with the invaders on Hayl's patio. Even the thunder of the riders couldn't smother the blast of rifle shots. Defenseless against the bullets, Karn guards dropped everywhere.

Then a Varz captain spotted Ixpar—and fired. Borj threw her to one side and the bullet missed Ixpar's chest, thudding instead into her shoulder. Strengthened by her rage, Ixpar wrenched out of Borj's grip and ran for Hayl's suite, ready to attack the invaders with her bare hands. As she passed a glass table on the patio, it shattered under the impact of a bullet.

Boots pounded behind her. "Manager Karn!" Borj shouted. *"Get down."* The captain tackled her and literally threw her over a retaining wall. Ixpar wrestled furiously, almost pulling free despite her gunshot wound. She felt no pain at all.

Borj shouted for help and another guard jumped over the wall. She grabbed Ixpar's legs and together with Borj managed to pin Ixpar to the ground. Helpless, Ixpar could do nothing but watch the Varz raiders.

They smashed the stained-glass doors fronting Hayl's patio and ran inside. Gunshots sounded and then the Varz guards reappeared, dragging Hayl. The boy was fighting, hitting with his fists, kicking with his legs, biting and scratching as the octet ran, half dragging and half carrying him to the riders.

A formation of Karn guards burst out of Hayl's suite and opened fire with their stunners, sending a slew of the intruders stumbling to their knees. The Varz guards answered with rifle shots and the Karn unit lunged for cover.

Motion flashed in Ixpar's side vision. Turning, she saw Kastora striding across a garden. Time seemed to slow down as the Senior Aide grabbed the stunner of a fallen guard. Even as

Ixpar shouted for her to get down, Kastora sighted on the guards carrying Hayl. In the same instant she fired, a rifle discharge cracked like thunder—and Kastora collapsed, blood splattering out of her torso.

Then the intruders reached their aircraft. They hoisted Hayl inside, and within seconds the craft was aloft.

A sudden silence filled the gardens. When Borj and the other guard relaxed their hold, Ixpar shoved them away, then vaulted over the retaining wall and ran to her Senior Aide.

"Kastora!" Kneeling by her body, Ixpar lifted her wrist, trying to find a pulse. "What were you doing, standing out in the open like that?" Her voice cracked. "Kastora, answer me."

The Senior Aide stared with sightless eyes at the sky. Blood no longer seeped out the wound in her chest.

Borj crouched next to Ixpar and checked for Kastora's pulse, then pulled back her eyelids. After what seemed like an eternity, she turned to Ixpar. "I'm sorry, Manager Karn. We can't do any more for her."

"No." Ixpar bent over her friend's body, pressing her hands against the wound as if that would fix it. When she pulled the stunner out of Kastora's grip, the Senior's hand fell limply to the ground. Her other hand was clenched around something else. Ixpar pried open the fist, revealing the box with the Suitor's Dice.

Gone. Kastora was gone. Her friendship, her wisdom, her dreams. All gone.

Standing up, Ixpar looked around at the carnage in the gardens. An ancient instinct was rising inside of her, burning so hot that a red haze clouded her vision, like a fog of blood.

A hand touched her shoulder. Spinning around, Ixpar almost socked a Karn medic in the jaw.

The woman paled. "I—I just meant—well, that."

Lowering her fist, Ixpar looked where the medic pointed. A hole in her shoulder was pumping out blood. While Ixpar blinked, the medic began to clean the wound. Ixpar knew she should feel pain, but only her anger was real.

Another aide appeared at her side, Anthoni, the fellow she had recently promoted to the top level of her Estate staff, making him the first man in Karn history to hold such a high position.

"I just came from Hayl's suite," he said. "The meds are treating his guards."

"How are they?" Ixpar said.

"Alive. But they'll be in Med for a while. Nesina took it the worst." He shook his head. "She went crazy when they grabbed Hayl. She wouldn't back off even after they shot her."

Ixpar swallowed. Guards trained to fight with stunners often plowed on after being hit, trying to do as much damage as possible before they passed out. She and Kastora had reacted the same way. Against rifles, that strategy was suicide.

Elder Solan came up to them, her lined face drawn and pale. "I cannot believe this happened. We must demand a Council Tribunal against Varz."

Ixpar disengaged her arm from the medic, putting up her hand when the woman protested. Then she drew Solan to the side. "Varz will refuse to convene a Tribunal."

"She can't refuse." Solan swept her arm out at the gardens. "Not only was this outrage a criminal act, it was stupid."

"Avtac never makes stupid moves."

"No Estate will support her after this."

"No?" Ixpar regarded the Elder. "What institution would you guard with your life, fight to the death to protect?"

"The Calanya, of course."

"The Calanya. Solan, I *kidnapped* Hayl. I had him playing Quis with Karn Calani. Including a female Calani, for wind's sake. Avtac's allies probably consider her use of force justified."

"Justified for what?" Solan watched an aide pull a blanket over Kastora's body. "All Varz had to do was demand a Tribunal against you."

As the orderlies lifted Kastora onto a stretcher, Ixpar spoke in a subdued voice. "It makes perfect sense. Hayl didn't want to go back to Varz. For many reasons, not the least being he knows what Avtac did to Kelric. Given access to a Speaker and a Tribunal, winds only know what he would say. Avtac needed a reason to justify attacking Karn and I gave it to her."

"You believe this attack had more than one purpose." Solan made it a statement rather than a question.

"Do you know what the riders that landed in the Calanya brought me? A copy of Sevtar's Calanya contract." Ixpar exhaled. "There is one reason and one reason alone why Varz doesn't control Coba. Kelric. Avtac means to get him back and she can only do that by force."

"Then she hasn't rescued a Calani." Solan paused as the orderlies carried Kastora's body by them. "She has started a war."

The Karn Skywalk arched into the Teotecs, ending at a hollow globe of tinted glass high in the mountains. Sunlight diffused through the sphere's polarized walls, gilding the chamber inside. As Ixpar drew nearer, she saw Kelric standing by one curved wall, staring out at the sky like a metal statue bathed in amber light.

At the sound of her footsteps, he turned. His gaze raked over the sling on her arm. "What happened?"

She paused just inside the chamber's entrance. "I got in the way of a bullet."

He shook his head. "I thought the only guns your people had were stunners."

"Things . . . change."

"And Hayl?"

"He went back to Varz."

A cloud drifted by the chamber, making a shadow inside the sphere. "I've given you war," Kelric said.

"We've always had it." Dryly she said, "That's all we used to do during the Old Age."

Kelric cupped his hands together. "Think of the Oath: 'You hold within your hands and mind the future of Coba.' Your world is a Calanya and the Restriction is your Oath." He dropped his arms. "When I crashed here that Oath was broken."

"You didn't create our aggressions."

"I've never known a people as quick as yours." He shook his head. "Coba has just begun to tap the knowledge buried in the Quis. It's going to break out like water through a collapsing dam, with my influence warping the flow. You have to take me out of the Calanya. Get me out of the Quis net."

"I need you now more than ever," Ixpar said.

"I won't be responsible for the destruction of a world."

She walked over to him. "We are responsible for ourselves, Kelric. That we've suppressed our violent tendencies doesn't mean they went away. It's time we faced that. Dealt with it."

He touched her sling. "I can see what I've given you."

Quietly she said, "You could have ruined Deha Dahl's life. You didn't. You could have brutalized Rashiva Haka. You didn't. You could have devastated Varz. You didn't. Even now, when you work with me to give Karn advantage over Varz, you marshal your dice to favor Karn rather than hurt Varz."

"I don't see your point. Why hurt Deha or Rashiva? They never wished harm against me. And why would I make tens of thousands of people in Varz suffer because their Manager is abusive to her Akasi? It's not their fault."

Ixpar watched his face. "All those years ago, you could have escaped Coba. You sacrificed your freedom, almost your life, so the Dahl escort could live." Her voice softened. "Yes, you've put yourself into the Quis. Your decency, your strength of character, your courage. Your capacity to love."

Kelric's face gentled, crinkling the lines around his eyes. He took her hand and for a while they just watched the sky that arched everywhere around them like an ocean of blue.

Far to the north the speck of a rider appeared above the mountains.

"Not another!" Ixpar strode to the com panel where the Skywalk met the chamber. But then she paused, her hand poised over the com. Something about the rider looked odd . . .

The craft drew nearer.

Nearer.

Nearer.

Its wings swept through the air in an impossibly huge arc.

A chill sped down Ixpar's back. "It can't be."

Kelric glanced at her. "You think this one is from Varz?"

"Not Varz." She took a breath. "Much higher in the mountains."

"There are no Estates higher than Varz."

"I know." Softly she said, "It's an althawk, Kelric. A giant althawk."

The bird glided closer until it was clearly visible, a beast with huge wings, glorious wings, their span outdoing a windrider. Brilliant red feathers edged its black wings like tongues of fire and the gold plumage on the rest of its body gleamed in the sun's pouring light. Ixpar could almost feel the gale that accompanied every sweep of those massive pinions. Talons as long as a man's arm curved under its legs.

"Gods," Kelric said, "It's beautiful."

"We thought they were extinct. It's the only one to come down from the mountains in a thousand years."

"Maybe it's the last of its kind. Searching for a mate."

After so long? she wondered. Had this magnificent hawk been driven from his home by loneliness, come to search the world for a mate he would never find?

Kelric touched her shoulder and pointed at the city. Tiny figures were running in the streets, waving at each other and the hawk. At the airfield, two riders were preparing to take off.

Ixpar switched on the com and an excited voice floated into the air. "Tal here!"

"Tal, this is Manager Karn. Ground those windriders."

"But there's an *althawk* up there. A real one! They're going to catch it."

"Tell them to let it go."

Tal paused. "Ma'am?"

"They aren't to catch it," Ixpar repeated. "I'll have anyone who tries thrown in jail."

The aide spoke in a disappointed voice. "Yhee, ma'am."

Kelric watched as she switched off the com. "You'll probably never see it again."

"I know." She came to stand with him. "But it would die in captivity."

The bird sailed closer until his shadow filled the sphere. For one instant he looked directly at them with his ancient gaze, his gold eyes hooded and inscrutable, so close now that had they been able to reach out, they could have touched his feathers.

Then he swept over the Skywalk, wheeling away into the freedom of an intensely blue sky.

40

Jahalla's Defiance

Rain drummed throughout the night on the windows of Hayl's suite. He sat in the corner of an alcove while the memory of his "rescue" marched through his mind. They had shot Nesina. *Shot* her. Riddled her through with burning metal dice.

Everyone at Varz had been so kind. So solicitous. It made him sick. Zecha had held him while he cried, and the doctors talked with Avtac in low voices about the supposed trauma of his experiences. He doubted they would be so understanding if they knew he was crying because he had seen them shoot his lover.

Avtac refused him the comfort of his friends. He still heard her voice: *You cannot return to the Calanya yet. We must avoid contamination to the Quis.* Not that it stopped her from trying to wring out every last bit of Karn Quis he had absorbed.

A door creaked. As Hayl looked up, Zecha appeared in the archway of the alcove. She came to sit by him, taller than him by almost a head.

"I couldn't sleep either," she said.

Hayl said nothing, acutely aware that she came with no introduction of Suitor's Privilege. The fact that she rarely requested it made him feel as if he wore an invisible gag.

Zecha poked her finger inside one of his curls. "I never thought I'd take a boy with yellow hair as my kasi." She sighed. "It's Haka, you know. In the desert, if a man smiles at a woman it's considered an invitation to his bed. But you yellow-haired boys from the north, you smile so easily. It makes a woman think the wrong things."

I ought to tell her about Nesina, Hayl thought. Maybe then she would leave me alone.

Zecha took hold of his chin, turning his face up to hers. Then she kissed him.

Hayl stiffened and tried to pull away from her. When she wouldn't let him go, he struggled harder, but with her stronger muscles she easily held him.

"So modest," she murmured. "Or is this the pretense of innocent youth?" A hard edge grated in her voice. "I'll take you no matter what happened at Karn." She fumbled with the laces on his shirt, undoing them with deft fingers.

Hayl tried to twist away, but he was trapped in the corner. When Zecha opened his shirt and stroked his chest, he nearly gagged. Working his arms up inside her embrace, he hit his fists against her shoulders again and again. She caught his wrists and held them together while she fondled him with her other hand. He kept fighting, trying to escape, but with no success.

After several moments the captain paused and considered him. "Maybe you aren't so worldly as rumor claims." She stroked his curls. "You must learn not to smile at other women, Hayl. It gives the wrong impression." Finally she let him go and stood up. "Try to sleep now. You need the rest."

The moment Zecha was gone, Hayl ran to the bathing room, peeled off his clothes, and dove into the pool. He soaped his body, cleaning every place she had touched him. Afterward, he put on the warmest clothes he could find and went back to the alcove.

It was time to make plans.

Avtac believed she had him secure. This guest suite jutted out from a corner of the Estate, with two sides facing the vertical cliffs that made Varz such an isolated—and forbidding—fortress. His escort guarded the other two sides. One of the cliff windows had a lock, but even had anyone been crazy enough to think Hayl would dream of opening it, Avtac believed his previous success had been a fluke.

His plan was simple: open the window, climb out, and creep along the ledge below it to freedom. At this hour most of Varz slept and the rain would keep anyone else inside. No one would see him running to the airfield. Once there, he would find a way to pay passage to another Estate. He could gamble for it. He didn't care that he had no idea how to survive on the Outside. He would rather spend the rest of his life a beggar than stay at Varz.

Only one problem remained. He had to climb out the window.

So he sat in the alcove, far more securely trapped by his terror than by the guards Outside his suite.

When he heard a clock chime Morning's Third Hour he knew he was almost out of time. Taking a breath, he crossed to the window and went to work. Every time he heard a board creak he tensed, afraid a guard was coming to check on him.

Finally the last pin clicked free.

Hayl froze, his palm lying flat on the door of glass. Then, with shaking hands, he pulled it open. Wind rushed in, splattering him with rain—he was going to fall, fall, fall, *icy air slashing past as he hurtled faster, faster, faster* . . .

With a gasp, Hayl cut off the image. He drew himself up to his full, albeit not so tall, height and took a deep breath. Then he carefully let himself out over the windowsill, turning so he faced the cliff, his breath coming in cautious gasps. As he lowered himself into the night, wind buffeted his body. He hung from the sill, paralyzed with fear, unable to move.

Finally he forced his toe to reach for a toehold in the basrelief of the wall. With excruciating care he descended. Rain made the stone slippery and wind played havoc with his balance. Once he lost his grip and slid an arm's length before he found another handhold. He had to bite the inside of his mouth to keep from screaming.

He kept climbing.

Eons later he reached the ledge. Built as a decoration, the shelf was too narrow for a boy's foot. He slid his toes along it and used wall projections for handholds. Bit by bit, fraction by fraction, he moved, praying he didn't reach a point where he had nothing to hold on to, or the ledge ended, or was broken, or—

His foot slid out over empty air.

Hayl nearly panicked. He had reached the end of the wall and a gap too big to step across separated him from the windbreak around the city. Maneuvering his head around, he looked along the tortuous route he had just traversed. He was too stiff with cold and fear to retrace his steps. Breathing in ragged gulps, he turned back to stare at the windbreak. He couldn't go back, he couldn't go forward, and soon his fingers would be too numb to grip the wall.

So he jumped.

He overestimated the distance and hit the windbreak in a jarring impact. Flailing for a handhold, he slid downward until his foot caught on a gargoyle and he flipped over its head. Grabbing for the statue, he caught a horn and wrenched to a stop, hanging in the air, his body swinging in darkness lit only by a faint glow from the city.

Struggling to stay calm, he probed for a toehold with his foot. He found one, another—and then he began climbing. Using drilled holes and grinning statues for support, clutching the wet stone, praying his hands didn't slip, he clambered up the wall.

When he reached the top, he slid stomach-down onto the wide expanse of stone and pulled himself across it, not even trying to stand. As he let himself down the inner side, he started to laugh; by the time he jumped to the ground he was shaking uncontrollably. He huddled against the wall, his laughter heaving out in huge breaths, until it turned into sobs.

Eventually the sobs trailed into silence. With a final gulp of air, he stood up and looked around. The cobbled street was empty. No one had heard him.

He pulled down his sleeves to hide his wrist guards and took off for the airfield.

Ixpar walked around the rider, scrutinizing it in the bright daylight. The gun turrets and cannons gave it a bristling appearance, like an angry hawk. Captain Borj stood in the hatch, her massive frame filling the opening.

"How did the test flights go?" Ixpar asked.

"It has good speed and acceleration. But it doesn't take g-forces well." Borj jumped onto the tarmac. "Do you really plan to use these riders?"

"If I'm forced to."

Anthoni appeared from behind the craft. "We just got a message from the airtower, Ixpar. A Varz rider has requested permission to land."

Finally, Ixpar thought. Although she had known Avtac

would refuse her demand for a Tribunal, she had called for it anyway, knowing it would provide invaluable information. In a Council Tribunal, the Managers sat as judges. The Quis Council chose six judges, two each for prosecution, defense, and neutrality. So in response to the call for the Tribunal, every Manager gave her preference as a judge. It meant stating where they stood on the hostilities between Varz and Karn.

In the tenday since she had sent out the call, every Estate but Varz had responded. Both Dahl and Bahvla pledged full support to Karn. Viasa chose neutrality, as did its secondary Tehnsa. More disturbing was that Shazorla, usually a Karn ally, also declared neutrality, followed by its secondary Eviza. Ahkah and Lasa confirmed their close ties to Varz with a pledge of support for the Ministry.

The biggest surprise came from Haka. Varz's staunchest ally chose neutrality.

Ixpar and Anthoni walked to the airtower and stood inside to watch the Varz rider land. As soon as it was down, a Karn octet armed with rifles surrounded it. The pilot opened the hatch and spoke with them, then handed the captain a scroll wrapped in gold suede and tied with a black cord.

As the rider lifted off, the captain brought the scroll to Ixpar. Tooled into the suede, the snarling black clawcat of Varz crouched next to the Ministry insignia, a combination that jarred Ixpar as much now as it had the first time she had seen it.

Ixpar sent Anthoni after Elder Solan and walked back to the Estate alone. Inside her office, she stood next to her desk reading the scroll.

Anthoni spoke from the doorway. "Elder Solan is here."

Ixpar glanced up. "Send her in."

Solan entered and closed the door. "Anthoni said you got an answer from Varz."

"Avtac refuses to convene a Tribunal," Ixpar said.

Solan didn't look surprised. "Refusing a Manager's call for a Council Tribunal will set an unpopular precedent. That could damage Varz credibility."

"I don't know what to think." Ixpar handed her the letter. "Tell me if it makes any sense to you."

As Solan read the scroll, her face furrowed. "Is this a joke?"

"I have no idea."

The Elder looked up at Ixpar. "Where would Avtac Varz ever get the notion you reabducted Hayl? It's a bizarre accusation."

"There are rumors he committed suicide."

"Winds, I hope not."

"You and I both." Ixpar paused. "It's the oddest thing, Solan—but I think I caught a trace of him in the Quis. It's so faint, though. I may be grasping at a ghost."

"Where is this phantom?"

"Viasa."

Solan frowned. "Why would Avtac send Hayl there?"

"Maybe she asked Khal Viasa to hide him while she accuses me of abduction again. It gives her a reason to refuse my demand for a Tribunal."

"If Manager Viasa has decided to support Varz," Solan said, "we are in serious trouble."

"I know." Ixpar indicated the letter. "Take this to the other Elders. I'll meet with all of you at Evening's Hour to discuss it."

After Solan left, Ixpar sat at her desk and rested her forehead on her hands. She longed to talk with Kastora, to hear her counsel. Then another image came to her, her mother, the late Atlena Karn, a tall woman with blazing red hair who had managed the largest Common House in the city. Ixpar could still hear her voice: *Look to the Quis, child. Unveil its secrets.*

Ixpar left her office and went to the Blue Alcove in her suite, then descended from there into the Memory of Karn. To walk through its cool halls was like stepping into the past. The identity of a race lay hidden here, just as it lay buried within the Quis.

But tonight she saw no answers in its history, only the record of a people plagued by their own violent nature.

Rev Miesa Haka walked next to the Calanya windbreak, using its shadows as a shield against the sun. After three years, he still loathed Haka. No lush mountains here. Just heat. And sand. It drifted through sculpted holes in the wall, blown by the keening gales Outside, the forever keening wind, until he almost believed he heard voices in its eerie song.

Rev stopped. That *was* a voice. It had called his name.

He looked through an opening in the windbreak. At first all he made out were clouds of swirling sand, like ruby-topaz powder veiling the land. Then he saw the woman; dressed in rough trousers and jacket, with her hood pulled up against the storm, she looked like a freight hauler from the docks.

He drew away from the wall, insulted. But when the hauler called him again, he paused. How did she know his name? He looked out the hole again.

The woman came closer. "Revi?"

He regarded her.

"Don't you recognize me?" she asked.

He shook his head.

She pulled back her hood—and she was a he.

"Hayl?" he asked. "Is that really you?"

"I've come every day for half a season, hoping to see you."

"Winds, Hayl! I can hardly believe it." Revi grinned. "Climb on over! Get yourself in here."

"Someone might see."

"No one's around. Come on!"

Hayl clambered up the wall and half slid, half climbed down the inner side. The instant he jumped to the ground, Revi threw his arms around him.

"Winds above." Hayl's voice came out muffled against his shoulder. "You sure got big."

They sat on the grass under a grove of jahalla trees and Rev listened while Hayl told him all that had happened since Avtac separated them. "So I got a ride to Viasa by playing lyderharp for the crew on a merchant rider," Hayl finished. "In Viasa I gambled at the market. It was easy. Outsiders can't play Quis worth spit. I used the money I made to buy passage here."

"Is that what you do now? Gamble?"

Hayl shook his head. "Men aren't allowed to gamble at the Haka market. Even if they were, I couldn't risk it. Someone will figure out I'm a Calani. I shouldn't have done it at Viasa."

At sixteen, Hayl looked almost as vulnerable to Revi as the

first time Rev had seen him, when he was five and Hayl an infant curled in his crib. "How do you live?"

"One of the Men's Houses took me in," Hayl said. "They give me meals and a room in return for chores."

"What if someone sees your Calanya guards?"

Hayl pushed up his sleeve, revealing a bandage that hid his guard. "I say I burned myself. I know I have to find a way to take off the guards. But once they're gone—it's final." He dropped his hands in his lap as if it hurt to remember what circled his wrists. "I hate it Outside, especially here. People act like I'm pole-dung because I have yellow hair. A kinsa-boss wants me to work for her and she won't stop bothering me. I used to be a Second Level Calani and now I'm nothing."

"Ask Rashiva for asylum."

"Manager *Haka*?" Hayl laughed harshly. "She'd pack me off to Avtac faster than you can roll your dice."

"Not if you tell her what you've told me."

"Not a chance."

"Hayl, I'm serious."

"You trust her that much?" When Rev nodded, Hayl exhaled. "You better be right."

The rider soared above the Teotec Mountains, piloted by Aka Karn, a merchant taking her cargo of spices to Bahvla. To starboard, she sighted an octet of riders flying in formation. Feeling gregarious, she switched on channel two of her com. "This is Karn *Greenbird*, calling octet north by east. Beautiful day, heh?"

The com crackled. "Varz *Nightrider* here. You're violating our airspace, *Greenbird*."

Violating their airspace? What did that mean? "I'm headed for Bahvla."

"The Bahvla lanes are closed," Nightrider said. "Pull off, *Greenbird*."

"Cuaz and Khozaar," Aka muttered. She flew in a large arc that took her away from the octet. Maybe she had better approach Bahvla along a different route.

The com spat static. "Pull off, *Greenbird*! This is your final warning."

"Pull off? I am pulling off. Pull off where?"

With growing apprehension, Aka realized the riders were closing in on her. Somehow *Nightrider* released a metal hawk from under its belly. When it became obvious the bird was going to commit suicide and fly into her rider, Aka tried to veer off. The hawk managed to graze *Greenbird*'s wing anyway—and an explosion rocked the craft.

"*Nightrider,* are you crazy?" she shouted into the com, struggling to keep *Greenbird* under control.

In response, *Nightrider* launched another false hawk and Aka just barely brought up her craft in time to avoid it.

Then she set course and ran back to Karn.

Rashiva Haka paced across her den. "It gets worse and worse. Abductions, accusations, and now this."

Her Senior Aide stood by the fireplace. "I would advise against giving Hayl asylum. He broke his Oath. Winds, he pulverized it. Avtac is the one who should deal with him."

Rashiva stopped in front of her. "I can't send him back to Varz. Not after what he's been through."

"If you keep him here you will antagonize the Minister."

"If I send him to Varz I will antagonize my conscience." Rashiva leaned one hand against the mantel and stared at the flames crackling in the fireplace. "There are times when I wish it was Ixpar who ruled in Varz and Avtac who Managed Karn. It would make this matter of alliances more palatable."

The Senior spoke in a low voice. "Take care, Rashiva. You never know who might hear."

The Manager looked at her. "Avtac has my loyalty, not my soul." She straightened up. "Hayl stays here."

Ixpar walked out of the hangar with Captain Borj. "Who was the pilot?"

"A merchant named Aka Karn." Borj unhooked her flight jacket. "She had already left Karn when we found out about the blockade. *Greenbird* barely made it back here in one piece."

Ixpar scowled. "I want armed riders on patrol along the perimeter of Karn airspace."

"I'll see to it."

As Ixpar headed to the Estate, she brooded. So. Varz was blocking every route into Bahvla. It cut Karn off from a crucial ally. Worse, Avtac's noise about Hayl's supposed reabduction had finally convinced Shazorla, normally a Karn ally, to speak in support of the Varz Ministry. That meant Ahkah, Lasa, Shazorla, and Eviza all stood behind Varz. And whatever Rashiva's personal feelings toward Avtac, Ixpar knew the Haka Manager put a high value on loyalty. In a confrontation, Haka would support Varz.

Viasa and its secondary Tehnsa still claimed neutrality. But the centuries of feuding between Bahvla and Viasa didn't bode well for Karn. If Manager Viasa broke neutrality it was unlikely she would side with a Bahvla ally.

It all added up to a gambler's roll of dice with odds Ixpar didn't like one bit.

Captain Tazza Varz piloted her craft with pride, soaring through the sky. They were two parts of a whole, she and *Nightrider*, and no craft could best them.

A buzz came from channel six on com, a line open only to the riders in her unit. "*VarzSun* here, Cap'n Tazza. We've got two riders coming up on port side. Looks like Bahvla."

"I have them on scan," Tazza said.

Com crackled on channel two this time, the line open to all riders within com range. "This is Bahvla *Clouddancer*. You're blocking our travel lane, *Nightrider*."

"These lanes are under Varz authority," Tazza said. "Go back to Bahvla."

Clouddancer's pilot swore. "You people have no right to hold an entire Estate prisoner."

Just try to get past us, Tazza thought. But the Bahvla riders headed back to their Estate like furpups cuffed by their dam.

That evening, while sunset blazed across the sky, Tazza spotted a Karn octet on the Bahvla-Karn perimeter.

A man's voice came over channel two. "This is Jevrin Karn, flying *Silverhawk*. Acknowledge, *Nightrider*."

Tazza laughed. Ixpar Karn must be desperate, sending boys

to do a woman's job. "You're playing in Varz airspace, *Silverhawk*. Pull off."

"We're headed to Bahvla," Jevrin said. "Suggest you pull off yourself, Captain."

Tazza scowled, annoyed by his tone.

A woman spoke on channel two. "Captain Borj here, *Nightrider*. We don't recognize your authority to block this lane."

Tazza's com buzzed on six, a secured message from one of her riders. "Cap'n, this is *VarzSun*. Shall we take them out?"

"Only on my order." Tazza switched to line two. "Borj, this is your last warning. Pull off."

In response, the Karn riders dipped together and crossed into Varz space.

"That's it!" Tazza said on six. "Let's go."

Her riders sheared toward the Karn octet. She sighted on *Silverhawk*—hold steady—there! He tried to dodge, but her gunfire ripped his wing. Just one more shot and—

A blast reverberated through *Nightrider*. These Karn birds had weapons! The rider pitched and went into a dive, losing altitude at an alarming rate. Tazza fought with the wings, playing the slats in and out, until finally they caught the wind with a jolt, slowing her plunge. She lowered the landing gear and aimed for a clear hill in the forest below.

Nightrider hit with a force that crushed Tazza against her safety harness. The screech of buckling metal pierced the air as the craft tore along the ground, until it flipped over and jerked to a stop, leaving her hanging from her seat. She unbuckled her harness and dropped to the overhead bulkhead, which had become the "deck." As the rider teetered back and forth, she made her way to the upside-down hatch.

Tazza shoved open the hatch—and saw flames racing along the fuselage. Throwing caution to the wind, she vaulted to the ground and broke into a run. Just when she reached the top of the hill, an explosion roared behind her. A second later the shock wave flung her into the air like a leaf on the wind. She hit the ground and tumbled down the other side of the hill until she thudded into a mound of dirt.

Tazza lay trying to focus her thoughts. She tried to move, but her body didn't respond. All she could do was listen to the flames consuming *Nightrider*. Another small explosion came from the wreckage and a drone filled her head. It wasn't until *VarzSun* flew overhead that she connected the hum to an engine.

After *VarzSun* bumped into a landing farther down the slope, its pilot jumped out and sprinted up the hill. She knelt next to Tazza. "Cap'n? Thank the winds!"

"Did you get the Karn riders?" Tazza asked.

"Six, maybe seven." The pilot slid an arm under her shoulders. "One dodged by us, but it took several hits. Another went back to Karn."

Tazza struggled to her feet. "And ours?"

In a subdued voice the pilot said, "We lost four." She helped Tazza limp to the *VarzSun*. "*Starbird* went back for crews to douse the forest fire."

Before now, keeping riders out of Bahvla had been almost a game to Tazza. No longer. Suddenly it was all too tangible, a grim reality brought home by the deaths today.

When *VarzSun* was aloft, Tazza looked down at the blaze of *Nightrider*'s demise. She would fly again. The deaths of her pilots wouldn't be in vain.

"No!" Henta Bahvla faced Jevrin from behind her desk like a fighter squaring off with an opponent. "Don't we have trouble enough? I can't get a single rider out of Bahvla and you're the only one who has made it in since the blockade started. Do you have any idea what that means? We don't have farms up here. Just trees, trees, and trees. I've got a fortune in lumber rotting out there on the docks while my city starves."

"Then you *must* give me the riders," Jevrin said. "I can show your guilds how to build guns and missiles. We can break the blockade."

"At what cost of lives? You limped in here with one rider and you left Karn with eight."

A shadow descended on his face. "They died for your Estate, Manager Bahvla."

Her voice gentled. "And Bahvla honors their memory. But

how many more will die if I give you what you want? You may not define it as such, but what you're asking for is an air force. Bahvla hasn't flown into war in a thousand years."

"You may have no choice. Not unless you renounce Karn and give in to Varz."

Henta blew out a gust of air. "I will give you an answer tomorrow."

After Jevrin left, Henta sank into her chair, weighing her thoughts:

I will not be a party to war.

I will not let Bahvla starve.

I will not submit to Varz.

Then just what would she do?

What?

Long after the sun had set, she sat brooding. She thought of Sevtar as she had once seen him, an isolated figure standing on the Calanya windbreak, staring out at the Teotecs with the wind blowing his hair. Now an entire world balanced on the verge of battle over this legend who wanted nothing more than to be left alone.

41

The Rising Tower: Souls Ascendant

When Borj's rider limped into Karn, the sole survivor of her octet, Ixpar mourned, both for the lost pilots and for the dying of a peace that had lasted a millennium. In the year since Kastora's death, Ixpar had come to recognize the violence that surged within her, a beast kept in control by a thin veneer of civilization. She saw that rage in Borj now as well, who had seen six, maybe seven, of her riders go down in flames.

After that day, the captain drove herself relentlessly, working with the ArmsGuild. Today, a season later, she stood with Ixpar in a warehouse and slid a gunbelt over Ixpar's shoulders.

Then she handed the Manager a gun, one larger and heavier than a rifle. "As long as you keep the lever depressed, the cartridges continue to feed in."

Ixpar nodded. At the far end of the warehouse, Anthoni was arranging a line of empty fuel canisters, and closer by Tal stood holding a clipboard.

"Ready, here," Anthoni called.

Ixpar waited until he moved out of range, then lifted her gun. Sighting along its barrel, she pressed the lever—and a roar of shots erupted, its echoes vibrating in the cavernous warehouse like thunder. Canisters flew into the air, riddled by bullets. Despite the teeth-jarring recoil of the gun, Ixpar continued to fire until not one container remained intact.

The silence that followed was broken only by the clink of one canister rolling into another.

"Cuaz above," Tal said.

Ixpar looked at Borj. "It works."

Borj watched her with a bleak, hard gaze. "So it does."

After they finished the tests, Ixpar walked back to the Estate with Tal and Anthoni, carrying the gun slung over her shoulder by its strap. At times like this she deeply missed Kastora's counsel. Although Solan had done well serving as both Senior Aide and Elder, the arrangement was temporary. It was time she trained a new Senior Aide.

As they crossed a courtyard at the Estate, Ixpar glanced at the aides with her. Tal perhaps? She had considered Tal as a possible successor, but concluded she lacked the necessary leadership qualities. As a Senior Aide, though, she might do well.

Anthoni is better qualified, she thought.

Ixpar halted, envisioning the backlash that would happen if she chose a man as her top aide. She had traded the Ministry for an Akasi and bards wrote embarrassing songs praising her supposedly passionate soul, but if she made a decision as sensible as choosing Anthoni for her Senior Aide, it would outrage all Coba.

"So what," Ixpar said.

"Manager Karn?" Tal asked. She and Anthoni had been waiting while she stood absorbed in her thoughts.

Ixpar handed Tal the gun and its belt. "Lock these in my safe and notify the ArmsGuild to set up their production as we discussed." She glanced at Anthoni. "I'd like to see you in my office tomorrow morning at Second Hour."

"Yhee, ma'am," he said.

The aides went to the Estate and Ixpar headed for the Karn Institute in the city. When she reached Ekina's lab it was dark, and at first she thought the physicist had left. Then she saw a dim red glow emanating from a table. As her eyes adjusted, she made out Ekina standing at the table, surrounded by a cluster of her students.

When Ixpar tapped on the door, the physicist looked around. "Manager Karn." She beckoned her over. "I hoped you would come today."

Ixpar went to the table. "Anthoni gave me your note."

"Just wait until you see," Ekina said.

The students drew back, revealing a glass tube stretched between two mirrors, one of which was only partially silvered. Light from the tube slipped through the partial mirror and made a faint red beam that was visible where it hit dust particles in the air. The beam ended in a small red dot on a screen a short distance away.

"Ah—what is it?" Ixpar asked.

Ekina looked as pleased as a chub cub after a feast. "That, Manager Karn, is a helium–neon-gas laser."

"Laser?"

"What Quis Wizard Bahr calls a light-sailor. We thought *laser* made more sense."

"Well, I'll be windblown," Ixpar said, evoking a ripple of gratified laughter from the students. "How did you get it to work?"

"It's the helium." Ekina tapped the tube. "With only neon gas we couldn't get enough atoms into high energy levels. Helium is easy to excite. So we pump up the helium and it pumps up the neon."

"Bahr will want to see this. I'll have the escort bring her."

"I'm curious to meet her," Ekina said. "You wouldn't believe some of the ideas she sends the Speaker over with."

"Try me," Ixpar said.

"Have you ever heard of metal changers?"

"They were popular back in the Old Age, weren't they?"

"That's right. Claimed they could change iron into gold."

Ixpar laughed. "Winds, Ekina, I hope Bahr hasn't got you started on that."

"She thinks she can do it. She calls it atom cracking."

Atom cracking? That sounded like Bahr. "How does it work?"

"You change the number of neutron and proton dice in an atom by splitting its nucleus. Crack it apart, so to speak. Bahr claims if a nucleus has more than two hundred nine nucleon dice, it splits spontaneously. This morning she sent me a Quis pattern for cracking uranium two hundred thirty-eight."

"Why would you want to crack uranium?" Ixpar wasn't even sure what uranium was, other than that Bahr's patterns predicted it existed.

"It could produce energy," Ekina said. "A lot."

"Do you think it will work?"

Ekina shrugged. "I'm not even sure how to test for it."

Ixpar drew the physicist aside, away from the students. "What about her idea for campfires? Can you build me a hand-carried laser that burns things?" She paused. "Like buildings."

Ekina stopped smiling. "Are you sure that's what you want?"

"Yes."

It was a moment before Ekina answered. "I'll see what we can do."

After Ixpar left the lab, she went to the Calanya and walked out to the parks with Mentar, telling him about the laser.

"You should tell Sevtar," Mentar said. "It might put him in a better mood."

"He is upset?"

"I am not sure. Earlier today he was standing by a window in the common room. Then he cursed and went into his suite. He hasn't come out since." Mentar spread his hands. "One never knows with him."

When Ixpar tapped at Kelric's suite, no one answered. Just as she was about to leave he pulled aside the screen. He simply looked at her, then left the screen pushed to one side and walked back into his living room, over to the liqueur cabinet.

As Ixpar followed him, closing the screen behind her, he poured himself a glass of baiz.

"If you want to play Quis," Kelric said, "you'll have to come back another time."

"Mentar thinks you're angry."

"Why should I be angry?" He turned to face her, holding his baiz as if he wanted to throw the glass. "I'm impressed. Astonished. It's remarkable how fast you people are regaining knowledge hidden in the Quis. I've never seen anything like it. From knives to machine guns in one generation." He downed his drink in one swallow. "What next? Nuclear warheads?"

Suddenly she understood. "You saw me in the courtyard with the gun we tested today."

He set down his glass and came over to her. "I hate being the cause of this."

She drew him into her arms. "Ai, Kelric. It's not your fault."

But as they held each other in the fading sunlight, she knew there was no solace even here in the Calanya, either for her or for Kelric.

The door of Ixpar's office slammed open and Anthoni burst into the room. "Two Varz riders—over the airfield—shooting." He heaved in a breath. "The tower is blind and city com lines are dead."

Ixpar was on her feet before he finished. "Get on Estate com." She ran to the vault and took out the machine gun. "Sound the alarm and have our defenses armed."

Anthoni grabbed her arm. "You can't go out there. You could get killed."

"Let go of me."

"Ixpar, for wind's sake—"

"Get on that com." She yanked her arm away, then slung the gun over her shoulder and ran out of the office.

It took only minutes to cross the city. Ixpar heard the boom of the defense cannons as she was running through the factory district near the airfield. The area around her lay in ruins: smoke roiled in billows, fires flared, cracks rent the pavement. Two Varz riders swept into view, flying in a strafing run, their blistering attack spurring an explosion in a nearby warehouse.

Then the Karn *Snowhawk,* a pride of Ixpar's air force, appeared in the sky, climbing above the smoke. It went at the Varz riders like an althawk defending its territory. As the craft engaged in the sky, Ixpar raced for the meager shelter of an awning.

One of *Snowhawk's* missiles caught an invader dead center, setting it off like a firebomb. As debris rained out of the sky, the second Varz rider fired. *Snowhawk* tried to veer off, but the missile caught its wing, blasting the slats. *Snowhawk* careened into a burning warehouse, caught the shredded remains of its wing on an upthrusting column of wood, swung around like a toy on a stick, slammed into a blazing wall—and detonated in a plume of orange and black.

Ixpar's lips drew back in a snarl. When the surviving Varz rider swept low over the awning where she had sought cover, she stepped out and brought up the machine gun. Standing with her long legs planted wide, she braced the gun against her body and fired at the craft's belly. Bullets stabbed its engines reckety-reckety-reckety, so loud that even in the chaos of the burning district the noise deafened her. The Varz rider lurched into a roof and met its death in a roaring balloon of fire.

Then the only sound was the crackle of flames.

Ixpar stood tensed, half expecting another rider to materialize out of nowhere. As her adrenaline slowed, the foolhardy nature of her actions soaked into her mind.

People were emerging from the shelter of nearby buildings, staring at her as if she were a reincarnation from the Old Age. She looked back at them in silence, fighting an inner war no one but she would ever witness. Her mind recoiled from the knowledge she had just killed another human being.

But the beast within her burned, its rage whetted, its thirst for vengeance unquenched.

A Fourth and a Sixth Level; they played Quis as never before known on Coba.

Mentar set an onyx rod into a column-of-time structure that represented Karn. Kelric placed a sapphire rod, the color of foresight, on top of the column. The structure persisted in evolving into a Karn Ministry despite it being implicit in the session that the Ministry was at Varz now rather than Karn.

Mentar studied the structures. "You play more like a man my age than yours."

Kelric glanced up, disoriented by Mentar's voice. "We're almost the same age."

The Fourth Level smiled. "You flatter me. I was fifty-six last season."

And I? Kelric thought. He had been thirty-four when he crashed on Coba and that was . . . fourteen years ago? No, that wasn't it. He had been at Karn for over three years now, so he had lived on Coba for sixteen. Sixteen years. He was almost fifty-one.

The Outside doors slammed open and Ixpar strode into the room, fiery hair flying around her face, her clothes streaked with ashes, a belt of ammunition crisscrossing her chest, and a massive machine gripped in her hand.

Discreet as always, Mentar withdrew from the alcove. As Kelric stood up, Ixpar stopped in front of him and spoke with no preamble. "If Varz ever succeeds in breaking through to the Estate, the first place they will come is here, looking for you. I'm going to move everyone, but I want you to stay in my suite."

"Then give me the machine gun," he said.

She stared at him like an oncoming tank that had run into a wall. "What?"

"Give me the gun. So I can defend myself."

"I can't do that. You're a Calani."

"For flaming sake, Ixpar. I used to be a Jagernaut."

"We only have this one."

"Then give me a rifle. Hell, a sword. Anything."

It took Ixpar a moment to absorb the concept. Then she said, "A rifle. Yes."

He nodded. "Why do you want me to stay in your suite?"

"It has access to underground halls that would be safe even if Karn were razed to the ground. I realize you may prefer not to share rooms. That what you feel—don't feel—" She looked as if she wanted to stop, but felt it was no time for reticence.

"I know I can never replace Savina. If you prefer I live in another suite while you stay in mine, I understand."

"No, don't move. But I have a condition." He brushed dried blood off a gash in her arm. "What do you think happens to an army when its commander fights on the front lines?"

"You're as bad as Anthoni."

"Karn needs your leadership. *You*, Ixpar. Not the Elders or your staff or your air force. You. You're irreplaceable."

Her scowl would have done justice to the wildest Kej warrior queen. "You want me to hide while Varz attacks my city?"

"Yes."

She started to speak, then stopped and regarded him with an odd expression. "If I had a successor you would also advise me to keep her protected, yes?"

"Yes. Of course."

"Then why did Imperator Skolia—your *brother*—have you fighting on the front lines?"

The question caught Kelric off guard. "He had his reasons."

"He lost his successor because of them."

His years on Coba had allowed Kelric to forget the deadly game of political intrigue that stalked the Imperial court. "My half brother chose three heirs: one of my older brothers, one of my sisters, and myself. Only one of us can succeed him."

Quietly she said, "The one who survives."

"Yes."

"He is a fool."

"He's many things. But a fool isn't one of them. He wanted the strongest of us for his heir."

"Only a fool pits kin against kin and throws away a man like you."

A childhood memory came to Kelric; his mother standing on a balcony, radiant as she waved to him, with his half brother Kurj towering next to her, the case-hardened dictator who had, incredibly, once been a baby in her arms. It was only here, on Coba, that Kelric had finally realized Kurj sought to tear him down because he feared Kelric would someday become him. It never occurred to him that Kelric had neither the desire nor the intention of following his half brother's violent path to power.

* * *

Elder Solan, First among the Seven Elders of Karn, leaned toward Ixpar from her seat at the conference table. "This decision of yours to make Anthoni Senior Aide is unacceptable."

"Preposterous," Elder Fourth said.

Murmurs of agreement came from the others. Elder Second's sonorous voice rolled out. "I fail to understand, Ixpar, why you do not pick someone better qualified than a boy."

"For wind's sake," Ixpar said. "He's not a boy. He's older than I am. And there is no one better qualified."

Elder Fourth puffed on her pipe. "You possess a staff of highly percipient aides. Surely you can find a more appropriate choice."

Percipient? Ixpar wondered if Elder Fourth ever talked like a normal person.

"He's unreliable," Solan added.

"I've always found him reliable," Ixpar said.

"He is too nice," Elder Sixth said. "He hasn't the necessary authority."

"Deficiency also exists in his diplomatic skills," Elder Fourth said. "This could cause acrimony."

Ixpar snorted. "He's simultaneously too nice and not nice enough? That's a feat."

"Consider how your staff will react," Elder Sixth said. "How he deals with them. It is crucial. As important as his competence. If they mistrust his judgment it weakens his authority. Weakens the Estate."

Ixpar crossed her arms. "Give him a chance to prove himself before you all bemoan the fall of Karn."

"And then what?" Solan demanded. "Perhaps you have a boy in mind for the Karn Successor too?"

"I don't have anyone in mind," Ixpar said. "I haven't found a suitable candidate."

Elder Third spoke. "There is another matter I find of more concern. Your proposal to build ground-based artillery in the city disturbs me."

"We have to do something," Ixpar said. "If Varz breaks our defenses again, they may go after people instead of factories."

Elder Fourth relit her pipe. "It seems to me the prudent

course of action would be to increase the number of riders on patrol and forestall Varz from reaching Karn in the first place."

"We don't have enough riders," Ixpar said.

Solan frowned. "We have as many as Varz."

"It isn't just Varz," Ixpar said. "Ahkah and Shazorla also have to be considered."

"Shazorla fly against Karn?" Elder Second rumbled. "Never."

"There is this matter of the perpetually disappearing Hayl Varz," Elder Fourth said. "Manager Shazorla seems to believe he is here."

Elder Fifth snorted. "I'll bet any roll of the dice Avtac knows where he is."

"We need to prove it," Elder Sixth said. "Prove she hides him. Then we might turn Shazorla from Varz. Back to Karn."

"What about Rashiva Haka?" Elder Seventh asked. "She still claims neutrali—"

"Meaningless," Elder Second rumbled. "If it comes to the test, Haka will remain loyal to Varz."

Elder Fifth leaned forward. "We have other allies. Dahl. Bahvla."

"Chankah Dahl has pledged a rider fleet," Ixpar said. "There's still no word from Bahvla."

"It has been a year since Borj's unit went down," Elder Third said. "If anyone made it to Bahvla we should have heard by now."

"How?" Elder Second demanded. "Any messengers would have to come on foot. Winds only know if they would make it."

Elder Fourth put down her pipe. "The situation appears to be this: we presently have only one viable ally whereas Varz has three at the very least, five if you include secondary Estates, and possibly seven should the alignment of Viasa and Tehnsa become manifest."

"In other words," Ixpar said, "we're in trouble."

42

Golden Nested Tower

Rohka Miesa Varz poked her head around the big clock at the entrance of the Children's Cooperative. No guardians in sight. She padded to the door, nudged it open—and she was out and free, trotting across the starlit plaza.

Tonight she would find the Magic. It lived in a place called Galerunner's Tavern on Juggler's Lane. Rohka wasn't sure what tavern meant, but she knew it was Magic by the way Guardian Jasina lit up when anyone mentioned a singer there named Tomi. The glow was inside of Jasina, a warmth in her mind that spread to Rohka and made her glow too.

While her mind danced with bright pictures of jugglers skipping over cobblestones, Rohka trotted through Miesa/Varz to Juggler's Lane. But when she reached it, she saw no jugglers anywhere. All the shops looked dark except for a place at the end where colorful lights and music spilled into the street.

After pondering, Rohka padded toward the building with lights. When she neared, she saw two fierce and burly women looming at its entrance.

Rohka hesitated. She hadn't expected the Magic to be guarded by giants.

"Well, I'll be a Quis cube." One of the giants knelt down to look at her. "Where did you come from?"

Rohka blinked, suddenly shy.

The woman smiled. "What brings you out here so late?"

"I came to hear Tomi sing," Rohka said.

The other giant laughed. "She may be young, but she appreciates true art."

"Come on back to the kitchen," the first woman said. "We'll get you a glass of tawmilk."

"Can I see Tomi there?" Rohka asked.

"The cook won't mind if you peek into the lounge." She stood up and spoke with the other giant in a low voice. The second woman nodded and set off toward Miesa Square.

"Is she going home?" Rohka asked.

The woman took her hand. "No. Just on an errand for me." She led Rohka around the side of the tavern. "Do you have a name?"

"Rohka."

The giant smiled. "I'm Chal."

Warm air and good smells filled the kitchen. Pots bubbled over the fireplace. In the door of a big icebox, Rohka saw her own reflection: a little girl with tousled yellow curls and a smudge on her cheek. She wiped at the smudge with her hand.

A plump woman in an apron bustled over to them. "What brings you back here, heh, Chal? No clawcats making trouble tonight?"

Chal grinned. "Caught me a clawcat cub." She nudged Rohka forward. "Instead of bouncing her out, though, I thought I'd bring her back for some tawmilk."

"Well, looky you." The cook bent over Rohka. "What a beauty. And look at those eyes. Never seen gold eyes before."

Rohka blinked up at the woman. "My greetings, ma'am."

The cook chuckled. "My greetings to you, little cub."

While the cook went for the tawmilk, Chal led Rohka to a half door and lifted her onto a stool. From her perch Rohka could see over the door into a room full of people and tables. A man on the stage was singing.

The cook brought Rohka a glass of warm tawmilk. "So." She settled her bulk on a stool next to her visitor. "What you say, little one? Is Tomi a right fine sight or what?"

"I guess so." Rohka's interest in the Magic was dimming. It had no jugglers or magicians, just a smoky room and a man who sang songs she didn't understand. She wanted to go home. It was such a long way, though. Maybe they would let her sleep here tonight.

Rohka curled her hands around her glass and drank the tawmilk. When she yawned, the cook picked her up and settled her into her ample lap, humming a lullaby as she rocked back and forth. Roca closed her eyes and snuggled in the woman's arms.

A commotion woke Rohka. She peeked over the cook's elbow to see Guardian Jasina hurrying in with the giant who had gone on the errand.

"Winds above, child." Jasina bustled over to her. "Do you know how worried we've been? What are you doing here?"

"See Tomi," Rohka said drowsily.

The cook chuckled. "She came to woo your intended, Jasina."

The guardian lifted Rohka into her arms. "The last time she went exploring we found her trying to stow away on a rider to Shazorla."

"Shazorla?" the cook said. "Whatever for?"

"Someone told her that suntrees there have real suns for fruit." Jasina smiled. "She wanted to see."

"Sunny trees," Rohka mumbled. She could feel Jasina's love for the singer. The Magic was back and now she knew where it came from. It was Jasina and Tomi together. Their warmth spread everywhere, making her safe and secure . . .

A gust of cold air woke Rohka. She found herself being carried through the streets of Miesa. Chal held her now and Jasina was walking next to them.

". . . unusual for a child her age to find her way around the city so well," Chal said.

"She's remarkably bright," Jasina said. "She has some odd ideas, though."

"Odd how?"

"Well, for one, she used to ask me why people thought one thing and said another."

Chal shifted Rohka in her arms. "Sounds like a good question to me."

Jasina smiled. "The thing is, she really believed she could hear people think."

Rohka remembered how she had tried to stop hearing thoughts after everyone told her it was impossible. But she still picked them up, like when Jon broke his toe and his yell bounced around her head as clear as if she stood right next to him instead of halfway across Miesa.

A rumbling swelled above them. When Chal stopped to look at the sky, Rohka looked, too, and saw three riders flying toward the airfield. A moment later, a big noise and a burst of light came from across the city. More noises boomed and the light got brighter.

"Cuaz above," Chal said. "They're *shelling* it."

"Why is the sun coming up over there?" Rohka asked. "That's the wrong place."

"It isn't the sun, honey," Jasina said. "The airfield is on fire."

"Why?"

Jasina drew them under a shop awning. "Not now, Rohka."

"Are we hiding?" Rohka asked.

"Just until they go away," Jasina said.

"Look." Rohka pointed up at the mountains and wiggled in Chal's arms, trying to get down. "There's more."

The new riders sped over the city, following the ones that had made so much noise and light. Jasina waited until long after they had vanished before she stepped into the street again.

For the rest of the trip back to the Cooperative no one spoke. Rohka caught a wisp of thought from someone about the riders being Karn. It confused her. Adults said Karn people were bad and Varz people were good, but that wasn't always what they thought. They were afraid of someone named Avtac and Avtac was at Varz.

Rohka knew Karn was important. Her father lived there. She wished he was at Miesa. She didn't understand why the evil people at Karn took him away, or why everyone said her mother had left on a long trip, when what they thought was that Savina Miesa had died.

Sometimes Rohka made pictures in her mind of the sun goddess Savina carrying her away to a magical cloud where the Akasi Sevtar lived. Suns grew on the trees and jugglers ran laughing down the cloud streets. It was a place where food never made you sick and gold eyes were normal and no one told you hearing thoughts was wrong.

In predawn dimness, Captain Borj walked with Ixpar across the Karn airfield. She pulled off her helmet, a bronze headgear shaped like the head of a clawcat. "The Varz defenses were too strong. We only managed one run over the airfield before they ran us off."

"Any casualties?" Ixpar asked.

"None." Borj paused. "We didn't lose any riders at Miesa either."

"Miesa? What were you doing there?"

"When we hit Varz, they brought in reinforcements from the Plateau. So we snuck out over Miesa while her defenders were at Varz." Borj tugged off her gloves. "We put out their airfield. Miesa won't be sending support to Varz for a while."

Although Ixpar knew the move made tactical sense, it disturbed her. Miesa barely claimed enough riders to support itself, let alone anyone else.

For the rest of the morning, Ixpar sat in her office reading reports from her commanders. At Midday she climbed up to her suite for a Quis session with Kelric. She found him asleep in the bedroom, and an uneasy feeling came over her as she watched the rise and fall of his chest.

She went back to the entrance and spoke to Eb, the captain of his Calanya escort. "Does Sevtar always sleep this much?"

"Usually," Eb said.

"Why? What does he do that makes him so tired?"

"Can't rightly say I know, ma'am. He spends most of his time playing Quis."

Ixpar frowned, then left the suite and went down to Med. She found her Senior Physician reading in the medical library.

"So," Shallina said. "Have you finally come for the physical I ordered?"

"This is about Sevtar," Ixpar said. "He sleeps too much."

Shallina spoke dryly. "There is no harm in sleep. You should try it sometime."

"Not this much. It's not normal."

The doctor closed her book. "I will look at him."

It was evening when Shallina came to Ixpar's office. "He's exhausted," the doctor said. "I don't know why. I found nothing wrong." She paused. "To be honest, I don't know what is wrong or right for a Skolian."

Ixpar put down her quill. "What do you suggest?"

Shallina cleared her throat. "I think you should, ah—ask Dabbiv Dahl to come here."

That threw Ixpar like a Quis die. Shallina's conservative approach to medicine usually had her denouncing Dabbiv's work. "Why?"

"Don't mistake my meaning," Shallina said. "I don't subscribe to these off-pattern ideas of his. But he is the only doctor on Coba who has had experience with offworlders."

Ixpar sent an octet of riders to Dahl that night.

Three days later, while Ixpar sat listening to her advisers argue in the Hall of Teotec, Anthoni brought her a message. She slipped out of the meeting and hurried with him to the airfield, reaching it in time to see her Karn riders landing, accompanied by a Dahl craft.

The heavyset man with gray-streaked hair who jumped down from the Dahl rider looked like a stranger. But the moment he smiled, Ixpar recognized him.

"Dabbiv." She returned the smile. "Welcome to my Estate."

The doctor bowed. "You look well, Manager Karn."

"Did you have a good flight?"

"For the most part. There was a bit of trouble near the end." Dabbiv adjusted his glasses. "For some reason an Ahkah patrol decided we were in their way."

"What happened?"

"Not much. They shook us around some, your Captain Borj shook them around some, and that was the end of it."

She laid her hand on his arm. "I know the risks you took coming here. You have my deepest thanks."

"I'm honored you think I can help."

They walked to the Estate with Anthoni and a retinue of guards. While Anthoni showed Dabbiv to his suite, Ixpar returned to the Hall of Teotec. Her commanders were still arguing, but they had migrated from the Opal Table to the wall map. Colored pins covered the map: red for enemy, blue for ally, gray for neutral. Red dominated: in the east it showed on Ahkah and Lasa, in the northeast on Varz and Miesa, in the west on Shazorla and Eviza. Karn made a splash of blue in the center, as did Bahvla to the north and Dahl to the south. Gray showed on Haka in the southwest and on Viasa and Tehnsa in the northwest. Air lanes networked the chart in blue, gray, and red.

Ixpar went to the map and pushed in a pin to mark the skirmish between Dabbiv's escort and the Ahkah patrol. The red marker encroached on the blue of the Karn/Dahl air lanes.

Elder Solan frowned. "At this rate, red will soon surround Karn."

Ixpar pulled out the red pin at Shazorla and replaced it with a blue one.

"Wishful hopes," Solan said.

"Soon to be fact." Ixpar regarded the Elder. "Whether Shazorla likes it or not."

Kelric sat in the Blue Alcove thinking Quis thoughts. In another part of the suite a door opened. He looked up, expecting Ixpar, but instead he saw the Calanya Speaker and an unknown man. After introducing the man as Dabbiv Dahl, the Speaker withdrew.

Dabbiv bowed. "My greetings."

Kelric wondered why Ixpar allowed a stranger to intrude on his privacy.

"Don't you recognize me?" the man asked. "Dabbiv. Your doctor at Dahl."

Kelric did recall an intense young doctor there. This man looked too old to be the same person.

After a moment Dabbiv said, "Would you prefer I came back later?"

Kelric had no desire to be poked at by more doctors. But Ixpar must have gone to a lot of trouble to bring Dabbiv here. For her sake he would consent to one more exam.

Ixpar found the person she sought in the office she had provided him, bent over the microscope he had invented.

"Dabbiv?" she asked.

He jumped to his feet, then grabbed some folders and slapped them down on the desk. "Manager Karn."

"Captain Eb told me you finished examining Kelric." Ixpar went over and pushed aside the folders, uncovering several texts, all with titles in Skolian. She picked one up. *"Cardiopulmonary Anomalies in Gamma Physiology."*

"Ah—" His face paled. "Yes."

"What does it mean?"

"Gamma refers to the breed of humans Kelric belongs to. *Cardiopulmonary* means heart and lungs."

"Imperialate hearts and lungs."

"Yes."

Ixpar set down the text and covered it with folders. "You should keep a neater office. You never know who might walk in."

The color eased back into Dabbiv's face. "I'll do that."

"How is Kelric?"

"I need more tests," he said. "It will take a few days. I've never done these procedures before, so I have to make sure I get them right."

Ixpar tensed. "You want to experiment on my Akasi?"

"The tests aren't experimental. Skolians use them all the time."

"You aren't Skolian."

He regarded her steadily. "If I don't determine what's wrong with Kelric—and believe me, something is wrong—it will do him far more harm than my tests ever could."

His words quashed Ixpar's last hopes that her worries were unfounded. "All right. But be careful."

Four days passed while Dabbiv ran his tests. On the fifth evening Ixpar found him waiting in her office, sitting at a table with his fingers steepled together.

She sat across from him. "What did you find?"

"Kelric differs from us far more than is obvious from his physical appearance."

"We take every precaution for him. Special diet, purified water—you've seen what we do."

"You can't change the ecosystems of an entire world." He lowered his hands. "Coba has poisoned him day by day, year by year, weakened his heart, digestive system, lungs, liver—everything. This world is far more hostile to him than we realized. But he has miniature biochemistry labs in his body, nanomeds. Coupled with something—a thing called bionech—they've kept him alive. Except they haven't been working right, not for years. Maybe not since he crashed here. It's gotten worse, until the meds themselves are poisoning him."

Ixpar watched his face. "And to heal him?"

For a long moment he looked at her. Finally he said, "If we had access to the resources of a full ISC medical facility, I think most of the damage could be repaired."

The room suddenly seemed too quiet. "There is nothing remotely resembling a full ISC medical facility on Coba."

"I know. I—Ixpar—I'm sorry."

"No." Her mind refused to understand. "No."

"I'll do all I can." Softly he added, "But it's like trying to stop a flood with a cup."

No. It couldn't be true. *Couldn't.*

"I haven't told him," Dabbiv said. "I thought it might be better if it came from you."

"How long?"

"It's hard to know exactly, with—"

"How long?"

He spoke quietly. "I doubt he'll live past this winter."

And though he continued to speak, Ixpar heard nothing else. Two seasons.

Two seasons remained for the legend that had changed her world.

That night, while the rest of Karn slept, she walked through the city, neither seeing nor caring where she went. It was deep in the silent hours before dawn when she returned to the Estate.

In the living room of her suite, she found an eerie Quis structure spread across a table. The longer she stared at it, the more patterns became visible, multiple threads woven together with an intricacy almost impossible to follow, the designs curled in haunting symmetries that whispered of precognition. She traced a thread in black, the pattern of a long, slow dying, and a chill breathed on her neck.

"You look tired," Kelric said.

Ixpar looked up to see him standing in the bedroom archway, dressed in a robe. "Did I wake you?"

"I'm glad you did." He came over to her. "Sometimes, when I'm falling asleep, I feel—strange."

Her eyes felt hot with unshed tears. "Strange how?"

He stroked her hair, looking at it as if it were a treasure he valued. "I wonder if I'll wake up again."

Ixpar's voice caught. "If you could have any wish, anything at all, what would you ask for?"

"Anything?"

"Yes. Anything." She waited for him to ask for the one thing she couldn't give: his freedom.

"To see my children," he said.

Later, while Kelric slept, Ixpar slipped out of his arms and went to the com in the Blue Alcove. She roused Captain Borj from her sleep and told her what needed to be done.

Then Ixpar descended into the Memory. As she walked through it, her tears fell like sand, leaving behind truths she had too long denied. She could give up the rule of a world for Kelric, wage for him the first war Coba had seen in a millennium, but she could no more make him love her, truly love her, than she could contain the spirit of a wild hawk.

43

Double Nested Tower

Rashiva walked with her retinue through Haka. A letter lay crisp in her pocket and crisp in her mind. New Ministers, Sixth Levels, war between the Estates, and in the midst of it all Ixpar Karn bid for the Calanya contract of a boy—a *Haka* boy—far too young to leave the Preparatory House.

Sevtar wanted to see his son, Rashiva was certain. From Ixpar's viewpoint, it would have been far easier to ask that Jimorla visit his father. Although the Preparatory House barred Outsiders from contact with its students, who could refuse such a request from a Sixth Level? Or Ixpar could have sent warriors to kidnap Jimorla. Considering everything else that had happened, it wouldn't have surprised Rashiva. Instead the

Karn queen chose the way of honor, making an offer for Imorla's Calanya contract.

Rashiva's Senior Aide was walking at her side. She touched Rashiva's arm as they passed a street leading to the airfield. In the distance, a battered rider rested in a repair bay.

"It comes from Shazorla," the Senior said.

Rashiva nodded. "Several limped in yesterday also."

"Crippling Miesa wasn't enough for Ixpar Karn, was it?" The Senior's voice hardened. "Now she adds Shazorla to the list."

Although Rashiva would never admit it aloud, she considered Ixpar's tactics inspired. Shazorla was a traditional Karn ally, a city and people Ixpar knew well. She had worked beautifully subtle patterns into the Quis, swaying Shazorla's already wavering citizenry to favor Karn rather than their uncomfortable new Varz allies. So at crucial times, crucial people in Shazorla looked the other way. By the time Rashiva had figured out what was going on, it was too late; Karn agents had sabotaged every maintenance bay, fuel tank, oil refinery, and rider-related factory in Shazorla. Its air force had been nullified without the loss of a single life.

"Karn grows more audacious each day," her Senior Aide said. "How much longer will you wait before you send support to Varz?"

"Until Varz needs it," Rashiva said. "Right now Avtac is doing fine without my help."

"She lost Shazorla."

"And Karn lost Bahvla."

"No one attacked Bahvla."

Rashiva scowled. "What do you call a blockade that cuts off an Estate from its food supply for over a year? Starvation, of an entire city. It appalls me."

"Miesa and Shazorla—"

"Lost their airfields. Shazorla has farms. Miesa has Varz. Bahvla has lumber. You can't feed people with wood."

The Senior fell silent as they approached the Preparatory House. The Elder Mentor was waiting at the arched entrance, cowled and cloaked, his face hidden behind a tasseled scarf. He bowed to Rashiva and preceded her into the House while

her retinue waited Outside. They walked through ancient halls
the Mentor's robe whispering on the cold stone floors.

At the Visitation Room the Mentor halted, leaving her to
enter alone. Inside, a thirteen-year-old boy stood poking at a
mobile of metal spheres that bobbed on the mantel. He was
unusually tall for his age, with the athletic poise of an acrobat
Black curls spilled into his violet eyes.

Rashiva closed the door behind her. "Jimorla."

Her son looked up, his face lighting in welcome. When he
came over and hugged her, Rashiva smiled. "You grow so fast
Soon you will go through the ceiling."

Obviously pleased, he pulled himself to his full height and
looked down on her. "Do you want tea? I'm an Initiate, so I
can have a Novice bring it."

"Tanghi would be nice."

Jimorla opened a side door and spoke to a younger boy outside. While the Novice went for tea, Rashiva sat with her son on
the sofa, and they talked about his life in the Preparatory House

"My Mentor thinks I'll be ready to apply to the Calanya in
six or seven years," Jimorla said as the Novice returned.

Rashiva waited until the boy poured them each a mug of tea
and left. Then she said, "Suppose someone made an offer for
your contract now?"

"Mother," Jimorla said.

"I'm serious."

"Why in a year of windless wogs would anyone do that?"

Rashiva tried not to smile at the idiom. "It happens." She
took a swallow of tea. "Say Karn made an offer."

He laughed. "I'd take a sword and go fight them."

"Jimi, I mean it. What would you do?"

"I would never go to Karn."

"Why not?"

"Because. It's Karn. Besides, Manager Karn cheated Varz
She used tricks to control the Quis."

Rashiva snorted. "I doubt Sevtar's contract forbids Ixpa
Karn from playing dice better than Varz."

Jimorla considered her. "Sometimes I think you don't much
like Minister Varz."

"Estate politics are complicated interdependencies. A Manager must retain objectivity."

"You always do that."

"Do what?"

"Talk like a law scroll when I say something you don't want said. And you know Manager Karn is worse than a dice cheater. She stole Hayl Varz. *Twice*."

"She did?"

"Well, he isn't at Varz."

"You have been there to check?"

"It's in the Quis," Jimorla said. "Someone stole him."

"That's right. Me."

He gaped at her. "You?"

"Hayl ran away from Varz. He asked me for asylum and I gave it to him."

"He's at *Haka*?"

Rashiva nodded.

"Then why does Minister Varz blame Karn?"

How did she explain Avtac to a child? "It's complicated."

"Are you going to talk like a scroll again?"

"Jimi, Manager Karn may not be our ally but she is an honorable woman."

"Why do you keep trying to make me like her?"

"Because she bid for your Calanya contract."

He gave an uneasy laugh. "This is a joke, yes?"

"No. She offers you a position coveted by Calani with many times your age and experience."

"It's a trick, then."

"I'm sure it is an honest offer."

"I don't believe it. What would Manager Karn want with me?"

Rashiva got up and went to the mantel, where the mobile drifted in circles. This was even harder than she had anticipated.

"Mother?" Jimorla said.

She turned to him. "Manager Karn wants to bring you to her Estate so you can meet your father."

"But he's here."

"No, Jimi. He isn't."

"I just saw him yesterday. He didn't say he was going anywhere."

"Raaj isn't—" She stopped as the words caught in her throat.

"Isn't what?" Jimorla asked.

She made the words come out. "Raaj isn't your biological father."

At first he showed no reaction. Then he gave her an uncomfortable smile. "Your jokes are strange today."

"It isn't a joke."

"You're right. It isn't funny. Father wouldn't think so either."

"Raaj knows all of this."

"You're making it up, yes?" He watched her with a heartbreaking look, as if willing her to tell him it was all a story. "The Mentors asked you to do it. This is some kind of test."

She spoke gently. "Your skin, your features, even the way you walk—it's just like him."

"Him?"

"Sevtar. The Sixth Level." She took a breath. "Your father."

Jimorla stood up, his fist clenched. "It's not *true*. Why are you doing this?"

"Who else has skin that shimmers like yours?" She went over to him. "Not Raaj."

"Father is my father. I don't want to hear any more."

"Ai, Jimi." Rashiva reached out to him. "I don't want you to be hurt."

He pushed her away. "Are you going to force me to live at Karn?"

"Not if you don't want to."

"I don't."

"Perhaps we could arrange a temporary visit for you."

"To meet him?" Despite his anger, anticipation leaked into his voice. "The Sixth?"

"Yes. The Sixth."

"And afterward I can come home?"

Relief poured over Rashiva. "Yes. Then you can come home."

* * *

A clamor woke Rohka. Everything was confusion. People yelled in the dark and a big rumbling roar shook the Cooperative. She scrambled out of bed and ran out of her suite, straight into a flock of little girls in woolly nightgowns who looked as scared as she felt.

A hoard of monsters poured into the corridor.

They were terrible, all leather and bronze, with metal faces like fierce beasts. As the monsters wrestled with the grown-ups, shouts filled the air. In the confusion, Rohka found herself trapped in a corner. She made herself little and flat against the wall, praying no monsters saw her.

Someone screamed and Rohka saw a monster scoop up a girl with yellow hair.

"Check her eyes!" someone shouted. "They're gold."

Rohka's confusion turned into terror. Only one girl had gold eyes. She bolted down the hall, trying to escape the turmoil.

Suddenly hands clamped around her arms. A monster hollered, "I found her," hoisted her up into its burly arms, and shoved its way through the melee.

Chill air blasted Rohka's face when they ran out into the night. Across the plaza, two riders crouched on the ground like sly birds ready to pounce.

"Let me go!" Rohka yelled. The monster's face looked like a helmet now, one covering a woman's head. She pounded her fists against the metal. "Avtac Varz will squash you flat. *Flat, flat, flat.*"

"Feisty little cub," the monster muttered. She reached the first rider and swung Rohka up to a woman in the hatch. The woman bundled Rohka into a seat while the monster jumped in and slammed the hatch.

A voice crackled from the com. "*Skyarrow,* this is *Windstar.* Scan shows two octets coming down from Varz. We've got to run."

"No problem, *Windstar,*" the pilot said. "We have what we came for."

The riders lifted into the sky. In dismay, Rohka saw her home, Miesa, recede into a scatter of tiny lights in the mountains.

* * *

When Kelric awoke in the morning, he found a mug of Tanghi steaming on the nightstand. He put on his robe and took the mug to an alcove that overlooked the gardens. While he sat drinking, Quis patterns evolved in his mind.

A new pattern evolved, one that had slowly taken form over the last three years, intertwining itself with the other shapes and forms of his life. He looked at the unexpected pattern and found it as clear as a mountain spring. When next he saw Ixpar, he would tell her of it. What difference it would make to her, he didn't know. But nevertheless, he ought to tell his wife he loved her.

The tramp of soldiers below his window fragmented his thoughts. They crossed the garden, one carrying a small sleeping girl with masses of gold curls tumbling down her back. Watching the girl, he felt a sense of familiarity, though he couldn't say why. Her image stayed with him, interwoven with his endless Quis thoughts.

Later another commotion drew his attention. A Calanya retinue was passing below his window, escorting a figure in the robes and Talha of a Haka Calani. It had to be a trick of light; no Haka Calani would be in Karn now. He was the height of an average Coban male, but slender like a boy.

A boy?

Kelric froze, suddenly understanding his reaction to the girl. *Like knew like.* Even a Kyle operator with a mind as injured as his own recognized the blooms that flowered from his own seed.

His children. Ixpar had brought his children to Karn.

A sense of urgency came over Kelric, a feeling that if he didn't go to Ixpar now he would forever lose the chance to tell her how much this meant to him and how he felt about her. He went to the Outside doors and made his escort understand what he wanted.

Captain Eb spoke to one of his guards. "You wait here. If Manager Karn comes, tell her the four of us took Sevtar to look for her."

44

King's Flight

Ixpar sat in the hatchway of her rider, looking out at the Calanya parks. Her craft was stripped to essentials, a runner designed for speed. It could easily reach the starport on one tank of fuel.

If Kelric stayed on Coba he would die. If he left, he would live.

Kastora, what counsel would you give me? Ixpar thought. Kelric wasn't the same man who, seventeen years ago, had intended to bring ISC down on them. What would happen if she set him free? Could she convince him to keep Coba's secret, to protect its anonymity? Her decision would affect the future of her entire world.

Shivering, Ixpar turned her face to the sun. Far in the north a flock of birds was arrowing toward Karn. It was odd to see them migrating in summer; they didn't usually come until autumn.

Very odd.

She jumped down from the rider and looked eastward—to see another cloud of dark forms headed for her Estate.

Ixpar swore, then took off running across the park. When she reached the Estate, she smacked her palm against the first com she found.

A voice floated into the air. "Tal here—"

"Tal, this is Manager Karn. Put Karn on alert. This isn't a drill! Do you understand? *Full alert.*"

Tal's voice crackled over the com. "I'm on it."

"Get me Commander Borj, Anthoni, Captain Eb, and Elder Solan on com. Contact Ekina at the Institute and tell her to meet me outside my office with the carbine. She'll know what I mean."

"Right away." In only a few seconds Tal said, "Commander Borj on three."

"I'm switching out." She switched to three. "Borj, fleets are coming in from the north and east. Go to the command center below the Atrium and put Code Four into action."

"On my way," Borj said.

"Good. Out." Ixpar switched to line one. "Tal, do you have Anthoni yet?"

"Line two."

Ixpar switched. "Anthoni, start the evacuation procedures for Karn. You're in charge."

"Understood," Anthoni said.

"Out." Ixpar switched to one. "Tal, what line is Captain Eb on?"

"I haven't been able to reach your suite. But I have Elder Solan on four."

Ixpar switched. "Solan, this is Ixpar. In the Blue Alcove of my suite you'll find an engraving that matches the lock sequence I taught you. The door it opens leads to an underground hall. Take the Calanya and Bahr down there."

"Understood," Solan said.

"Switching out." Ixpar went to one. "Tal, have you got Eb?"

"There's only one guard at your suite. She said the others left with Sevtar to look for you."

Ixpar swore. "Then get on every line, contact every guard, whatever is necessary—*but find him.*"

"Yes, ma'am. What shall we do with Jimorla Haka?"

Winds above. "Manager Haka's son is here? Already?"

"He arrived early. I just sent an aide to tell you."

Rashiva must have learned of the Varz attack plans *after* the boy left Haka. If any harm came to Jimorla, nothing would stop Haka's wrath. But the only truly safe place on Karn was the Memory where she had sent the Calanya. How could she reveal, to the son of a hostile Manager, a secret kept by the Ministers of Karn for two millennia?

Still, he was Calani. Almost Calani. He was also a hostage worth his height in jeweled Quis dice. "Send Jimorla with the Calanya. Tell everyone it's a storage room and have Jimorla kept under guard. I don't want him wandering around down there."

"And Rohka Miesa?" Tal asked.

"Saints almighty, Tal. She's already here too?"

"Yhee, ma'am."

"Send her with Jimorla."

"Right away," Tal said. "I have Elder Solan on six."

"Out." Ixpar switched. "Solan, what's going on?"

"I'm at your suite," Solan said. "We found the chambers and took the Calanya down. We're waiting for Sevtar now."

"Any word on where he is?"

"Not yet. I sent more guards to look for him."

"Let me know as soon as they find him. Out." Ixpar switched to one. "Tal, do you have Commander Borj?"

"Line three."

Ixpar switched. "What's the situation, Borj?"

"The fleet coming from the north is Varz," Borj said. "East is Ahkah, with support from Lasa. Altogether, they outnumber us about two to one."

Ixpar grimaced. "Where did Avtac get so many riders?"

"My bet is that she pulled her octets off the blockade."

"Any word from Bahvla?"

"None."

"What about Dahl?"

"The Dahl forces stationed here are up with our riders," Borj said. "I sent a runner for reinforcements, if Manager Dahl has any, but I doubt it will reach Dahl before tonight."

"Any sign of a Haka fleet?"

"Nothing so far."

"Keep me posted. Out." Ixpar switched to one. "Tal, have they found Sevtar?"

"Not yet," Tal said. "But Ekina is at your office. She says she has what you want."

Where was Kelric? "All right. Go to the command center and stay on the com lines. I'll be there as soon as I can. Out."

Ixpar took off running. She found Ekina standing in front of her office, holding a monstrous gun with cooling-coils around its barrel and a heavy metal stock. A power pack sat at her feet.

"Is it accurate?" Ixpar asked.

Ekina's face was flushed from running. "Accurate? We've hardly even *tested* it yet. I never expected this monster to come out of those Calanya patterns."

Ixpar took the laser carbine, hefting its bulk in her hands. "How do I use it?"

Ekina strapped the power pack around her waist and indicated a button on the gun. "Push that and it fires."

Ixpar slung the gun's strap over her shoulder. "You better go to the command center. You'll be safe there."

"You're coming, aren't you?"

"As soon as I get a look at the situation." Before Ekina could protest, Ixpar took off again.

She went to the outside balcony that circled the Observatory dome. In both the north and east, she saw a sky dark with windriders: Varz and Karn, Ahkah and Dahl, all engaged in battle. Nowhere did she see the Haka emblem of a rising sun. To the west, lines of people wound into the Teotecs as they evacuated Karn.

A shadow cut across the steepled roofs of the city, a lone Varz rider arrowing for the Estate, the first to break through the Karn defenses. Her lips drawing back in a snarl, Ixpar raised her gun, sighted on the craft—and fired.

The violent flare of light produced by the carbine bore no resemblance to the harmless red beam she had seen in Ekina's lab last year. This pulse streaked to the rider and exploded the craft in a blast of white light. An instant later the sound wave of its detonation slammed against Ixpar.

"Spirits help us," she whispered as molten metal showered the empty streets.

Sunlight diffused through the Atrium, falling across Kelric and his escort as they walked past the plants and waterfalls. The serenity felt oddly fragile, like blown glass.

A guard ran into the hall. "Captain Eb! Varz fleet—coming in—get to Manager Karn's suite."

Kelric immediately turned with his guards and they ran for the staircase that swept up from the Atrium. In the north, he saw a hoard of riders swarming toward Karn.

Two Varz warcraft suddenly soared out from behind a nearby tower and skimmed low over the Atrium, breaking its glass with the vibration of their passage. An explosion blasted through the balcony above them, destroying the top of the staircase. Kelric and his guards spun around and raced back down into the Atrium. At the bottom, they ran to the landing of a stairwell that descended to a more protected floor.

When the whistle of falling bombs pierced the air, only Kelric recognized the sound. His warning shout was smothered by an explosion and the floor heaved under his feet. As he fell, one of his armbands caught on the staircase banister, wrenching him to such a fast stop his shoulder nearly pulled out of its socket.

Then the band yanked off his arm and he fell down the stairs. Glimpses of rail, floor, ceiling, all flashed by as he tumbled. As an explosion rocked the stairs above him, he hit the floor and rolled over, gasping for breath.

Kelric scrambled to his feet in time to see a curtain of flame sweeping across the staircase. Behind and within it, he could make out the frantic forms of his guards trying to smother their burning clothes and escape the inferno.

"Sevtar!" Captain Eb shouted. *Get out of here!*

Kelric had no intention of leaving them to die. He beat at the flames, shielding his face with his arm as he struggled to reach the guards.

With a deafening crash, the landing above him collapsed. The steps crumbled next, toppling in succession as the area disintegrated in a thunder of falling walls. Chunks of debris shot into the air, mixing with clouds of plaster. Kelric staggered, coughing, eyes watering, skin blistering, forced back by the searing heat, until he backed up through the door arch behind him.

It was cooler in the marble corridor outside the stairwell. He sagged against a wall and slid to his knees, drawing in huge breaths. Then a rumble swelled behind him. Twisting around, he saw the walls of the corridor toppling inward like a wave running up a pipe.

Kelric lurched to his feet and took off, running past burning archway after burning archway, trying to outrun the destruction. When he found a stairwell untouched by fire, he took the wide steps three at a time. At the top he pulled open the door, and a gale shoved him in the chest like a giant hand. Leaning into the wind, he pushed his way onto a balcony—and looked out over a nightmare.

Karn was in flames.

The darkening sky boiled with riders, roaring in the chaos of battle. Ashes swirled in the air, whipped into a shower of powder by the wind. Smoke billowed out windows, rolled across lawns, rose in great oily clouds that spread a gray pall of crackling soot over the city.

Kelric clenched the balcony rail, staring out over the scene. "No," he said. "I won't be the cause of this." He raised his head and shouted at the riders battling in the sky. "Do you hear me? *I will not be the cause of this.*"

The rail burst into flame, tongues of fire consuming the wood. Within seconds the entire balcony had ignited. Racing the flames, Kelric backed away and ran down the stairs, out again into the marble corridor. He kept going, past arches that opened onto debris, until finally there were only smooth marble walls that went on and on, unending, as if he were doomed to run down the tunnel forever while Karn burned.

He came out into a foyer he recognized; he was near the old Calanya. He kept running, following familiar halls this time.

Inside the Calanya, he found tables toppled and screens hanging in shreds. Every room was empty, but when he neared the exit to the parks he heard voices. He slipped outside, hiding behind a hedge. Across the gardens, an octet of Varz warriors stood gathered by their riders, towering women in bronze and leather armor with beast helmets over their heads.

Nearer by, an empty Karn rider sat on a lawn. Sleek and stripped to essentials, it had the streamlined grace of a runner built for speed.

Staying low behind the bushes, Kelric crept toward the runner. When he reached the end of the hedge, he paused. Then he sprinted into the open.

Shouts erupted behind him and a bullet whizzed past his arm, kicking up the dirt ahead of him.

"Don't shoot, you idiot!" someone shouted. "He's a Calani!"

"*Six* bands!" another voice yelled. "*That's him.*"

A stun shot hit Kelric's arm, numbing his burns, and another caught him in the knee. His breathing came in labored gasps but he never broke his stride. He would rather die from heart failure than go back to Varz.

The open hatch of the rider loomed into view. As Kelric vaulted into the cabin, boots pounded behind him. He spun around, planted his foot in the armor-covered chest of the warrior reaching for him, and shoved. As she flew over backward, he slammed the hatch.

The rider's weaponry was crude but recognizable: two cannons at about 20 millimeters and two machine guns at 12 to 13 millimeters, though he couldn't be sure about the numbers given his lack of proficiency in Teotecan units. Although it could take a payload of one bomb, its bay was empty, another indication the runner was meant to go fast.

He taxied across the lawn, jolting on the uneven ground until he gained enough speed to lift off. As he soared into the sky, he looked down and saw the warriors staring up at him, helmeted faces blurring as they receded into dots. They could probably have no more imagined a Calani flying a rider than they could picture life without Quis.

It wasn't until he flew low over the gardens, strafing the bushes, that they dove for cover behind walls or in the Calanya. He came around again and riddled their riderless riders into oblivion.

He wasted several moments looking for the runner's neutrino transmitter before he realized the Cobans had yet to develop the technology. But he understood the screen with moving Quis dice; it was the Coban equivalent of radar.

That realization saved his life. In the same instant he interpreted the Quis pattern, it showed a Varz rider coming at him from behind. Kelric threw his rider into a roll and then a flat turn, a desperation move to evade the oncoming gunfire. Then he pulled into a steep climb.

The craft passed only a few hundred meters from him, at an angle that allowed neither of them a good shot. Emblazoned on its hull was the Varz clawcat and the name *Nightrider,* followed by a Quis symbol for resurrection. *Nightrider Resurrected.*

Kelric kept climbing, taking advantage of his better speed. Or what he thought was his better speed. At the lower altitude *Nightrider* had made such a clumsy turn that Kelric wondered if the craft was damaged, but as they climbed *Nightrider* gained on him.

As soon as Kelric realized he faced a fighter better equipped than his for high altitudes, he rolled over his runner, sky and horizon careening past his windshield until he was upside down. He pulled on the stick and the rider arced through the air in a reversed half loop, spots dancing in his vision from the g-forces.

The loop brought him down on the tail of his pursuer. But he had only flown a rider once, hadn't piloted anything for sixteen years, and had never flown a craft without a computer. He misjudged and came out to *Nightrider*'s port side, his gunfire riddling its wings. *Nightrider* spread its slats like giant mechanical feathers, letting most of the gunfire pass through them instead of hitting solid material.

They were farther out now, above the Teotecs. *Nightrider* came at him again, in a half loop to reverse its course. Still above the Varz rider, though just barely, Kelric went up in a half loop as well. At the top, he flipped his runner over and went into another half loop. The g-forces nearly knocked him out, but his biomech took over and moved his hands, rolling the rider right side up at the top.

The Varz craft followed on the first loop, but when it tried to reverse direction and chase him into the second, it stalled. As the craft floundered, losing speed, Kelric went into a dive, coming in on its tail. Dead-on target this time, he fired with everything he had—and *Nightrider* exploded in a black and orange billow of heated gases and flame.

Kelric stared after the remains of *Nightrider* as they showered out of the sky. Drawing in a breath, he saluted his fallen opponent. Then, adrenaline still pounding, he took his rider south, out over the Teotecs.

Gradually, as Karn disappeared in the mountains behind him, the pound of his heart eased, calmed, quieted. Finally he absorbed what had happened.

He was free.

45

Queen's Fire

The ruins of the Atrium lay open to the sky. Ixpar stood at their edge, staring at the destruction, the laser carbine hanging from her hand. The Varz riders that destroyed the command center below the Atrium had been too accurate for luck; they must have known its location.

"Ixpar." Borj beckoned from a side hall. "I found a working com."

She went over to it. "Ixpar here."

"Manager Karn!" Tal shouted. "You're alive!"

"Where are you?" Ixpar asked.

Tal spoke in a calmer voice. "In the Lower Levels, in generator room six. We've set up here the best we can. Most everyone from the command center made it here. But we can't find Borj."

"She's with me. What's the situation?"

"The Varz air units are withdrawing."

Considering how Varz had so far pulverized Karn, they had no reason to retreat. "Any reports of foot soldiers?"

"From everywhere. They're swarming all over the city."

Ixpar grimaced. So. Varz was moving in to occupy Karn. Intact, even partially, it was a far greater prize than reduced to rubble. "Tal, have units posted on the Estate perimeter. I'll send Borj to coordinate it. We have to hold the Estate."

"Understood, ma'am."

When Ixpar reached the generator room, she found Tal taking reports: casualty lists, damage, sightings of Varz soldiers. No word from Elder Solan, but that might not mean anything; the Memory had no com. She had to believe that silent meant safe.

"Manager Karn," Tal said. "Message from Commander Borj."

She leaned over the com. "Ixpar here."

Borj spoke flatly. "The Haka fleet is here. And it's big."

Ixpar sank into the chair behind her. Karn's last hopes had just gone up like chaff under a firebomb. "Are they landing soldiers?"

"Actually, no." Borj paused. "It's odd."

"Odd how?"

"Their air force is holding over the mountains. No, wait— one rider just broke away. It's headed for the Estate."

Ixpar glanced at Tal. "Have that rider escorted to the Calanya parks."

Borj spoke over the com. "It could be a trick."

"I have to trust my instincts on this one, Borj." Ixpar turned back to Tal. "Have two octets meet me in the Calanya parks."

The aide stared at her. "You can't go out there."

"This is something only I can do."

When Ixpar reached the Calanya parks, she saw a trio of Karn fighters circling in the sky. On a lawn below, Karn soldiers surrounded a Haka rider. Ixpar jogged toward them, past the wreckage of several riders near where she had left the runner. Whoever destroyed the Varz warcraft had apparently caught her runner as well.

When Ixpar stopped in front of the Haka rider, its hatch opened and a Haka aide jumped to the ground. "Manager Karn." She bowed deeply. "We request a pattern of truce."

It was an ancient request, coming from the Old Age. The pattern of truce: a temporary ceasing of hostilities long enough for foes to negotiate.

"Pattern granted," Ixpar said. She had no doubt the rider carried a diplomat to negotiate Jimorla Haka's release. They had wasted their time. She had no intention of giving up the boy. He was all that stood between Karn and defeat.

Rashiva Haka appeared in the hatchway.

Ixpar stared at the Manager. Had she lost her senses, coming onto hostile territory during a battle?

The desert queen jumped to the ground. "Manager Karn."

Ixpar nodded. "Manager Haka."

Rashiva didn't bother with formalities. "My son?"

"He's safe."

"Take me as your hostage," Rashiva said. "Let Jimorla go."

It was a more than reasonable exchange. But Ixpar didn't dare risk unsealing the Memory in the midst of battle. "I can't do that."

Rashiva stiffened. "If he isn't released within an hour, my fleet has orders to join Varz. You know Karn will have no chance then. Let him go."

"You better give your people new orders," Ixpar said. "Because neither you nor Jimorla are going anywhere."

For a long moment Rashiva looked at her. Then she said, "To stop their attack I must talk to them."

"You can do that from the Estate." This had to be a trick. Rashiva would never let herself be captured so easily. Ixpar turned to a Karn captain. "Make sure this craft vacates the parks." She tilted her head toward the Haka aide. "She goes with it."

The aide said nothing. Ixpar had seen the fierce loyalty of Rashiva's staff to their Manager. If this one let Rashiva be taken so easily, she had been ordered to do it. Why?

Ixpar considered Rashiva. Then she gestured as if she were ushering the Manager to a Council function rather than making her a prisoner of war.

Rashiva came quietly. Surrounded by Karn warriors, she and Ixpar crossed the parks to the Estate. At the entrance to the Lower Levels, Rashiva paused. She stood dark and proud, watching her captor with an unfathomable gaze. "Ixpar."

"Yes?"

"Jimorla's father——?" Rashiva stopped, her silence broken by the distant sounds of artillery.

Then Ixpar understood. A promise bound Rashiva, one as strong as her allegiance to Varz. *In return for your Oath.* With those words, she had sworn to Kelric a vow she still honored. Incredible as it was, Rashiva apparently believed protecting Kelric meant keeping him free of Avtac. The Haka Manager let herself be captured so her fleet could refuse to fight without losing honor.

"Sevtar is with his son Jimorla," Ixpar said.

Rashiva nodded. "Thank you."

After the octet took Rashiva down to the Lower Levels, Ixpar activated a wall com.

"Tal here," a voice said.

"This is Manager Karn. An octet is bringing Manager Haka down to you. Warn all units. No one is to fire on them."

"Then it's true? Manager Haka really is our prisoner?"

Ixpar blinked. "You already knew?"

"We intercepted a signal between Haka and Varz," Tal said. "Varz wanted to know what's going on. Haka said they couldn't do anything because you had their Manager."

Let Avtac puzzle that one out. "I'm coming back down—"

Ixpar never had a chance to finish. A blast shook the hall, caving in the entrance to the Lower Levels and knocking her to her knees. Shielding her face with her arm, she squinted into the dust and saw an Ahkah octet striding toward her. Helmets protected most of the warriors but those with bare faces wore looks of triumph, like hunters who had trapped the ultimate prey.

"Take her alive," someone ordered.

I refuse to be Avtac's prize, Ixpar thought. Then she hefted up the laser carbine and fired.

In the confined hall the light was blinding, the heat tremendous. When her vision cleared she saw only fused slag where a moment before a corridor full of warriors had stood. Stunned and nauseous, she struggled to her feet. When she heard the rumble of boots nearby and voices with Ahkah accents, she slung the carbine over her shoulder and took off in a limping run, wincing from the burns on her legs.

Ixpar lost the soldiers in a maze of halls she knew like a well-worn Quis pattern. Smoke filled the corridors. Like most Estates, Karn had been built primarily from stone, which meant the fires came from furnishings, drapes, and paneling as flames gutted her home.

Varz had penetrated the Estate defenses. Given that Karn soldiers were armed with rifles, a few even with machine guns, either the Varz troops were better trained or else outnumbered hers. Based on what Jevrin and her Quis spies had picked up about Varz and its allies, she knew Karn had the edge in military strategy, which meant Varz took its advantage in numbers.

She came across evidence of fighting: bullet-ridden walls, smashed statuary, broken windows. More sobering were the corpses, two from her own troops and one from Varz. She knelt next to them, silent, in honor of the lives they had given up.

Then she ran on, looking for an unblocked entrance to the Lower Levels. What she finally found was an operational com. She smacked her hand against its switch. "Tal?"

Commander Borj's voice snapped out. "Winds above, Ixpar, where are you?"

"Near the Hall of Teotec. What's the situation?"

"Anthoni got a message through," Borj said. "They completed the evacuation before Varz broke our defenses. The people are safe. In the city, the worst damage is to the airfield, factories, and guild warehouses."

"What about Haka?"

"Still holding in the mountains."

"Any word of the Calanya?"

"Nothing—what?" Borj paused. "Tal is getting a message from the Varz fleet."

Smoke seeped into the alcove and swirled about Ixpar's legs. "What message?"

Tal answered. "It's for you. It reads: 'If you surrender immediately and release Manager Haka, we will spare Karn. Refuse and we will raze your city. Be reasonable, Ixpar. You have lost. Avtac Varz.' "

Ixpar grimaced. "Borj, how much longer can we hold out?"

"Our forces have gradually been pushed back. The Lower Levels haven't been breached, but it won't be long. The rest of our defenses are gone. The Varz ranks are depleted, but ours are even worse." Borj made a frustrated noise. "If we just had fresh troops and riders, we could beat them back."

"Then find fresh troops and riders."

"We don't have them."

Ixpar clenched her fists. "Avtac can't have taken Karn."

"She must have used every rider she had," Borj said. "Took them off the blockade, off Ahkah, even off Varz. She gambled—risked leaving her flank undefended and threw everything she had at us. And she won."

"She hasn't won yet."

"Ixpar, we have no choice. We must surrender."

"While I live," Ixpar said, "I will never yield to Varz."

"Then you condemn Karn to destruction. We don't even have enough riders left to protect the evacuees."

No. Ixpar wanted to shout the word. Yet if she refused to surrender, a people and a city with a history over two millennia old would be destroyed in one day.

It felt like ages before she finally responded, though she knew it was only seconds. "Very well. Ask for terms of surrender."

Tal answered in a subdued voice. "Yhee, ma'am."

Quietly she said, "Refuse to tell them what happened to me. When they pressure you, 'give in' and reveal that I escaped the Estate."

"We'll make it believable," Borj said. Quietly she added, "And you had better make it truth. Fast."

"Yes." Ixpar took a breath. "Out."

She switched off the com and limped into the smoky hall. Borj was right; she had to get off the Estate. Although Avtac apparently gave orders to take her alive, Ixpar had no doubt the Minister intended to have her executed, in public, for all to see.

Boots sounded nearby. Ixpar slipped into an alcove just before a Varz octet entered the hallway. After that, it became a deadly game of hide and run as she evaded the troops that had come to secure her Estate. At one point she stood trapped behind a door, a handspan away from a Varz captain talking on com. What she heard made her teeth clench: Karn had fallen. Estate, city, and citizens were now secured. Soon the conquering Minister would come to take possession of her prize.

After the captain left the alcove, Ixpar slipped into it and scraped her fingers along the seam where one wall met the floor. She found the niche she sought and pushed its switch. A clink of pins answered from within the stone, just as it had done all those years ago when, as a child, she searched out the secret tunnels of the Estate, never knowing that game would someday save her life.

Without a torch, Ixpar had to feel her way in the dark. At the end of the tunnel she nudged open its stone door, verifying the area was clear. Then she walked out onto a balcony filled with amberwood chairs. The Hall of Teotec lay below her, intact.

Heat puffed across her back. Turning, she saw flames advancing toward her across the wooden balcony. What in a dice cheater's hell was going on? According to what she had heard from the Varz captain, the Estate had been made safe for occupation, its fires doused.

As the flames pushed forward, she backed into the balcony rail. Behind her, she heard the great double doors in the Hall open. She spun around to see a Varz octet striding between the great portals. Her first thought was that she was trapped; she could neither go down into the Hall now nor retreat through the flames.

Then she saw who strode among the guards.

Avtac.

That was when Ixpar knew beyond a doubt that something had gone wrong. Avtac would never have walked into a hall she knew was burning, nor have come on the Estate if her forces believed any danger existed, either from fires or enemy warrior queens.

You haven't won yet, she thought to Avtac. As long as I am free, you can never rest. I will raise a new army to destroy you.

Ixpar raised her carbine and fired at the ruler of Coba.

The instant she moved, the Varz octet saw her and lunged toward Avtac. The blazing flash of the carbine filled her vision, and when her sight cleared, she saw flames roaring in the Hall of Teotec, consuming tapestries, furniture, and the glossy wood paneling on its stone walls. Timbers supporting the balcony were burning as well, listing to one side—

And the entire balcony tore away from the wall.

Ixpar fell, aware of a lurid glare on all sides. For one instant she was floating. Then she smashed into the Opal Table, and it cracked in two with a great moan of burning wood. She struck the floor with agonizing force, pain searing her arms, back, legs, especially her thigh where a burning shard gashed it. Struggling to breathe, she lurched to her feet and stumbled toward the Calanya dais. Made from bare stone, it was almost the only place in the Hall that wasn't burning.

"Hold," a voice commanded.

She froze. Above her on the dais, Zecha Varz stood wreathed in smoke, her rifle aimed at Ixpar's head.

Ixpar lunged at the dais, wrenching her body around in

midair. The blast of a gunshot cracked so close that she felt it crease her arm. Then she slammed into Zecha and they fell to the ground, wrestling for the gun, rolling over and over on the dais, Zecha under her, on top, under, on top. They both had the rifle now, each gripping its stock, straining to gain control of the weapon pressed tight between their bodies.

As they wrenched the gun around, Ixpar worked her finger onto the trigger. She pulled it and the rifle barked, its recoil shoveling the stock into her hip.

Zecha swore, grabbing her knee. Then she gave a giant heave and yanked the gun out of Ixpar's hands. The captain scrambled to her feet, but when she tried to stand her leg crumpled and she lurched forward, teetering on the edge of the dais.

Then she fell.

Like a toppling pole, Zecha pitched down the steps and rolled into the inferno that had been the Opal Table. Engulfed by fire, she screamed and thrashed while her clothes burned. As Ixpar staggered to the edge of the dais, heat slammed her in waves. Stumbling on her injured leg, she fell to her knees, sweat pouring down her face while flames roared all around her.

Zecha rolled across the floor and out of the blaze on the far side of the Hall, into a tiled area the fire couldn't reach. Her movements had smothered the flames, but she lay still, silent and crumpled, a disturbing contrast to her previous frenzied motion.

"So we add murder to your crimes," a voice said.

Ixpar turned her head with a start—and looked up into the bore of her own laser carbine. Far up the length of the gun, Avtac watched her like an iron statue brought to life.

Ixpar spoke hoarsely. "Kill me and you're the murderer."

"Kill you? And make you a martyr? I think not." Crimson light edged the planes of Avtac's gaunt face. "When my Tribunal finishes with you, this golden warrior-goddess image of yours will be slag. Then you go to the guillotine." She prodded Ixpar with the carbine. "Get up."

Ixpar climbed to her feet, a straggle of hair falling into her eyes.

"Where is Sevtar?" Avtac said.

"Where you won't find him."

"Don't be obstinate, little girl. It will be less painful for you if my search is short."

Ixpar gritted her teeth. "Go rot in a Lasa whorehouse."

A muscle under Avtac's eye twitched. Then she swung the carbine and slammed the barrel into Ixpar's injured leg. With a gasp, Ixpar reeled backward to the edge of the dais. The steps dropped away beneath her and she fell, tumbling toward the Opal Table, almost into the crackle of flames and heat.

Avtac walked over and planted a foot on either side of Ixpar's hips. She raised the laser, holding it like a club. "Now. Sevtar."

In her side vision, Ixpar saw flames ignite a chunk of wood. "All right." As she spoke, she heard a distant rumbling. "I'll tell you where he is." She grabbed the blazing chunk and hurled it at Avtac's head.

The Minister easily dodged, but her motion made the carbine slip and her thumb hit the firing stud. Ixpar clamped her eyes shut, then opened them to see melted stone clattering down from a jagged hole in the hall's vaulted ceiling. While Avtac was still blinded by the flash, Ixpar jumped to her feet and ran to the Calanya dais.

The rumbling she had heard was swelling in volume, its thunder filling the hall. *What was going on?* Avtac would never have come onto the Estate unless her troops had ensured it was safe, yet it sounded as if the destruction had begun again. Above the clamor in the hall, she heard the unmistakable roar of riders above Karn. Fighting. *Fighting?* It was impossible, yet it was happening.

The rumbling on the Estate grew louder, until it drowned out even the riders. The entire Hall of Teotec was shaking. Plaster flew off the walls and windows cracked. As Ixpar stood in the Circle of the Calanya, her feet planted wide to keep her balance, the far wall of the hall bowed inward. In a nightmare of slow motion, it collapsed, peeling away like a giant wave.

Pillars toppled, one after the other, massive stone trunks crashing over in clouds of debris. Avtac stood in the midst of the chaos, seeing now, staring upward as, with formidable majesty, the Hall of Teotec thundered down around her.

Dropping down within the Circle, Ixpar shielded her head

with her arms. Debris richocheted off the rail above her and dust swirled around her body, thick with ashes and flakes of stone. The Hall's collapse roared like the judgment of an avenging deity.

Gradually the thunder lessened. Became a growl. A rattle. A trickle.

Amid swirling clouds of dust, Ixpar rose to her feet. Ruins open to the sky surrounded her. In the entire hall, only the Calanya dais remained intact.

She still heard the riders. They filled the sky, far more than she had thought either Karn or Varz had left. Although she looked up, she couldn't see well enough, with dust and tears in her eyes, to make out the symbols on the craft. She had no idea what rider belonged to what Estate.

But that didn't dilute the miracle.

They flew circles, loops, rolls, dives, other combat maneuvers. But they weren't fighting.

They were playing Quis.

Ixpar found Avtac's body beneath a mountain of rubble. She knelt by the late Minister, her head bowed, listening to the roar of the dice game above her. Why the battle started again or how her forces had managed to recoup, she had no idea. Only one fact blazed in her mind. They had switched from death to dice.

The patterns were obvious. Each windrider identified itself as a particular Quis piece. They probably kept straight who was what using a com channel open to everyone. Soaring in perilously close formation, the riders flew the same moves they had been using to shoot each other out of the sky, but now instead of firing they let the combat maneuvers represent structures. Even without access to their com chatter, Ixpar recognized some of the patterns. She could only imagine the multitude of transmissions going on as the air- and ground-based forces coordinated the session.

Afternoon faded into evening and still the Quis session continued. Only when twilight deepened did they bring it to an end, with the same awe-inspiring display of aeronautical skill that had marked the entire session.

Still Ixpar continued her vigil by Avtac's body, hidden in the encroaching night that shrouded her Estate. A dusty mist seeped into the ruins of the Hall and softened the contours of destruction.

Some time later footsteps approached. Ixpar raised her head to see a wraith coalesce out of the mist and shadows, a figure cloaked in veils of dust.

"Manager Karn?" Anthoni asked.

Numbly Ixpar said, "Why aren't you with the evacuees?"

"It *is* you." Anthoni came toward her, clambering over the debris. "We've been searching everywhere. Manager Viasa even—"

"Manager who?" Ixpar asked.

"Manager Viasa. And Jevrin."

"Jevrin?"

"He's been in Bahvla. He brought the Bahvla/Viasa fleet."

"A Viasa/Bahvla fleet?" Her mind began to function again. "I've never heard of Bahvla and Viasa cooperating on anything."

"It's a first." Anthoni reached her, slipping and stumbling on piles of broken stone. "Apparently Manager Viasa felt that starving a city, even Bahvla, was an outrage. She had mountain climbers smuggle in supplies, and Jevrin helped both Estates arm riders and train pilots. When Varz pulled off the blockade, Viasa and Bahvla launched their air forces."

"Those were the riders I heard fighting?"

"Yes." He paused. "The Varz forces were decimated. With the reinforcements, we gained advantage. Varz knew they had lost."

She heard the hesitation in his answer. "But?"

"Our numbers and theirs were close. Too close."

"Meaning?"

"To win, we would probably have had to wipe them out, and would have lost most of our forces as well. It would have been a massacre on both sides."

"So they played Quis. In the sky."

"Yes. Karn far outplayed Varz."

Ixpar nodded. And so Varz saved face, allowing its forces to back down, without humiliation, from a final battle they all knew would end in mutual carnage. "A worthy combat."

Anthoni spoke quietly. "We had a report that Minister Varz came onto Karn just before news of the reinforcements reached her fleet. But we've found no sign of her."

"You can stop looking. She's here."

"Here?"

The words felt like dust in Ixpar's mouth. "Yes. Here. Buried. Dead."

Anthoni spoke in a subdued voice. "Varz is finished, Ixpar. We won."

She looked at the ruins of the Hall from where she had once ruled Coba. "Did we?"

46

The Tower of Olonton

When the voice first crackled over the com, it sounded almost unintelligible. Nearly two decades had passed since Kelric had heard his own language. The message repeated again and again, distant, impassive, remote.

". . . identify yourself. This zone is Restricted. Starport grounds are closed to natives. Please identify—"

"I'm an Imperialate citizen," Kelric said. "Do you read?"

The recording continued to repeat, an automated message from an automated port. His rider arrowed through the dusk unchallenged by more than a mechanical voice.

Towers rose out of the desert like obelisks. No defenses surrounded them, only a low wall. He landed by an outcropping of rock and jumped down from the rider, warm wind ruffling his hair.

Then he walked to the starport.

It didn't even have a gate, just a wide gap in its wall. He stopped short of the opening and stared at the sand-covered street on the other side. Wind brushed sweat from his forehead and whispered across the desert.

Kelric looked back at the mountains. Up there, hidden in the peaks, an Estate had raged in flames because of him. He could never undo what he had rent here. But he could give Coba a promise.

Protection.

He would say nothing that might bring ISC to this world. For as long as he lived, he would keep his silence, in deed, in word, and in mind.

He guarded more than Coba: he also protected his children. He had to make a choice; trust Ixpar with them or take them into the life-and-death intrigues surrounding the Imperial dynasty. He could never undo the damage that dance of interstellar politics had wreaked on his life, nor could he know what would happen when he returned, almost two decades from the dead, to face his half brother, a man who had murdered his own father for the rule of an empire and would see Kelric dead if he perceived him—or his children—to be a threat.

Kelric had never seen Jimorla and had spent only one winter with Roca, yet they had forged a link so strong that even here in the desert he felt them, alive and secure in Karn. Part of him wanted to go to them, to return to Karn, though it meant giving up his life. Another part wanted to leave Coba and return with backup regardless of the Imperial attention it would bring. And it *would* draw notice: given his long absence, his family and the Assembly would have him watched every moment—if they still existed, which was in no way certain considering the volatile nature of the interstellar situation when he had disappeared.

Until he knew what he faced in his own future, Roca and Jimorla were safer here in anonymity. But knowing it was in their best interest to stay made it no easier to leave them. Perhaps the time would come when he could return with a title no one would dare defy. Imperator.

No matter what happened to him, someday Coba would have to face the Imperialate. If his sense of Coba was true, Roca and Jimorla would grow up strong and self-assured, ready to face their heritage rather than diminished by it, two miracles hidden in obscurity where none of his opponents would think to look. Should the Imperialate ever descend on Coba, Roca could claim her right to the line of Rhon succession; her DNA carried indisputable proof of her identity.

Until then, he could only do what his heart felt was best for the wonders his seed had grown.

"Ixpar, protect them. Make them strong for the day when they claim their heritage." His words swirled in the wind as tears ran down his face. "Take care of them for me."

Then he stepped across the invisible line that separated Coba from the Imperialate.

Anthoni found Ixpar as she was preparing to enter the Dawn Chamber. Silent and grim, he handed her a ring. When she turned it over, she found the inscription: *To Captain Eb Karn, for her years of service to the Ministry.*

Ixpar swallowed around the sudden lump in her throat. "Where was it found?"

"In the runs near the Atrium."

Her fist closed around the ring. "And Sevtar?"

Anthoni pulled a Calanya armband out of his pocket. As Ixpar took the partially melted circlet, she saw the name.

Sevtar.

A roaring filled her ears. "There would have been more gold than this."

"There was." Anthoni struggled to speak evenly, but his voice caught. "All melted."

She stared at him. "It could have come from anything. A vase. A molding. The stair banister."

"Ixpar, I—I'm sorry."

The roaring cut off, leaving her in dead silence. She turned numbly and limped into the Dawn Chamber.

They were all there, the Managers of Coba, gathered around a makeshift Opal Table: Dahl, Haka, Shazorla, Eviza, Ahkah, Lasa, Bahvla, Viasa, Tehnsa. Only the Ministry chair remained empty.

Ixpar went to stand at the Karn chair. When she was in place, a door opened across the chamber and Stahna Varz entered, a tall figure dressed in the blue cloak of mourning.

She took her place before the Ministry chair and swept her gaze over the assembled Managers.

"We meet today," Stahna said, "to end this war of Estates. We begin with the Council's call for a ballot of confidence. The ivory cube supports the Varz Ministry, the ebony cube a Karn Ministry."

A ballot of confidence? "I was not informed of this," Ixpar said.

"Perhaps," Stahna said. "In any case, the law forbids you and me to vote. Do you protest this?"

"No." It made no difference. Even if the vote went in her favor, Ixpar knew Varz would never relinquish the Ministry.

Stahna spoke. "Dahl?"

Chankah set a black cube on the table. "Dahl supports Karn."

One by one Stahna called the roll and one by one the Managers played their dice: black from Bahvla, Viasa, Tehnsa, Shazorla, Eviza. Haka and Ahkah set down white cubes, but in an unprecedented move the Lasa Manager voted against her primary, placing a crystal ring of neutrality.

Ixpar heard their voices, saw their dice. None of it registered. Her mind was numb.

When the vote was done, Chankah Dahl spoke. "The ballot favors Karn."

Stahna Varz watched them with the same iron gaze that had made her predecessor infamous. "A trade was made in good faith by Varz. A Sixth Level for the Ministry. So. Sevtar is at Karn. The Ministry stays at Varz."

Ixpar spoke. "There is no Sixth Level at Karn." She took the armband from her pocket and set it on the table. "He is dead."

In the silence that followed, the only sound came from the tall clock ticking by the door.

Finally Henta spoke. "Ixpar—I'm sorry."

Chankah swore softly. Then she turned to Stahna. "Hasn't there been enough conflict? End this. Return the Ministry to Karn."

"I will relinquish the title," Stahna said. "If a condition is met."

That caught Ixpar by surprise. She would never have expected Varz to give up what cost so much to attain. "What condition?"

"That for your successor," Stahna said, "you choose a girl born, raised, and educated at Varz."

"That's absurd," Henta Bahvla said.

"You might as well demand that Karn hand the Ministry back to Varz after one generation," Chankah said.

"It's worse than that," Khal Viasa said. "Such an agreement would also give control of Karn to Varz after one generation."

Rashiva spoke. "Then let it be. Varz gained the Ministry in a fair trade, one *instigated* by Karn. The title belongs where it is."

Chankah leaned forward. "A Varz Ministry has no support."

"My condition stands," Stahna said.

Henta snorted. "Do you honestly believe we would allow such a condition?"

The Ahkah Manager spoke. "And do you honestly believe this Council can rob Varz of its rightful title?"

"The condition is an insult," Chankah said.

"An outrage," Henta said.

"Ludicrous," Manager Shazorla put in.

Ixpar listened to them argue. When the debate ebbed, she said, "I accept the condition."

Silence.

Then they all spoke at once, their voices piling over one another. The debate raged on and on, but Ixpar neither wavered nor explained. Late that night, with the Council as witness, she signed the documents and once again became Minister.

As Ixpar left the Chamber, Rashiva joined her. They walked together through the scarred halls of Karn.

It was Rashiva who broke the silence. "Sevtar will be mourned by many."

Ixpar swallowed. For the rest of her life she would wonder why he had chosen to leave her suite that day. "I will have Jimorla brought to you."

Rashiva's shoulders relaxed. After a moment she said, "The boy Hayl is in my Calanya. Fourth Level, if you are willing to grant him a Karn Oath for his years spent here."

So. It was true, the rumors she had heard; Hayl had been at Haka. Knowing that all along wouldn't have prevented the war; Hayl had only been an excuse Avtac used, one she would have bent to her purposes regardless of what Karn claimed. Had Rashiva intended to negate Avtac's strategy she would have done so long ago.

In any case, it wasn't Hayl's fault he had become a pawn. "Yes," Ixpar said. "I will grant him a Karn Oath." Eighteen years of age and Hayl was, after Mentar, the ranking Calani among the Twelve Estates.

They walked in silence for a time. Finally Ixpar said, "Captain Zecha survived. My Tribunal sentenced her to prison."

Rashiva raised her eyebrows. "Varz will demand her freedom."

Ixpar suddenly felt tired. "And Karn will challenge Varz." She doubted the irony was lost on Rashiva, that as long as the Council fought over Zecha's fate, the captain would remain locked in the prison she had once controlled.

They parted at the Haka guest suite, Rashiva going in to await the return of her son, a sign of good faith, while Ixpar went on alone to the North Tower. She climbed the spiral stairs and paused at the top, acutely aware of the guards watching her. Then she opened the door to the tower room.

Inside, a Hakaborn boy sat in a window seat gazing out at Karn. As soon as Ixpar saw him, her heart leapt: the shimmer of his skin, the cast of his features, the way he rested his elbow on his knee—it was so hauntingly familiar that the tears she had fought all day surged against her defenses.

He turned with a start, then rose to his feet. He was tall for his age, already the height of a grown man. Emotions rippled across his handsome face: curiosity, apprehension, shyness. True to the ways of the desert, he gave her no smile. In him, she already saw the Haka mystique that evoked such fascination from women throughout the Twelve Estates.

"Jimorla." Ixpar bowed. "Your mother's escort waits for you."

Relief washed over his face. As he crossed the room, she reached to open the door. But her hand halted at the handle. She couldn't make herself take this final step that forever cut her last tie to Kelric.

The boy hesitated. "Manager Karn? Are you all right?"

Although Jimorla had yet to take an Oath, Initiates rarely spoke to Outsiders, let alone the Manager of a hostile Estate. Hearing him, the familiar lilt of his voice, was too much. Ixpar's voice caught. "You look so much like him." She reached to cup his cheek, but managed to stop her hand before it touched his face. "Jimorla, my offer for your contract stands. I would like you to come here. As my—my—Calani."

"But I haven't finished my studies."

"I can wait."

"I have to talk to my parents. To my Mentor."

Ixpar nodded. "I will write them." Then she made herself open the door. As Jimorla stepped Outside, his escort surrounded him in an implacable bulwark and he watched her from behind that fortification like a cipher. His guards swept him away. Just before he disappeared down the stairs, he looked back—and his smile flashed like a promise.

Then he was gone.

Ixpar exhaled. One final visit remained before she could retreat to her suite, to face her grief in private. She went down the stairs, crossed several halls, and entered another suite. As she closed the door, a small girl with glorious golden hair came padding into the living room. She stopped and regarded Ixpar with large eyes shimmering like liquid gold.

"Who are you?" Roca asked.

"Manager Karn."

The girl bit her lip. Then she went to an alcove. She climbed up on a ledge and sat looking at the floor, her legs dangling in the air.

Ixpar sat next to her. "Roca? What is it?"

The child blinked as tears gathered in her eyes.

"Are you upset with me for taking you from Miesa?" Ixpar asked.

The girl blinked harder.

"Ai." Ixpar felt like an ogre. She lifted Roca onto her lap. "I won't hurt you."

"Minister Varz got hurt." Roca looked up at her. "She got killed."

How could the child know? "The fighting is over now."

"But why my father? Why is he gone?"

"I—I wish I knew." I will care for you and love you as if you were my own, Ixpar thought. You have my oath.

Roca relaxed in her arms, almost as if she had heard the vow and trusted Ixpar enough to find it reassuring. Two big tears rolled down her cheeks. "My father had the Magic with you, Minister Karn. With you and me and the boy."

"The Magic? What is that?"

"Like Jasina and Tomi. The Magic that makes you warm."

"I don't understand, Roca."

"I felt it everywhere. Before he was gone. His thoughts filled up the whole world."

His thoughts? What did she mean?

Then Ixpar realized Roca had called her Minister Karn. Not Manager, but Minister. Yet the child had never known her as Minister and only the Council yet knew the title had reverted back to Karn.

Ixpar swallowed. "Is hearing thoughts the Magic, Roca?"

"No."

"Can you explain it to me?"

"The Magic is what makes people want to say 'I love you.' "

Ixpar's eyes felt hot. "You think your father had that with me?"

"I felt it." She spread her small arms as if encompassing the world. "Everywhere."

Ixpar cradled the girl, aching to believe her. Could it be true what Kelric had told her, that his daughter was a telepath? Rhon child, he called her. Rhon. Child of a House that ruled an interstellar empire.

Through his daughter, Kelric had left them a priceless legacy. Ixpar had seen it the moment Stahna Varz stated her condition for relinquishing the Ministry. In that instant Ixpar had chosen her successor.

Stahna believed Varz had triumphed, but in truth all Coba had won. The Restriction wouldn't last forever. Someday the Imperialate would come. But Coba would be ready. The conquerors would find this world ruled by a golden-eyed woman who bore the right to claim her place among the Rhon.

For she who will lead my people, Ixpar thought, is heir to the stars.

Appendix I

The Estates

Quis rank
first tier: Karn, Varz
second tier: Haka, Dahl
third tier: Ahkah, Bahvla, Viasa
fourth tier: Miesa, Shazorla
fifth tier: Eviza, Tehnsa, Lasa.

First tier Estates have the strongest Quis and thus the most power. Second tier Estates are also forces to be reckoned with. Third tier has less clout, but still considerable influence. Fourth has respectable Quis with moderate influence. Fifth is weak. Prior to its destruction, Hahvna was third tier. Kej was destroyed before Quis became prominent.

Primary Estates, in order of influence: (Kej), Karn, Varz, Haka, Dahl, Viasa, Bahvla, Ahkah, (Hahvna), Shazorla, Miesa. The Haka/Dahl and Viasa/Bahvla rankings are close and hotly contested.

Secondary Estates, in order of influence: (Primary in parentheses): Eviza (Shazorla), Tehnsa (Viasa), Lasa (Ahkah).

Estate symbols:
Ahkah: A stalk of silkcorn grain crossed by a needle threaded with blue silkcorn yarn.
Bahvla: A rosewood tree: black bark, rose highlights, emerald leaves.
Dahl: A suntree: gold bark, pale green leaves, gold fruit.

Eviza: A jahalla tree plumped by water: yellow bark, green-gray leaves, red and yellow flowers.

Hahvna: Two children holding hands, a girl and boy, each in blue pants, a white shirt, and gray boots.

Haka: A large red-gold sun rising over a red desert.

Karn: A giant althawk in flight, with black wings edged by red feathers and gold eyes.

Kej: A warrior's spear with a jahalla shaft and a stone spearhead.

Lasa: An airbug.

Miesa: The sungoddess Savina in her sky-blue althawk, pulling the gold chariot that carries the sun.

Shazorla: A crystal carafe edged with gold and full of rosewine.

Tehnsa: A grayrock castle high in the mountains, wreathed in mist.

Viasa: The Grayrock Falls, a spectacular mountain waterfall.

Varz: A clawcat on a mountain cliff, silhouetted against the sky.

THE ESTATES

Ahkah: a sprawling eastern Estate with a large population. Its Managers are infamous for their business acumen. Primarily agricultural, Ahkah is also known for its garment industry and pleasant climate. It allies with Varz.

Bahvla: a small northern Estate in a region of dense forest. It derives most of its support from its lumber industry, in particular the sale of rosewood. Bahvla and Viasa are the only Primary Estates within visible distance of each other, and they maintain a long-standing feud, though no one remembers exactly why. Bahvla is a strong Karn ally.

Dahl: an attractive holding about midway between Shazorla and Ahkah. Known for its lovely climate, it supports a number of industries including orchards, carpentry, and tourism. A powerful Estate, on par with Haka, it has long been Karn's strongest ally.

Eviza: a small agricultural holding near Shazorla, with a population similar to Haka but less conservative. Secondary to Shazorla.

Hahvna: formerly northwest of Dahl, Hahvna was destroyed by an earthquake in year 422 of the Modern Age. Most survivors went to Dahl, a few to Bahvla. Until its demise, it was the largest exporter of ceramics and goods for Children's Cooperatives. It allied with Karn.

Haka: a desert holding legendary for the ferocity of its Old Age warrior queens and the mystique of its men. It exports silicate compounds and is known for exquisite stained glass. The most conservative Estate, it still enforces laws from the Old Age, including the Propriety Laws for men. The Hakaborn, those with a long Haka lineage, top its hierarchies. The black eyes, glossy black hair, and dusky complexion of the Hakaborn is one Coban standard for beauty (the other being Miesan).

Haka is a powerful Estate, on par with Dahl. In the Old Age it was a staunch Kej ally. After Karn destroyed Kej, Haka swore allegiance to Varz, which was just beginning its rise to power and its millennia-long challenge of Karn.

Karn: a large cosmopolitan Estate generally considered the center of civilization. It is known for scholars and accomplished Quis players, exports most machinery used among the Estates, and draws many tourists. Its autumn foliage displays spectacular colors, and in spring plumberry vines cover the city in flowers.

Year One of the Old Age dates from the year Karn was built. Its Manager also serves as Minister and as such rules the Estates. Throughout history, Karn and Varz have been bitter enemies.

Kej: an ancient holding south of Haka, the only Estate ever built entirely in the desert. At its height, Kej surpassed all other Estates in power. It existed in an almost continual state of warfare and fought Karn in a savage series of battles known as the Desert Wars. They ended in Year 632 of the Old Age, when Queen Odana Kej kidnapped a Karn Akasi and made him her Akasi. In retaliation, the Karn queen raised one of the largest armies ever known among the Estates and burned Kej to the ground.

Lasa: a small holding near Ahkah. Notorious for seamy gambling houses and corrupt Quis, it is considered the least desirable Estate. Secondary to Ahkah.

Miesa: a small northern Estate. Among the oldest holdings, it dates from the early Old Age. Miesans tend to be small and are known for breathtaking beauty, with exotic yellow hair and blue or gray eyes. During the Old Age, warriors often came down from Varz to raid Miesa and kidnap its men, though prisoners were usually released after a few days. The raids continued well into the Modern Age, until finally Miesa appealed to the Quis Council. After passage of the Consent Law, which made raiding illegal, the harassment of Miesa's men by Varz's women tapered off.

Miesa is Ward of the Miesa Plateau, which supports the Jatec Mineral Flats, a main source of minerals and inorganic chemicals among the Estates. In the Old Age, Miesa controlled the Plateau's output and claimed great wealth; in modern times Varz has gradually taken control. Miesa allies with Varz.

Shazorla: a large holding famed for its vineyards and rosewine. Although most geographers classify it as a desert Estate, it is actually in the Shaza foothills of the Teotecs. It tends to ally with Karn, more rarely with Haka.

Tehnsa: a small holding above Viasa known for fine rock sculptures and frazzled Managers. Secondary to Viasa.

Varz: a northern fortress on the apex of Mount Skywalk, at the highest altitude of any Estate. Infamous during the Old Age for its armies, it remains known for fierce hunters. Strict immigration laws, and a climate that is colder in summer than some Estates are in winter, hold down the population. Its citizens tend to fair coloring and are tall even for Cobans, women and men both averaging well over six feet. In the Old Age they were even taller and looked more Hakaborn, but centuries of raiding the Miesa Men's Houses introduced Miesa traits into the population.

Varz does a strong commerce in goods: stunners, knives, honed discuses, javelins; furs from snowtigers, clawcats, silver talopes; lumber from icefirs. Second in power only to Karn, it has long disputed Karn's right to the Ministry. After the fall of Kej, the most violent Old Age battles took place between Karn and Varz.

Viasa: a northern holding above the spectacular Grayrock Falls, in a dense forest known for perpetual mist. As Ward of the Viasa-Tehnsa dam, it has sole rights to sell electricity, making it one of the wealthiest Estates despite its small size. Viasa has no strong political ties but leans toward Varz. Its feud partner, Bahvla, can be seen in the southeast when the fog lifts.

Appendix II

Glossary

Unless otherwise specified, words are Teotecan. Italicization of a word indicates it also appears in the glossary.

Abbreviations: *Arch.*—Archaic; *Io.*—Iotic; *Lysh.*—Lyshrioli; *Myth.*—Mythology; *OS.*—Old Script; *pl.*—plural; *Qs.*—Quis; *Sk.*—Skolian; *sl.*—slang; *Uc.*—Ucatan. Languages defined below.

advantage *Qs.* Having the highest-ranked dice within a structure. Player with advantage takes possession of the structure.

airbug Small insect with blue wings.

airplant Diurnal mountain plant topped by a blue *airsack*.

airsack Pouch on an *airplant*. In the day it fills with air, raising the head of the plant to the sun; at night, the pouch loses air and the head bows over.

Akasi *OS., pl.* **Akasi** *Calani* who is also a Manager's husband.

alchemist's gamble *Qs.* A risky move intended to convert one structure into another.

amberwood Rich gold wood from Dahl suntrees.

ascendant *Qs.* Situation where player is gaining *advantage*.

atom cracking Nuclear fission.

augmented spectrum *Qs. Spectrum* with white, gray, and black dice.

Avtac *Myth.* Goddess of iron.

bar-builder *Qs. Builder* made with bars arranged according to length as well as *order,* both increasing together.

blown-glass Quis die *sl.* Fragile person or thing.

bone *sl.* Fondness for something. *Got a bone for slithering snakes:* likes to spy on people.

Borj *Myth.* Ancient race of giants said to dwell in the desert. A Borj was as tall as twelve women standing on each other's shoulders.

brews *sl.* Upsets, causes agitation or anger.

bridge *Qs.* Dice structure joining two others. Player with highest-ranked structure gains possession of all three.

bridge of Olonton *Qs. Sunsky bridge* made to offer another player sanctuary.

builder *Qs.* An unbroken curve of polyhedrons, all the same color, arranged according to *order.*

Calani *pl.* **Calani** A man who lives in a calanya as a dice player.

Calanya *OS., pl.* **Calanya** 1. Group of Calani living in seclusion. 2. Buildings and parks where Calani live. 3. *Arch.* In the *Old Age,* a male harem.

camouflage *Qs.* Any dice structure hidden by structures or surfaces of similar appearance.

carn-abi *OS.* One who guards or wards. May derive from the Tozil word *chabi:* to care for, watch over, guard.

chabiat k'in *Uc.* "The day is guarded" or "the day is watched over." 1. A spiritual thing, a guarding of life. 2. The life a warrior gives in battle by offering her own to save another.

Chankah *Myth.* Goddess and harbinger of change.

circle *Qs.* Ring of dice that captures a structure by enclosing it.

clawcat 1. Giant mountain cat known for ferocity. 2. Female warrior. 3. Feminine woman.

Coba *Myth.* Goddess of eternity. Mother of *Jahlt, Mox, Avtac,* and *Hayl.*

color *Qs.* Dice attribute. Color determines *rank* according to the optical spectrum, with red lowest and violet highest.

column of time *Qs.* Cylindrical structure that represents the passage of time. Its flat base is the past and the cylinder is the progress of time from past to future.

continuity law *Qs.* 1. Applies when player loses a game in one move due to playing a dice with the wrong *color, dimension,* or *order.* If his opponent opens the next game with the same die she played in the last, he must fix his previous move using a piece that (a) has the same attributes as the misplayed die and (b) outranks his opponent's die. 2. *sl.* Dilemma with no solution.

cream pheasant Large bird with ivory plumage marked by gold spots that resemble eyes. Prized for its tender meat.

crooner *sl.* Crazy person who tells stories, usually a convict.

Cuaz *Myth.* Wind god known for his capricious nature. See *Savina.*

descendant *Qs.* Situation where player withdraws from play, either by leaving game or making moves that don't affect main structures.

Deha *Myth.* Goddess of air and storms. Craftiest of all deities. Mother of *Cuaz* and *Khozaar,* both sired by *Mox.*

desert tower *Qs.* *Tower* made with "desert" colors: ruby, topaz, and gold. Although generally lower in *rank* than a tower with more colors, it ranks higher when determining *advantage* over other desert structures.

dice cheater's hell *Myth.* Underground cave where people who cheat at Quis go when they die. They are made into human dice and used by fog spirits to play Quis.

Dice Queen 1. Estate Manager. 2. Superior player; a dice wizard.

dimension *Qs.* Dice attribute. Rods, rings, and so on have one dimension, flat dice have two, other dice have three. Rank increases with dimension.

dismantle *Qs.* Capture another player's structure in a way that requires she remove it from the playing area.

double circle *Qs.* *Circle* made by one player to prevent a second player from encircling a third player's dice.

drumbug 1. Slow-flying bug with round, flat body. Makes a booming noise at twilight. 2. *sl.* Dull-witted person.

Elder Mentor Man in charge of a *Preparatory House.*

flat-stack *Qs.* *Stack* of flat dice, all with same shape.

grand spectrum *Qs. Spectrum* with ten or more dice.

halften Fifth day of a tenday cycle.

hawk's claw *Qs.* Structure shaped like a talon. The player who owns the closed claw also owns any structure within it.

hawk's fire *Qs. Hawk's claw* that captures a tower. Player making the capture can topple, dismantle, or ravage the tower, or leave it intact. See *ravaged tower* and *toppled builder.*

hawk's flight *Qs.* Half arch. It has a high rank because it is difficult to construct a stable arch that is supported on only one side. Gives *advantage* over any structures below it.

hawk's rage *Qs. Hawk's fire* that ravages a tower.

Hayl *Myth.* God of the hearth. Son of *Coba* and *Sevtar.*

hazelle *OS., pl.* **hazelle** 1. Long-limbed animal with gold antlers and white hooves. Known for speed and beauty, hazelle live in the mid to upper ranges and are prey to *claw-cats.* 2. Desirable man.

hazelle colt 1. Young *hazelle.* 2. Desirable youth.

Henta *OS.* Matchmaker.

High Quis Sessions played by Managers and Minister during Quis Council. It is considered the highest form of Quis. Some scholars believe Quis among high-level Calani equals High Quis, but the claims can't be verified because Calani live in seclusion. Modernists suggest the Oath is used to deny Calani the influence commensurate with their Quis expertise.

hot-light sailor Laser carbine.

hyella Pale blue reed found near desert oases. An iridescent orb floats on the tip of a mature hyella.

icefir Tree found at high altitudes, with needled branches that resemble frozen lace. Named for ability to survive ice and snow.

Initiate Boy in *Preparatory House* who has qualified to study Calanya Quis. See *Novice.*

inverted tower *Qs.* An upside-down *tower,* with the lowest *rank* pieces at bottom and the highest at top.

Iotic *Io.* Ancient language from *Ruby Empire* now spoken only by scholars and Imperial nobility.

Ixpar *Myth.* Goddess of War. Unlike most Coban myths, which date from the Old Age, tales of the war goddess pre-date known history.

jahalla Sparse angular tree with yellow bark. Given water, its leaves and limbs expand with stored moisture and its flowers blossom. Its seeds are used to make *java-cream*.

jahalla's defiance *Qs.* Structure that challenges the patterns established by dominant players in a session.

Jahlt *Myth.* Goddess of silence.

java-cream Dark cream, smooth and rich, made from javalla beans, which are the seeds of the jahalla tree.

kasi *OS., pl.* **kasi** Husband. Derives from *Akasi*.

Kelric *Lysh.* God of youth and hope.

Khal *Myth.* Spirit of water holes and fog. Daughter of *Avtac* and a mortal man, Edarque of Kej, renowned for his strength and intellect.

kinsa Male prostitute.

kinsaborn Having a kinsa for a father.

kinsa-boss Female pimp.

Khozaar *Myth.* Wind god known for his great beauty. See *Savina*.

kicked-mote emitter Laser.

kya *Sk.* Title meaning "born of the House of." Used by Imperial nobility. "Kelricson Garlin Valdoria kya Skolia, Im'Rhon to the Rhon of the Skolias" literally translates as "Son of *Kelric*, named in honor of Garlin, descended from the Valdor's line, born of the House of *Skolia*, heir to the Imperator, with the right to use the title 'Rhon.'"

Lady Death *Myth.* Spirit who takes the living through the membrane between the realms of life and death.

Lyshriol *Lysh.* Home world to Valdoria branch of the Rhon. *Lyshrioli:* People or language of *Lyshriol.*

metal changer Alchemist.

Mox *Myth.* God of spices and love, father of *Cuaz* and *Khozaar* by *Deha*. Known for causing mischief. *She's bedeviled by Mox:* she's in love.

multiple builder *Qs.* Structure consisting of several *builders*, made by players working in cooperation.

nested tower *Qs. Tower* shielded within another tower. The larger tower protects the smaller regardless of who owns it. A nested tower is captured by toppling the structure around it or making a *bridge* into the protecting tower.

Night's First Hour The hour after sunset. See *temporal calendar.*

Night's Midhour Moment halfway between dawn and dusk.

Novice Boy in *Preparatory House* who is not yet an *Initiate.* A Novice who fails his Initiate exams usually leaves the House.

Oath of Olonton Document in which Estates pledged to settle political conflicts with Quis rather than war. See *Olonton.*

Old Age Millennium when Estates came into being. Characterized by constant warfare, the Old Age ended with the signing of the *Oath of Olonton.*

Old Script Hieroglyphic language used in the *Old Age.*

Olonton *Uc.* 1. Peace, in particular that which came when Quis replaced warfare. See *Old Age.* 2. Heart.

orb's circle *Qs. Circle* that captures a orb enclosing it.

order *Qs.* Number of sides on a *Quis* die. The higher the order, the higher the *rank.*

Pattern games *Qs.* Quis used to solve equations.

pattern of truce 1. *Qs.* Pause in a session so opponents can negotiate. 2. *Arch.* Pause during battle so foes can negotiate.

phalanx *Qs.* Structure made from wedges and used to penetrate an opponent's defense.

podbag Withered *airsack.*

pog Small amphibian with mottled green, pink, and blue skin. Lives in mountains. *I'll be a pog on a pole:* I'm amazed.

pole-dung Excrement from *scumrat.*

Post-Quis Deconstructive Thematics Scholarly theory of modernist criticism that claims Quis is used to control male aggression and sexuality by sublimating it into the dice network. The theory is considered seditious by the women on the Quis Council. However, it creates less controversy than might be expected, mainly because no one can figure out what the heck "Post-Quis Deconstructive Thematics" means.

Preparatory House Elite boarding school that trains boys for the Calanya. See *Initiate, Novice.*

Primary Estate Self-supporting Estate with an independent vote in the *Quis Council.*

Propriety Laws Laws from the Old Age that are still followed in HaKa.

The require that a man a) never smile at a woman unless she is his wife, b) never go in public without female chaperones, c) always wear full-length cowled robes in public that cover him from head to toe, d) and always wear a *Talha* scarf in public that covers his face, leaving at most his eyes visible.

pug *Sk.* Skolian cussword.

queen's coup *Qs.* Any strategy hidden until it is implemented, at which time it gives the player significant *advantage*.

queen's fire *Qs.* *Hawk's fire* made from *queen's spectrum*.

queen's gamble *Qs.* Ultimate *rumrunner's gamble*. Most queen's gambles have a high enough rank to capture even multiple *towers*.

queen's spectral tower *Qs.* Vertical *queen's spectrum*. Outranks any horizontal structures it touches, such as a *starburst* or *spectrum*.

queen's spectrum *Qs.* *Spectrum* made with five or more polyhedrons arranged by number of sides, as in a *builder*.

Quis Council Coban governing body, composed of the Minister and Estate Managers.

Quis net Network formed from all dice players on Coba. Users access it by playing dice.

Quis table Small round table supported by fluted pedestal. It may have carvings or mosaics around edges, but the playing area is unadorned. *She has no Quis table:* She is eccentric.

Raaj *Myth.* God of the earth and all growing things.

Ralkon *Myth.* Goddess of wisdom.

Rashiva *Myth.* Goddess of fire.

ravaged tower *Qs.* *Tower* that is harmed during capture but kept as a tower rather than converted to a new structure. Considered a brutal move, it offers no *advantage* over gentler moves, such as keeping the tower intact, or toppling or dismantling it.

Raylicon *Io.* Planet. Birthplace of *Ruby Empire* and Imperialate.

reopen *Qs.* Reenter a session after leaving it.

Rhon *Sk.* Descendant of the *Ruby Dynasty* who carries a full set of paired Kyle genes.

Roaz *OS. Old Age* philosopher whose writings are considered a source of wisdom.

rock's chute *Qs.* Rectangular *rock's well.* Although difficult to capture due to its stable architecture, it is low in rank because players can continue moving pieces of theirs captured inside it and perhaps gain their release.

rock's well. *Qs.* Hollow cylinder built from stone dice.

roll *Qs.* Take out dice for a *Quis* session. *Rolled right sharp:* Looks good; is good. *Roll the red die:* Have sex.

rosewood A glossy black wood with red highlights that comes from the darkrose tree. Also called *darkwood.*

Ruby Empire *Sk.* Fragile interstellar empire that existed five millennia before Skolian *Imperialate.* Ruled by the Ruby Dynasty.

rumrunner's gamble *Qs.* Any structure built with great risk and substantial potential payoff. *Rumrunner's folly:* A failed gamble.

sailing-light device Laser.

Savina *Myth.* Goddess of the sun. Savina rides a blue althawk that pulls a gold chariot carrying the sun. She has two *Akasi,* the wind gods *Cuaz* and *Khozaar.* See also *Sevtar.*

scowlbug 1. Beetle with elongated mandibles. 2. *sl.* Angry person.

Scowl Laws *sl.* The Propriety Laws.

Scribe 1. Scholar who records Estate affairs. 2. Historian.

scumrat Small animal with greenish fur and buck teeth that lives in sewers.

Secondary Estate Subsidiary Estate with no independent voice in Council. Must ally with its *Primary* or abstain. See Appendix I.

Second Season Winter.

Sevtar *Myth.* God of the dawn. A giant with skin made out of sunlight who strides across the sky, pushing away the night so *Savina* can bring out the sun.

shylark Small bird with feathers the color of a human blush.

Skolia *Sk.* 1. Family name of the *Rhon.* 2. The Imperialate.

Skolian *Sk.* 1. Imperialate citizen. 2. Imperialate language used as an interstellar standard.

slither *sl.* Spy on someone.

slow-syrup Sweet syrup made from suntree sap.

snowfir Tree with white bark and blue-green needles, found only at high altitudes.

Speaker's Privilege Granted by Manager to let someone talk with a Calani. Usually only given to his kin.

spectral tower *Qs*. Vertical spectrum.

spectrum *Qs*. Five or more dice of same shape arranged in an unbroken curve according to the colors of the rainbow.

starburst *Qs*. Star-shaped structure that breaks a *circle*. The star's spokes extrude into the circle and "burst" it.

strokes *sl*. Pleases. *Strokes Haka pink:* pleases Haka.

Suitor's Dice Jeweled dice given by a woman to a man to initiate courtship.

Suitor's Privilege Granted by Manager to let a woman court a Calani.

sunsky bridge *Qs*. Bridge made from yellow, gold, and blue dice. Used by one player to suggest a cooperative venture with another.

suntree Deciduous tree with gold bark found in Dahl region. Produces a gold fruit prized for its sweet taste.

switch *Qs*. Any move taking a player to a new stage of play within a session.

Tálha *OS*. A long, woven scarf similar in shape and length to a muffler, usually bordered with tassels. Worn for the *Propriety Laws*, or as protection against blowing sand and the sun.

talope Hardy deerlike animal with silver fur.

tas *OS*. Leafy plant found around Shazorla. *Tas stick:* cigarette made by rolling tas leaves in colored paper.

taw Large plant with succulent stalk.

tawmilk Sweet milk made from taw stalks.

temporal calendar Calendar that specifies the exact time, every day of the year, for various moments throughout the day. Used by Cobans, who measure hours relative to sunrise and sunset.

Teotecan *Uc*. Modern language spoken in the Estates.

Teotecs *Uc*. Mountain range where most Estates are located.

ticklefly Iridescent green fly with fast-beating wings.

toppled builder *Qs*. *Tower* laid flat by an opponent, making it a builder (and thus lower in rank).

toppled chute *Qs.* *Chute* laid flat by an opponent, making it horizontal rather than vertical (and thus lower in rank).

toppled spectrum *Qs.* Toppled *spectral tower.*

tower *Qs.* Vertical *builder.* Dice are stacked in decreasing *order,* with the highest order piece at the bottom.

tower of Odana *Qs.* *Tower* of red dice meant to initiate seduction, most often made by a woman for a man.

tower of Olonton *Qs.* Structure that transcends all others in a session yet causes no harm. Considered the most difficult structure to make, it is rarely seen even in high-level Calanya Quis.

tower of souls *Qs.* Tower of black dice. Dismantles any structure within a distance of one dodecahedron.

Tozil *Uc.* Some scholars claim this is the correct name for *Ucatan.* The origins of both words were lost in the chaos prior to *Old Age.*

treeclam Mollusk that lives on trees in the lakes region around Viasa. Considered a delicacy.

Ucatan *Uc.* Hieroglyphic language predating Old Script.

upper level *sl.* Brain; mind. *Slow in the upper level:* Stupid.

Valdoria *Lysh.* Family name for *Lyshriol* branch of *Rhon.* Valdor: Bard or singer.

Viana *Lysh.* Goddess of fertility, beauty, and love. Her hair is the night sky.

wing-ivory Ivory made from the bones of a small *althawk.*

yhee *OS.* Formal form of word *yes,* often used to indicate respect.

yip *sl.* Informal form of the word *yes.*

Note: The chapter headings are named for Quis moves, or in a few cases, for Quis pieces. Taken altogether the chapter titles form a complete Quis session.

Appendix III

THE RUBY DYNASTY

Boldface names refer to members of the Rhon.
The Selei name denotes the direct line of the Ruby Pharoah.
All children of Roca and Eldrin Althor Valdoria take Valdoria as their third name.
All members of the Rhon, and only members of the Rhon,
have the right to use Skolia as their last name.

= marriage   + children by

Lahaylia Selei = **Jara**

Dyhianna Selei = ¹· **William Seth Rockworth III**
(separated)

+ ²· **Eldrin Jarac**

Althor Izam-Na

Havryl Torcellei

Denric Windward

Del-Kurj   **Chaniece Roca**
(fraternal twins)

Sauscony Lahaylia =

=

Taquinil Selei

'Akushtina = **Althor Vyan Selei**
(Tina)   (born 3 years after
Santis   end of *The Last*
Pulivok   *Hawk*)

Jaíbriol Qox I = Zara Qox
+ ?

Ur Qox = Viquara Iquar
+ Camylliia

=

Jaibriol III

*Genetically, Kurj was made from the DNA of Jarac and Roca. However, he considers

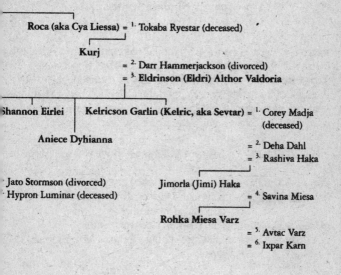

Roca (aka Cya Liessa) = [1.] Tokaba Ryestar (deceased)

Kurj

= [2.] Darr Hammerjackson (divorced)
= [3.] Eldrinson (Eldri) Althor Valdoria

Shannon Eirlei   Kelricson Garlin (Kelric, aka Sevtar) = [1.] Corey Madja
                                                             (deceased)

       Aniece Dyhianna

                                                         = [2.] Deha Dahl
                                                         = [3.] Rashiva Haka

Jato Stormson (divorced)   Jimorla (Jimi) Haka
Hypron Luminar (deceased)   = [4.] Savina Miesa

                      Rohka Miesa Varz

                                                         = [5.] Avtac Varz
                                                         = [6.] Ixpar Karn

Jaibrol Qox II

Rocalisa   Vitar   del-Kelric

Tokaba Ryestar his father.

Appendix IV

Timeline for Skolian Imperialate

Dates are given in Earth years for ease of comparison with Earth history. The **Imperial Calendar,** used in the Imperialate, sets Year One as the year the Imperialate was founded (A.D. 1904). A much older dating system, the Iotic Calendar, begins with the year humans arrived on Raylicon. Disagreement exists, however, as to the exact date of the first Raylican settlement.

circa 4000 B.C.	Group of humans moved from Earth to Raylicon
circa 3600 B.C.	Ruby Dynasty begins
circa 3100 B.C.	Raylicans launch first interstellar flights; rise of Ruby Empire
circa 2900 B.C.	Ruby Empire begins decline
circa 2800 B.C.	Last interstellar flights; Ruby Empire collapses

.
.
.

circa A.D. 1300	Raylicans begin attempts to regain lost knowledge and colonies
A.D. 1843	Raylicans reattain interstellar flight
1869	Aristos created
1871	Aristos found Eubian Concord (aka Trader Empire)
1881	Lahaylia Selei born
1904	Lahaylia Selei founds Skolian Imperialate and takes Skolia name

2005	Jarac born
2111	Lahaylia Selei weds Jarac
2119	Dyhianna Selei born
2122	Earth humans achieve interstellar flight
2132	Earth humans found Allied Worlds of Earth
2144	Roca born
2169	Kurj born
2204	Jarac dies; Kurj becomes Imperator; Lahaylia dies; Eldrin Jarac Valdoria born
2206	Althor Valdoria born
2210	Sauscony (Soz) Valdoria born
2219	Kelricson (Kelric) Valdoria born
2237	Jaibriol Qox II born
2258	Kelric crashes on Coba (beginning of *The Last Hawk*)
2259	Soz meets Jaibriol II (beginning of *Primary Inversion*)
2274	Domino War begins
2276	Traders capture Eldrin; Althor Valdoria dies; Domino War ends; end of *The Last Hawk*
2279	Althor Selei born
2328	Althor Selei meets Tina Pulivok (beginning of *Catch the Lightning*)

About the Author

Catherine Asaro grew up near Berkeley, California. She earned her PhD in Chemical Physics and her MA in Physics, both from Harvard, and a BS with Highest Honors in Chemistry from UCLA. Among the places she has done research are the University of Toronto, the Max Plank Institut für Astrophysik in Germany, and the Harvard-Smithsonian Center for Astrophysics. She currently runs Molecudyne Research and lives in Maryland with her husband and daughter. A former ballet and jazz dancer, she founded the Mainly Jazz Dance program at Harvard and now teaches at the Caryl Maxwell Ballet School in Maryland. She also wrote *Primary Inversion*, *Catch the Lightning*, and *The Radiant Seas*, all science fiction novels set in the same universe as *The Last Hawk*. She can be reached by E-mail at asaro@sff.net, and on the web at www.sff.net/people/asaro.